D1351885

Psychic Surveys: Book Four

Old Cross Cottage

ALSO BY SHANI STRUTHERS

EVE: A CHRISTMAS GHOST STORY
(PSYCHIC SURVEYS PREQUEL)

PSYCHIC SURVEYS BOOK ONE:
THE HAUNTING OF HIGHDOWN HALL

PSYCHIC SURVEYS BOOK TWO:
RISE TO ME

PSYCHIC SURVEYS BOOK THREE:
44 GILMORE STREET

BLAKEMORT
(A PSYCHIC SURVEYS CHRISTMAS NOVELLA)

THIS HAUNTED WORLD BOOK ONE:
THE VENETIAN

JESSA*MINE*

Psychic Surveys: Book Four

Old Cross Cottage

'It's not wise to linger at the crossroads…'

SHANI STRUTHERS

Psychic Surveys Book Four, Old Cross Cottage
Copyright © Shani Struthers 2017

The right of Shani Struthers to be identified as the Author of the work has been asserted by her in accordance with the Copyright, Designs and Patents Act 1988. All rights reserved in all media. No part of this publication may be reproduced, stored in a retrieval system, or transmitted in any form or by any means, electronic, mechanical, recording, photocopying, the Internet or otherwise, without the prior written consent of the copyright holder, nor be otherwise circulated in any form of binding or cover other than that in which it is published and without a similar condition being imposed on the subsequent purchaser.

Authors Reach
www.authorsreach.co.uk

ISBN: 978-0-9957883-0-5

All characters and events featured in this publication are purely fictitious and any resemblance to any person, place, organisation/company, living or dead, is entirely coincidental.

For Rachel and Mark Bell and their very much loved Old Cross Cottage.

NORTH AYRSHIRE LIBRARIES	
07396031	
Bertrams	31/05/2017
	£14.99
B	

CANCELLED

Acknowledgements

I say it every time but I really do mean it, thank you so much to all my beta readers for reading and amending early drafts of Old Cross Cottage, without you there'd be so many mistakes and plot holes! Thank you also to my editor, Jeff Gardiner, I'm chuffed to be working with you still and also Gina Dickerson, not only a wonderful author (as is Jeff!) but also a demon cover designer – and I mean demon in the nicest possible way! This book is dedicated to Rachel and Mark Bell who own Old Cross Cottage but again, I'd like to say thanks to them for the wonderful, if seriously spooky, weekends spent there!

Foreword

A huge thank you to all those who've been with me from the beginning of the Psychic Surveys journey – I really appreciate your support. I envisage six books in total in the series with several companion novellas, each one covering a separate case and different areas of psychical ability. You can jump in at points other than Book One (The Haunting of Highdown Hall) but please note certain story elements do continue from book to book. Whichever you choose to do, I hope you enjoy the ride!

Prologue

SO still.

In the early hours of the morning, with the moon hiding behind thick layers of viscous cloud, it's dark – hiding the fork in the road that lies ahead.

And on that road stands Old Cross Cottage, as alone as it's ever been.

A beautiful cottage, or it could be, if the pink render were not so mottled, if the thatched roof was a little tidier, if the picket fence that surrounds it was more welcoming instead of standing like a series of soldiers on guard. To the side of the porch is a plaque, as worn as the house – *Old Cross* inscribed upon it in black letters which twist and turn at angles. Diamond leaded windows, symmetrical but on a slant, indicate the cottage is listing, the ground beneath trying to bury it, perhaps.

A noise interrupts the stillness. Not a dog barking in the distance, unsettled and anxious, nor an owl in the trees presiding over the cottage and over the ancient village of Canonibeare itself.

This is a sound from within.

A shuffling backwards and forwards stops then starts again. Becomes urgent. As though someone is trapped and desperate for escape. But no one's at home.

No one living.

Another sound: a door opening and then just as quickly slamming shut. The action repeats not once but twice, then a third time. A voice? Could it be? Muffled and unintelligible, lips working furiously as words tumble out. There's crying too; stifled sobs. So pitiful it would tear your heart in two to hear it – so *hopeless*.

The door bangs again. The crying abruptly ceases.

A bruised sky dawns.

All is still again at Old Cross Cottage.

So still.

Chapter One

"WE'RE all going on a summer holiday—"

Ruby winced. "Cash, you sound as if you're in pain."

Leaning back into the passenger seat of her old Ford, he continued to sing, a satisfied smile on his face. "No more working for a week or two—"

"Even the dog's barking at you!"

Not that he'd be able to hear Jed – the ghost dog – only she could. And it wasn't barking exactly, it was a kind of howling, as painful as Cash's singing.

"Fun and laughter on our summer holiday—"

"Since when have you been a fan of Cliff Richard anyway?"

That almost got him, he'd faltered, missed a beat.

"And technically it's spring. British Summertime doesn't start for another month."

"God, you're pedantic, Ruby."

At last, an answer! "You know what, right now I'll consider that to be a blessing. Seriously, I was just about to make a diversion and go in search of some duct tape."

Before he could respond further, she asked him to stick the sat nav on. They'd got as far as they could without expert guidance.

"So you've never been to Lyme Regis before?" she asked, watching him from the corner of her eye as he leant forward to retrieve the 'shat nav' – his pet name for it – from the glove box. Once it was in his hands, he keyed in the details for the village of Canonibeare, asking Ruby several times for confirmation of spelling – 'Canoni-what?' – before attaching it to the windscreen. They had another half an hour or so to go – time in which she planned to keep him talking, not singing. She could only be expected to suffer so much. "Have you even been to the county of Dorset?"

"Have I even been…? Yes, thank you, Miss Davis, I've driven through it loads of times, being as it's on our doorstep."

"What? It's one hundred and fifty miles away!"

"Don't be so small-minded, that is on our doorstep, relatively speaking."

"Relative to what?"

"To if we were living in America, or Russia, or… Europe. An Italian friend of mine, Enrico, thinks nothing of driving a two-hundred mile round trip for a night out."

"So, I'm small-minded, is that what you're saying?"

"And I can't sing, is that what you're implying?"

"I implied nothing. You *can't* sing. That's more of a statement, I believe."

"Ruby," his hands clutched at his heart, "you know how to wound a man."

"Yeah, and don't you forget it."

After a brief moment of companionable silence she started speaking again.

"So come on, where's the best place you've ever been?"

"The best? Ah, that's difficult. I love any kind of escape, discovering new places, new people, and different cultures. Abroad, I suppose it's got to be Jamaica." That was no surprise, his mother was born there, and he'd talked about it fondly before. "The vibe's so laid back, music fills the air. It literally fills the air, Ruby, and the food … ah, it's amazing, as is Aunt Hilda's homemade rum. Man, that stuff is powerful!"

He'd also mentioned the rum before, how he and his brother, Presley, had stolen mouthfuls of it when they were kids and the adults weren't looking, how it soon became obvious what they'd done due to the fact they could barely stand, let alone walk! They'd only been to their mother's homeland a couple of times; there simply weren't enough funds for more visits. She'd raised them alone after her husband, their father, abandoned them when Cash was barely two – an English man; he'd simply upped and left with little to no contact since, and started another family. Not that Cash seemed bothered by it. He, his brother, and mother were a tight unit.

"What's number one over here?" she continued.

Although they'd been together for nearly a year and a half, she still enjoyed finding out about him – his memories mingling with hers to form a common history. This was *their* first holiday together – a whole week in a village a few miles outside of Lyme Regis, in a place called Old Cross Cottage, belonging to Rachel and Mark Bell and offered rent-free – well, free in a sense, in return for services rendered at least.

"Scotland, it has to be Scotland," Cash was saying, nodding his head as if to add weight to that fact. "It's magical, Ruby, it really is. I'm talking about the Highlands and Islands. I was eight, Presley was ten and Mum borrowed a friend's camper van, we took off for the whole summer, roamed from place to place like nomads. Not that you'd have known it was summer, it was freezing and poured with rain at some point every single day, but it was brilliant, still brilliant, sitting in the camper van with the door open and a cup of tea in your hands as you stared at the wilderness, feeling alone but never lonely. At one with the world, d'ya know what I mean? Connected."

"I do know what you mean," replied Ruby, overtaking a camper van and wondering at the synchronicity of it. "It sounds spiritual almost."

"Yeah, it was, no almost about it."

Ruby had rarely travelled as a child. Raised with no father on the scene either, it was her grandmother who looked after her in the main after Jessica, Ruby's mother, had suffered a breakdown due to her own psychic experiences. She'd had a day trip here or there with Gran, visited castles, country parks and stately homes, but never ventured too far. She'd made up for that as an adult somewhat, spending weekends away with friends and former boyfriends and usually favouring the West Country.

"Thirteen," Cash noted, interrupting her train of thought. "Lucky for some."

"Thirteen what?"

"Miles," he answered. "That's all we've got left. What shall we do about groceries? Bridport's the closest town, there's bound to be a supermarket there, we can stock up. Talking of rum, I fancy a bottle of Captain Morgan and I can whip up jerk chicken tonight if you like. We'll get kindling for the fire too. I know it's May but blimey, I don't think the weather-gods do!"

Ruby checked her watch. It was a nice idea but...

"I'll tell you what, let's just get to the cottage shall we? Drop the bags and do the shopping later." She glanced briefly at him. "And jerk chicken sounds wonderful. We can get some Coke too, to go with the rum. Oh, and chocolate.

Loads of chocolate."

"Aero or Galaxy?"

"Both. And Dime Bars."

"Dime Bars too? Ruby, you're a girl after my own heart!"

Dear Cash. He was so easy-going, so accommodating. He didn't suspect a thing. Guilt began to nag, tapping away at some inner door and refusing to desist. As for Jed, she could feel his eyes boring into the back of her head. He wasn't impressed with how dishonest she was being either, far from it. As a non-psychic, Cash couldn't 'see' Jed, but that didn't seem to matter; there was a bond between them, a real and tangible thing. Cash talked to him just as he would a living dog, even holding the door open for him on occasions should Ruby happen to mention he was trotting along behind them. It was just one of the things she loved about him: his sweet, almost too good to be true nature. But it wasn't an act, he *was* good, he was true, and she was lucky to have him.

Which of course increased her guilt further.

"Cash…" she began, deciding to come clean.

The phone rang.

Her mobile, attached to the dashboard, was within easy reach. Noting it was Theo, her friend and colleague, left behind to take care of Psychic Surveys, Ruby's Lewes-based high street business, specialising in domestic spiritual clearance, she thought it best to answer. If there was a problem with work she should know about it. Taking her eyes off the road for a few seconds, she reached across.

"Rubes! Watch out!"

"Huh? What's the matt…? Shit!"

They were on a single carriageway, going via the town of Bridport; the traffic they'd encountered was sparse given it was just before noon, when a car approaching from a side road shot straight out in front of them. It was so sudden, so unexpected, even Jed was taken by surprise. She'd have expected her protector – at least that's how she thought of him – to bark or something in an attempt to alert her. Instead, Cash reached out, one hand turning the steering wheel to the left, the other yanking up the handbrake. Just as well because in her panic Ruby had closed her eyes and removed both hands entirely as she brought them up to cover her face. They were going to hit the car, there was no way they'd miss it. The next sound she'd hear would be the screeching of brakes, the crash of metal, thunderous in her ears, a roar like no other, it would be deafening. Why the hell hadn't the driver waited for her to pass? What the heck was he playing at? He or was it a she? She hadn't actually seen. All she'd registered was a flash of red – the colour of the car itself, or the driver's jumper or jacket? Red for danger, danger, danger...

"Bastard!" It was Cash's voice, not the sound of colliding metal. "What a complete tosser!" Twisting round to look behind him, he yelled, "Hey, where do you think you're going, come back, come back!"

"Cash, he's not coming back, not for love nor money."

Facing the front again, Cash was clearly shaken. "I can't believe he didn't stop, check that we're okay. He's just driven off and left us here."

'Here' was in the bushes. They'd veered off the main road, gone onto the verge, and come to a grinding halt amidst a bank of greenery. Ruby looked at the foliage squashed against the car and was immediately grateful for such a soft cushioning. If they'd had the misfortune to hit a tree trunk, she doubted either of them would be talking right now, let alone calling the driver a variety of names. She also breathed a huge sigh of relief they hadn't hit anyone. It wasn't a pedestrian walkway they'd mounted but even so, there could have been a cyclist, or a rogue jogger.

Which didn't bear thinking about.

Jed leapt forward to lick her face.

"All right, all right, Jed. You can stop, it's fine."

Even though her hand went straight through him, she attempted to bat him away. He refused to be put off, however, intent on apologising for being caught off guard.

"Jed, we were *all* caught off guard."

She turned to Cash. "You okay?"

"Yeah, yeah." His voice was calm but his skin, caramel in colour thanks to his exotic heritage, was decidedly ashen. "What about you?"

"I'm okay," she replied, a slight tremor suggesting otherwise. "Thanks to you." Exhaling, she shook her head in dismay. "Closing your eyes and taking your hands off the wheel in a crisis probably isn't the best reaction in the world. Sorry."

A smile made him looked less bewildered at least. "Rubes, when it comes to battling demons and sending spirits to the light, you're second to none. When it comes to more practical matters, such as driving, leave it to me."

"No it's all ri—"

"Seriously, Ruby. We've only got a few miles to go and well… as much as I love Jed, I don't want to join him in the hinterland just yet."

"The accident wasn't my fault!"

"You were about to answer your phone."

"On loudspeaker."

"Even so."

"I'd checked what was on the road ahead, there was nothing, absolutely nothing. That man, woman, or whatever

– an idiot for sure – just came out of nowhere."

"Nowhere?" Cash looked back at the road, so did she, neither of them able to see where the road branched off from this particular vantage point.

"Lucky though," she reconsidered.

"Lucky? Why?"

"That the road was as empty as it was."

Cash couldn't disagree with that.

"Where is everyone?" Ruby asked. The subsequent quiet was unsettling.

Cash shrugged. "It's midday, Friday, people are working I suppose. We're bound to see more life as we get closer to the town." In no mood for pondering it further, he added, "Come on, swap over. I want to dump the bags and get to Bridport. I'm starving. We can grab some lunch as well as food for tonight. Fill the cupboards."

"You and your stomach," Ruby replied, as she climbed out of the car. The bushes had completely blocked Cash's exit, giving him no choice but to clamber into the driver's seat. Whilst he shunted the car back and forth she stood in the fresh air, breathing great gulps of it. Her view ahead was clearer now. Off the main drag, there was a road to the left and one immediately opposite it. *That bloody driver*, she fumed again, wondering not only where he'd come from but also where he'd gone. Disappeared into thin air apparently, as though he'd been conjured up.

Conjured?

Ruby shook her head.

Remain down to earth, stay grounded.

An ironic thought really, considering her profession.

* * *

As Cash was driving, Ruby decided to call Theo back. Whilst she waited for her to pick up, her mind started to run riot: a client had complained that a spirit they'd sent to the light had returned, full of angst and upset – the spirit and the client both. Or perhaps there'd been more bad publicity about Psychic Surveys in the media. After recent happenings at 44 Gilmore Street, that was a constant worry. Quickly she reminded herself that press attention had rapidly died down following that particular case, current issues taking over as current issues tended to do. Besides, any publicity was good publicity, right? After a lull, business had revived, big time.

"Hi, Theo, how are you?"

"Fine, darling, fine. And what about you, is everything all right?"

The way she said it caused Ruby to frown.

"Darling…" Theo prompted.

"Yeah, yeah, we're okay. Almost at Lyme Regis. Well, the village of Canonibeare, which is just outside it."

"And the journey, how's it been, uneventful, or…?"

Ruby gasped. "Theo! You know, don't you? We almost crashed the car." Cash contradicted her use of the word 'we', but she ignored him. "Come on, Theo, spill!"

"Darling, darling, calm down. I don't know any such thing. I just sensed a frisson in the air around me, that's all. So, you've had a bit of an accident?" There was a slight pause and then she gasped too. "Good Lord, don't tell me this is a direct line from the other side! You meant it when you said you were okay, didn't you?"

Bursting into laughter, Ruby assured Theo she had. "But it was a close call and… well, Cash, saved the day, he steered us to safety – literally."

"Bless that boy," Like Jed, Theo had a real soft spot for

him. "I'm glad to hear it. Erm... does he know yet, by the way?"

"No."

"Hadn't you better—"

"Yeah, yeah, I will. Soon. Is business okay? Any problems?"

"Business is just fine, sweetie. I'm busy prioritising cases at the moment, a phone call's come in from the Brookbridge Estate, I think that's going to top the list."

"The Brookbridge Estate? Again?"

"Again," Theo confirmed.

The Brookbridge Estate was a new housing estate built on the grounds of a former asylum, Hellingly Hospital to be precise. Although a few of the buildings were still in NHS use, including a high security wing for the mentally ill, it now comprised mostly two-, three- and four-bedroomed houses, billed as 'ideal homes for families and couples in the glorious Sussex countryside.' Ruby and the Psychic Surveys team had been called to the site numerous times, to deal with spirits both real and imagined. The split was about fifty-fifty when it came to the real deal.

"What's the problem this time?" Ruby asked.

"One of the residents has been complaining of unusual activity in her home, but not only that, it's happening in her entire row of houses. All those affected, her neighbours basically, corroborate her story. I'm off to do the initial survey on Monday and then probably the three of us will go a day or two later and, if things haven't been sorted before you get back, we can all wade in together and do battle."

Battle? In truth, Theo had as much empathy with the long dead patients as she had. Of those that remained, most of them were traumatised still, what they'd suffered at the hands of sadistic 'professionals' having been far from nurturing.

"Not all 'professionals'," Theo remarked, reading her thoughts – one of her unique – if unsettling – psychic abilities.

"No, of course not," Ruby agreed, but there were reasons why some people craved to be in a position of authority; unsound reasons. "Apart from Brookbridge," Ruby continued, veering off subject again, "is everything else under control?"

"Aye, aye, captain, it's all hands on deck."

Theo's next words, however, caused the smile to dissolve on Ruby's face.

"Ruby… you will take care won't you? This may sound silly but I called you because the colour red flashed in my mind. I don't know… it worried me."

Red for danger, danger, danger…

"I'll take care, don't worry."

"And take care of Cash too."

"I will."

"And Jed."

"Of course Jed."

"Surround yourselves in white light."

"Yes."

"All of the time."

"All of the time," Ruby repeated.

"Should you need help, call. We'll drop what we're doing, come down."

"I know you will."

Not just her friends and colleagues, the Psychic Surveys team – Theo, in her seventieth year and bursting with energy, the decidedly more solemn Ness and Corinna, the youngest of the four and forever cheerful – were her allies.

"One more thing before I ring off, darling."

"What's that?" Ruby asked.

"If you're mixing business with pleasure, take a leaf out of my book."

"Which is?"

"Err on the side of the latter."

Chapter Two

HAVING bypassed Bridport, Cash veered off the main road towards Lyme Regis, travelling on a country lane that led to Canonibeare. Rachel had said they'd see the house directly in front of them after about two miles or so, positioned on a crossroads. It was painted pink apparently with one of those chocolate-box thatched roofs, and *Old Cross* adorned on a plaque to the side of the front porch.

As Cash negotiated blind bend after blind bend, Ruby tensed, her mind imagining another car flying towards them, causing a head-on collision this time – no one steering it but fate. Mercifully, the coast remained clear.

"This Canoni—" Again Cash faltered. He really couldn't get his head round the name.

"Canon-i-beare. What about it?"

"Exactly that, what about it? Why'd you choose it in the first place? Why not somewhere in the centre of Lyme Regis? I hear they've got good pubs there."

"There's a pub in the village too."

"Is there? That's a relief. Let's just hope it's not full of *The League of Gentlemen* types who stare at you 'cos you ain't local."

"Cash!" Ruby pretended to be offended by his un-PC remark. "As for why I chose it, I'm sure I mentioned it belongs to a friend of a friend of mine. It's really historic apparently, just like the village itself, dating back to medieval times. The countryside is lovely too, you can see all the way to Pilsdon

Pen from one of the rear windows."

"What the heck is that?"

"It's the highest point in Dorset."

"Oh." Cash seemed impressed. "And you got it dead cheap?"

It was an unfortunate choice of words but Ruby nodded that that was correct.

"Even so, I want to pay half of whatever it cost."

"I've told you, it's my treat."

"Ruby—"

"No, Cash, I insist." After all, what was one half of nothing?

"Well, I'll pay for the shopping and meals out instead."

"We'll see," she replied, grateful that the road opened at last to reveal the crossroads. A flash – not of red this time, but pink, a muted shade – caught her eye. "There it is! Old Cross Cottage, to the left there. It's the pink one."

"Pink?" Cash frowned. "It's practically green in places."

"It *is* old, Cash."

"You're not kidding, it's one step up from a mud hut."

"Cash!" Now she really was offended. For her, the cottage held a certain appeal.

"I'm joking," he said, smiling. "It looks great, Ruby, honestly."

She couldn't help but smile too. Cash's light-heartedness was something she loved. Pointing again, she directed him to the side of the cottage, the side that faced the road that led to Wootton Fitzpaine, according to the signpost that stood to the right of the crossroads. The front of the cottage faced the road that led to Lyme Regis.

"Park over there, there should be enough room if we tuck the car in tight."

He did as instructed; she the one clambering over the gear stick to the driver's side this time as once again trees and bushes hemmed them in.

"Sorry, Rubes, I didn't think. I should have let you out beforehand."

"No worries, Cash, I can take a bit of karma on the chin."

On terra firma, Ruby stood and smoothed down the jumper she was wearing and shrugged her denim jacket back on. Cash was right earlier when he'd mentioned the weather-gods, there was a definite nip in the air. She'd go as far as to say it was colder here than ever. A shiver ran through her as she stared at the somewhat lichen covered exterior of the cottage, hoping it was clean and welcoming inside at least. She looked forward to the log fire Cash had talked about. And a rum and Coke, and his jerk chicken and just being with him... But first there was business to deal with.

Each carrying their respective bags, they made their way round to the front of Old Cross Cottage. Overhead clouds were beginning to obscure the sun and the whistle of birdsong seemed razor sharp with no traffic to mask it.

Before entering the low gate that separated the cottage from the road, Ruby took in her whereabouts. There was another cottage on the other side of the crossroads, *New Cross Cottage*. As its name suggested, it was a more recent building than the one they were staying in. Although no expert, she guessed it had been built around the 1950s. Opposite was a driveway leading to a farmhouse, although the farmhouse was too distant to be seen; just the sign for it, *Grange Farm*, hanging from a post.

Walking slightly further into the lane, she peered both left and right – there were houses dotted on either side, all occupying their own plot of land, and what appeared to be some sort of community hall. It was a village, a normal village, very pleasant in fact, but with one abode that wasn't as normal, that was troubled. Certainly the coldness in her toes and fingertips seemed to be spreading, tingling at first, almost pleasantly, before rushing onwards to engulf her limbs, her torso, and her heart.

"Ruby, you okay?"

"Yeah, good, all good," she assured Cash.

"You seemed a bit lost for a moment."

Lost? That word seemed apt somehow.

Cash shifted his gaze to the cottage. "You sure you want to stay here, Ruby?"

"Well… yeah, why?"

"Because it… you know… could be a bit spooky."

Ruby raised an eyebrow and immediately he relented.

"Yeah, yeah, I know, spirits don't always inhabit the most obvious places." He paused, thought for a second. "I still haven't seen one in our local Tesco though."

"That's because you can't see spirits, Cash."

"See, there you go again, being pedantic. How does Jed feel about this?"

"About what?"

"Staying at a spooky ancient cottage in the middle of nowhere."

"It's hardly in the middle of nowhere."

"But we could have stayed in Lyme Regis, actually in the town, where it's a bit more buzzing."

"Sorry, am I hearing right? You don't fancy being stuck in the middle of nowhere, with just me and the dog for company, going to bed early, getting up late, perhaps returning to bed in the middle of the day, perhaps not bothering to get up at all…"

Cash moved closer, his arm going round her. "I could be persuaded I suppose."

"*Easily* persuaded," she corrected, hugging him back.

"It's not as if there's much else to do around here."

"Oi! You'll sleep in the coal bunker if you carry on!"

"*If* there's a coal bunker. Seriously though, we can't stay in bed all day, it's impossible."

"Impossible? Why?"

"Who'd let the dog out?"

Rolling her eyes at his joke, she indicated for him to follow as she moved from his embrace to the front door. Jed hung back, his head cocked to one side in that way he had when he was trying to figure something out.

It'll be all right, Jed, Ruby assured him.

He didn't look convinced.

"Have you got the key?" Cash asked, falling into step beside her.

"The key?"

"Yeah, it's a small thing, usually made of brass, steel or iron and used primarily to open locks. We'll need it to get in."

"Oh, the key," Ruby replied, her mind working overtime.

"Don't tell me you've forgotten it?"

"No... I..."

"So where is it?"

"Erm..."

"Oh, hang on, of course, it's in one of those key safes isn't it, probably in the porch somewhere. I'll need the code in that case."

"The code?"

Cash stopped and stared at her; clearly amazed she was being so dense.

"Ruby, what on earth is the matt…? Christ!"

"Cash? Are you okay?"

When he didn't answer, she swung round. He was looking at the window, the one to the left of the porch. She didn't need to draw on her psychic ability to know who was inside, but despite that she felt the hairs on the back of her neck stand to attention as she stared too at the thick gloom that lay beyond.

Even Jed was agog.

She should have told him, told *them*.

"There's someone in there, Ruby," Cash whispered. "I saw a shadow."

"A shadow?"

"Yeah, honestly. I'm not joking."

She reached out. "Cash, it's—"

"And footsteps. Bloody hell, I heard footsteps inside!"

"Cash—"

Again he refused to let her explain.

"They're coming closer, towards us."

His eyes were fixed on the door – which also looked pretty ancient, as solidly built as the surrounding walls, the brass furnishings on it in dire need of a polish. It began to open… moaning as it did so, as though it was all such a terrible effort.

"Bloody hell!" Cash swore again, his mouth falling open.

Jed started to whine.

Briefly Ruby closed her eyes. *Oh, bugger!*

A figure appeared. A woman, quite a bit older than Ruby, in her mid-forties or thereabouts, her face pale, her hair too and falling in waves around her shoulders. There was nothing scary about her, quite the contrary – she was pretty in the most wholesome of ways. Earthy, Ruby would describe her as, such appeal reinforced by the natural shades of clothing she wore, all sage greens, and browns.

"Rachel?" Ruby checked.

She could feel Cash's eyes bore into her but she wasn't yet brave enough to return his gaze, didn't want to see the confusion nor the accusation in his eyes. Instead, she took a deep breath and remained entirely focused on the woman, who was holding out her hand, looking thrilled to see her, who greeted her, as all those who have had a genuine encounter with the paranormal, tended to greet her.

"Miss Davis, from Psychic Surveys? Oh, thank God you've come, thank God!"

* * *

Standing to one side, Rachel invited Ruby and Cash in – Cash having to dip his head because the doorway was so low. Rather than race ahead, as he usually did, Jed stayed close to Cash, the pair of them united in confusion.

Ruby guessed that Rachel's overall demeanour was one of calm, but in this moment a gnawing of the lower lip signalled agitation. She led them straight through to the kitchen, where her husband, Mark, was waiting. As tall as his wife, with dark hair and a close-cropped beard, his serious expression reminded her of Ness.

After they'd all shook hands, the obligatory tea was offered, Cash accepting a mug as well as her. They were then invited to sit at the sturdy oak table; two sets of iron candleholders, minus the candles, its only decoration.

Whilst Rachel and Mark busied themselves, Ruby could feel Cash's eyes boring into her. Not ideal, as she was also trying to tune into the atmosphere, to see what she could sense. But she couldn't avoid him any longer; she had to look his way, offering a rather pathetic smile as she did so. Oh God. He looked furious! The accusation she'd feared written all over his face. *You lied to me.*

She swallowed, desperate to offer an explanation or an excuse, but she couldn't. It would have to wait. Rachel and Mark were her first priority.

"Here we are." Rachel returned to the table with a breeziness that was slightly forced. "Good strong Darjeeling to fortify us. I've put sugar and milk on the side."

Rachel sat opposite Ruby and Mark sat opposite Cash, Jed on the floor, glancing upwards at the ceiling every now and then.

"I didn't realise two of the Psychic Surveys team were coming down," Rachel said. "That's great, really great. What's the saying? There's strength in numbers."

Ruby was about to answer but Cash beat her to it.

"I'm not part of the team."

"Oh?" Rachel was clearly taken aback.

"I'm on holiday. Or at least I thought I was."

"Holi—?"

Ruby intervened. "What Cash means is that he's not a psychic investigator, he works in IT. Although, erm... er..." She winced. This was no time to start stuttering. "I thought it'd be nice to have some company whilst here and you know, perhaps see a bit of the countryside. It's... er... such lovely countryside in Dorset, isn't it? So different to the rolling hills of Sussex, although obviously there are rolling hills here too, quite a few of them, in fact. And they've got names, haven't they? What's the one I was telling you about, Cash? Oh yeah, Pilsdon Pen, that's it. "

She skidded to a halt. It was hardly a good idea to start gabbling either. Taking a deep breath, she tried again.

"Only I'm here to investigate your claims of paranormal activity at Old Cross Cottage, as we agreed, but Cash Wilkins is my partner. We're... erm... a couple."

And then there's Jed, should she tell them about Jed? Appear even dafter?

Rachel and Mark continued to stare at her.

"Right, well, I'm glad we've got that sorted," Ruby declared, bringing her hands together in a resounding clap, the way Theo often did when wanting to move a subject on. "I know we've spoken on the phone, Rachel, but can you tell me again what you've been experiencing here." Jokingly she added, "No detail too small."

To her dismay, their faces remained straight.

After another brief silence Rachel did as Ruby had asked – mercifully. "As you know we bought this cottage mid last year, intending it not only for family holidays but also to rent on occasion to family and friends. We got it for a good price, a bargain really for this part of the world. I immediately fell in love with it; the thatched roof, the location, even the fact that it's painted pink! It's like something I've dreamed about, but that dream," she paused, took a breath, "it's turning sour. The thing is," again she paused, tapped her fingers against the table, another sign of agitation, "Mark and I reckon it's haunted. Call me weird but I believe in ghosts, always have done, the whole paranormal thing makes sense to me, that we're spiritual beings and funnily enough, it doesn't actually scare us that much, does it, Mark?"

Mark, who was clearly a man of few words, simply shrugged in response.

"But here's the rub, we've got kids, and they refuse to come here anymore. Not ideal, considering the reasons behind the purchase. And my kids, even though we've told them not to, they've told their cousins the kind of stuff that's been going on, exaggerating it even, and well… everyone's scared stiff now, making excuse after excuse not to visit. When we do manage to force a gathering of some sort, they have 'experiences' too." Again she looked towards Mark for confirmation. "In one of its incarnations, in the nineteenth century, the cottage was a pub, and at least two of us have woken in the night, including myself, to hear the clink of glasses downstairs and the sound of people talking. It's not loud or anything, more like a low hum."

"And you don't think about going down to join them?" Cash asked, his tone dry, bored even. Normally he'd have a field day with the puns a haunted pub could illicit.

"This cottage is cold at nights, believe me, you don't want to move unless you have to. My sister would agree. She's the one who heard them on another occasion."

Like Mark, Cash shrugged. "Oh well, it gives a whole new meaning to being haunted by spirits I suppose."

Ah, so he hadn't been able to resist after all! Ruby stared at him, tried to catch his eye, but he was looking elsewhere. "So, erm… what else?" she prompted.

Rachel twisted round and pointed. "More stoic than us, my brother did actually brave the cold to come down one night for a glass of water, he walked into the kitchen, and there, where the wall is, saw a man dressed in breeches and a waistcoat, hurrying alongside it. The man didn't look at him, didn't even seem to know he existed, he was… just going about his business, I suppose."

"What happened to the man?" Ruby asked.

At last, Mark spoke more than half a dozen words. "According to Rachel's brother, he came out of nowhere and disappeared into nowhere too."

24

"Interesting," commented Ruby, just like the car that had nearly crashed into them.

"And then there's the random banging of doors," Rachel was in her stride now, no longer hesitating. "That happens quite often and, before you suggest it, we've checked for draughts, breezes, and subsidence, the latter's the only possible cause. But even then, we don't think so, not when you take everything else into account. We've heard whispering, that was when it was just the two of us – our children are old enough to stay at home you see, so lately it's just been Mark and I visiting. And it's not just any sort of whispering either; it's frantic. Going back further, my niece screamed herself hoarse once insisting someone was in the room with her."

"Did she actually see anything?" asked Ruby.

"No, it was just a feeling she got, a *strong* feeling, but like my brother, my friend Gail saw something, this time in the bedroom upstairs, a figure standing at the window. It wasn't very clear, a shadow really, again dressed in old-fashioned clothing and with his back to her. Thankfully he didn't turn around – she'd have probably had a heart attack if he had. Instead, she closed her eyes and when she opened them he was gone. There's scratching too, scraping, like there's rats in the rafters, but there isn't, we've had it all checked, and my son swears blind he's been prodded awake on at least two occasions. Worst of all though, is the crying. It's so… Oh, it's awful."

Even the mere recollection had caused Rachel's eyes to shine.

"Do you get a sense of who it is crying?" Ruby asked.

Rachel looked at her. "No, that's just it, I don't. This is really hard to explain but it's like a *suggestion* of crying, not the full blown thing, does that make sense?"

"It does," replied Ruby – the actual *act* a suggestion but the emotions attached as strong as they ever were.

Having finished her tea, she sat back in her chair, and took a moment to think about what she was going to say. Not rushing, but taking her time.

"First of all, Rachel, Mark, I don't think you're weird for believing in spirits, how could I? I'm a psychic. Spirits are not just my business, they're part of my world. Secondly, there *is* an atmosphere here and my initial impressions are of slight unrest. If I could just explain, there are four main types of haunting, the first two being residual and intelligent. A residual haunting is a playback of a past event, a recording. With regard to the man your brother saw, you're probably right when you say he didn't seem to be aware of him, he's probably no more than an imprint on the atmosphere, playing as though on a loop, over and over again. The pub sounds could be the same thing: mere recordings. An intelligent haunting, however, is when a spirit is aware of and able to interact or communicate with the living."

"In what way?" Mark asked, leaning forward, interested at last.

"Commonly they move or hide objects, send signals through mediums such as the Ouija board, which we don't recommend you try by the way, and automatic writing, which is slightly less risky but should still be carried out or supervised only by someone who knows what they're doing. If the spirit can muster up enough energy, they might even try to communicate verbally, or laugh, or cry, as you've described."

"Why is the Ouija board risky?" Again it was Mark asking.

"Because the Ouija *invites* spiritual contact. It's like a magnet, attracting entities in the near vicinity, some of which may not be entirely human." She paused for a second, tried to find a polite way of putting it. "They're more *mischievous* than that."

"You mean something over and above what's already here?"

"Exactly."

"Well, we won't be doing that," he decided. "What's here is more than enough."

Eager to get back on track, Ruby explained that she thought it was a mix of both residual and intelligent hauntings at the cottage.

"No wonder the damned place was cheap," Mark sighed. Rachel on the other hand looked even more upset.

"But it is something you can deal with? You won't just... abandon us?"

"Rachel, if I abandoned clients or spirits I wouldn't be in the business I'm in for very long and, as you know, Psychic Surveys has a very good success rate."

Rachel sat back in her chair, only slightly more at ease.

"What about past owners, do you know any and if so, have you contacted them to ask about any unusual experiences?" Ruby asked.

Rachel shook her head. "We don't know any, I'm afraid. All we know is that it was empty for a long while before we bought it, empty in a manner of speaking of course." She waved one hand around. "The décor's very old-fashioned as you can see, it needs a lot of updating. The thatch above needs replacing too, which is another nightmare actually, I've found out it's going to cost a fortune. In many respects Old Cross Cottage is a project as well as an investment, but we knew that when we took it on. We're in no particular hurry, we'll see to everything over the years, until we've got it how we want. We intend it as a family heirloom you see, something to pass onto our children and for them to pass onto theirs, an idea that's only going to work if we can get rid of what's here. And yes, you're right, I have sourced a few mediums and Psychic Survey's seems to be amongst the best."

"And the cheapest," Mark added. "Some of them are extortionate."

"We try to oblige on both counts," Ruby assured them.

"And it's a week you're staying for?" he checked. "That was the deal."

It was indeed.

Staring at Cash, Mark seemed to acknowledge his presence, appreciate it even. "I think it's best the young lady has company. We don't mind you staying as well."

"Too kind," mumbled Cash, again his sarcasm was clear to her at least.

"Right," said Mark, standing up, Rachel too, their chairs scraping against the flagstone floor. "I think it's time for the grand tour. Follow me."

Chapter Three

RACHEL was right, the décor throughout Old Cross Cottage was old-fashioned, but Ruby didn't mind it, quite the opposite in fact. She only hoped that when they remodelled it to twenty-first century standards it retained something of its charm.

Charm?

Could a rundown cottage be described as such? That would depend on who was doing the describing, she supposed. There were some who'd see this as too much of a project, who'd run a mile at the prospect of renovation. Like Rachel, she'd love a shot at it, but owning one home, let alone a second was not likely on her wages.

The kitchen itself had a low-beamed ceiling – Cash at six foot tall stood just below it – and rough plaster walls that had been whitewashed, although the paint was patchy in a few places. Other than that it housed all the amenities you'd expect: an oven, a hob, a dishwasher and a washing machine – as well as cupboard doors painted a startling cobalt blue and blue gingham curtains at the window.

Leaving the kitchen they re-entered the room they'd previously been ushered through, a parlour combined with an entrance hall. She hadn't really noticed before but here the atmosphere was heavier, more complex, but not threatening.

Rather, there was comfort in it. When Mark announced this was where the pub lounge – or its equivalent – used to be, Ruby wasn't surprised. For many it *would* have been a place of comfort, somewhere to mingle and catch up on the day's events.

"It's also of course where the pub noises stem from," Rachel elaborated. "Our bedroom might not be directly above but that doesn't stop us from hearing them."

"They're a rowdy lot then?" Cash commented. Standing right beside him, she could sense his anger. And she was angry too, with herself, for being so deceitful. Theo's perennial adage, *honesty is the best policy,* ringing painfully in her ears.

Focusing on her surroundings, or at least trying to, Ruby took it all in: the window seat with its worn red cushions, threadbare in places, a fake leather sofa, surprisingly modern, that sat opposite an inglenook fireplace, more narrow beams above her head, whitewashed walls and a bookcase in the corner. Four framed pictures hung on the far wall, including a depiction of the cottage itself; amateur, but sweet, captured by a previous occupant perhaps. Every single one of the frames was crooked and her fingers itched to straighten them. There were light sconces too in the shape of faux flames that for the moment remained unlit. Whilst making a mental inventory, she also endeavoured to connect psychically with whatever it was that was here, but her concern over Cash seemed to be clouding the process.

Both men and Rachel had to dip their heads as they left the parlour, only Ruby, slightly shorter than the three of them, was able to walk straight through. To their right was a staircase, the treads uneven and very wide, precarious to negotiate, especially after one rum and Coke too many. Mark noticed her checking them out.

"Those boards, they're coffin lids they are."

"Wha—?" she answered. "Seriously?"

Stealing a quick glance at Cash, even he looked alarmed.

Rachel quickly explained. "Not *used* coffin lids, there's no inscriptions on them or anything. But our friend Lesley, who's an architect, said that's what they could be, due to their unusual width and shape. From the stairs upwards they're everywhere."

"It was probably a job lot going begging in one of the yards around here," Mark said, agreeing with Rachel. "A novel use for them if you ask me."

"Erm… yeah," Ruby replied, wondering about that theory. After all, people died every day, so where he got the 'going begging' angle from she didn't know.

There was a gap between the parlour and the second room, home to another sink and a downstairs toilet that was tucked away. As she passed through it, Ruby thought of it as a sort of 'no-mans land' – although where that phrase sprang from she didn't know. Nonetheless it was benign enough if a little stark. Arriving in the second lounge, she saw this was much larger than the first with an oriental rug, its colours once bright perhaps but now washed-out, covering almost the entire width of the flagstone floor and another inglenook, the log burner in it more impressive than the first. She smiled; Cash was going to enjoy teasing a fire into life in that – if he stuck around that is – a second thought that caused her smile to fade. Instead of a light-fitting dominating the centre of the ceiling, there was a hook.

"What's that doing there?" Cash asked before Ruby could.

"Yes, it's odd isn't it?" Rachel replied. "We think this was originally a cold room for the pub, you know where they hung the meat, prepared the food, that kind of thing."

"And no one's thought to remove it since?"

"Evidently not."

"Will you?" Ruby asked Rachel. "Remove it, I mean."

"One day," Rachel said, nodding. "Meanwhile, it's useful for hanging a decorative lantern from, which is something I must do actually, it'll help to soften the room a little. Anyway, what's interesting is that behind the door to the left of the fireplace is another staircase, hidden almost. It's tiny, but it leads directly to our bedroom."

The winding treads of this particular staircase reminded her of those you'd find in a castle turret, each of them having to concentrate as they climbed higher.

"This is the main bedroom," Rachel explained, once they'd reached the top, "where you can sleep if you want. It's the largest room upstairs."

Ruby felt it immediately, a presence, but a vague one, as if whoever it was had sensed her too and stepped deeper into the shadows, of which there were a considerable amount, one small deep-set window not allowing for much light.

"Is this where you hear the crying?" she asked.

"This is where we've heard the pub noises, as I've already said, and yes, where I've lain in bed and heard crying too and, just lately, the whispering. But it doesn't seem to be coming from inside the room. The sounds seem to... *drift* towards us."

"So where have figures been sensed or seen?"

"One was in the room next door, come and I'll show you."

The room leading off the main bedroom – the area directly above 'no man's land' – instead of a corridor, was used as another bedroom. It was narrow with room enough for just a single bed and a chest of drawers, a simple wooden mirror adorning the wall. Claustrophobic, it wasn't somewhere she'd choose to sleep.

"This was where my niece sensed someone in the corner," Rachel explained. "Like I said, she didn't actually see anything but she got the impression it was a child, a huddled child, her knees brought up to her chest, her arms wrapped round them."

"A *huddled* child?" Ruby repeated, finding the description a pitiful one.

"That's right, needless to say she didn't last very long in here after that. A kid herself, she ran across the landing and bunked in with her mum and dad instead. The next morning, all three of them left after breakfast and haven't been back since."

Leaving the bedroom, they reached the landing, Ruby glancing down those coffin lid stairs. Across from them was another bedroom, with twin beds in it this time and a wardrobe, behind which several long-abandoned cobwebs were festooned.

"Has there been any activity in this room?" she asked.

"Not so far. It's in the next one that Gail saw a figure at the window."

The fourth and final bedroom had a double bed, wardrobe, and a chair. Really the entire cottage was sparsely furnished, with peeling paint in a lot of places and spiders, the ones she always referred to as 'daddy-longlegs', that shake furiously when you blow on them, occupying several nooks and crannies. Despite Gail's 'visitation', the atmosphere was less heavy in here. In fact, Ruby realised, it was a bit of a contrast to the rest of the upstairs. Although she'd only thought of the single bedroom as claustrophobic, in retrospect, she realised the main bedroom and the twin bedroom had had that same feeling.

33

"Does the cottage have a cellar?" she asked.

"No. And there's not much of an attic either, it's pretty much as you find it."

"I see."

"Well, that's it," Rachel stated, "there's just the bathroom and then we're done. First thing we did when we bought this place was put in a new shower. It works quite well actually; you won't go short of—"

Instead of continuing, the colour drained from Rachel's face.

Mark noticed immediately. Moving closer, he put his hand on her arm. "Rach, what is it, love, what's the matter?"

"Didn't you hear it?" she whispered. "Surely you heard it?"

"Heard what?"

Like Mark, Ruby was confused. She hadn't heard anything either. Glancing again at Cash, she studied his face to see if he'd been privy to whatever it was that had alarmed Rachel. His bewildered shrug indicated otherwise.

Jed?

Jed was looking around, gave a quick bark, and then crept closer to Cash, practically sitting on his shoes, as though the floorboards suddenly offended him.

"Rachel," Ruby repeated Mark's question. "What did you hear?"

"Words," her voice was trembling as much as she was, "I heard words. Not whispered, not vague, but as clear as anything, screamed in my ear. *Get out! Leave!* The voice, it was so… angry, so… insistent." She clung to Mark too. "I'm not making this up, honestly I'm not. Why would I? I *heard* it."

"I believe you," Ruby replied, although to be honest, she wasn't sure if she did. She hadn't heard a thing, only the incessant sound of birdsong in the distance. And yet… there'd definitely been a presence in the main bedroom, and the cottage had a cloying feeling about it generally. She needed to focus, because whoever had come forward might just as quickly retreat, just like the entity she'd sensed in the main bedroom. As for the words, what were they exactly? A warning or a threat?

"Rachel, was it a man or a woman who shouted?"

"I… I don't know. It was so quick it was hard to tell."

"It's okay, don't worry."

Explaining briefly to the Bells what she intended to do, Ruby closed her eyes, before she did taking note of the fear on Rachel's face, *genuine* fear. She had said that the paranormal didn't particularly bother her, but being threatened, whether by someone living or someone dead, was never pleasant.

Hello, my name is Ruby Davis, I'm a psychic, which means I'm able to sense those in the spirit realm, the deceased in other words, those who have passed. Who's here? Tell me – a man, a woman, or a child? Who was it that shouted?

Silence came back at her.

Do you know you've passed?

Odd question some might think, but it was astounding how many insisted they were still very much alive.

Talk to me, please, I'm here to help you. I mean no harm. There's no need to hide.

Jed whined – the only sound to break the silence.

I can help you. I can walk with you to the light. The light is home.

His whine becoming a full-blown bark again, she opened her eyes and stared at him, her canine companion – her guide.

What is it, Jed? What's the matter?

He continued to bark, staring at the space before him – an *empty* space.

"It's getting cold in here." It was Rachel, still shaking.

"Ruby, are you okay?" It was Cash; the first time he'd spoken directly to her since he'd discovered their trip to Lyme Regis was not strictly a holiday.

"I'm fine," she replied, grateful he'd moved closer too. This cottage and who haunted it remained a mystery. One in which she had a week to crack.

Observing her startled clients, she explained that on occasion it took time to make a connection.

"But I'm stunned you couldn't hear whoever it was that shouted." Any semblance of Rachel's calm demeanour had vanished. "I'm not the psychic one, you are!"

"It's never that cut and dried."

"Well, what is it then?" Mark asked, his tone perhaps overly-challenging.

Ruby was about to reply but Cash beat her to it. "It's a gift, Mr Bell, that's what it is. And Ruby's excellent at what she does, as your wife has already pointed out from checking the testimonials on her website no doubt. I've seen her in action and I agree with every word, wholeheartedly. But like Ruby said, it's not cut and dried. Spirits don't always choose to reveal themselves to the most obvious person, hence why a lot of non-psychics can sense spirits, why they see them, why they can hear them too. The whole material-spiritual mix, it's just that, and as such it gets mixed up sometimes."

Impressed, Ruby stared at him. She loved it when he stuck up for her, loved the fact she had someone who would do that so readily.

Mark was silent but only for a moment. "All we want is a nice place to visit, a haven. As open-minded as we are, we don't need all this ghost malarkey."

"No one really needs it, Mr Bell."

"Okay, well… there you have it, we agree on something. You'll provide us with daily updates I take it?"

"Absolutely," Ruby answered, "if that's what you want."

"It is."

"Then yes, I'll email or phone every day."

Mark led the way to the main staircase, looking as eager as Rachel to beat a retreat and they stood once more in the parlour. Rachel grabbed her jacket, hanging by the side of the front door and wrapped it round her as though it were a blanket.

"I'll be glad to get out of here," she said, "which is a terrible shame because you know, despite everything, I love it here. It could be wonderful."

Ruby agreed. It could be everything they wanted.

Mark also put on his jacket. "We're returning to Worthing. Thankfully it's only a three-hour drive, if there's an emergency we'll be straight back."

"We'll be fine, I'm sure," Ruby replied, striving to appear confident, for their sake as much as her own.

Ruby and Cash walked with them to the door, where Rachel faltered before handing over the key.

"You said there are four main types of haunting, residual and intelligent hauntings being two of them, what about the third and fourth?"

Ruby was surprised, for some reason she hadn't expected her to ask. Should she tell her? Theo's words rang once again in her ears. *Honesty is the best policy.* Yes, she'd tell her but she'd play it down. "There are also poltergeist hauntings, which are believed to be the result of psychokinesis, therefore the power to move objects with the mind, on a conscious or sub-conscious level."

"And commonly associated with teenage girls?"

"That's right," Ruby replied.

"And the fourth?"

The fourth? How could she play down the fourth?

"Ruby?" Rachel prompted.

"The fourth is demonic."

* * *

After they'd both wished Rachel and Mark a safe journey – particularly in the light of their near crash – Cash closed the door and turned to Ruby.

"So come on, why didn't you tell me what this was all about? A holiday, my arse!"

Easy-going on the whole, there were occasions when Cash wasn't, with this – understandably – being one of them.

"The thing is—"

"I mean you lied, Ruby, that's what gets me. You *lied*."

"I didn't lie!" Ruby protested, following him into the kitchen where he proceeded to pace up and down the flag-stones. "I was just… economical with the truth."

Cash came to a standstill, the look on his face incredulous. "No, Ruby, you lied. You said to me you wanted to go on holiday, take a break; that you *needed* a break, after Gilmore Street, after what happened with your mother, after High-down Hall. Come to think of it," he paused and did exactly that, thought about it, "I was there for all of that too, so I needed a break as well. And it's just one week, one measly week and instead what do I find out? That this isn't a holi-day at all, it's another bloody job!"

Every word he was saying was true. She could carry on

making excuses, or she could admit culpability. Once again, she chanced the former.

"Cash, we're busy at the moment, so busy. This case came in and I... well, I thought it'd combine the best of both worlds, you know, work and pleasure." Remembering Theo's words, she added, "A fair bit of pleasure really. I mean it doesn't feel *that* haunted here. It's mainly residual I think."

"Oh, you do, do you?"

"Yes."

"Dismissing entirely the spirit that shouted in Rachel's face."

"*If* such a thing happened."

"Do you know something, Ruby?"

"What?"

"For a believer you're the biggest bloody sceptic there is! I didn't get the impression Rachel was lying, not in the slightest."

"Oh, Cash..."

He ignored her beseeching tone. "I just wish you'd been honest. And now here I am, spending a week in a bloody haunted cottage, involved in what for you at least, is a busman's holiday. I love you and what you do, Ruby, but really, I think I'd have preferred a Premier Inn!"

"Cash, what have I told you? The age of a building doesn't matter when it comes to grounded spirits, not really. I bet you a fair few Premier Inns are haunted too."

"Oh, really? The only thing that haunts me about the Premier Inns is those camp adverts by Lenny Henry! Put it this way, we'd have had more of a chance of escaping the paranormal by staying somewhere a little less dated than this, that doesn't have as much baggage attached and you know it!"

Just as he'd paced the floor, Ruby began to do so too, her hands clenched into fists by her side. She could hardly believe it. How had she let it come to this? They were arguing about Premier Inns. Who cared about Premier Inns?

Having to calm her breathing so she could speak, she also forced herself to stand still. "Look, Cash, this is my job, it's what I do, despite what I said, there are no holidays as such. Wherever I go, whatever I do, there's always something – whether it's a Premier Inn, an ancient cottage in an ancient village or a five-star hotel on the island of Mauritius!"

"You've never been to Mauritius!"

"No, I know I bloody well haven't, but what I'm saying is that even in a place like that I'll bet someone pops up from the spirit world and wants my attention. They always do, *always*. That's my life, my damned life. A curse, a blessing, call it what you will, it's a mix of both, I can see and the fact is, as much as I want to sometimes, I can't un-see. Don't you get it? Do you really not get it, after all this time together? I'll spell it out for you. THERE IS NO HOLIDAY FOR ME. NOT NOW. NOT EVER!"

Her voice had risen to a crescendo. Each word fired like arrows from a bow.

"Ruby!" Cash shouted back.

"What?" Her voice was still a growl.

"You're in my face. I mean… right in my face."

She blinked. He was right. She was. There was barely an inch between them. How come she was surprised? Why hadn't she noticed she'd drawn so close? Quickly, she took a step back. "Oh, I… sorry, I…" No more words would come. It was as though she was spent. The supply dried up.

Cash stayed where he was, a series of emotions flitting

across his face. Ones she couldn't fathom. Or perhaps didn't want to. He then left the kitchen, igniting a cold spark of fear within her.

"Where are you going?" she asked.

Was he planning to grab his bag, which was still by the front door and hitchhike back to Lewes? Was what she'd done – lying to him, making up excuses, yelling in his face – so bad as to warrant it? She gulped. Of course it bloody was!

"Cash!" she yelled, racing after him.

He didn't pick up his bag, which was something she was grateful for, but he did yank open the door and storm right out of it.

"Where are you going?" she yelled again, desperate for a response.

At last she got one; words thrown back at her.

"I'm going for a walk. Come on, Jed, you can come with me."

Chapter Four

DAMN!

Why'd she done it? Withheld the truth? Yes, she'd been afraid he'd make a fuss if he found out, but was that really reason enough? She considered herself to be an okay kind of person, kind, compassionate and generally thoughtful instead of thoughtless, but there was this whole other side to her – a side she wasn't so sure about – that would rear up and take over sometimes, make decisions she'd live to regret, just as she was regretting this one. She could be obstinate, insular, hot-headed, easily obsessed; all qualities unique to her or inherited? And if the latter, then from her mother or her father – the father she'd never known? That made sense somehow, unknown qualities from an unknown source – a warped kind of sense.

Her head fell back on her shoulders as she sighed.

Stop making excuses for yourself, Ruby, and start taking responsibility.

It was self-administered advice that stung.

Regarding Cash, she'd give him time; give him space.

And apologise, that's something you haven't done yet. Say you're sorry.

Of course she would, just as soon as he returned.

With a bit of luck, this case might be over before it had

even begun, a flash in the pan. That's what she hoped for, what she'd taken a gamble on, like so many cases before it. And if not, if it took a little longer, well… she'd strive to maintain some kind of balance – make it her goal. There'd be time off to go fossil-hunting, to walk along the coast and laze all afternoon in pubs, she'd make sure of it; plenty of time.

But whilst alone, she may as well work.

Which room in the cottage was the most active? The parlour downstairs for sure, where the pub used to be, and the main bedroom and its adjoining single bedroom. The double bedroom, the one where Rachel had experienced someone shouting at her, had seemed so much lighter – ironically. In which case, it might be the better one to sleep in. She'd ask Cash; let him make the decision, if – *when* – he returned.

Deciding to initially survey the parlour, she crossed over to the sofa and sat down, the cushion squeaking slightly in protest. Her back straight and her feet placed slightly apart, she closed her eyes and took several deep breaths before tuning in.

Listen for pub noises, try and feel the atmosphere, the laughter, the chatter, the emotions of regular visitors, extreme emotions in particular, happy or unhappy.

An echo, there was a definite echo. This was a place for locals to gather, a hostelry, *Old Cross Inn* the name that flashed in her mind. Nice to see the building had retained its name down the years. There was bellowing laughter – the energy very masculine, no evidence of femininity to soften rough edges. Slaps on backs, a coughing fit, pungent ale, and tobacco smoke – the latter so thick you could choke on it. No wonder someone was coughing so furiously. There was a dog at her feet, not Jed, this one was bigger, a wolfhound, his fur long and coarse, his nose sniffing the ground, licking at a pool of liquid and then recoiling. Shades – that's what they were, just shades. The man in the kitchen, the one that Rachel's brother had seen, was he something to do with the Inn? The landlord perhaps? If so, what was that room? A snug? Perhaps. The bar had been in the parlour, against the far wall, an impression of a man behind it, tall and proud, wearing the old-fashioned clothing Rachel had described – a waistcoat and breeches. Not a haunting as such but *haunting* certainly. Such replays could easily be mistaken for the real thing.

Deciding she'd sensed enough pub activity, Ruby broke the connection. Rising, she went through the door, past the main staircase and 'no man's land', straight to the second sitting room. It was actually an attractive room, but that hook needed removing. Repeating the process of earlier she took a seat and tuned in. Nothing. The atmosphere was dense but also curiously empty – 'numb' was the word that sprang to mind. It was a numb room, the feelings experienced in here dampened down with effort going into making sure they were. Why?

Standing again, she wondered whether to use the hidden staircase to go upstairs or the main staircase. Two to choose from in a cottage seemed like overkill.

It was two cottages once.

Startled, Ruby looked around. Who had fed her that information? Certainly she hadn't formed that thought of her own accord; it was another voice, a whispering. And was it true? Again, something she had yet to find out. But she could easily imagine it being two cottages. Was that before it had been a pub or after?

"Who are you?"

Usually Ruby communicated with spirits in thought but as she was on her own, she decided to speak out loud, the familiarity of her own voice comforting somehow.

"Come forward and tell me more. I don't mean any harm, I just want to help."

There was silence. Such a lot of silence, removed as she was from the hustle and bustle of everyday life. Even the birdsong had died down. It was a silence that was...

Maddening.

"Who is it? Are you male, female? How old are you?"

Usually she gleaned a sense of the person behind the voice but not this time.

Give them time. Give them space.

That thought was hers and exactly what she'd told herself to do regarding Cash, to just... be patient.

Rising, she decided to venture upstairs via the main staircase, wincing as her feet touched down on coffin lids acting as floorboards. They might be offcuts, but what a strange sense of humour someone had to employ them.

Cruel.

"Is that it? It was cruel humour?"

Again, there was no reply. She felt like the wolfhound she'd just sensed, waiting under the table to be thrown mere scraps. Fighting against frustration, she reached the landing, staring at doors behind which lives had once been lived. Not as muted as in the living room, there was anger in the air, and sadness – sometimes separate, sometimes entwined – a terrible sense of bewilderment too. Were such emotions still being experienced or were they simply ingrained into the building, as much a part of it as the bricks and beams that held it together? Nothing was clear.

The lack of light upstairs wasn't helping matters; it was as though the cottage shied away from the sun, the copious trees surrounding it protective but overly so – the boughs needing to part a little so that the sun could filter through.

Walking over to the only window on the landing, rectangular in shape with the obligatory light sconce above it, Ruby bent to peer down the lane, hoping to see Cash and Jed returning already. The lane was empty, stretching into the distance as well as from side to side – the fourth path not visible from this angle.

As she stared, the sense of loneliness was crushing.

Straightening up, she took a deep breath and made her way to the room with the twin beds, noting dust motes dancing in the air as her presence disturbed the stillness.

Maybe this would be a good room to sleep in, she mused, *there's nothing to stop us pushing the two beds together, and we could bring a cushion up for Jed...*

A scream! In the confines of her head, ricocheting from side to side.

"I'm here!" Ruby cried. "Don't worry, please don't worry. I can help you."

The scream didn't come from the twin bedroom, but elsewhere in the cottage. Hurrying into the double bedroom, she stood looking wildly around. There was no sense of anything. She'd head to the main bedroom instead, passing the single bedroom en route. Such a strange little room – a corridor really, one she didn't want to linger in, that Rachel's niece had *refused* to linger in. Even so, she took in the rough walls, the furniture – such heavy pieces – and the mirror that hung there.

It didn't start here.

Again, the words formed in her head.

"Where did it start?"

No reply but this time she got the gist, she should carry on walking.

In the main bedroom she spoke again.

"If you're in pain, I can help. I can walk with you to the light. The light is home –where you should be, not here, not anymore, confused and suffering. Let me help."

With the silence enduring, she felt like screaming too.

Patience, she reminded herself, *you have to have patience.*

Sometimes her job really was straightforward, other times it was far from it. Some spirits needed only the slightest encouragement to move onwards. But there were some who hid, who toyed with you, and some who were downright violent. There was no violence yet, but she was definitely being toyed with.

Tread carefully.

Her own thought but she could sense that someone was in agreement with her – a threat behind that agreement or concern? Of course she'd be careful. She also had to appease Cash. The thought of toggling between the living and the dead made her feel tired all of a sudden, exhausted even. Her gaze fell longingly on the bed, placed dead centre in the room with its back against the far wall. It wouldn't harm to kick off her shoes and lie down for a bit, take a nap perhaps, just a quick one, whilst Cash was gone. Glancing at her watch, it was after three, not late but it had been a long day already, what with the drive, the near crash, and the games being played... Games. Perhaps that was the wrong word. Games implied fun.

Unable to think further, she moved closer to the bed. It was comfortable, lumpy in places but whilst on it she manoeuvred her body so they didn't affect her. The pillow was soft too, her brown hair fanning out against the cream of its cover. She yawned, turned on her side, and closed her eyes, sleep taking no time at all to arrive.

* * *

"Mary! Mary! Come home now. It's supper time."

Mary looked up from what she was doing: making daisy chains under the shade of an old oak tree, a favourite place of hers, where she often came to sit and relax.

She knew she should go straight away, heed her mother's distant call, but it was nice where she was, cool. In the cottage it'd be cool too, but dark, it was always so dark and she preferred the light. Nonetheless, her mother wouldn't suffer disobedience, and so she finished the chain, popped it onto her wrist, and admired it for only a few seconds before pushing upwards to stand beneath the boughs.

"Mary, I'm warning you! Come in."

"Yes, Mam." Why she bothered to answer she didn't know. Her mother's voice was strident, her own less so. She'd never be heard from the field she was in, as far from the cottage as she was ever allowed to roam. She'd love to go further, explore the great expanse of evergreen countryside that surrounded them; the hills, the meadows, more fields, so many of them, but her mother wouldn't hear of it. 'You're too young,' she'd say. 'Seven years is no age, stay by my side.'

Besides which there were chores to be done – sewing clothes, cleaning, and the kneading and baking of bread. It's a wonder she managed to snatch any time alone.

Leaving the tree behind, Mary broke into a sprint, life's energy pulsing through every vein and sinew, a raw thing that she identified with. As she ran through the tall grass, the dress she was wearing – made of linen and a dull brown –

flapped against bare legs. Around her face, her fair hair did the same. She'd prefer trousers if she were honest, like the boys in the village wore, and to have her hair tied back, or better still, cut short, but her mother had looked horrified when she'd suggested that.

The ground was firm but not muddy although it had been a wet summer, which was a good thing; it meant crops for the farmers and the promise of plenty to eat when the days grew short. That wasn't always the case; sometimes they only had bread to chew on and a hunk of cheese. With no garden, her mother couldn't even tease her own vegetables from the ground. But they had a roof over their heads, which was the main thing. And it was a decent cottage with a good-sized bedroom for them to sleep in, and down the narrow winding staircase an inglenook fire in front of which they'd huddle during the evenings, together, just the two of them, as it had always been. She hadn't known her father, but there were rumours in the village. He was a gentleman apparently, well heeled, and it was he who paid the rent in return for favours of a kind Mary couldn't fathom. The children would laugh and snigger about it. Sometimes their parents scolded them; sometimes it was as though they were laughing too. Not having a father made her different, not an outcast as such, but she had no real friends, no one who would ever come and invite her to play. Her mother was indignant of course, told a different story – that she'd been decently wed; that her husband had died of pneumonia when Mary had been but a baby – a sorry business it had been, tragic; that she managed the rent herself, thanks very much.

They'd moved a couple of times in Mary's short life, settling in Canonibeare, the name of the village she was born in as unpronounceable as this one and much further west apparently. Whenever Mary summoned the courage to ask about her father, studying her mother's face intently as she answered, she'd notice her gaze would avert when speaking of their wedding day and the pride he took nine months later in the birth of his only child. Recalling his death, she'd mutter how she missed him, missed everyone. But who was everyone? Her mother wouldn't say, at that point she'd beg tiredness or insist there was work to be done instead of chatting idly. Her reluctance to elaborate caused Mary to wonder. Could the rumours be true and her mother was lying? If so, she decided she didn't mind. She liked the idea of her father being some sort of gentleman, in turn it would make her a lady, and also, it exalted her mother. If such a man had looked upon her, admired her beauty – and Mary thought her very beautiful with chestnut hair falling in waves around her shoulders, green eyes, and a fulsome figure – it meant she was more somehow. Not just a woman who laundered and mended other people's clothes to make ends meet, who sold fresh bread from her oven and who struggled as all common women struggled. She was Ellen – a name that was beautiful too. She was special.

"Mary!"

"I'm coming, I'm coming."

The cottage in sight, Mary slowed from a gallop to a trot and took a well-earned breather. There'd be supper to eat and then more laundry to wash, hung out to dry in front of the fireplace and from that strange hook in the ceiling above them. A hook she fervently wished wasn't there, that set her imagination on fire. What had it been used for? Hanging meat apparently. When the cottage and that which adjoined it had been one building – an inn – and their dwelling room its larder. Whenever she looked at it, all she could see was a carcass waiting to be hacked.

Her eyes caught sudden movement. The Old Cross – the name of the inn – had been closed for a few years, and, once separated, that half had stood empty. There was some kind of tragedy attached to it apparently, a death, which meant no one wanting to frequent it thereafter. Even if she felt lucky to live where she did, she hated one thing and that was living so close to something abandoned. Again, her imagination would run riot as she lay beside her sleeping mother in the dead of night, conjuring a whole host of horrors. As well as the cry of night owls, she'd fancy she could hear whispering, just the other side of the wall, soft but persistent, able to penetrate through plaster and lath, a desperation in it. And once there'd been crying – heart-wrenching sobs that had made her cry too. Someone was trapped – the person who'd died there perhaps, and now a ghost? When she'd told her mother what she feared, she'd laughed. 'Away with you, Mary, it's empty. There's no one there at all.'

Except now there was. There definitely was.

There was movement at the window, someone tall and thickset – a shadow that turned and noticed her too.

Mary's breath caught, as her eyes grew wide.

Who is it? Who's there?

"Mary!"

Her mother's voice: it was so near and yet so far.

"Mary!"

Becoming even more distant as she retreated, fed up of waiting for her errant child.

Mam, don't go! Please, don't go!

The door to the abandoned cottage opened, slowly, so slowly, its rusty hinges creaking in protest. And still Mary stared, unable to tear her gaze from the shadow sure to materialise, from the darkness intent on revealing itself, to her, only to her…

As if… as if I'm the chosen one.

A burst of air rushed upwards and she was able to breathe again, her chest heaving at the suddenness of it, but her feet betrayed her next and refused to move.

Rooted to the spot she was such easy prey.

"Mary?"

It wasn't her mother calling this time.

Chapter Five

"RUBES, Rubes, wake up! What's wrong? You're thrashing about like a harpooned whale. What the hell are you dreaming about?"

As Ruby surfaced she sat up, her face, her entire body drenched in sweat.

"Ruby!"

"Hang on, Cash, give me a minute. Just… give me a minute."

The dream, about a little girl called Mary, who used to live here, or at least in this part of the cottage when it had been divided into two, had been so vivid, not like a dream at all, like watching a film or rather playing a part in a film – a form of method acting, feeling every emotion intensely. Could Mary be whom she'd initially sensed – the 'huddled child' even? And if so, was she trying to communicate with her? Ruby forced herself to remember as much as she could, in case, as dreams do, it faded.

"Pen and paper. Cash, please, get me a pen and paper. Quick."

Time was of the essence – already details were on the slide.

Instead of pen and paper. Cash produced his mobile phone and clicked on the notepad app. "Here, use this."

Without further exchange she started scribing: *Mary, aged*

*seven, lived in the second half of the cottage (smaller half),
mother calling her, running towards the cottage (from the east?),
different, she was different, not quite an outcast but lonely, no
real friends, rumours about her father, mother defensive about
rumours, bedroom she slept in, it was the MAIN bedroom (the
bedroom I fell asleep in), other cottage empty, abandoned, whispers, crying, trapped, no longer empty, shadow, the door opening, someone there, someone calling her. Not her mother. Not
Ellen.*

And the hook, Ruby reminded herself, the one in the living room below, directly below in fact, Mary hated it. She
scribbled another note: *imaginative child.*

"Ruby, what's going—?"

"Tragedy." The green of her eyes met the brown of Cash's.
"There was a tragedy here. And because of it the pub closed
down and the building was subsequently divided into two
cottages, probably because it changed ownership, but that
side," she nodded towards the dividing wall, "stood empty,
and then... well, then someone moved in, a tall, dark – and
weird – stranger."

If Cash looked bemused so did Jed. They were both staring at her.

"What the hell are you talking about?"

Ruby was quiet for a moment, wondering how to explain
further and then she laughed. Suddenly that was all she
wanted to do, break the hold that the dream had had over
her, dissolve the tension it had built up, lighten the load.

"Ruby!"

"Sorry, Cash." Oh God, she had to pull herself together
but it was so good to laugh. Whilst sleeping, she'd felt caught
in a vice, unable to do anything but journey alongside the
main protagonist. She'd already acknowledged it as an

intense experience, but it had been painful too. She shook her head. No, that wasn't quite right. What was to *come* was painful; she sensed that as much as Mary had.

At last Cash's face cracked, joined her in laughter, his earlier anger beginning to dissolve. Seizing the moment, she leant forward, grabbed him and he rolled back with her on the bed. As Jed always did during such moments, he disappeared.

"Ruby, you harlot, unhand me!" Cash protested as he nonetheless started nuzzling at her neck, the touch of his lips causing her to squeal instead.

There was much wrong at Old Cross Cottage, so much yet to discover but for now what they were doing would inject a bit of positive energy into the otherwise leaden atmosphere, offset what was here, balance it, if only for a short while. And, as his hands started roaming, what they were doing felt very good indeed.

* * *

Cash had spent about twenty minutes trying to coax a flame from the logs in the inglenook fireplace, only mildly cursing as initial attempts proved fruitless. At last it roared into crackling life, each flame the shape of a golden petal, leaping higher and higher, competing with each other in a battle to draw the chill from the air.

Satisfied, Cash retreated to the sofa where Ruby was waiting for him, a woollen throw that had been on the back of the sofa draped across her legs. Reaching for the glass of red wine that she'd poured for him earlier, he joined her under the throw, the pair of them staring at the mesmerizing sight before them whilst taking long slow sips. Just in front of the fire, lay Jed, also seemingly content.

It was Ruby who broke the silence.

Snuggling into Cash, she murmured, "I take it you've forgiven me?"

"Hmm," he said, making her wait for an answer. "I suppose so, although don't get me wrong, you've still got plenty of making up to do."

"Plenty?"

"Yeah, but I think you'll enjoy it somehow."

"Maybe I will, maybe I won't. That depends doesn't it?"

"On what?"

"On the give and take. I'd like a little more giving next time please."

"Ruby! Are you calling me a selfish lover?"

"I'm just saying. That's all."

He placed his glass on the table. "You're a cheeky mare! I give as good as I get."

Laughter turned to giggling. "Now there's an incentive if ever I heard one!"

He leaned closer, the nuzzling about to begin again, but her stomach rumbled, ruining the moment entirely. Still giggling, she pushed him away, complaining how hungry she was, ravenous in fact.

"Yeah, me too," Cash agreed. "And there's no food in the house."

"Nothing at all, not even a packet of left-over pasta or something?"

"Believe me, I've checked. There's some fruit in the bowl, a packet of lemon and ginger biscuits that are two months out of date and this bottle of red." He looked over at the bottle, which was also on the table, as if scrutinising the label. "I hope Rachel and Mark won't mind us nicking it. It's a Morrisons special, so not too expensive."

"We won't nick it, we'll replace it, but we do need to eat. What shall we do? Head into Bridport and stock up, like we planned."

Cash didn't look enthralled at the prospect. "But it's so nice by the fire."

He was right, it was. As cosy as she'd hoped it would be. *Together, just the two of them.* She felt safe here, in this part of the cottage, and Mary had too, until… until what? That was what she had to find out. Glancing at the hook, she shuddered. She just didn't get why it'd been allowed to remain. Again, Mary's thoughts regarding the offending object were uppermost in her mind, of how vividly she'd imagined a carcass hanging from it, a dead thing basically. *More* dead things…

Shrugging the blanket off, Ruby stood up and made a decision.

"We can get the fire going again when we come back plus I'll need to dig out my sage sticks, get them cleansing all those dark corners."

"What about your crystals?"

"I've bought a big chunk of rose quartz with me." It was a stone that Theo swore by, meant to promote peace and healing. "I'll place it in the parlour I think. If you close the door to the burner, that'll keep it ticking over nicely until we return from the pub."

"The pub?"

"Yeah, let's go and see what it's like. They're bound to do food there."

"Really?" Still Cash didn't look too keen.

"Cash, we're talking about the prospect of eating here, you know, filling your stomach, like you love to do. I can't believe you're even hesitating."

"Steady on, Rubes, I'm not that bad!"

"You are!"

Jumping up too, he grabbed her hand. "You're right, I am. Come on, and you, Jed. I don't suppose they object to ghost dogs in the pub."

"What you can't see…"

"Can't harm you."

Not strictly true but even so… And whilst at the pub, depending on how friendly the locals were, perhaps she could ask about the cottage, see what people knew about it, in particular the 'tragedy' that may or may not have occurred at Old Cross.

Mary, we're going now but we're coming back. Don't worry – we'll be back.

As they headed out the door, it was Ruby that was flooded with worry – her own emotion, Mary's, or the other entity that was here? Again, it was less than clear.

* * *

Rachel had previously told them that the pub was about a ten-minute walk if you followed the road. Alternatively, you could take a short-cut through St Winifred's churchyard, which Cash preferred to do.

Ruby shrugged. "Okay, if you're man enough."

"Of course I am, besides, if anything rises from the grave, just tell it to get lost."

"Get lost? And that would make me great at my job, wouldn't it?"

"Oh, all right. But tell it to wait until we're on our way back at least. Any spook worth its salt should realise nothing comes between a man and his pint."

"But if it's a female spook, the chances are she's not going to give a damn."

"Ah, the fairer sex, they can be so irrational at times."

"We are who we are, Cash," Ruby replied, pushing the church gate open, the touch of the wrought iron so cold against her hand. "Even in death."

As she spoke, Cash looked at her and even though night was falling she could tell he was frowning, her words having had an impact, although that hadn't been her intention. They'd simply slipped out. She wasn't even sure she believed it; death *could* change you – often for the better.

St Winifred's was an imposing building – its fifteenth century tower looming a couple of hundred yards in front of them although a good selection of sagging gravestones, some fancy, some plain, lay much closer. To the right of them was a large tree that looked as ancient as the village itself, under which yet more graves sheltered and further up the path was a bench, where a person could sit and reflect.

"Feel anything?" Cash asked as they ventured forwards.

Ruby tuned in – were there any souls still lingering? Churchyards were often a magnet for spirits, not necessarily those who'd been buried in the grounds but those that wandered too: trying to make sense of death by drawing a little closer to it.

Having reached the bench, she suggested they sit, just for a few minutes. Closing her eyes, she focused. Around her the birds continued to call to each other – crows amongst them she realised, their cawing always so distinctive.

Mary, is this where you were buried?

Jed jumped onto the bench beside her, seemingly wanting to be close.

Is there anyone here who needs help?

If there was, they were proving as elusive as those in the cottage.

Don't be afraid, if you're here come forward.

The dog barked.

That's all I want to do, help you if you need it.

Nothing. The coast was clear. No Mary, no darker energy either – it was peaceful. Really very peace—

GET OUT! LEAVE!

The words were screamed in her face, accompanied by a rush of hot air, as if they'd been spoken by a living being, not someone deceased.

Mary?

When there was no reply, Ruby turned to look at Cash, who was staring the other way and therefore hadn't registered there was cause for alarm. Jed barked again, and moved even closer if such a thing were possible. He'd be *in* her at this rate.

"Shall we go?" Cash said, starting to rise. Quickly she laid a hand on his arm and told him to wait.

"Have you made a connection?"

"Possibly."

Staring frontwards again, she silently addressed whomever it was that had shouted, reiterating that she only wanted to help, but the atmosphere, only briefly eddied, was still again. For several minutes she persisted but the churchyard was empty, quite empty. Instead she tried to process the emotions that had been expressed – anger; there was obviously anger, or was it more than that – rage? *Outrage.* That seemed a better fit. Whoever had said it was outraged.

A plan started to form.

She'd return in daylight, tour around the headstones and

note down any belonging to females called Mary as well as Ellen to see if she could learn anything that way.

Her stomach rumbling again, she clutched at it. There was no point in hanging around. They could wait all night for the same thing to happen again – longer even.

It might just be a one-off.

They'd almost reached the pub before she realised it wasn't a one-off. *Get out! Leave!* Those were the exact words Rachel claimed had been shouted at her too.

Chapter Six

ALL heads did indeed turn and look at them as they entered The Plough, all six of them to be precise, including the barmaid and a collie – the latter the cause of great excitement for Jed. Immediately, he ran up to the living, breathing canine and started to sniff. The collie bristled initially and then relaxed, deciding to let its ghostly counterpart just get on with it. Ruby couldn't help but marvel at how accepting animals were of the spirit world; clearly the collie had deemed Jed harmless.

She smiled at those who stared in her direction but none smiled back. Immediately, paranoia surged. Did Rachel and Mark know these people? Had they told them they'd invited 'ghost-busters', as she and her colleagues at Psychic Surveys were so persistently called, to stay at Old Cross Cottage, their intent to 'exorcise' it? And if so, were they horrified by that fact... amused even?

Before her thoughts could start galloping ahead, Cash whispered to her.

"Here's something a bit different for you."

"Different?" she whispered back. "What do you mean?"

"I mean this place, it's got about as much atmosphere as the moon."

"The moon? But... Oh right, yeah, I get it!"

In the same affable manner as Jed, Cash sprang forward.

"What a lovely pub!" he declared, the lie evident to Ruby at least. "And look, you've got a menu board. Thank God! You wouldn't believe how hungry we are."

The startled silence continued – even both dogs looked taken aback by such relentless enthusiasm. As for Ruby, she held her breath waiting to see if a response would ever be forthcoming. The seconds ticked by, one, two, three, so many she lost count and then she breathed in relief as the barmaid began smiling too.

"Aye, we've plenty to keep you fed here, lad, decent portions an' all. But it's a pint you'll be wanting first, what can I get you?"

He'd done it! He'd broken the ice. Cash – the light to her darkness – had softened any tension there might have been. *You could have imagined there was tension, Ruby.* True, but as much as she cherished her gift, used it to reach out, to try and help, it set her apart. Again Mary's words came to mind. *Not an outcast as such.* Ruby knew what she meant. She wasn't an outcast either, but at times she got a sense that she almost was – and almost was difficult enough to deal with.

She realised Cash was talking to her. "Glass of wine, Ruby, or a rum and Coke?"

"Erm… rum and Coke, please."

"Come and get it, then."

With a start she realised she was still standing by the entrance and had to make a concerted effort to push forward. She really did feel like Exhibit A. The rest of the pub's inhabitants, all men, were still sizing her up but the barmaid – she'd introduced herself as Louisa – seemed to be warming to them. Cash had busied himself asking about local attractions and she was telling him about the town of Lyme Regis, the

Jurassic coast itself and nearby Abbotsbury, home to the world's only managed colony of nesting mute swans apparently and 'well worth a look'.

"Where you staying?" She asked that question of Ruby specifically as she handed over her drink.

"Rachel's cottage, just on the edge of the village."

"Rachel's?"

"Old Cross Cottage," Ruby corrected.

"Ah. Supposed to be the oldest house in the village that is. Used to be a pub too, once upon a time."

"So I gather. Do you know the new owners, Rachel and Mark?"

Louisa leaned against the bar and shrugged. In her early- to mid-forties, she had vivid green eyes, almond in shape and pretty golden highlights in the brown of her shoulder-length hair. A kindly face, it wasn't forbidding at all, although they'd all looked that way initially. "They've been in here once or twice," she was saying, "they seem nice enough, very quiet, gave 'em their drinks and they went and sat down. Doubt they'll be here long though, no one stays long at Old Cross Cottage."

"Oh?" Ruby's interest peaked dramatically and she was annoyed when Cash nudged her to look at the board and pick something to eat.

"Cash—"

"I'm having sausage and mash with onion gravy. What are you having?"

Even more annoyingly, one of the other customers was holding his pint up for a refill, capturing Louisa's attention entirely. Ruby gritted her teeth – *so near and yet so far.* That had been another of Mary's sentiments – when her mother had been calling her, when, fed-up with no reply, she'd retreated, when the child had noticed someone at the door to the other cottage, mimicking her mother, calling her too…

What happened afterwards? How could she find out?

"Ruby?"

"Erm… yeah, yeah, I'll have sausage and mash too, please."

As Louisa hurried off to the kitchen with their order, Ruby allowed Cash to steer her over to a table by the window, although there was no view as such, not now that night had fallen in its entirety, it was just a void beyond, an immeasurable black hole. They were the only ones occupying a table, the rest remained at the bar including Jed, snuggled happily against the collie, both of them wagging their tales in unison. Ruby did her utmost to hide her frustration, a fixed smile on her face as she listened to Cash reiterate in full the holiday tips that Louisa had given him.

When Louisa finally came over with their food, Ruby decided it was now or never.

"Louisa," she said airily, as the woman bent slightly whilst laying their plates on the table. Only briefly did she notice Cash's eyes widen at the ample cleavage on display as she did so. "You said Old Cross Cottage has had quite a few owners in the past. I was wondering about that, it's such a lovely home, really quaint with lots of character. Is there a particular reason why, do you think?"

Cash had managed to avert his gaze, diving into his mash instead, but a part of him was listening, his eyes flickering upwards whilst he waited for Louisa to reply.

"Well," Louisa sighed, straightening up. "It's a funny old place really, got a bit of a history to it. Used to be the pub as I said, until 1900 I think it was, the turn of the century. This place took over from 1904, although you wouldn't think it would you? Unlike Old Cross, there's nothing original here, it's been rebuilt extensively during that time." Pausing, she inclined her head to the left. "See over there? Used to be a lovely fireplace with one of them huge oak beams lying across it. But it took up too much room, didn't it? They got shot of it, put in that paltry burner instead; stupid thing hardly chucks out any heat. Still, we've got central heating I suppose. Mustn't moan."

The wood burner she referred to was indeed less than impressive; to either side of it positioned yet more empty tables.

"Get busy do you?" asked Cash in between mouthfuls.

"Sometimes," Louisa replied. "The Saturday night quiz draws them in. You should come along, give it a go."

"A quiz? Yeah, we might do," Cash replied.

Eager to get back on track, Ruby asked Louisa again about the 'history' of the cottage, and indicated for her to perhaps take a seat. A quick glance at the bar revealed all pint glasses were filled so hopefully the woman could spare a minute or two.

"May as well, I suppose," said Louisa, responding to Ruby's gesture. "Take the weight off me feet, ache like a bugger they do."

Settled in beside her, she needed no further prompting and started talking about the cottage happily enough.

"So, Old Cross was a watering hole until 1900, don't ask me how long it was beforehand though, maybe forty, fifty years, maybe longer. And it was a popular pub too, according to local legend, the last ever landlord much-loved, initially anyway. Towards the end, he started to become withdrawn, depressed even. No one ever knew the reason why. He just… changed, didn't he? Hanged himself."

"Hanged himself?" An image of the hook in the living

room flashed into Ruby's mind. "In the cottage you mean?"

"No, no, not in the cottage," Louisa answered, dispelling that notion. "Underneath an oak tree, in one of the fields hereabouts. They cut his body down and brought him back to the Inn, laid him out for a week apparently and on the bar of all places, before deciding what to do with him. Sort of killed the spirit of the place I'd imagine. Who'd want to drink at a bar where a body's been laid out? I only hope he'd been plugged up properly, I'd hate to think of all that seepage if not."

"Yeah, gross!" Cash mumbled, clearly not grossed at all as he continued demolishing his food. In contrast, Ruby's plate lay untouched, her mind digesting information instead. Was the landlord's death the tragedy Mary had referred to?

"Do you know the landlord's name by any chance?"

"Everyone round here does, it was Thomas Ward, an upstanding member of the community if ever there was one. Even so, he's not buried in the village, on consecrated ground, you know, on account of him being a suicide."

"Where was he buried then?"

"God alone knows."

Which might indeed be the case, thought Ruby. Still keen to extract as much information from Louisa as possible, she asked what happened to the pub after Ward's death. "The cottage got divided into two, I believe?"

"That's right, it did, well, so the story goes. But the front cottage, where the bar had been, never really got lived in. The rumour was it was haunted by the ghost of Ward, which is just plain daft. Who believes in ghosts, I ask you?"

"Ruby does," Cash piped up again, "that's her business. She moves ghosts... sorry, she doesn't call them that she calls them spirits, to the light. Grounded spirits I mean, the ones that get stuck here. I've seen her in action too, plenty of times. She's good, very good. An expert in the field and bloody well-regarded."

Ruby's mouth fell open and she had to try hard not to kick him under the table. Louisa had just declared herself a non-believer, yet still he had waded in and told her what they were doing here. She knew he meant well, that he was proud of her, that she should be proud of herself. She *was* proud of herself but even so, he needed to rein it in sometimes, not be so gung-ho about such a controversial subject.

As his words couldn't be retracted, all Ruby could do was glance at Louisa to gauge her reaction, dreading the worst, that they'd be chucked out of the pub, banned even. To her surprise, she looked as impressed as Cash intended her to be.

"Really, you're an exorcist are you? You're with the church?"

"No, not the church," Ruby quickly corrected, "I'm not affiliated with any religion, but I am a psychic and I run a business, a *high street* business, specialising in domestic spiritual clearance. We have, as Cash says, a good reputation."

"Well, well, well." Louisa sat back in her chair and crossed her arms under her chest. "I don't believe in ghosts, I've just said. But... maybe it's 'cos I've never seen one. Is that what you're doing at the cottage, searching for ghosts?"

Ruby shook her head, not sure if Rachel and Mark would want that sort of information disclosed. "We're on holiday, that's all. And I, erm... I like history too. That's why I'm asking about Old Cross. Out of interest, nothing more."

Louisa raised an eyebrow – an expression on her face that indicated well enough she didn't believe her. Even so, there was no spite in her manner. Because of that, Ruby considered it safe to continue probing.

"So… you were saying that the house became two cottages, but only one was really lived in, the back cottage so to speak."

"Yeah, and then at some point it became one property again, the dividing wall knocked down and that's the way it's been ever since. I've lived in this village all my life and I've only ever known it as one cottage. But like I say it's had a succession of owners, no one's ever lived there properly, a few years perhaps but no more than that. It's mainly a holiday let. A lot of places round here are, especially in more recent times, people moving out of the sticks and into the cities. Going where the jobs are."

Ruby supposed that was true. "And you don't happen to know the names of any other past tenants who lived there, after Ward I mean, when it was two cottages?"

At that Louisa did look surprised. "Why should I?"

"I was just wondering."

"No, 'fraid not. No one of any importance though."

'No one of any importance?' Those words jarred.

A sigh escaping her, Louisa pushed back her chair and rose to her feet. "Oh well, it's been interesting talking to you, but I'd better get on with the job I'm paid to do." She glanced over at the four souls that lined the bar. "That lot, they're permanent fixtures they are, they'll be wanting a top-up round about now and another one in about forty-five minutes – honestly, I can set my watch by 'em. Anyway, been good chatting to you. Regarding what you do, have you got a website? I'll look you up."

Ruby gave her one of the business cards she kept in her bag and taking it, Louisa winked. "You never know, I might need your services one day."

Chuckling, she wandered back to the bar. Ruby thought

again about giving Cash a discreet ticking-off regarding his earlier indiscretion but decided against it. In some ways her heart swelled even more with love for him because of it.

As though cottoning onto her train of thought, he looked up, straight into her eyes. She smiled and he did too – her connection with him once more rock solid. About to open her mouth, to say something – maybe even get a bit soppy – he beat her to it.

"Not hungry after all, Ruby? Don't mind if I pinch a bit of yours then, do you?"

Chapter Seven

ARRIVING back at the cottage, the three of them spent another contented hour in front of the fire, finishing off the last of the red wine. In between drinking, Cash insisted on fiddling with his iPhone whilst Ruby simply lost herself in the beauty of the flames, able to forget for a while that she was indeed working. Her glass drained and the heat making her drowsy, she was about to suggest they go to bed and get a relatively early night. In the morning they could explore some more – Lyme Regis first and then the churchyard – when Cash thrust the mobile in front of her.

"What is it?" she asked, slightly taken aback. "A text from Presley or something?"

"Look at the screen properly, Ruby."

She did as instructed, leaning closer. Against a black background was what seemed to be some sort of radar, neon green in colour – the detector sweeping around it at breakneck speed. Below the radar was a series of ever changing numbers and above it one word spelt out in red: *warm*. As she stared, a faint blue blob appeared on the far left of the radar.

"What is it?" she asked, still confused.

"It's *Ghost Discovery*."

"Ghost what?"

"An app, *Ghost Discovery*, it's designed to detect paranormal activity by using various sensors." Warming to his theme, he began to elaborate. "I've been reading about these apps, some of them are rubbish, but this one's regarded as a bit of a classic and has got some good reviews. The sensors hunt for changes in the atmosphere and only give readings when a definite pattern's been found. And that word at the top – *warm* – that's the word it's detected, otherwise known as spirit speak. And it's not wrong is it? It has warmed up in here. Also, you see that blue blob? That's the spirit it's detected. When it's blue it means it's a weak presence, green is medium and red is strong. So right now, it's erm… yeah, it's weak."

Unable to resist, they both turned to look where the 'blob' was supposed to be, right by the door. Ruby tuned in; there was nothing there.

"Okay," she asked, "if it can pick up a spiritual presence, how come there's no blob on the radar where Jed is? He's a spirit if ever there was one."

"And he's in front of the fire, is he?"

"Correct, so, technically, he'd show up at the top of the radar, but there's zilch."

Cash did indeed look perplexed. "Perhaps spirits of a canine variety are exempt?"

"Weak argument, Cash, very weak." Exasperated, she leant back into the sofa. "What a load of tosh! I can't believe you're bothering with something as stupid as that. It's a gadget, as useless as most other gadgets that claim to detect the dead."

Cash refused to be deterred. "Ah, come on, Ruby, there's no harm in it. I mean, I know technically it *is* a load of tosh, there's no hardware in a phone to pick up infrequencies in the atmosphere, and the words are all pre-programmed, but at the very least it'll be a laugh. Let's leave it running and see what happens, how many blobs appear. You can then use your psychic powers to cross reference."

"It's psychic ability, Cash, not powers. I'm not Wonder Woman."

"You are to me, sweetheart."

Ruby snorted. "Honestly, you tell me off for trying to combine work with a holiday and yet the IT specialist in you is never far from the surface is it?"

Cash favoured her with a grin. "We're two of a kind."

"Maybe, but you're more into my job than I am at the moment!"

"Well… if it's fun it won't seem like work, will it? But tomorrow is definitely a day off. We'll go into Lyme Regis, get fish and chips, walk along its famous prom."

"Cobb," Ruby corrected.

"What?"

"The bit you walk along, that juts out to sea, is called the Cobb. I've seen it in that film *The French Lieutenant's Woman*, you know with Meryl Streep. She stands right at the end of the Cobb, staring forlornly out to sea, praying for her man to return."

Cash shook his head. "Never seen it."

"Well, like your app there, it's a bit of a classic."

"Okay, sounds good. Whilst we're here, perhaps we should hunt down a copy."

"Yeah," Ruby replied, warming to that idea at least, "that'd be fun." She was about to suggest there might even be a copy in the cottage, in one of the cupboards in the parlour, when a voice that belonged to neither of them nearly scared the wits from her: a male voice, uttering one word and one word only: *cold*. Yet again it was right. As though on a yo-yo, the temperature had plummeted suddenly, despite the fire.

"Who was that?" Ruby breathed, her eyes as wide as plates.

"Sorry," Cash said, holding up his iPhone in a gesture of surrender. "I've just found the volume on this app, it speaks the words as well as displaying them."

"Oh, for God's sake!"

"Hang on, there's a red blob, it's picking up a strong presence, again to the left of us. Do you think it's accurate? Can you feel anything? It really has got cold in here!"

Red. Why did it have to be red? Red meant danger, always danger.

Exhaling again, certain she'd see plumes of mist appearing in front of her and surprised when there wasn't, Ruby closed her eyes and tried to focus. Was someone really there, standing by the doorway, staring at them? Could the app be right?

Hello? Can you hear me?

After a few seconds she tried again.

Let me know if you can hear me? Say something.

It was growing warmer again.

Don't go, please. Mary, is it you?

If it had been strong, it had also been fleeting.

"Turn it off, Cash," she said at last, "it's nothing more than a distraction."

"Okay," Cash replied, in reluctant agreement. Before he could, however, another word flashed up and the computer-generated voice spoke again.

Don't.

* * *

In the double bedroom – the room Cash had chosen – Ruby lay awake and listened to his gentle snores. Jed had been gone for the last hour or so, to wherever it was he went when he wasn't by their side, but he'd appeared again several minutes ago, turning three full circles, as was his habit, before settling at the foot of their bed.

Despite *Ghost Discovery's* instruction, she had persuaded Cash to switch it off – pointing out that it was hardly conducive to seduction. At the mention of that particular word, or rather the promise of it, he'd positively dragged her up the main staircase, intent on getting said seduction under way. Afterwards, they'd chatted for a while, Cash occasionally listening for sounds of the 'ghost pub' as he called it from downstairs, insisting that if he did hear anything, he'd join them for a glass of Captain Morgan. Finally he fell asleep. Ruby was tired too but her brain refused to switch off. After lying with her eyes determinedly shut for the best part of an hour, she decided to go to the bathroom, once again recoiling inwardly at the touch of those strange floorboards against her bare feet. As she attempted to tiptoe across the room, several of them creaked, causing Cash and Jed to gently stir. Twice she stopped and waited for the floorboards to settle before continuing.

At the door, she eased it open, wincing as that creaked too, and stepped onto the landing. The bathroom was to the left and she was about to turn towards it when something to the right caught her eye. It was a shape, a shadow – darker even than the pitch that surrounded her – and not tall, but childlike, darting swiftly from sight.

Ignoring the demands of her bladder, Ruby decided to follow, wishing she could flick a light on but that really would disturb her slumbering companions. Besides which, she was growing used to the gloom, her eyesight adjusting. As she bypassed the stairs, she thought she heard a sound from below – the clinking of glasses, a stifled laugh, as Rachel had described, drifting towards her.

Shades, she reminded herself, *they're just shades of a time long gone.*

The shadow might well be the same – nothing more substantial to it than that.

In the single bedroom she came to a halt. A sliver of moonlight had crept in, only barely illuminating it. This had been part of the front cottage, she was sure of it.

His cottage.

Ruby's breath caught.

"Whose? Tell me."

Come.

Steeling herself, Ruby pushed forwards into the main bedroom, into a darkness that moonlight had forsaken. Although she could barely see the furniture within, she was drawn towards the bed as surely as if someone was guiding her. She knew she'd have no trouble sleeping now. Tiredness seemed to wither her.

Reaching down, she drew back the blanket, still ruffled from earlier, and, climbing in for the second time, she closed her eyes.

* * *

Her feet obeying at last, Mary picked up speed, ran back to the cottage, to the safety of its thick walls, the fireside, and her mother's arms. *Run, Mary, run.* Flying through the cottage door, she pulled it shut, before slumping in relief.

"Oh, decided to show yourself, have you? Look at your hair! It's all over the place. We need to keep it braided, Mary,

I've told you. You look like a child from the gutter."

A barbed comment, but she barely noticed it.

"Mam, there's someone next door. Who is he?"

Despite the fear his presence had invoked, Mary couldn't help but notice how weary her mother looked. There were shadows under her eyes and she was slightly hunched instead of standing tall. Little wonder, she worked so hard, they both did, sometimes from first light until late at night. She was fair though, would give her daughter plenty of breaks to go outside, the fresh air always so welcome. But it concerned Mary that she herself never fetched a break, sometimes not even on a Sunday. She'd rise, bundle them both off to church, where they'd stand at the back – always – and then hurry home again, often without speaking to a single soul. As young as she was, that irked Mary. The others in the village seemed happy enough to acknowledge Ellen as they handed over clothes to be washed or mended, or wanted a loaf of her oven-fresh bread, but other than that, not a word. She shook her head; refused to get side-tracked. There were more pressing matters to attend to.

"Someone's next door," she repeated.

Ellen didn't look surprised.

"Do you know already?" Mary asked.

"There's gossip hereabouts. A man, come down from the north he has. What he wants here I'll never know. Nothing much for anyone."

"Then why did we move here?"

"Oh, don't start that again." Ellen flapped her hand in the air as she said it, turning her back to lay the small table they'd sit at to eat. "Come on, the stew's getting cold."

Mary did as her mother instructed, the chair scraping against the flagstones as she pulled it out. Picking up her wooden spoon she couldn't help but ask again, in the confines of her head at least. *Why* had they moved here? Other children had grandparents, uncles and aunts as well as parents, where were hers? Why were they so alone in the world? And who was their new neighbour, a man who'd called her by her name? Remembering that fact she almost choked on a lump of meat.

"Mam," she said again, "he knew my name!"

"Who did?" Seated too and eating, her mother seemed to have forgotten what they'd been talking about.

"Next door, the man, he knew my name. How come? I've never met him!"

Ellen paused. "I... I don't know. Mebbe he heard me shouting. God knows I was out there long enough."

That was true. That could explain it. Even so, there was still a chill in the pit of Mary's stomach, ruining her appetite, making her feel shivery suddenly, and quite ill. Her supper barely touched, she pushed it away and crossed the room to sit in front of the fire, trying to draw warmth from it – her actions causing Ellen to frown in concern.

"Let's get you upstairs to bed. I'll lie with you for a while, just until you doze off."

Ellen was as good as her word and Mary escaped her worries into a series of dreams, all of them vague, as dreams often were, but with a sense of running, as if from room to room, as though she were trying to find a way out... and failing.

The final dream must have frightened her because it shook her from sleep. Who'd been chasing her? A shadow? If so, it had been relentless in its pursuit.

One hand reached out in the darkness for her mother, but the bed was empty. She'd gone downstairs again, to sew by candlelight no doubt, her eyes becoming redder and redder.

Her poor mother, she should leave off, come upstairs, and join her again. How she longed for the comfort of such a familiar figure beside her. Especially when the whispers started, so easily penetrating the divide between the two cottages, another voice amongst them – *his* voice.

"Mary... Mary..."

Chapter Eight

PROPELLED from sleep too, Ruby opened her eyes. She was surprised to see the bright light of a sunny morning filtering through the flimsy curtains, blue stripes as opposed to the gingham of downstairs. How long had she slept for? She checked her watch. All night. And she'd dreamt again, about Mary.

Lying on her back, she made a conscious effort to breathe deeply and evenly, striving to recall every detail of what she'd seen. It was much easier than last time, scenes not fading at all, nor the emotions. Poor Mary, she'd been so afraid.

Was she experiencing a visitation dream? A spirit – Mary in this case – finding it easier to communicate when a person was deeply asleep and therefore no longer focused on the physical. Under such circumstances, they had a captive audience. In her mind, she ran through characteristics typical of this type of connection. It was vivid – check. It felt real – check – *very* real. When spirits chose this medium it wasn't because they wanted to engage in idle 'chit-chat', they came with a clear purpose in mind, a message. Ruby thought about that one. Yes, there seemed to be a clear purpose to the dreams, Mary giving her a unique insight into her life, kick-starting from a perceived point of crisis. Check. Most definitely check.

Rising from bed at last, Ruby padded over to the wall and laid her forehead against it, imagining the whispers Mary had described. After a few moments she left the main bedroom and stood on the other side of the wall in the single bed-room. That it was a bedroom at all was wrong. It seemed more like a bridge of sorts, a link between somewhere good to somewhere... not so good.

Is this where the man had slept, the one who called Mary's name, tormenting her? In the dreams, Ruby had witnessed the first couple of times it had happened, but there'd been more occasions. She knew that without having to be shown. Was Mary's tormenter still here? Was he the one responsible for the weight of the atmosphere in the cottage? More to the point, was he the one who'd shouted at Rachel and then sub-sequently at Ruby in the churchyard? In which case his words were most likely to be a threat. With no clear handle on anything, she could only guess. He could even have passed into the light, only his residual energy left behind, whilst Mary, his victim, still suffered.

Are you here, Mary? Is anyone here? If you are, speak to me, do something.

The curtains at the window rustled slightly, but a slight crack in the windowpane could account for that. Beneath her the floorboard creaked, one of those damned coffin lids, but then again so many of them creaked, it was more usual than unusual.

"Please, I *know* someone's here."

There'd certainly been plenty of activity before, according to Rachel and Mark; the suggestion of a huddled child in this room, a clear view of a figure in the double bedroom, the sounds from the pub below, scratching, scraping, whispering, crying even – terrible crying. So why was it all so quiet now, as if, with their arrival, the cottage had tensed – only the child venturing forwards and that through dreams?

What are you all so afraid of?

A door banged. A sudden but muffled sound – the kitchen door perhaps and a possible indicator that what was within was becoming bolder. She hoped so. They had one week and already twenty-four hours had gone – hardly the flash in the pan case she'd hoped for! Even so, it'd be nice to put right what was wrong here, another success to bolster their reputation further. And that's what she wanted, to spread her wings with cases across the UK, not be confined to the area in which she lived. *You could even go international.* Wouldn't that be something?

Realising she'd become distracted, she was about to call time on her efforts, for this morning at least, go back to Cash and crawl into bed beside him, perhaps they'd spend the morning there, not venture into Lyme Regis until much later, maybe stay in bed all day… when she was thrown against the wall – a spectral hand responsible but no less powerful because of it, managing to dispel the air from her lungs.

"Listen…" Ruby began, seizing the moment, trying to reason with whoever it was, but she was interrupted when the spirit yelled the very same word.

LISTEN!

And then it fled, leaving her alone.

* * *

The sun was shining on the three of them as they parked the car off the main drag in Lyme Regis and proceeded to walk towards the beach.

"There's loads of nice shops here," Ruby commented and Cash agreed. "We should explore them after lunch."

Lunch was fish and chips obtained from one of the beach stands and eaten overlooking the harbour, Cash having to finish hers as the portion was so generous and Jed looking enviably up at him all the while. Watching him munch away too, her familiar friend, guilt, nagged at her. She hadn't told Cash about what had happened in the single bedroom. It wasn't that she was concealing information this time, or that she was worried about frightening him; he was made of stern stuff. She was just trying to get it straight in her head first.

The spirit had been so insistent – *Listen!* But listen to what, and to whom? She didn't get the impression it was Mary who'd pushed her – it had been too powerful for that, Mary's tormenter then? A place with that much history could hold any number of spirits. And yet... one thing she did know, the cottage, although tense, was beginning to stir, but slowly, very slowly. As for connecting via dreams, it was hardly the most practical way to keep in touch with the child; she could hardly sleep 24/7!

"I'm done," Cash announced, having made an impressive dent in her portion too.

"You amaze me, you really do."

"Nice of you to say so," he replied, getting up to find the nearest bin so he could discard the remains of their meal. "What have I done to deserve such praise?"

She fell into step beside him. "You eat so much and yet there's not an ounce of fat on you."

"That's because I'm a lean, mean, eating machine."

"I wish I was," she pinched her waist. "I've been putting on a few pounds recently."

"That's contentment that is," Cash said, hugging her briefly.

"So you'll still love me if I grow to be the size of Moby Dick?"

"'Course I will. You and me, we're destined to grow old

and obese together."

"Obese?" Ruby screwed her nose up at that particular prospect. "Are you saying your appetite is going to catch up with you one day?"

"Everything catches up with us at some point, doesn't it?"

She nodded. That did indeed seem to be the way.

On the Cobb now, walking along the elevated stone path, as it weaved gracefully into the sea, she decided to tell him about what had happened.

"Cash—"

"Ruby—"

Clearly he had something to say as well.

"Go on," she conceded.

Glancing at him, she was surprised to note him hesitating. "Cash?" she prompted.

"Well… it's… erm." He retrieved his iPhone from his jacket pocket before continuing. "I know it's a load of nonsense, but I kept *Ghost Discovery* running last night on silent and – this is really clever actually – you can access the list of words that it's detected during that time. It makes pretty interesting reading."

Ruby groaned audibly. "Cash, I've told you, we don't need stuff like that. It's commercial crap."

"I know, I know, but hear me out, or rather hear the device out."

Before she could protest, Cash pointed to one of a series of benches lining the lower half of the Cobb wall. "Come on," he prompted.

Taking a seat beside him, Jed having wandered off to sit at the feet of whoever else was eating fish and chips al fresco, she couldn't deny she was curious. Yesterday, in the living room of Old Cross Cottage, the device had been strangely accurate. Unlike Cash, she knew nothing about IT but those who built such programmes were, in her opinion, fiendishly clever and maybe they incorporated some magic of their own. For a moment, before he began speaking, she wished they truly were on holiday, no case to crack at all. The day was calm, the sea too, lapping gently against the shore. On her lips she could taste sea salt – different to the salt she'd put on her chips, tangier, and above her a collection of gulls circled high and low against a clear blue sky. *It's the calm before the storm.* The saying came to mind but she dismissed it. Right now, a storm of any kind was hard to imagine, despite what had happened that morning. She loved it here, in Lyme Regis, at the cottage...

"Right, here we go, are you listening?"

"Oh, yeah, sure, go on."

"Okay. This is in the order they were recorded: *cold, warm, don't*—

"We've already had those."

"I know, I know, I'm starting from the top."

Ruby shrugged as a light gust of wind blew her hair back, causing her to shiver. She nestled into Cash as he continued with his list.

"*Dark, cold* – that's the second time for 'cold' – *mixed, beat, realise, wrong, pushed, ruined, blamed, two, indulged, king, break, tales, stubborn, malleable, desperate, judge, blessing, aligned, mine, taller, finer, fault, hers.*"

After he'd finished reciting the words, he sat back against the bench. "So what do you think? Impressive, eh?"

"Impressive?" Ruby pondered. In a way, she supposed so, some words more than others, more emotive she supposed, but that was probably a deliberate ploy on behalf of the designers. The game would be more fun that way. And that's what the app represented – a game – whereas what they were up against was all too real. The time had come to tell him what she'd experienced too. "Cash, you know that dream I had on the first day we got here, about Mary?"

"Yeah, you jotted down a few notes about it on my phone."

"That's right, well, last night, I couldn't sleep. I got up to go to the toilet but got side-tracked. I saw a shadow, a child I think, possibly Mary, possibly just a shade, but I followed it, all the way to the main bedroom. Whilst in there I felt tired, really knocked out, so I lay on the bed again and went to sleep. I had another dream about Mary, picking up from where the last one left off – there was more concerning her fears about the man next door – she felt he was homing in on her. She heard or imagined she heard him calling her name through the wall that used to divide the cottages. Well, when I woke, I got up and tried to keep the connection going but couldn't. Instead, I went through to the single bedroom and tried to connect there. Apart from a door banging down-stairs, there was still nothing happening, or so I thought. I was about to give up, go back to our room, sneak back in beside you, when I was assaulted, a voice yelling in my face, telling me to listen. It could be the same voice that Rachel heard, that I heard in the churchyard. I've no sense who the voice belongs to, I don't think it is Mary, but if I'm wrong, then maybe it's a warning."

"About what?"

"About a darker presence. It's vague, barely detectable but it's there, and maybe it's not just residual, but intelligent too. She could be warning us about that."

"Or it could be the darker presence itself?"

"It could, in which case it's more likely to be a threat."

Having listened intently, Cash looked from her to his phone again. "Do you think this could be from Mary too?"

Ruby shook her head. "I think she's connecting by dreams at the moment – that's her chosen medium. That thing you've got there, with its weird random word generator, it could muddy the waters and confuse us further."

"I'm not sure, Rubes, I think it could be a useful tool."

"Useful? Go on then. Try and make sense of those words."

"Erm… okay, it's *dark*, it's *cold*, I'm *mixed* up, I'm *beat*. I *realise* that I was *wrong*. I was *pushed*, my life *ruined*, I *blamed* so many people, but it was actually *two*. I was *indulged,* like a *king,* and my heart, it would *break*, *tales* spinning round in my head… What's the matter, why are you looking at me like that?"

"Because it's gobbledygook."

"I think I did a pretty good job actually."

"You would!"

"Ruby, come on, you've been wrong before."

Typical Cash – he didn't mince his words. She came to a decision. "Look, leave it running if you want, but I'm going to pursue more tried and tested channels."

"Such as?" Cash shut off the phone and put it in his pocket.

"Such as the churchyard at Canonibeare. Let's have a quick scout around the shops like we said we would and then go back there. I want to check all the gravestones with the names Mary and Ellen on them whilst there's still daylight."

"Fair enough," Cash agreed, "but can we do one thing before we hit either the shops or the churchyard?"

"What's that?"

"Get an ice-cream, I don't know about you but I could murder a Mr Whippy!"

Chapter Nine

THE sea air had taken its toll on all three of them as they arrived back in the village. Cash excused himself from the churchyard trawl and went back to the cottage for a nap instead, Jed cottoning on and following him, clearly thinking an afternoon slumber the most brilliant of ideas. Suppressing a yawn as she watched him disappear inside, she had to admire his complete lack of apprehension. There were many people who wouldn't dare enter a cottage that was regarded as haunted either alone or with an army behind them. Even after he'd closed the door she carried on surveying the cottage, imagining herself to be standing in the exact same spot that Mary had stood, the moment she'd skidded to a halt when she'd noticed someone in the cottage that had previously lain empty, when she'd heard him call her name.

I'm here now, Mary. I'll help you. Don't be afraid.

But the trouble was Mary was very afraid.

Sadness rose up in Ruby, causing her earlier good mood to plummet. Dealing with a vulnerable child, a *fatherless* vulnerable child, she could certainly empathise with her. She felt anger too – the first stirrings – against the spirit that had yet to show itself; the dark presence. If he was the one who had terrorised her…

She checked herself – if he was and he made contact, then

that would be a good thing, it would go a long way to getting this case sorted. But right now it was just about Mary, searching for a clue to her identity somewhere other than the cottage.

Turning on her heel, she experienced a strange sense of disorientation, momentarily wondering which path to take.

Straight on, Ruby, the church is straight on.

Of course it was, past the village hall and a few more houses that lined the road, mostly detached, all the way to the looming tower. That brief disorientation played on her mind though. The cottage was set on a crossroads – could that be one of the reasons behind its chequered history – its in between location, set neither here nor there, and its inhabitants drawn to it for that very reason? It'd be the law of attraction in action again – like calling to like. When she'd first spoken to Rachel about the cottage, it had seemed a standard case, not dissimilar to many on her books. She'd been busy dealing with Gilmore Street at the time but even so, she'd kept thinking about Old Cross Cottage and had devised a way to bump it to the top of the pile – *lied* to get here, she'd been that keen. Obviously attracted too.

Her mobile started ringing. Reaching for it, she saw it was Theo again.

"Hello, sweetie, how are you?"

"Hi, Theo! I'm fine thanks, checking up on me are you?"

Theo laughed, her usual booming sound. "Darling, I would have thought you'd be checking up on *me*, or the business at least, not the other way round."

Ruby laughed too but somehow didn't buy that. Theo *was* checking up on her, which meant she was still worried, that she could sense something.

"Are you calling from the office?"

"Perish the thought! I'm at home but I'm off soon to my eldest son's for dinner with my raucous grandchildren. Just relaxing I suppose – remember that concept?"

"Hang on… actually, I'm not sure I do."

Despite joking, Theo's voice grew sombre. "Tell me it hasn't all been work so far."

"It hasn't, don't worry, we've spent most of today in Lyme Regis actually, having a bit of lunch, looking round the shops, that kind of thing. We're back in the village now though. Cash and Jed have gone for a nap and I'm off to the churchyard."

"As you do," Theo commented dryly.

"As *we* do. You've hung around your fair share of cemeteries in the past."

"'Tis true, 'tis true. I can't deny it. It's all part of the job. So come on, tell me what you've found out so far and why you're heading there."

Ruby filled her in, not just regarding personal experiences, but what Louisa had said too.

"So it was a pub until 1900," Theo reiterated, "at which point in time the landlord – a certain Thomas Ward – hanged himself under a nearby oak tree. His body was duly cut down and laid out at the pub for a week before it was decided what to do with it, thereby ruining the mood of the place. The property changing hands, it was divided into two cottages, which were then rented out."

"That's right," Ruby said, her feet crunching against gravel.

"In which case, Mary is post 1900 at least, as she lived in one of those rented cottages with her mother. When did the cottage revert back to one dwelling again?"

"I've yet to find that out but I get the impression she lived there pretty much soon after, judging by her clothes and the cottage interior; the early 1900s for sure."

"Studying images from that era will help. What's the Wi-Fi like where you are?"

"Not great, it dips in and out and Cash didn't bring his laptop."

"Oh? That's unusual for him."

"Well, he did think we were on holiday…"

"Ah, of course, and so he left it behind. You've got your mobile though."

"I have, but you know what a headache it is checking details on such a small screen."

Theo snorted. "I have absolutely no idea of the hell it is, dear girl! I use my phone purely for calls and texts. Heavens," she added, "even that's enough to make me giddy at times. Look, why don't you ask Rachel if she has access to the title deeds or the Land Registry? They could well show the chain of ownership at Old Cross Cottage. It might be easier for her to access that sort of information than us."

"I could do but Ellen was a tenant, not an owner."

Theo sighed. "That does rather complicate matters." They both knew that records of tenants were only kept for seven years once they'd vacated a property. Pre-World War Two, the chances were they hadn't been kept at all.

"Census records might help though," decided Ruby. "Theo, on Monday, when you get a chance, could you check them online and see if there's mention of an Ellen who lived in the village, possibly a seamstress? It'd be helpful to have a surname."

"You're going to the churchyard to find that out, aren't you?"

"Hopefully, but in case I *don't* find it out."

"Of course I will, but, Ruby, census records dating that far back are often incomplete too. Plus, if the arrangement was informal…"

"The rumour was that her rent was paid for her."

"Because as a lone woman she couldn't possibly support herself?" The sarcasm in Theo's voice was evident.

"A common view back then, I suppose."

Theo paused. "And you got all this from a dream?"

"I've had two dreams so far."

"It seems to me just carry on dreaming if you want to find out more!"

True, but cold, hard facts were always useful.

"What's your feeling regarding Ellen?" Theo asked.

"She seems to be a proud working woman, able to defend herself well enough against the rumours. As I said she appears to be a seamstress, plus she took in washing, and baked and sold bread. Anything to make ends meet, I suppose."

"You don't sense her spirit at the cottage?"

"I sense someone but it's dark, very dark."

"And Ellen's not dark?"

"Not from what I can gather so far but he certainly is."

"The man who terrorised Mary?"

"That's right and he wants me to leave, so he can carry on tormenting her. But I won't let him, Theo, I won't let him!"

"Darling, calm down!"

"Calm down?" Ruby questioned.

"Yes, sweetie. Surely, you're aware you raised your voice just then?"

"Did I?" To her ears she'd spoken normally. She apologised, despite her confusion.

"It's fine, and… well, I understand why you're getting so het up, any case involving a child is always harrowing, just ask Ness. Actually, scrub that, don't ask Ness. She doesn't like to talk about the work she did with Sussex Police before she met us – she gets very tetchy indeed. Honestly, love, I feel sorry for Mary as much as you do. Now… going off-piste, there's something else on your mind isn't there?"

"Something else?"

"Yes, something about a crossroads."

Ruby stopped in her tracks. "Theo, I honestly thought a person had to be within a certain range before you could read their thoughts!"

Theo laughed again. "That's almost always the case. I suppose the bond between us – the *connection* – is strong, which might account for it. But it's not a constant thing, it comes and goes, often leaving me just as bemused as you are."

"Not quite," denied Ruby, she couldn't get her head round it at all. "I was just musing about the crossroads, that's all. The cottage sits where the four roads meet and I was wondering at the significance of it. I've heard it said a few times before that a crossroads is a sort of in between place, somewhere neither here nor there."

"That's absolutely right," replied Theo and Ruby could just imagine her blue eyes twinkling as she warmed to such an interesting subject. "Legend has it that a crossroads attracts the lost and the lonely, those that don't necessarily fit society's mould. They're also the haunt of ghosts, black dogs and other creatures of a supernatural bent, your archetypal devils, demons and witches."

"Black dogs? They got that right. Jed seems to love it at the cottage."

"And you, Ruby? Do you love it?"

Ruby paused. "The dark presence aside it's okay I suppose, cosy enough." Realisation dawned, "Oh, come on, Theo, you're not saying that I'm one of the—"

"Lost and lonely? To be frank, yes I am, on occasion."

Like Cash, Theo didn't mince her words either, but before Ruby could respond, the older woman continued speaking. "The belief that a crossroads is an in between place is a universal one. It's where the veils between worlds are thought to be much thinner, which can lead, of course, to the source of our bread and butter: good old paranormal activity, with souls getting trapped and even time itself playing on a loop. Hence why so much that happens at a crossroads is residual."

"That makes sense," Ruby said, stopping again, at the gates of the church.

"Crossroads were also sometimes the burial sites for murderers and criminals."

"Why was that?" Ruby asked.

"Simple really, it was believed that the different paths leading away from a crossroads would confound the restless spirits, thus stopping them from returning to haunt the living. Maybe it was effective, maybe it wasn't. The act of burying murderers and criminals at a crossroads was outlawed in the early 1800s, but suspicion often outweighs the law, so you can bet your bottom dollar the practice was carried out for many decades afterwards and always under cover of the night."

Listening to what Theo was saying an idea started to form. "What about a crossroads being a burial site for someone who was murder*ed* rather than the murder*er*?"

"The child?"

"Yes."

"Ruby, you don't know what happened to Mary, not yet."

"It's obvious."

"It's not. What's more, we'd need concrete evidence to get

the powers that be to do anything about it, not psychic speculation."

Ruby sighed – she was right.

"I know it's frustrating, darling, but remain objective and presume nothing."

"Okay, I'll try, I promise."

"And don't get too comfortable at Old Cross Cottage. Superstition aside, it's not wise to linger at the crossroads. Do your job and come home. Just… come home."

Chapter Ten

ONCE again Ruby was puzzled. It wasn't just the way Theo had ended their call, with such strange words about coming home, it was the way in which she said it too. There was such sadness in her voice, a resignation almost. Of course she was coming home, in six days to be exact. Why would she doubt otherwise?

Do your job.

Theo had also said that and that's what Ruby focused on. Pushing open the wrought iron gate with its ornate pattern of swirling circles, a single crow eyeing her cautiously as she did so, she did a quick scan. There really were a lot of gravestones – and some of them would be impossible to decipher, although hopefully the ones post-1900 would be in reasonable enough condition. Mentally, she divided the churchyard into quarters, which should make it easier to examine each segment thoroughly. She also resolved to work in a clockwise motion. To walk the other way, anticlockwise or widdershins, as it was known, was considered unlucky, another ancient superstition and one she decided it was just as easy *not* to put to the test.

An infuriatingly popular name – back then especially – there were several Mary's even in that first quarter, two of whom fitted the suspected time frame – born in the late

1800s or early 1900s and having died as children – one was ten and the other was twelve. She had no idea yet when Mary had died, her torment could have endured for several years. Again, it was painful to think that that might be the case but she'd also heed Theo and see it simply as fact, nothing more.

Quickly deciding she needed to do something more constructive than just read names if she was going to get anywhere today she stepped forward, touched the first headstone she'd come across and held onto it with both hands. Closing her eyes, she concentrated, repeating the procedure with the second headstone.

On both occasions various impressions hit home, some gently, others with a little more impact. Nonetheless, all were fleeting and none caused her undue concern. She witnessed a ball game of some sort, laughter, a present given at Christmas or it could have been a birthday that elicited squeals of delight from the recipient, a walk up the path that ran beside her to attend Sunday service, stomach pains that quickly became excruciating, a fever that burned, a shortness of breath, the trees around turning from autumn red to skeletal, a grey sky, dying but peaceful, strangely peaceful, accepting, as a child accepts so much. Other flashes too, from those who'd stood by whilst each coffin was lowered into the ground, the agony, and the tears, the grief over a life cut short. Tragic, all of it was tragic, but it was nothing to do with *her* Mary, they were simply memories left behind, emotions taking time to dissipate.

Thankfully the number of children called Mary that had died in childhood dwindled in the second and third quarter, although certainly there were plenty of other children who'd been whisked away on the wings of a dove or some other divine carrier during the 1800s and 1900s, to rest forevermore. They were awful times really, Ruby surmised, so often disease struck, and with medicine not as widely available as it is now, it could quickly get a stronghold. People may curse the NHS in current times, but she thought they were still lucky to have at least a semblance of it. In other countries around the globe that wasn't the case and death was rife there as well. Whilst musing on this sorry matter, she also kept an eye out for any markers with the name Ellen on them, but whilst there were various Helens and even a couple of Eleanors, there was no evidence of an Ellen. Scanning the Eleanors in particular, wondering if Ellen was a pet version of that name, the dates of neither of them fit: one had died in 1891, the other in 1900. Soon she was in the final quarter, examining the last few graves that nestled beneath that ancient, gnarled tree – a yew it looked like, regarded as sacred by the Druids, who had planted them prolifically on consecrated ground, with early Christians continuing the tradition.

Ruby paused for a moment. She was reminded of when she'd first encountered Mary in the dream; she'd been sitting with her back against a tree – not a yew, it was an oak – nestled too. When she'd heard Ellen calling her, Mary had run back home from which direction? The east? That was the impression she'd got. On tomorrow's agenda would be a trip out that way, to see if she could find the oak tree. Sitting under it might help strengthen their connection. But first she needed to seek out the Marys in this section: there was just the one – Mary Weaver – who was born in 1897 and died in 1947, aged fifty. Not her Mary either. Even so, she drew closer.

Adopting a now familiar stance, she stood with her legs

slightly apart, leant forward and placed her hands on the cold, hard tablet.

"Bloody hell, I've seen it all now!"

Ruby almost jumped a foot into the air, wondering who the heck had spoken – the woman whose name was on the grave, aggravated that she'd been disturbed? It wasn't of course; it was a living, breathing lady, middle aged and dressed very smartly, in a pleated navy skirt and a close-fitting burgundy blazer, staring at Ruby with something akin to amusement rather than horror.

Swiftly, Ruby removed her hands from the grave and stood up straight, attempting to explain herself. "Sorry, I was just trying to—"

"Tune in?"

Ruby was astounded. "Well… yes." How could she know that?

The older woman laughed – a raucous sound not dissimilar to Theo's laugh. "You're staying at Old Cross Cottage aren't you? Louisa told me about you, told the whole village by now I should think. You're a psychic. Said you've got an impressive website, lots of people on it testifying that you're the real thing."

Still Ruby was lost for words. "Erm… thank you. Yes, yes, I run a high street consultancy, specialising in domestic—"

"Spiritual clearance, I know, I've had a look at the website too. So, come on, what are you doing here? Is something up with…" she paused and leant forward to read the name on the gravestone that Ruby had been holding onto, "Mary Weaver?"

"No, no," Ruby stepped away from the grave as if trying to prove her point. "Mary's… at peace. It's very peaceful here, in fact. It's… lovely."

The woman looked around her, "It is, it really is. I often come here to sit and contemplate – makes me feel lucky to be alive. Reminds me to make the most of what I've got left as well. You're a long time dead, in't it?"

Not always, thought Ruby but nodded in amiable agreement.

The woman held out her hand. "Grace Comely's the name, pleased to meet you."

"I'm Ruby Davis," Ruby took her hand and shook it, "pleased to meet you too."

"Are you enjoying your stay at the cottage?"

"Yes I am, thank you."

"Good, not on your own though, Louisa said you've got a chap with you."

"Yes, yes, I have, Cash, my… erm… boyfriend."

Grace frowned. "Cash? What sort of a name is that?"

"It's after Johnny Cash, his mum's a fan."

"Oh, is she? I preferred Elvis myself."

"Erm… Cash's older brother is called Presley."

There was a sparkle in Grace's eyes. "Presley, eh? Seen it all and heard it all now too. There's nowt so queer as folk. Anyway, you specialise in ghost clearance?"

"Yes, although I tend to call them spirits not ghosts."

"Why's that then?"

"It's more respectful."

Grace's tone grew haughty. "Oh, I wasn't trying to be disrespectful or nothing."

"Sorry, I didn't mean to imply—"

"I'm sure you didn't. Here's the thing, I've always thought there was a bit of an atmosphere in my house. There's a spot in the spare bedroom that never warms up you see, no matter what. Strange feeling in there, I'm telling you, not spooky as such, I don't mean that, but it's different to the rest of the house. If you've finished hanging onto gravestones, do you fancy coming over to check it out? I only live up there, just through the churchyard and along the lane." Before Ruby could say whether she fancied it or not, Grace started walking. "Follow me. I'll lead the way."

* * *

The one aspect of Ruby's job that Cash remained consistently concerned about was her going into strangers' houses with no back up – often she'd carry out initial surveys on her own. She had to admit, right now, she could see his point. Grace might be an older lady but who knew who lived with her – living or dead. Since the Gilmore Street case, she'd become less blasé about such concerns.

Following Grace through the front door of her semi-detached cottage, she began to relax – it appeared that Grace lived alone. The décor was very feminine, bordering on the chintzy but also very comfortable, lived in, the atmosphere calm despite the suspicion of a lingering spirit, not unsettled like it was at Old Cross Cottage. There the atmosphere was simmering. How long before it reached boiling point?

"Fancy a cuppa first, do you?"

They were in the kitchen and Ruby glanced at the wall clock – she didn't want to be gone too long in case Cash woke and was worried by her absence, so she declined. "Is it okay if we go straight to the room you were talking about?"

"Fine with me. What about fees? I'm only asking you as a favour really…"

Ruby waved a hand in the air in a show of nonchalance. "Don't worry, no charge. We'll just… see what's going on, shall we?"

With Grace leading her from the kitchen, they climbed a narrow set of stairs to the upper landing – like downstairs, it was light and bright with two bedrooms to choose from, all clean and clutter free, no coffin lids beneath your feet but plush carpet in a tasteful shade of oatmeal. It was the farthest bedroom Grace walked towards, the one with just a single bed in it, a chest of drawers, and a mirror, the configuration the same as that of the single bedroom at Old Cross Cottage. No sooner had she thought it, than it hit her – a flash of insight. Not to do with this bedroom, to do with the other one. What had it been? A bridge, a link... a cell? Yes, that was it! It had been a cell, or as good as, with rags on the bed and a glass knocked over, its contents – nothing fancier than water – soaking the floorboards. And in the corner was a shadow, that of a child, legs drawn up to hide her face, trying to make herself small, smaller still... to disappear.

Shocked, Ruby had to reach out and hold onto the doorframe.

Mary, is that you?

The image, like an old, old photograph, like a dream in fact, was fading. Ruby screwed her eyes shut, tried to keep it in her mind's eye, but it was gone, as fast as it had arrived. She opened her eyes to find Grace staring at her aghast.

"Well, it's a bit odd in here I know," she said, "but I didn't think it were that bad!"

* * *

An hour later, back in the kitchen, Ruby tried to process what had so recently happened, accepting a cup of tea this time from Grace.

First there'd been the flashback – prompted by the similarity of the rooms she'd guessed and serving to increase her concern for Mary. And then there'd been Annie.

Grace was right when she'd suspected a presence in the bedroom. It was that of an old lady sitting by the window in her rocking chair, her hands ever busy with knitting what looked to be a jumper. Recovering from the flashback, she'd asked the old lady for whom the item was intended. It took a few minutes to get an answer. 'My Samuel of course, loves to come visiting he does, spend time with his grandma.'

Studying her clothes, her demeanour, Ruby thought she was again someone who'd lived in the 1900s, not residual, the fact that she'd replied meant her spirit was very much intact, but not because of trauma, far from it. This was a lady content to sit and wait; a very patient lady. The shame was she might wait forever.

Giving Grace a brief explanation of who the spirit was, Ruby asked if she might have a few minutes on her own in the room. Grace complied, saying she'd wait in the hallway. Having left the room, however, she didn't close the door behind her, but stood keeping an eye on proceedings. Ruby didn't especially mind, she was used to curious clients and so continued regardless. The old woman seemed to be in no doubt that she'd passed, 'But here is where I sit and here is where I'd like to stay.'

"Isn't it lonely?" Ruby asked.

Busy hands came to a standstill. "I won't be lonely if my grandson comes. Strapping lad he is, fine lad. Like his father before him."

"The thing is, I don't think he *can* come and visit, not anymore."

The woman had turned to her then, some of the light in

her already pale eyes dimming. "Whatever do you mean? Why not?"

Ruby had taken a breath, if she said why the woman's obliging manner might change. Again the image of a simmering pot came to mind and how easy it could start to boil. Although torn, she decided she had to do what was right, and that was to spell it out for her – after first finding out her name, which the old lady gave willingly: Annie Trenwith. A name that rang a bell – Ruby had to think for a moment and then she realised, it was one of the names she'd read in the churchyard.

Before explaining, Ruby thought she'd chance her luck.

"Do you know Old Cross Cottage, another house in the village?"

"The one that stands at the crossroads?"

"That's it, that's the one." Ruby had felt both excitement and guilt – not really sure of the ethics involved in pumping a spirit for information concerning a separate case.

Annie shook her head. "Bad place, that's what it is."

"Is it? Why?"

"Should be razed to the ground."

"Because of Mary?"

Annie's hands had started to shake. Immediately Ruby felt guilty about causing her upset and reached out, no matter that there was nothing substantial to lay her hand upon. "It's okay, I was just asking that's all, I'm staying there—"

Annie whipped her head back round, a lightning quick movement that belied the age she was presenting as. "I do want to go, I've been ready for a long while. But I'm scared you see."

"What of?"

"Which road to take."

Ruby frowned. Had talk of the crossroads confused her?

"Take the road that leads to the light."

Annie stood, the movement again sudden, her knitting falling from her hands, disappearing because it was no longer needed. "My grandson's not coming, is he?"

"No. He's not."

"And I shouldn't be here."

"That's right, but only because you've somewhere else to be, your true home."

Still Annie looked worried, agitated even. "If he does return, be sure to tell him, won't you? I was there for him. I didn't turn away. And I'm proud, so very proud."

Ruby's heart cracked a little to witness such fierce love and loyalty.

"I will."

"So many died, another grandson included."

"Another grandson?"

"But he shouldn't have. There was no need."

"What happened to him, Annie?"

"I suspected but I never knew. That's the trouble you see, I never knew. Not for certain."

"I don't understand what you're talking about."

"I blamed myself."

"For what?"

"I should have listened."

Listened? There was that word again.

"Annie…" There was such conflict on her face, such sorrow.

"Some souls, they'll always remain lost."

"Your grandson?"

"No!" At that intimation Annie grew fierce, "not him. He was good and true! A brave young man, not afraid to stand up for king and country, for what's right."

Ruby stood her ground. "If that's so, then he'll be in the light too, waiting for you."

As quickly as it had flared, all fierceness left her. "You're right, yes, yes, I know you're right." Looking directly ahead, she said, "I walk straight on, do I?"

"If that's where the light is. Can you see it?"

Annie's eyes narrowed. "Can't you?"

"Well… no, not at the moment. Sometimes I can, but not always."

"Not always," Annie echoed.

"Annie—"

"You have to know, don't you, which path to take?"

Ruby nodded.

"You have to make your choice, and live and die with it."

Live and die with it? "Yes, yes you do."

"Will you walk with me?"

"Of course," Ruby replied, rising too. Oh, how she longed to quiz her further, to have her explain such crypticness, but if she was finally ready to go she shouldn't delay her.

Standing shoulder to shoulder, they started walking, Ruby just a few paces before her journey ended, Annie continuing so much further. Just as the old woman left for good, she spoke again. It took a couple of moments for Ruby to register her words but when she did the hairs on her arms rose for the second time that day.

"Poor Mary," Annie said, as the light enclosed her.

Chapter Eleven

RUBY might be more confused than ever, but Grace was thrilled.

"The whole house feels different, it feels like… mine. All mine. For the first time in over thirty years! Oh, I'm so glad you've got rid of it, I really am."

It? Ruby had told her several times already that the spirit's name was Annie, but unless you could see and hear one of the deceased, she supposed it was easy to dehumanise them, to think of them as just that, an 'it'. As she rose to go, she decided the main thing was customer satisfaction and regarding that, Grace fit the bill. The woman was grinning from ear to ear as she waved Ruby goodbye.

Back in the churchyard, Ruby sought out Annie's grave and paid closer attention to the inscription:

Annie Trenwith
1881-1950
Sleeps with Angels

She did now at any rate. If she'd been born in Canonibeare and died here – which was very likely as migration at that time wasn't as common as in later decades – she'd have known both Mary and Ellen, and perhaps the man who'd moved in next door. And if so, that was the first step in dating the era she'd lived at the cottage, post 1900 but before 1950. Ruby also thought of Annie's last words – *Poor Mary.* What had happened to her that Ruby had yet to find out? What agonies had she endured that, even in death, a fellow villager felt such sorrow for her?

Ruby did a quick calculation in her head – 2016 minus 1950 equals sixty-six. If Annie were saying 'poor Mary' because Mary had died, that would have been at least sixty-six years ago. Did anyone in the village that was living still remember Mary? Or perhaps they knew *of* her, just as they knew of Thomas Ward, another village tragedy who'd passed into myth if not the light. What should she do? Knock on everyone's door and ask? She'd already asked Louisa about the cottage, and Grace, and neither had mentioned anything about Mary. It looked like the girl hadn't even made it to myth status. Her story forgotten, as so many were. As she'd been doing when discovered by Grace, Ruby leant forward to touch Annie's grave – wondering about the residue left behind. She closed her eyes, waited for flashbacks to fill her mind. World War, that had been uppermost in Annie's mind, she'd lived through both of them, seen young men sent to the front, her brother during World War One, her grandson during the second. With the former, there was jubilation, he'd come home; with the latter, as Ruby knew already, he'd gone missing in action – those that waited behind for him hope*less* instead of hope*ful.* So young, he was. Younger than eighteen? Ruby thought so. He'd lied about his age as many did, a fine, strapping lad as Annie had described him, he'd have been easily believed. She saw Grace's spare room, this time Annie's version of it, not a spare room, but her bedroom, overlooking the fields, or at least it did then – a fine view, lush and green. And there was Annie, waiting and waiting, until the war was over, until her life was over. But never hope, not in Annie's case, because hope sprang eternal. Annie had asked Ruby to tell him she'd remained constant, praying for his return day after day as she'd sat by the window – not the prodigal son but the prodigal grandson. It gave her pleasure to think she could do the deed herself now that she'd passed too.

What about the other grandson, the one who needn't have died? What about Mary?

But try as she might, Ruby could pick up no further clues.

Deciding it was time to head back to the cottage – she'd been gone long enough – Ruby called Rachel en route.

"Hi," Rachel greeted, "how are you, any progress?"

Ruby assured her they were making headway but asked her to look into the dates the cottage had become two dwellings and when it had reverted back to one.

"That's significant is it?" Rachel asked.

"It could be."

"I wonder how I go about it."

"There's a chance the information could be in the Land Registry or in the title deeds, both of which are probably available online. Everything is nowadays. Don't worry if you can't find out, it'd just be handy to know that's all."

"I'll certainly do my best. I've had a quick word with the Estate Agent about the people who owned it before us too, a couple from London apparently. Like us, they used it as a holiday home. To be honest, I don't think they visited much; the place was infested with spiders when we got it. We had to have it fumigated."

And yet still plenty remained. It's a good job Theo wasn't working on this case alongside her. Try as she might to deny it, she was terrified of spiders.

"Do they know anything more about them than that?" enquired Ruby.

"Greg, that's the name of the agent we dealt with by the way, had to dash out, but I can always ring back again."

"I'd really appreciate that, thank you."

"Do you mind me asking how such information could help?"

"No, not at all," answered Ruby. "If a spirit's grounded, there's often a very human reason behind it. I need to know as much about the history of the house as possible if I'm going to fit together all the pieces."

"Makes sense," Rachel agreed. There was a slight pause and then she spoke again. "Look, if you can't sort the problem out I'm not going to hold it against you or start bad-mouthing your company. I'm just really appreciative you know, that you're giving it a shot. Your job... I don't envy you. It can't be easy."

Ruby was appreciative too, for Rachel's kind words; there were plenty who wouldn't be as gracious. It made her even more determined. "I'll do my best, Rachel, you can be sure of that. We really are making steady progress."

Rachel thanked her and ended the call. Ruby was only a few yards from the cottage when she saw the door open, slowly, ever so slowly... Her chest constricting, she found it difficult to breathe. Was this another flashback, Mary taking over again?

Still she continued to stare – her eyes wide as she ground to a halt, imagining not the tarmac but a dirt track beneath her feet – the ground as unappealing suddenly as the coffin lids, an energy pulsating through it that was like the steady beat of drums.

Who's there? Who are you? What did you do to Mary?

Was this the moment she'd get a glimpse of the darker presence?

A familiar face appeared before her. No, this was not the moment. Nor was it a flashback. It was Cash, looking downright perplexed.

"There you are, Ruby! I was about to come and find you. To be honest, I've only just woken up, around ten minutes ago. The thing is… I had a dream."

* * *

Later, settled in front of the fire, Ruby started reading about dreams via Google.

"Apparently it's a way of consolidating memories, regulating emotions and figuring out what you'd do in a threatening scenario."

"I'd guessed the first two," Cash answered, "but what do you mean by the third?"

"Well, according to *Scientific American* the threat simulation hypothesis suggests that dreams provide a sort of virtual reality environment. They refer to a study of children in two different areas of Palestine, which showed those who live in a more turbulent environment have a much higher incidence of threat in their dreams."

"And their reaction to that threat?"

"Is almost always relevant and sensible apparently, involving plausible solutions. It *teaches* them I suppose, offering them something of a trial run."

"A trial run? In which case, I failed mine pretty spectacularly."

"Better gear up for the real thing then, hadn't you?" she

teased.

Thinking about it though, she'd have probably done the same as Cash had during his nightmare: run and hid.

"I felt so helpless, you know," Cash endeavoured to explain again, "so… not small, I wouldn't say small but… insignificant in the face of such… fury. Yeah, that's it, insignificant. Whoever was after me was so full of anger, they were terrifying."

"And it was this house you were in, in the dream I mean?"

"Definitely, although it looked different to how it is now, there was even less furniture and it was much darker, colder too, that's the thing I remember most, it was bloody freezing. I wanted to find a cupboard, somewhere to squeeze myself into, where I could curl up in a ball, hide my face and pretend it wasn't happening."

Just like Mary had done in the flashback.

"And the next thing you know you've woken up?"

Cash nodded. "I heard a dog barking, probably from the farm up the road."

Clocking Jed's oh-so-innocent face she raised her eyebrows. "Maybe," she responded. It was her turn to stoke the fire. Rising from the sofa and heading towards it, she glanced sideways. "Bit odd if you're channelling Mary too, isn't it?"

"Or I could be channelling you," Cash pointed out.

Picking up the poker and prodding at logs, she asked what he meant.

"Well, Mary's at the forefront of your mind, you've been talking about her since the afternoon we arrived, so my dream could have been a reaction, that's all."

It was a fair point.

"And your phone?" she asked, still not believing in it but checking for good measure. "Any more activity on that?"

Cash grabbed his phone, which was on the table in front of him. "I forgot to leave it on whilst I was sleeping and to be honest I haven't bothered with it since. I'll turn it on now if you like."

Ruby shrugged. "May as well." About to suggest they make something for dinner, a crash coming from the direction of the kitchen startled them both.

"What the hell…?"

Cash got to his feet and flew out of the room, Ruby at his heels.

"What is it, Cash?" she said as he entered the kitchen just ahead of her.

"I don't know," he said.

Standing beside him, she looked from left to right. There was no obvious sign of any damage but there'd definitely been a crash, as though a chair or some other object had been hurled against the wall in temper.

"Let's check the cupboards," she suggested, "a shelf might have collapsed."

A closer inspection showed no such thing.

Upstairs a door banged followed by the sound of footsteps running across the floorboards.

"Blimey!" said Cash, his face a picture of bewilderment.

Before investigating, Ruby regarded Jed, her barometer in times such as this. He was staring at the ceiling, his ears flattened, his body in pounce mode.

"Come on," she said, slightly nervous, she had to admit.

Still Cash led the way, negotiating the uneven stairs with impressive ease, before coming to a brief halt on the landing. Taking a few steps forward, the floorboard below his foot creaked louder than usual, drawing both their attention downwards.

Lying in the centre of one wide tread was a scrap of mate-rial, brown in colour and easy to miss as it was camouflaged so well against the brown of the boards. Jed materialised and started sniffing around it, momentarily clawing at the boards before backing away. In a second he'd disappeared, clearly having had enough excitement.

It was Cash who bent to retrieve the scrap, examining the rough material before handing it to Ruby.

"Where did that come from?" he asked.

"Mary," Ruby replied, certain the red tinge on one of the frayed ends was blood.

Chapter Twelve

DESPITE steeling themselves for more phenomena, the rest of the evening passed peacefully. Ruby tucked the linen scrap into the pocket of her jeans, wanting to keep it near. In a strange way it gave her comfort, as though she were keeping Mary herself near – and perhaps she was; although what did surprise her – apart from the appearance of the scrap itself – was that it elicited no flashbacks. Despite holding it in her hand for a fair while it was quite benign. Frustration – that was the name of the game. The psychic game anyway.

Cash's spaghetti carbonara went some way to appeasing her. Events seemed to have given them both an appetite as they ploughed their way through a sizeable bowlful each, drank more wine, white this time, their new topic of discussion the crossroads itself rather than dreams. She related what Theo had told her about the subject and he in turn asked whether she'd heard the old Robert Johnson song.

"Robert Johnson? Was he in The Cure?"

The look of disgust on Cash's face was absolute. "Clearly, you haven't."

"Go on then, oh music maestro, enlighten me."

"Johnson was a blues singer from the Mississippi Delta. In the 1930s he recorded a song called the *Cross Road Blues*." He paused, shook his head. "Have you seriously never heard of him, Ruby?"

"No I haven't, and stop looking at me as though I've just crawled out from under a rock."

"But he's a legend, the greatest folk blues guitar player that ever lived!"

Ruby had to smile at how indignant he was.

Continuing to elaborate, he told her Johnson was an itinerant musician, not earning much, just travelling from place to place, playing his songs, scraping by. "He was a terrible guitarist, not amazing at all, until he *was* amazing that is and seemingly overnight. Legend has it that he sold his soul to the devil, whom he met at the crossroads, close to where he lived in the Delta. He referred to the devil in a lot of his songs, but *Cross Road Blues* is perhaps the most famous. The lyrics go something like this…" to Ruby's dismay, he burst into song again. "*I went to the crossroads, fell down on my knees. Asked the Lord above, have mercy, now save poor Bob, if you please.*"

Tempted to cover her ears, she pointed out he'd asked the Lord, not the devil.

"Yeah, but it was the devil who heard him and made a pact: fame and brilliance in return for his soul."

"He's a greedy bastard that devil."

"He is, but you could also say he's fiendishly clever. Anyway, he was granted fame and brilliance, but sadly all too soon the debt was due and Robert Johnson joined the 27 Club – who knows, he might even have kick-started it."

"The 27 Club?" She'd heard of it before, but needed reminding.

"He died at the age of twenty-seven, just like Jimi Hendrix, Janis Joplin, Jim Morrison, Kurt Cobain and Amy Winehouse, the list goes on and on. It makes you wonder if all the exceptionally talented have some sort of due to pay. Hey," he said, suddenly thoughtful, "you're twenty-seven next birthday, aren't you?"

"Yeah, I… Cash, what are you trying to say?"

Cash held his hands up. "Nothing, nothing, I'm just pointing it out that's all."

"Oh, right, well thanks for that! I'm not sure I needed it pointing out to be honest."

He reached across and squeezed her shoulder. "Nothing's gonna happen to you."

"And why's that? Because I'm not exceptionally talented?"

"Not musically anyway, you're as tone deaf as I am!"

"Finally, you admit it! Come on; finish the story, what happened to Robert Johnson? How did he die?"

"In violent and mysterious circumstances. There are several accounts of his death but it's generally believed the jealous husband of a woman he kept flirting with in a bar laced his whiskey with strychnine. Other reports insist you can't disguise the taste of strychnine; he would have detected it, also that it would have killed him almost straight away whereas he took three long days to peg out. Whatever happened, and I don't suppose we'll ever know for sure, it only served to fuel the legend of him being in league with the devil."

"Fascinating stuff," Ruby concurred.

"It is," Cash said, taking a swift sip of wine. "But of course regarding Johnson and the crossroads, it's allegorical."

"What do you mean?"

"He wasn't singing about an actual crossroads, despite music fans descending on the Delta in their droves ever since, trying to find it. Currently the most likely site is set between Highway 61 and Highway 49 but that wouldn't have existed in Johnson's time so it's all a pile of claptrap."

He paused. "Mind you, if we ever find ourselves in Mississippi, we've got to head there all the same, get our photo taken, you know… just in case." He shook his head. "No, when Johnson sang about the crossroads he was talking about a man's need to make choices, the most fundamental one being, of course, between good and evil. Like you're always saying, there are two wolves inside us: one evil and one good. Which wolf wins?"

"The one you feed the most," Ruby answered, thoughtful too.

Even someone like Annie must have faced that dilemma. Like most people, she must have had dark thoughts about the war and all that it had taken from her, thoughts that forged new pathways in her mind. That pit of anger was so easy to fall into, and once you had, it was sometimes difficult to emerge. Such paths had confused Annie, part of the reason for her being grounded Ruby realised, and why mention of the crossroads had agitated her. Not that she'd physically lived at the crossroads – *lingered*, as Theo had put it – unlike Mary, unlike Ellen, unlike Thomas Ward and Mary's tormentor too, the one who'd willingly aligned himself with evil.

Aligned?

Ruby sat up straight. "Cash, those words that *Ghost Discovery* picked up, one of them was 'aligned' wasn't it?"

"Yeah, I think so. Why?"

"I… no reason. Just keep the app running, you know in the background. On mute."

"So you believe in the power of the app now, do you?" Cash was grinning again, either thinking she was an idiot or that he'd got one over on her.

"Let's just say it's interesting and I'm desperate."

"Desperate?" Cash mused. "That was another word the app picked up."

* * *

Looking forward to a long lie-in the next morning – exactly what Sundays were made for – Ruby couldn't believe it when there was a knock on the door dead on nine.

Who the heck is that?

Such was her shock it took a moment to register that she'd woken in the double room she shared with Cash, and had slept soundlessly and dreamlessly. She couldn't work out if she was disappointed because of it or relieved.

Disappointed, Ruby, definitely disappointed.

She needed to maintain contact with Mary not lose it.

Before she could contemplate further there were three more raps at the door, each one more determined than the last.

"Cash, Cash," she said, jolting him awake. "There's someone at the door!"

"Go and answer it then."

"No, I can't, I'm not dressed, and my hair, it's all over the place… *you* go and answer it."

"What about my hair?"

"You haven't got any!"

Not strictly true, but he kept it close cropped, giving him a slightly thuggish look, which she sometimes teased him about.

Cash finally sat up. "Oh, for God's sake, Ruby, ignore it and they'll go away."

Ruby sat up too. Maybe he was right – there'd been a bit of a break between the third and final knock. They could settle down again, drift back to sleep, or maybe not, drift

119

into something else, something more exciting, being as they were both awake…

A fifth knock scuppered thoughts of that nature.

"Cash, please. I can't answer the door looking like this!"

Cash groaned audibly before peeling back the covers. Shuffling into his jeans and tee shirt, which were lying over the arm of the room's only chair, he left the bedroom and made his way downstairs, Jed curious, but not enough to follow him.

"Those floorboards really give you the creeps, don't they, boy?" she murmured.

Since finding the scrap of linen, she'd noticed he tended to materialise on the bed whilst upstairs, disappearing entirely before materialising again downstairs – avoiding the floorboards if he possibly could. Perhaps Rachel and Mark ought to think about replacing them too at some stage, along with removing the hook.

Whilst she waited for their unwelcome visitor to depart, she looked over at the window, tried to imagine a figure standing there, as Rachel's friend had claimed she'd seen. If it were Mary's tormenter, she'd have thought she'd feel unsettled in this room, ill at ease, but she didn't. This was the room she felt most comfortable in.

Pulling the sheet up under her chin, she prayed Cash would hurry back to the warmth of their bed. A good night's sleep had given her an appetite, for something other than breakfast. First though, she'd have to check if Cash had slept without dreaming too, or rather without *remembering* his dreams. And also the words that *Ghost Discovery* had recorded.

From below the muffled voices continued. Was their visitor a salesperson of some description, trying to flog something? She glanced again at her watch. No way, it couldn't be, not at this hour and on a Sunday too. Maybe it was Grace Comely, unsure that Ruby really had succeeded in moving Annie on and wanting her to come back and double check. Oh, what a pain if it was – the last thing she needed was to be distracted. Not when they only had a few more days in which to investigate what had happened to Mary, and to use that information to coax her forwards. If it was Grace, she'd have to be firm, as regarding her case, she *knew* she'd succeeded.

The voices had stopped.

Oh good, it looked like Cash had succeeded too. Any minute now she'd hear the front door closing and footsteps on the stairs, signaling his welcome return. She lay back amongst the pillows, positioning herself provocatively and waited... and waited.

Instead of the front door closing and Cash appearing, all she heard was his voice calling her name from the bottom of the stairs.

"Ruby, you'd better come down."

What!

Ruby sat up again and, wrapping the sheet around her, left the comfort of their bed and tiptoed across the landing, the floorboards making their usual racket. Keeping her voice low at least, she stood at the top of the stairs and hissed back.

"Cash, I can't, I'm not dressed remember."

"Well, get dressed."

"No! Tell them to go away."

"I can't. He won't."

He? So it wasn't Grace at least.

"Well, who the bloody hell is *he*?" she hissed again.

"It's the vicar, Ruby, of St Winifred's, the local parish

church."

* * *

By the time Ruby got downstairs, Cash had made a pot of tea and was pouring from it into the vicar's cup. The scene would have been a pleasant one, had their visitor not been sitting as though he'd just been impaled upon a red-hot poker. In contrast, Cash looked relaxed, asking how many sugars he took; one lump or two?

Indicating for Jed to move aside, so she could pull the chair out, Ruby sat down.

"Hello, Vicar, erm... what a pleasure it is to see you."

Ruby winced as she said it, hoping the vicar couldn't see that she was lying through her teeth. Not that she had anything against vicars, or priests, or nuns, far from it, but usually they had something against her. And this one was no exception.

Rather than respond straight away, the vicar sat as if in quiet contemplation. A man with distinctly 'sandy' colouring – even his eyes were light beige in colour - she got the impression he wasn't especially tall, more her height than Cash's. Nonetheless he seemed formidable, his developing scowl indicating a foe rather than a friend.

At last he cleared his throat – his voice, when he spoke, soft but as clear as church bells, each word perfectly enunciated.

"It has come to my attention that you've been involved in certain... practices in this village. Practices that we don't normally condone."

There was no beating about the bush. He was as straight talking as Theo, as Cash, as... well, most people she'd met in the village.

Before she could answer, Cash sat down and raised an amused eyebrow.

"Ruby," he said, "your witchy ways getting you into trouble again?"

Ruby shot him a warning look before focusing again on the vicar. "Look, Vicar…"

"You may call me Reverend Martin."

She frowned. Wasn't 'Reverend' a term you bestowed on a minister of Christ out of respect, not something the actual person was supposed to bestow upon themselves? She could be wrong, but actually she didn't think so. "Look, Vicar," she repeated, "I'm really not sure what you're referring to but—"

"Grace Comely is who I'm referring to and your supposed exorcism of a spirit at her home yesterday afternoon."

"Exorcism?" Cash made a show of looking impressed. "It sounds so much more sinister than a cleansing, doesn't it, Ruby?"

He was right – it did. And it was also a practice carried out solely by the church, tethered to the restraints of religion. Which is where they differed. Hers was more of a holistic approach, combined with psychic ability, no restraints applied. Even so, it wasn't the first time she'd clashed with the church, and rather than be riled by his obvious admonishment of what she'd been doing, she attempted to explain.

"I encountered Grace in the church grounds yesterday, we got talking and—"

"What were you doing in church grounds?"

"What was I doing?" It sounded as if he were appalled that she'd had the temerity to set foot on sacred ground. "I was looking at the graves."

"Strange behaviour," he commented, resting his elbows on the table and joining his hands together as if in prayer – a defence somehow, just as he might wield a cross as a defence against a vampire, if such creatures existed.

Ruby stared at him, at the smattering of freckles that covered his hands and face, should she make an excuse for her behaviour or come clean and tell him exactly what she'd been doing? Emboldened or incensed – which should she be?

"Okay, vicar or Reverend, whatever you like to be called—"

"As I've said, Reverend will suffice."

God, he was so superior, wearing his religion like armour.

"I was looking for a gravestone belonging to a child called Mary, a child who I think lived in the early 1900s, in this very house in fact, Old Cross Cottage, and who died here – as a child – due to tragic circumstances."

"Why on earth—"

It was Ruby who interrupted now. "We've been asked to investigate paranormal phenomena by the new owners of this cottage because there's been unusual activity experienced by them and their extended family members. That's what I do; I'm a Psychic Investigator. I run a high street business in East Sussex called Psychic Surveys, a successful business, with plenty of satisfied clients. I don't work within the boundaries of religion; I adopt a more holistic approach. And yesterday, when I was in the churchyard, Grace stopped to ask me what I was doing. That's how we ended up at her house, how I moved Annie Trenwith on, the spirit of a woman who used to live there and most probably a former parish member."

The Reverend Martin looked confused. "Annie Trenwith? I've never heard of her!"

"Then perhaps you ought to take a closer look at the graves you preside over," suggested Cash. "Get to know your flock a bit more… dead or alive."

Unclasping his hands, the Reverend Martin exhaled dramatically. "So, you're employed by the new owners of this cottage? People with more money than common sense, I'll bet. I can't do anything about that I suppose, it's their prerogative, but what I won't have is you inflicting your superstitious nonsense on the rest of us."

"Superstitious nonsense?" Ruby echoed. "Pot, kettle and black come to mind."

"I hardly think you can compare some tin-pot moneymaking scam to what the church has been doing for over two thousand years!" the Reverend spluttered.

Tin-pot moneymaking scam? The cheek of it! "This may come as a surprise to you, but people like me have existed for thousands of years too," Ruby countered, "and we've been persecuted by your lot for most of that, but not now, not any more, times have changed. People are no longer terrified to seek alternatives, fearing they'll be hung, drawn and quartered, crucified or burnt at the stake if they do. What I choose to do for a living works, it bloody well works. And what's more, it's for the greater good – something that should please the church not affront it!"

The Reverend's complexion, no longer pale, suffused with colour as he jumped to his feet. "If there's a spiritual presence in a home, it's the church and the church alone that should be called in to deal with it, not some... some... charlatan."

Ruby got to her feet too, Cash, she noticed, staring at both of them in a state of abject bewilderment.

"There are a lot of people in the world who'd call you a charlatan too! I've got no problem with the church, I really haven't. We just provide an alternative approach that's all, one that's not bound in red tape. But I'll tell you something; at this rate I could develop a problem. I'm sick of such narrow-minded, bigoted clap-trap!"

"Outrageous! This is outrageous!"

The Reverend leant over the table at exactly the same time that Ruby did, the tips of their noses almost touching.

Cash, who'd risen too, shoved his hands between them. "That's it, break it up you two, time for a group hug."

"A group hug?" Ruby spat the words at him. "What are you talking about?"

"All right, all right, that's going a bit far, I admit, but come on, we're adults here, or at least we're supposed to be. Surely we can agree to differ!"

"I'd suggest our differences are too great!" the Reverend Martin responded with as much venom as Ruby. "I repeat, whatever practice you're involved with in this village, I'd like you to keep it to yourselves and not interfere with my parishioners."

"Grace approached me!"

"And you charge for your services—"

"I never charged Grace!"

"But you do, as a matter of routine. I've checked your website, you've a sliding scale apparently—"

"That's right, because this is my *job*. It's how I earn a living. Just as you get paid for the job that *you* do. Oh, and let me think, you get living accommodation thrown in, don't you, and a uniform to wear that asserts your authority over us all and which you can use to full effect whenever it is you're preaching from the moral high ground."

"Moral high ground? I'm a man of God!"

"We're *all* from God, vicar, that's the point I'm trying to make here!"

"Enough!" Cash's fist on the table made them both jump.

"Cash!" Ruby admonished, but her voice sounded less sure

of itself.

"Just stop, Ruby, okay, stop. You're as bad as he is."

"What!"

"Neither one of you is bothering to listen to each other, all you want to do is attack. The way you're behaving actually embodies all that's wrong with the world – past, present, and future. You need to sit down, drink some of that damned tea I made you and start again." Cash made sure his glare included the Reverend too, the sandy little man withering under such scrutiny and sinking down rather than sitting on his chair. "Go on, drink!" he ordered. "That's fine Darjeeling tea that is."

The Reverend Martin duly picked up his cup and sipped.

"And you, Ruby, I don't hang around making tea because it's a fetish of mine."

Grudgingly, Ruby obeyed too, only once glancing at Jed, who was looking back at her with a less than impressed expression that matched Cash's. Annoyed, she turned away. She'd swear he and the dog were morphing into each other!

Very much employing what she did in a paranormal situation, Ruby took a few measured breaths and tried to calm her heart rate. The Reverend Martin seemed to be doing the same. She was soon composed enough to speak again.

"Is the reason you're here because Grace complained about me?"

The Reverend twitched slightly before answering. "Erm... well... ah..."

"Did she or didn't she?" asked Cash, still refereeing.

"No, not complained."

"What then?" Ruby asked.

"She... appeared satisfied with what you'd done."

Relief surged through Ruby. That was certainly the

impression she'd got too.

"So, where's the harm?"

The Reverend faltered. "Because—"

"Because, ironically, you don't believe in psychical ability, do you? A man whose very profession hinges on a belief in the unseen."

"*Faith*," he corrected.

"Okay, okay, faith," Ruby granted. "But you see, the thing is, for me, and for people like me, it's not the unseen. I *can* see beyond the material world, those that linger here for a whole variety of reasons instead of returning to the light."

"Heaven, you mean—"

"I mean the light. It's what I call it."

"Now, now you two," Cash warned, clearly concerned the situation was going to deteriorate again.

Ruby took another sip, another breath and leaned back in her chair. She was curious. "Being so close to God, a *spiritual* being, have you never experienced anything out of the ordinary?"

"Of course not… well… no, not really."

"Not really? You don't seem so sure."

"I am sure," the Reverend insisted, twitching once again.

"But you'll readily condemn me because of my experiences, because I use the ability I was born with to help, not just the dead but the living too."

"I'm not condemning you, I simply can't condone it."

"Can't or won't?"

"I just think it's best if any other parishioners approach you, you politely turn them away. We don't want the atmosphere in our peaceful village unsettled."

A bang from upstairs, as if a large book had been dashed to the floor, was as loud as Cash's thump on the table earlier.

Elsewhere a door slammed and at one of the kitchen windows, the glass began to shudder in its frame.

All three of them looked in the various directions the sounds had come from.

When Ruby turned back she noted confusion in the Reverend's eyes and something else... a trace of fear.

"There's been no peace in this village for a long time," she said. "And you know it."

Chapter Thirteen

THE Reverend Martin thankfully had to depart to take Sunday morning service, but, after his initial outburst and the subsequent unnerving disturbances, his manner had been considerably more subdued, apologetic even, unless Ruby was imagining it.

When she'd closed the door on him, Cash had stood looking at her.

"What?" she'd practically barked at him.

"I know you've asked Theo and Rachel to find out more information about Old Cross Cottage, but you know what, it'd be handy to access parish records."

"Parish records? They're probably online too."

"Even so, it might take the Reverend to interpret them."

"I'm sure it's not rocket science, Cash, *I'll* be able to interpret them."

"There you go again, getting uppity—"

She drew back. "Uppity?"

"Yeah. Because you know what, you can be bloody self-righteous too at times."

She swallowed as she stared at him, unsure how to respond.

"Look, all I'm saying is why make an enemy of him, of anyone for that matter?"

It was a good point, one that caused her to withhold any further retort. Following him back into the kitchen, she sat as subdued as the Reverend had, finishing off her cold tea whilst Cash fried bacon, eggs, and tomatoes with a healthy side of granary.

Whilst Ruby ate she continued to worry. Today was Sunday, giving them five full days including this one to solve the case – plenty of time and yet not enough.

Breakfast over she was about to head upstairs when there came another knock at the door. As startled as she'd been earlier that morning, she looked at Cash. Was it the Reverend? Stomping back after service, not quite done with her.

Before he could stop her, she rose from the table and hurried to the door, she'd be firm but fair – stand her ground but not start another fight – or at least *try* not to.

"Look, Vicar…" she said, yanking the door open a little too enthusiastically she had to admit, judging by the startled looks on the faces of the two women standing in front of her. She coughed. "Oh, I'm sorry, I… erm… wasn't expecting you."

The woman on the left, middle-aged but with black bobbed hair similar to Ness's was the first to recover, introducing herself as 'Edyth with a y', and her daughter as Jennifer, also dark-haired and perhaps a year or two younger than Ruby.

"Right, okay, hello, Edyth, hello, Jennifer. How can I—?"

Before she could get any further, Edyth stepped forward, pulling her daughter with her. "Expecting the Reverend again, were you? We saw him hurrying away from here just before church this morning," she said with a conspiratorial wink. "Ooh, I bet he caused a hullabaloo, didn't he? A bit straight-laced he is at times, bless him." Abruptly she laughed, a high-pitched sound with the potential to burst eardrums. "Bless him!" she repeated. "D'ya see what I did there?"

Her daughter was laughing too, both of them looking very jolly indeed as they made their way further into the house to stand beside Ruby in the parlour. Cash, who was observing in the kitchen doorway, appeared as bemused as Ruby felt.

"Erm…" she tried again, "can I help you?"

"Well!" Edyth commented, looking not at Ruby but around her. "I've wondered what it looked like in here nowadays." She turned to Jennifer, "Haven't you, love?"

Jennifer shrugged. "Not especially."

"Oh, I have, you know, the house that's not a home."

"Not a home?" Ruby questioned. "What do you mean by that?"

"It's a holiday rental isn't it," Edyth clarified, "and has been for such a long time, when it's not stood on its lonesome that is. I have to say though, if I was coming here on holiday, I'd want a few more comforts than this. Bit basic, isn't it?"

"Really?" As far as Ruby was concerned it had comforts enough.

Edyth nodded and nudged Jennifer so that she nodded too. "And I wouldn't want the ghosts."

Ruby started. "The ghosts, what do you mean?"

"That's what you're doing here, isn't it? According to Grace Comely anyway and Louisa at the pub, you're ghost hunting."

Ruby looked at Cash who was still looking startled. "I—" Again she was interrupted.

"There's been a suicide here," Edyth announced, rather imperiously.

132

"Yes, I know, Thomas Ward, in 1900."

"It's him that haunts the place?" Jennifer asked, wide-eyed.

Ruby was curious. "How do you know it's haunted?"

"How do you know it's not?" Edyth shot back.

"Look," Ruby said, wanting very much to get rid of them so that she could have a shower and get the day underway. The plan – as yet undiscussed with Cash but hopefully he'd acquiesce – was to find Mary's oak tree, to follow her senses until she found it. "This is all very interesting, but I need—"

"Tell her about the other man," Jennifer was the one nudging her mum now. "Go on, the one that did used to live here, back in the nineties. Tell her what happened."

All thoughts of a shower evaporated. "What happened?"

"Strange one he was, never mingled," Edyth said, her tone deliberately ominous.

Jennifer concurred. "An outsider if ever there was one."

"An outsider?" Ruby queried, an outcast in other words.

Cash stepped forward. "Well, you've got my attention," he said. "Come into the kitchen and I'll put the kettle on. You can tell us over a nice cup of tea."

* * *

It turned out that Mr George Taylor had lived at Old Cross Cottage from 1989 until 1993 – four years, and something of a record, at least in its recent history. He died, aged fifty-nine, having committed suicide. Like Thomas Ward, it hadn't been at the cottage. Rather he'd gone to some nearby cliffs known as Golden Cap – a National Trust beauty spot apparently – and thrown himself off from there, his body dashed against the rocks as the hungry waves waited below to devour him.

"Quite a few throw themselves off Golden Cap," Jennifer confided, reminding Ruby of its Sussex equivalent, Beachy Head. That too seemed to draw the desperate like a magnet. As of course, did Old Cross Cottage.

"Did you know George?" Ruby enquired further.

"Jen didn't, she was too young, but I knew of him. Saw him come and go at times, always with his head down, striding along, looking very determined, very purposeful. Used to say 'hello' to him but nine times out of ten he didn't bother to reply."

"Did any of you ever come knocking on his door?"

It was a good question Cash had asked; after all, they'd certainly come knocking during the short time she'd been in residence.

Edyth looked at Jennifer – or Jen as she was now being called – and then back at Ruby, not so imperious now, a bit sheepish. "No, well… like I said, he was a strange fella, kept himself to himself, and made that plain. I think one or two people tried, we're a friendly lot after all in Canonibeare, but no chance of being invited inside."

Or even barging their way in, as Edyth and Jennifer preferred.

Edyth wasn't taking much notice of her tea, having taken a sip and declared that she preferred a decent drop of Yorkshire and not some foreign muck – a statement that had Cash having to bite hard on his lip to stop from laughing, muttering instead about the wonderful tea plantations north of Watford as he poured a mug for himself. Jennifer, however, sank hers happily enough and, wiping her mouth with the back of her hand, urged her mum to tell them about the locks.

"Oh, yes, the locks," Edyth said, nodding voraciously. "Actually, this isn't about Mr Taylor when he was alive, it's more about what they found after he'd died."

"Okay," Ruby nodded too. "Go on, tell me."

"Well, he must have suffered from paranoia or something, 'cos when the cottage was cleared afterwards – not by his family, he didn't seem to have any, none that were interested anyway – a few of us helped out with removals."

"Kind of you," Ruby muttered, she could just imagine them scuttling over.

"Well, you've never seen anything like it," she continued blithely. "The locks I mean. There were so many of them, two at least on the inside of the front door, big 'uns, you know, them mortice ones, top and bottom. Also, the windows were nailed down, every last one. There was even a lock on one of the bedrooms upstairs."

"Upstairs? Which one?"

"The door that leads to the biggest bedroom."

"Is that the bedroom Mr Taylor slept in?"

"Don't think so, his personal stuff was in the room directly above us."

Edyth's eyes darted upwards and so did Ruby's – she meant the double bedroom, the one she and Cash were occupying. Interesting.

"Do you know what he was so afraid of?"

"I haven't got a clue. And when we found out, there were some who felt quite insulted, me too if I'm honest. We're not that bad he needed to go to such lengths!"

Ruby smiled at Edyth's supposed joke, and so did Cash. "Did you find anything else out of the ordinary whilst you were… helping out?"

"No, it was all very Spartan in here, a bit like it is now.

And lonely, that's what it was, such an air of loneliness the cottage had about it. Always has had, before Mr Taylor, during and afterwards. I felt bad about him, you know? When I found out what he'd done, the guilt was terrible. I should have made more of an effort. Like I said, he didn't seem to have no family."

"Was he buried at St Winifred's?" Ruby asked.

"Yes and afforded every respect."

"Who buried him?"

"The Reverend Martin, he was brand new to the village then, held a lovely service he did, just me in attendance and a few other villagers."

Cash looked impressed. "So, the Reverend Martin's not all bad then?"

Edyth shook her head. "I'd say his bark's worse than his bite. He's just... passionate about the church that's all. Straight-laced as I've said but not in every respect. Believe me, there are some vicars who'd refuse to entertain suicides, who insist that taking your own life is still a sin, that it foils God's plan for you."

"It's ridiculous, isn't it," Cash continued, "to view despair as a sin."

"Totally." Jennifer answered, her shy but penetrating smile causing Cash to fidget a bit – once he'd cottoned on, that is, to just how penetrating it was.

"What a terrible feeling it must be, to exist on the outside of life, to feel as though you haven't been included." Edyth's shiny eyes revealed the sensitive soul she really was. In the next breath, however, she was back to her old self. "Goodness, look at the time, it's near on midday! I need to go home, get the roast on. Him indoors is a stickler for routine, likes to eat bang on three and then spend the rest of the day in front of the TV, pretending he's watching it, but really he's snoozing."

"You're as bad, Mum!" Jennifer accused.

"I know, I know!" Edyth jovially conceded. "I'll tell you something though, there's nothing better than putting your feet up on a Sunday afternoon. It feels legitimate somehow, doesn't it? As if that's exactly what you should be doing." Rising, she and her daughter made their way back to the front door, Ruby and Cash in tow.

At the entrance, Edyth paused. "No overkill on the locks nowadays is there?"

"Not particularly," Ruby agreed, "and I've opened a couple of windows upstairs, they're certainly not nailed down. Can't vouch for the others though."

"I hope they're not, a place needs ventilation, the air gets so stale otherwise. And what about the main bedroom, the lock been removed there too has it?"

"Yeah, there's no lock now."

"Strange to have one indoors though, especially in a room you're not sleeping in." Before Ruby could issue any type of answer, Edyth invited both her and Cash to The Plough that evening, for quiz night.

"I thought it was last night?" Cash said, frowning.

"It's usually on a Saturday but there weren't enough punters in, everyone staying at home, according to Louisa, to watch that new drama on BBC1, you know, the one about Ruth Ellis, the last woman in Britain to be hanged. Sad about her, it is. I reckon that David Blakely was a cad the way he treated her. He deserved to be shot!"

Not knowing the case particularly well, Ruby could only nod politely.

Intending to thank her for the kind invite but decline it,

Cash waded in.

"Well, in that case, we'd love to come, although I warn you, when it comes to quizzes, I'm a bit of an ace. Sure that won't upset some of the locals?"

Jennifer's laugh was breathless. "Oh, it won't, they'll appreciate the competition." She sighed, or it could even have been swooned. "I'm so glad you can come."

"That's settled then," Edyth declared. "Eight o' clock it starts, don't be late."

When she'd gone, Ruby ran her hands the length of the front door, feeling a slight rough patch in a rectangular shape on the top half of the door as well as on the bottom. Beckoning for Cash to come closer, she pointed to it.

"I wonder what he was trying to keep out," she mused.

Cash ran his hand over the rough patches too. "Or what he was trying to contain."

Chapter Fourteen

"WHAT is the name of the robot in the 1951 science fiction film classic *The Day the Earth Stood Still?*"

"Erm… er…" Jennifer muttered.

"Don't worry, I know it," Cash replied.

Ruby rolled her eyes – of course he did, just like he knew the answers to every single question the compere had asked so far. Jennifer, Edyth, and Edyth's husband, Bob, were in awe of him. Regarding answers, Ruby was as much in the dark as Jennifer.

"What was Belize called until 1973?"

Jennifer looked expectantly at Cash, who nodded his head to show he knew this one too. Ruby, meanwhile, was struggling to think where Belize was on the world map.

"The fastest computers in the world can now perform 1,000 trillion calculations per second, also known as 'Floating Point Operations per Second'. What is the acronym for this?"

An IT question – it had to be! As Cash scribbled down the answer, she discarded her pencil; it was of little use to her. He'd be insufferable later; she knew it, getting every single question right. He really was such a geek sometimes.

Taking a sip of rum and Coke, she attempted to drown her sorrows. There'd been a good turnout for the quiz, which led her to the conclusion that part two of the Ruth Ellis drama must be the following Saturday instead of running on consecutive nights. Jed was off canoodling with the collie again – Dollie; Jennifer had said her name was, 'Dollie the Collie' – who seemed as happy to see him as he was to see her, and in the far corner sat the Reverend Martin, surrounded by Grace Comely and several other women of maturing years, who were staring at him in a manner similar to how the Campbells were staring at Cash, as though he were their guiding star.

Despite feeling like a spare part, she smiled, inwardly at least. The Reverend hadn't acknowledged her yet, but actually she and Cash had received a hearty welcome from a fair few locals when they'd arrived, even some offers to join other teams beside the Campbells, which Jennifer had looked alternately stricken and furious about. Cash had tactfully declined, insisting they'd be just fine with Edyth and co. And, despite the questions being infuriatingly beyond her capability, she couldn't help but think what a nice event it was, appreciating the sense of community it evoked, the *inclusion*. News of her profession had obviously spread like wildfire but – the Reverend aside – not one person had treated her as leprous because of it, although, she supposed, the night was still young.

Straightaway, she admonished herself.

Enough with the paranoia! Just enjoy the moment.

As the compere droned on and on – they had seven more questions to go to complete thirty before switching papers with the other teams to get them marked – her mind returned to George Taylor. From what she'd been told, she couldn't imagine him enjoying a night like this, not in Canonibeare. There was a good chance he'd never even set foot in the pub. Which begged the question why come here, to a close-knit community, if you weren't going to throw yourself into the mix? Surely, you'd be more anonymous living in a city; totally anonymous in fact, if you chose to be. Living amongst an endless supply of people meant you could blend in, become part of the urban wallpaper. Although George had travelled a few miles to commit suicide, his spirit could well have returned to the cottage, his last abode.

Worried that that might be the case, she had tuned in after Edyth and Jennifer had left, sat in the double bedroom whilst Cash was in the shower, looking towards the window where Rachel's friend had seen the shadow of a man standing.

Is it you, George? Are you still here?

Although there was no reply she heard shuffling on the landing, it wasn't Cash, he was still in the bathroom. It wasn't Jed either – still doing his utmost to avoid the floorboards. He'd be either downstairs or running in some Elysium field.

Going to investigate, it was all quite still. She decided to inspect the door to the main bedroom instead, do what she'd done downstairs with the front door, and try to figure out where the lock had been. Walking through the single bedroom to reach it, she thought she caught a glimpse of movement, but turning towards the bed, there was nothing, no huddled child. Disappointed, she'd sighed. Although the wood panelled door between rooms looked as if it had recently seen a lick of paint, the shade a chalky cream and embedded in an oak frame, it was still an old, old door; certainly Ruby thought it pre-dated George, maybe even Mary and Thomas Ward. Still in the single bedroom, she ran her hand over that side of the door – it was smooth enough.

She inspected the other side and found the same. Retracing her footsteps, she closed the main bedroom door behind her, walked back through the single bedroom, and pushed the door open to the landing. Immediately, she'd had a flashback – not Mary, but a man, George Taylor she presumed, just a vague impression of him as opposed to anything more substantial, hammering away furiously as he fixed something to this door. Not on the inside, where she was, but on the landing side. Examining it, sure enough, there was a rough patch. She remembered Edyth's words, *'The door that leads to the biggest bedroom.'* Well, technically, she'd been right. As for Cash's words regarding what George was trying to keep in as opposed to keeping out, they'd never seemed so pertinent: the sweat had been pouring off George as he worked.

And then it struck her.

Were you psychic, George? Is that what set you apart from society, or what you felt set you apart? Could you sense what was here and been worried by it?

No, that was the wrong word; he hadn't been worried, he'd been terrified.

Could it be that George was the one warning them to leave, not Mary? That would make more sense. After all, why would Mary want her to leave? Her story hadn't yet been told.

If it was George, he refused to say. All she'd been able to pick up regarding him was residual stuff. Frustrating for her, but if he'd moved on, she'd be glad of it.

When Cash had finally finished in the shower, she'd had hers and then they'd gone in search of the oak tree. It had been a lovely day with clear blue skies overhead and only the lightest of breezes. Cash had treated, with some amusement, her expectation that she'd be able to find one specific tree amongst so many.

And damn it, yet again he'd been right.

They'd walked east, in the direction she'd sensed Mary had come from when running back towards the cottage, using a compass app on the iPhone to guide them. East had taken them across a couple of fields in which resided oaks galore. Veering to the left and to the right, she'd looked round in despair. How the heck was she supposed to find 'Mary's tree', as she'd dubbed it? Do what she did with the gravestones and go and hug each one? It was an idea she only briefly contemplated. Hoping Jed might 'sniff' the right one out, he seemed baffled too. Giving up after an hour or so, they'd gone back to the cottage and checked the list of words on *Ghost Discovery*: *dark* – that was the third time for that one – *want, content, taken, enough, truly, craven, fault, images, float, memories, bear, choice, everywhere, shut, child, mother* – the latter two causing her to take the phone from Cash and study it.

Content and *craven* were at odds with each other, total odds. *I need something more concrete* she'd whispered in the general direction of the phone, *the name of the man who tormented Mary would be good, tell me his name.* But all that happened was the radar kept spinning, *dark* and *memories* thrown up again, and a weak presence indicated as being just behind her.

Handing the phone back to Cash, she reminded herself *Ghost Discovery* was a game, just a game and now here she was, at the pub, involved in another one.

"Ruby, Ruby, come on, you should know this one!" Cash was pointing at the last question on the sheet. Edyth, Jennifer, and Bob looking expectantly at her too.

"Erm… what is it? What's the question?" she asked, even as she was looking down and reading it. *Whose story led to the first-ever televised exorcism back in the 1970s?*

She stared into the distance, trying to think.

"Is it to do with the Enfield Haunting?" Cash asked.

Ruby shook her head. "No, that had news coverage but was never televised at the time, not as far as I know."

"Who'd want to televise an exorcism anyway?" Bob commented.

"It's not the sort of thing I'd go in for," Edyth declared.

Jennifer snorted. "Mum, you'd be first in line to watch it!"

"I wouldn't," she denied. "I wasn't. I was around in the 70s, and never heard of it."

Exorcism, exorcism, Ruby pondered, whilst they continued to talk, *can't see it being on English TV, not in the 70s, it must have been America.*

"We need an answer," Jennifer nudged.

"Time's running out," Edyth agreed.

Tell me about it. "Okay, okay, I think Gran did say something about it, she wasn't overly impressed as far as I can recall. Not with the exorcism as such, but with it being blasted into so many living rooms – she was concerned about the ethics involved. It's strange, but I keep wanting to say David Beckham—"

"The footballer!" Jennifer gasped. "He'd have been a kid in the 70s, I'm sure of it."

"I know, I know, it's nothing to do with him or his family," Ruby quickly replied. "But the surname, it's similar."

"Can't you draw on your psychic powers for the answer?" Bob asked, using the same phrase that Cash had, although she wouldn't tell him off at least.

Who was it, Ruby? Try and remember what Gran said.

Beckham... Becks... Beck... Becker...

It was as if a light bulb came on in her head.

"The Beckers! It's the Beckers story!"

"Ruby!" Cash hissed. "Keep your voice down, don't tell the entire pub."

"Oh, sorry, sorry," Ruby apologised, leaning forwards and whispering instead. "But I remember now, Edwin Becker was the man who got exorcised, him and his wife, Marsha, and it was in their home in Chicago and yes, Gran was *very* disapproving."

"Did it work though?" Jennifer asked, nothing less than wonder on her face.

Ruby shrugged. "I don't know, I've never actually watched any footage on it."

"There must be something about it on the net," Jennifer continued, turning to her mother. "We're going to have to find out if there is, give it a watch."

Edyth looked as disapproving as Gran once had but she conceded nonetheless. "If you insist," she replied.

"So, we're going with the Beckers, are we?" Cash checked.

Ruby nodded and time was called.

As the papers were gathered up, Cash sat back in his chair. "Well, if you're right, Ruby, I reckon we've got ourselves a perfect score."

Jennifer beamed. "That'll be an all-time first, won't it, Mum?"

Edyth nodded, looking delighted too.

There was a rush for the bar, Cash joining the scrum to buy a second round as the Campbells had footed the bill for the first. About to engage her newfound friends in conversation, Ruby noticed several people wandering not in the bar's direction but in hers. As they approached, she also noticed the Reverend noticing, and could just imagine him cursing under his breath at the antics of his wayward flock.

"Hello, Ruby in't it?" a man with a red face and red hair to match asked, holding out his hand. He'd been one of the men that had propped up the bar on Friday night, who'd initially glared at her. Far from glaring now, he was smiling, introducing not only himself as 'Ben' but the equally robust woman standing by his side as 'Sarah.'

"Hi, hi there," Ruby said, shaking hands with her too. "My grandmother's called Sarah." Slightly lame, but she didn't know what else to say to these people.

Aside from Ben and Sarah, there was Maggie and Guy, another ruddy-complexioned couple, and Liza – 'as in Minnelli' she'd informed them – who announced that Louisa and Grace had also told her all about Ruby and that she was 'dead impressed.' Unsure whether Liza meant the pun or not, Ruby had simply smiled as they pulled up chairs and joined her and the Campbells. A few minutes later, Cash returned from the bar with a drinks-laden tray, noted the five extra people and, heroically concealing a crestfallen look, offered to buy them drinks too.

Finally, when each and every one had a pint or glass of something before them, conversation turned to Old Cross Cottage, and whether it was indeed haunted.

"'Cos that's what you're here for, in't it?" Ben insisted, "I know you've said you're not, but your sort can't help yourselves can you, and that cottage, we've always thought it a bit strange, haven't we, Sarah?"

Sarah looked askance at Ben and frowned. "Yeah, I suppose we have, although… it's not just the cottage, but where it's located."

"Oh?" Ruby glanced at Cash as she leant forward. "What

do you mean by that?"

"This is a quiet village," she said, just as Edyth once had, "tucked away from the madding crowds. Nothing much happens, but if it does, it tends to happen there."

"At the crossroads?"

"That's right, yeah."

"What happens exactly?" Ruby pressed.

"See! You are ghost-busting," Ben declared, taking a break from supping at his beer, "I knew you were! Want all sorts of information, don't you?"

"Ben, I—"

Cash stepped in. "No, she's intrigued that's all, same as me. Can't help it really, it's an interesting history the cottage has. Shame there's no ghosts there."

"No ghosts?" Ben queried, looking like he'd been slapped in the face.

"Not as far as we can tell," Cash said, shrugging. "There'd be more phenomena at a Premier Inn we reckon."

"But... but Grace said—"

"Oh yeah," Cash interrupted, "there was a bit of action at Grace's but that's it so far. We're just intent on having a good week, really, enjoying ourselves. Now, what was that you were saying about the crossroads, it's a bit dodgy is it?"

"Well, erm... yeah," Ben said, encouraging Sarah to divulge all.

It turned out there'd been several accidents there over the last decade, concerning either vehicles or bikes and once upon a time a tractor.

"Trouble is," Guy said, joining in the conversation, "you get a lot of bored teens in these parts, once they learn to drive they take to the roads for a bit of a thrill, make like Lewis Hamilton they do or who's that other one? Damon

Hill, that's it, only without the skill or the training. Watch out for 'em, they speed down these lanes, especially at night, and well, the crossroads is where most accidents happen."

"Aye, it is, it is," Maggie agreed, as did Liza and Edyth. "Been at least two deaths there that I can remember."

"Deaths?" Cash repeated, clearly shocked by that fact.

"Oh, yeah," Guy nodded his head in a suitably grave manner. "I'm going back maybe twenty years ago now, but a girl got thrown from her horse on the exact spot where the four roads meet, broke her neck she did. Tragic it was, so tragic."

"And the other death?"

"That was a car crash, someone passing through late at night, going too fast, he'd had a tot to drink as well, collided with a local."

"The local was okay?" Ruby checked.

"Jack? He was fine, shaken though, as you can imagine. That were around nine years ago and he's not driven since, put him off it did."

Cash looked at Ruby as though making sure she was absorbing all this information. She certainly was, remembering the rhythm of the ground beneath her feet – the earth's energy, she supposed – as she'd stood at the crossroads and how compelling it had been. Even so, she hadn't detected any lingering spirits there – no girl thrown from a horse, no drunk driver.

"I don't suppose any of you know about a child called Mary who used to live there, do you? I mean you wouldn't have known her personally, she lived there in the early 1900s I reckon, but have you heard of her? She lived with her mother, Ellen."

No sooner had she blurted out the words than she

regretted them. They'd know she was lying now – or rather Cash had been lying – and that she was indeed ghost hunting, as they'd no doubt call it. But she'd been unable to resist, it was a much older history she needed to get to grips with than the one being discussed. To her surprise, no one immediately jumped in with 'see, I knew it, I was right all along', instead they conferred with each other to see if anyone did indeed know anything.

And drew a blank.

"But you know who you could ask, don't you?" suggested Maggie.

Ruby looked towards the Reverend Martin, who seemed to immediately sense her eyes on him and lifted his head to glare back. "Yes, yes, I do know, thanks," she answered, cursing that the fount of all knowledge had to be him.

Chapter Fifteen

RUBY, Cash and the Campbells had indeed won the competition – a perfect score, as Cash had predicted. There was no prize as such but the Campbells couldn't have been more pleased. Jennifer practically threw herself at Cash, wrapping her arms around his neck and clinging on whilst thanking him profusely. Edyth too had given him a hug and Bob had shaken his hand so enthusiastically, Ruby half expected his arm to be torn clean off. The thought of which was still making her giggle as they weaved their way back to Old Cross, the pair of them supporting each other as Jed ran ahead.

"How many rums did you have to drink?" Cash asked, doing the lion's share of supporting she had to admit.

"Don't know, lost count, but one too many I reckon."

"You can say that again."

With her free hand she batted him. "Hey, you can talk! You downed every single one of those drinks that the Campbells bought you."

"I was merely being polite," Cash insisted. "It was their heart's desire to reward the golden boy, the hero du jour, the brightest star in the—"

She batted him again. "You wouldn't have got a full house if it weren't for me."

"Ruby, it was a pub quiz, not bingo!"

"Oh, yeah, yeah, so it was. I get confused, so confused."

Even though she was decidedly drunk, the fact she'd said those words at the exact moment they passed St Winifred's with its silent churchyard wasn't lost on her. In fact, they seemed of the utmost relevance. She was totally confused by this current case: who Mary was, whether she was being warned by a second presence or threatened, and whether that presence was Mary's tormenter, as she'd come to think of him, or the landlord, Thomas Ward. And if it was Ward, what terrible sadness had driven him to commit suicide? As for the oak tree, where the hell was it? "And does it matter anyway?"

"What?" Cash's question made her realise she'd spoken out loud.

"Oh, nothing, I was thinking about the oak tree, whether it matters if we find it or not. But there's also the crossroads to consider never mind the cottage itself. I'll tell you something, we won't be leaving on Friday if we can't piece it all together."

"We'll have to, I'm playing a gig Friday night remember, at The Lamb in Lewes."

Ruby screwed her eyes shut, tried to remember. "That's right, so you are." A drummer in his brother's band, *Thousand Island Park*, it promised to be a good night, with Corinna in tow, plus several mutual friends. She was only glad Cash was placed firmly behind his drum kit as opposed to joining his more vocally gifted brother at the mike. A thought that elicited more giggles: Cash and his singing.

"What's wrong with you?" Cash asked but he was giggling too, the pair of them, coming to a standstill in front of Old Cross Cottage, clutching their stomachs they were laughing so hard and loving every minute of it. It felt good, *vital* even, bringing light and laughter to a place that light and laughter had often overlooked.

Whatever this place is, if the myths and legends are true, nothing is beyond the light, nothing.

In that moment, she truly felt it – they were winning.

We just have to keep drinking, that's all!

Again, she bellowed with laughter, causing a bird – a crow probably – to take flight above her, its wings beating indignantly.

"Oh, Cash," she said, when she was able to. "I love it here, I really do."

"What here?" Cash said, straightening up too. "At the crossroads?"

Ruby looked down. He was right; she was in the middle of it, dead centre. "I actually meant the cottage," she answered. "The cottage, the village and the lovely time we had in Lyme Regis yesterday. This is our first holiday, Cash, our very first."

"Ha!" Cash moved closer to her. "It's a holiday of sorts, remember."

"Even so, we're not having too bad a time, are we?"

"No, of course not." His arms around her, he hugged her to him. "Where's Jed?"

"Jed? He's sitting on the porch I think, waiting for us."

"Is he? Do you think he'd mind waiting a little longer?"

"What for?"

"For this," he answered, pulling her towards him.

As his lips met hers, his tongue teasing at first, deliberately hesitant, taking his own sweet time to rouse her, Ruby didn't think Jed would mind at all.

* * *

Mary couldn't believe it. Ellen had let him into the cottage; she'd actually let him in! And right now, this very minute, they were downstairs, the pair of them, talking and laughing – her mother particularly, laughing at every single word he said.

Sitting at the top of the narrow staircase, Mary hugged the newel post to try and stop herself from shaking. Why had her mother done such a thing, allowed him into their sanctuary? Was it a one-off or would it happen again?

She hoped not, she *prayed* not.

"Mary, come down and meet our new neighbour."

She didn't want to meet him, she didn't want to go anywhere near him. Remembering how he'd called her name, the first time she'd become aware of him, but afterwards too, his voice drifting through the walls in the dead of night, seeming to envelop her, her skin crawled. There was just something so… *wrong* about him. A sensation that was hard to explain to a mother burdened with the harshness of everyday realities. She had less and less time for what she'd call her daughter's frivolous imaginings. Since moving to this cottage, Ellen had had to work harder than ever. But she wasn't working now. For him she'd put work aside.

"Mary! Will you please come down?" From strident, Ellen's voice became girlish again. "Oh, that child! I'm always yelling for her, I am. You've probably heard me. In fact, I know you have. You know her name too, don't you? She told me."

There was a low murmur in reply but not one that Mary could understand, and then more laughter from her mother. She'd have to obey or risk being dragged down. Ellen wouldn't stand for what she'd perceive as rudeness. She was a proud woman. *Too proud,* thought Mary, finally relinquishing her hold on the newel post.

Descending the narrow stairs, she hesitated at the sliver of door that separated the stairwell from the main living area. Never before had she hesitated, normally she'd burst through, eager to sit by the fire, to be with her mother as they sewed or baked, to relish the busy but secure atmosphere. *It should be just us in there, just us!* She was almost in tears as she thought it, tears that she roughly wiped away.

Reaching out, her hand touched the cold hard wood in front of her – listened to it groan as though it were reluctant too, as slowly, slowly she pushed it open…

* * *

It wasn't a door that divided them now, it was a wall – the one she used to lie on the other side of, in the big bed beside her mother. Now she was on the opposite side, whilst *he* took her place.

In the corner, huddled against it, the tears poured down Mary's face. As thick as the walls were, she could hear them, moaning and yelling out. *She's in pain, just as I am!* But then her mother would start laughing again, confusing Mary, adding to her pain somehow – pain that he was the cause of.

Why had her mother listened to him?

"But he's right," Ellen had said when she'd protested. "A man and a woman need their privacy. And you're only next door, not far away, not at all. It's one big house really, *our* house. In the morning you'll come back, we'll work together, like always."

"No!" she'd screamed. "I don't like it next door. That's his house, *this* is ours."

"Mary, stop it!" Ellen had raised her voice too. "I… this is my chance, our chance, to be respectable in the eyes of others, I'll have a husband and you'll have a father. Yes, Mary, you heard right, he's asked me to marry him and I've accepted."

"No!" It had been a sob this time, anger turning to despair in the face of such a revelation. "Please, Mam, no." She'd looked at Ellen then, noticed she was in turmoil too and seized her chance. "Why do you want to marry him? Why can't it just be the two of us? Like it's always been. We were so happy."

"*He* makes me happy," Ellen insisted, "and together we'll be a family." She'd stepped away from Mary then, as if remaining close would make her falter even more. "I know we've been getting by, but how long can we do that, eh, without a man? And the villagers," she'd sighed then, bit down so hard on her lip that Mary feared she'd draw blood. "I'm sick of the rumours, sick of them! And sitting at the back of the church, snubbed, because I don't fit their idea of respectable. I've nothing to be ashamed of. Your father was a good man, do you hear me, a good man!"

"My father was a lord!"

"No!" Ellen screamed as loud as her. "He was a good man but he was no one special. Forget your fancy ideas, that you're special too, above others somehow. You're not, and nor am I. And because we're not, there's no choice. I'm going to marry him."

And so she had, not even two months to the date of when he'd first arrived, ousting Mary, placing her next door – his idea, all his. He the one who'd initially taken her there, 'to settle her' he'd said, gripping her by the arm as he pushed her up the stairs, the treads uneven, the boards almost black in colour and so much wider than her feet. She hated it at once, as much as she hated him; the atmosphere neither warm nor comforting but so very stark. She'd only had time to glance at the room downstairs as he'd rushed her through it, wondering where it was that the landlord's body had been laid out after he'd hanged himself. Once an Inn, a strange smell lingered – like the smell of beer, but stale. Everything was so stale.

At the top of the stairs, he'd pushed her again, through another door immediately to the left, behind which lay a small room with a single bed in it, a table and a mirror. That was it, nothing more. There weren't even curtains at the window.

"Stay here," he growled, "and don't go wandering."

His eyes, surrounded by thick skin that was gnarled and pitted, bore into her.

"You hear me?" he barked again, coming closer.

Who was he? Just a labourer, that's all, another labourer – finding work on one of the farms around here. Ellen had said they were no one special – that she should dispense with such notions – but nor was he. How had her marrying him increased their standing? At church, when they all went together, they might not have to sit at the back anymore, they had crept forward several pews, but that was it, the sum of what he'd done for them. As before, no one went out of their way to engage them in conversation, they could expect just a few cursory words from the vicar on occasion, nothing more. They were still at the edge of the village, in every sense.

"Oi!" he said, his hand on her again, shaking her. "I said d'ya hear me?"

"Yes," Mary replied at once.

"Yes, Father!"

"Yes, Father." She gritted her teeth as she said it.

His hand lingered, not for a moment, longer than that, and then he snatched it back as if her skin were red hot and it burnt him. Hurrying to the door, he intended to leave her there, in that barren room, without a light. Even so, she wanted rid of him.

He paused, not quite done with her yet. "You don't want to go wandering, see. Not in this house. There's something here, besides me."

Her eyes widened. The shuffling, the whispering that she'd heard, long before he'd moved in, that he couldn't possibly be responsible for – who was it?

What was it?

"Will I be safe if I stay in here?" She cursed the whimper in her voice.

"*Only* if you stay in here. This is your room now, Mary, all yours."

Finally taking his leave, she realised: this wasn't her room; it was her prison.

* * *

Her head in her hands, her cheeks drenched with salty tears, Mary huddled in the corner again, hardly daring to open her eyes, screwing them shut.

As she'd suspected, as he'd said, there was something else here. When her mother at last quietened down, whilst she slept with that man beside her, then this part of the cottage would ease into life, intermittent shuffling on the landing outside, frantic whisperings, muffled conversations below and then a sob, as heart-wrenching as her own. Night after night it would happen, so many nights spent here, and still she hadn't grown used to it. Oh, how she longed for daylight, because with it came release. He'd take her back to work alongside her mother, who barely even acknowledged her anymore, as if she daren't somehow, her eyes averted. When at last he'd go to work, leaving them alone, Mary would plead with Ellen. Oh, the times she'd plead!

"Mam, look at me, please."

Eventually Ellen had lifted her head, the change in her shocking. There was no longer even a trace of laughter on her face. She looked tired, so tired, more than that, exhausted... and afraid. The cries emitting from her mother's bedroom at night, the squeals, lately there'd been a different tone to them.

"Is that a bruise under your eye, Mam?"

Immediately Ellen had lowered her head again. "Just get on with your work. We do what we have to do, to get by."

"But we're working harder than ever. Why, when he works too?"

"He... I don't know what he does with his wages. I don't ask, Mary, and neither should you. Now stop your jabbering and get on."

Since that day, she'd seen other bruises on Ellen too, not on her face, not again, but on her arms, whenever she rolled up her sleeves to do the laundering, some of them as black as the darkness that so often surrounded her. And then he'd come home, expect to be waited on like he was indeed a lord, and they'd scurry round after him, Ellen eager to please, Mary sullen but obeying, for the sake of her mother, not wanting to give him reason to bruise her further – waiting for him to stir himself after supper, to haul her back to his side of the cottage, to imprison her yet again.

And there she'd sit, in that cursed room, dreaming of the oak tree, of the days when she used to linger beneath it, soaking up the sunshine, idling the time away, making daisy chains. There were never any breaks now; no time to feel the wind in her face as she ran across fields, the grass soft and swaying beneath her feet. The cottage was her universe, *his* cottage – and, like the night, something to be endured.

More tears burst from her eyes and instead of holding her head she clasped her hands together, her lips moving fervently in a rapid succession of words. She'd pray, just like the other one that was here prayed – both of them, fuelled by desperation.

Please, please, please, help me. If you're listening, please help, I'll do anything, anything you want, just as long as you help.

Please, you have to help!

Chapter Sixteen

"RUBY, what are you doing in here?"

At the sound of Cash's voice, Ruby opened her eyes, blinked several times before sitting up and looking round her. She was not where she expected to be, in the bed she shared with Cash, neither was she in the main bedroom – she was in the single bedroom, just a sheet covering her. Racking her brain, she had no recollection whatsoever of how she got here. The last thing she remembered was tumbling into bed with Cash and engaging in some very frenetic sex. Afterwards, she'd dozed in his arms, feeling very mellow indeed.

The dream, Ruby, the dream!

It hadn't just been one dream this time; there'd been a series of them.

Straightaway, vivid images crowded her mind, filling it in daylight as surely as it had done at night and with them the emotions attached – Mary's despair, her helplessness in the wake of that man who had barged his way into their lives. What was his name? She racked her brains for any mention of it and could find none.

But Mary was frightened of someone else too, the one who shuffled, who sobbed, who prayed.

Not her tormentor then, he'd still been alive. So who was it, and why?

"Argh, my brain!" she moaned, cradling her head as Mary had cradled hers.

Cash sat beside her. "You've been dreaming again?"

She nodded.

"Bad dreams?"

"They weren't pleasant, Cash. What that girl went through was awful." Briefly she explained the dreams to him, her eyes watering at the recollection. "In the dreams I lose myself, I'm her instead. She was just a little girl, and that man, whoever he was, terrorised her, and the mother too, after first seducing and marrying her. God, I can't believe he banished Mary from her own house, made her stay in this half of the cottage, in this bedroom, every night, alone, feeding her stories about how haunted it was. I'll tell you something, unlike George, he didn't need to fix a lock on the door, she was rooted to the spot with terror."

There was a grave expression on Cash's face as he listened. "The other presence you're talking about, Mary's ghost, if it's someone sobbing, could it be a woman?"

Ruby frowned. "That's a bit sexist, Cash."

"I'm just trying to work it out, that's all."

"You and me both," she admitted. "Well... it can't be Ellen, poor deluded Ellen, because she was still alive when all this was going on too. It could be Thomas Ward, of course, or..." she paused, bit her lip. "There is a third presence, one that's deep in hiding, if it's a later addition then it could be Ellen, but I don't know, Cash, I said this to Theo, she's just not dark enough. It's more likely to be Mary's jailer."

"Or it could have nothing to do with any of them?"

"Call me psychic, but I think it's connected." She smiled weakly at her attempted joke. "Don't get me wrong, Cash, there are many shades at Old Cross, many layers, several dimensions even, it's… a special place, this house at the crossroads, but the one I've tuned into revolves around Mary. This is all to do with her."

Cash nodded as though somehow he agreed. "Okay, I've got another question for you: if Mary was picking up on ghosts, was she psychic too?"

"It's a really good question, but actually she might not have been. Children are more open to psychic experiences in general. The shutters haven't yet come down, not like they do when we move towards adulthood and material concerns take over."

"Like eating, drinking, clothing yourself, scratching a living, that kind of thing?"

"Exactly."

"Not that the shutters ever came down for you."

She laughed. "I'm aware of that." Although, to be honest, there'd been a time when she'd shut down to a certain extent, as a child, when her mother had dabbled with the occult and conjured something that was as far from human as it was possible to get. Ruby had swallowed such a horrific memory, imprisoned it too, watching helplessly as her mother withdrew from her, just as Mary's had, but for very different reasons. Or were they so different, Ruby wondered, when you examined them – both Ellen and her mother, Jessica, had been dealing with demons of sorts.

"Actually… hang on. Children are more open to psychic experiences in general, I just said that, didn't I?"

Cash frowned. "Yeah, yeah, you did. So… what are you getting at?"

"Well, Mary, alone in the dark, would have been very open to suggestion." That idea developing, she reminded herself that Mary had been considered an imaginative child.

And night after night, with nothing to distract her, she could have indeed started tuning into the spiritual world, or at least *imagining* all sorts of things to do with the spiritual world. Hence why the house came alive at night for her. "It's just a theory, Cash," she said, after she'd explained. "She could have demonised the spirit that was here because of fear, but one person she didn't exaggerate was her tormenter, I'm certain of that. And, I know Theo said I shouldn't presume, but I'm also certain her torment continued, ending in yet another Old Cross tragedy." She sighed in anguish. "If only I knew his name, the man who did this to her."

"William," Cash replied. "I think his name was William."

* * *

Before Cash would reveal how he knew the man's name, he insisted Ruby pull on some clothes and follow him downstairs. "I need breakfast, I'm starving."

"But Cash—"

"Ruby, you know me well enough by now, I won't make any sense on an empty stomach. Here," he handed over the kimono-style wrap that she'd brought with her, "come downstairs and I'll reveal all after you've made us a fry-up."

"Me? But you usually do the cooking!"

"Not on holiday I don't."

As he turned to leave the room, she sighed again, as long and as loud as she could to let him know that she wasn't impressed with his teasing. To her annoyance, she was completely ignored. He wasn't teasing, she realised. He meant it. She was in charge of breakfast. Rising from bed, she shrugged the wrap on, tying it at the waist before smoothing her hair. Moving across to the mirror that hung just above the chest of drawers, she stopped. Unlike the other two items of furniture, the mirror looked old, the glass within it slightly mottled. Hesitating still, she eventually decided to check her appearance in the bathroom mirror. Whilst there she could also brush her teeth – kill two birds with one stone, so to speak.

In the kitchen, a few minutes later, it was clear Cash was sticking to his guns; he wasn't going to say a word until she'd delivered breakfast. Retrieving the ingredients from the re-frigerator, she'd never fried food so quickly in her life.

"And toast, don't forget the toast," he commented.

"Oh, the bloody toast," she swore, setting two plates on the table and hurrying over to the toaster. "You can make a fresh pot of tea though."

"Coming right up," he replied, pinching her bottom as he sidled past.

Back at the table, she waited for him to consume at least half his breakfast before threatening him with dire retribu-tion if he didn't put her out of her misery.

"How the hell do you know his name's William?"

"Well…"

"Cash, I've done what you want, I've been patient enough!"

Cash set down the piece of toast he'd been chewing on just a tad too leisurely. "Okay, okay, keep your knickers on, Rubes. Actually," he leaned sideways as though to double check, "you haven't got any knickers on, have you?"

"Don't get side-tracked," she warned, trying not to get side-tracked too.

As he sat up straight again she was surprised to note how quickly all amusement left his face. He was deadly serious again, and in the blink of an eyelid. "So you've been dreaming, connecting with Mary that way, and, as you know, I had a significant dream. When was it? Saturday?"

"Yeah, you went for a nap when we came back from Lyme Regis."

"That's right. Similar to what you've been experiencing, I was me but I was also someone else, hiding, terrified of facing what was in this cottage with me, its fury."

"And I said it was a bit odd if you were channelling Mary too."

"Yeah, well I've been thinking about that, Rubes. I don't think I am channelling her. I think I'm a man, definitely a man. Having said that, there are similarities to Mary. I'm curled up in a ball as well, trying to make myself small, to disappear. Also, you said Mary was praying, well so was I – sorry, I should stop saying that, I mean *he* was praying, holding his hands together, his lips moving as if begging to be heard."

Ruby frowned, how strange they should both channel figures that mirrored each other's actions. That's if Cash was indeed channelling something and he wasn't suffering from suggestion either. "How do you know it's William and not Ward?"

"That's where *Ghost Discovery* comes in," he said, reaching for his phone. "As soon as I woke up, I switched it on. I forgot to do that last night, too drunk—"

"And too horny!"

Cash laughed. "Yeah, that as well. Anyway, within seconds a word flashed up—"

"William," Ruby said before Cash could.

"Correct."

Ruby pushed her half-eaten plate of breakfast away. "And that's it, that's why you think the third presence here is a man called William?"

"I know you dismiss this as a game, Ruby, but—"

She held her hands up. "No, I'm not dismissing it, honestly. But it is a bit… fantastical, believing in an iPhone app. I know I asked it for a name, but even so."

Cash looked from her to his phone. "You're calling *this* fantastical?"

"Yeah, yeah, all right, me and the app both." Her smile fading, she frowned. "Okay, let's roll with it, the elusive and darker presence may well be William, and if it's all entwined, he could be the one who tormented Mary. If you channelled him whilst dreaming too, he's scared, he's praying. That's the bit that doesn't make sense, what's he got to be scared of? Mary I can understand, the poor child was and still is traumatised, but if William's the same, then it must be divine retribution that terrifies him. There's also Mary's 'ghost', as you called it, potentially the suicide Thomas Ward; three spirits to coax forwards basically – all of them in considerable distress." Having got that straight for the pair of them, her thoughts turned to the day ahead. "I'll get onto Theo and Rachel later, see what information they've been able to dig up. Meanwhile," she sniffed a couple of times, "I'm in dire need of a shower."

Cash was on his feet and round the side of the table in an instant.

"Me too. Do you think it's big enough for two?"

* * *

Having taken Louisa's advice, Ruby and Cash visited the swan sanctuary at Abbotsbury, spending a pleasant morning there before lunch at The Anchor Inn in Seatown – a gorgeously rustic pub set right on the coast and close to Golden Cap. After they'd finished their soup with fresh crusty bread, Ruby suggested a walk.

"Golden Cap… Golden Cap…" mused Cash, grabbing his jacket as they left the pub to start the steep trek uphill. "Ah, I know what you're doing!"

"Can't get anything past you can I?"

"Not anymore. George Taylor might not be at the cottage, but he might not be at rest either. He could be forlornly wandering the cliff-top as we speak."

"Forlornly is right. I just want to double-check."

Cash nodded. "I take it that Jed's with us and is enjoying the walk too."

"Funnily enough, I've just seen him. He ran way ahead of us and then disappeared, straight over the edge of the cliff."

Cash stopped in his tracks. "Shit, is he all right?"

Ruby burst out laughing. "He's fine, Cash, he's already dead, remember? He probably saw a seagull or something and is chasing it." Tilting her head to one side, she added, "I suppose in a way he can fly too, his spirit at least."

"Jed with wings, I love it." Sighing, he added, "I wish I could see him, Ruby."

"If you're channelling William, your extra sensory ability might well be developing."

"Really?" He'd looked pleased at that. "I could even rival you one day?"

"Be careful what you wish for," she warned.

Linking arms with him, they continued to climb. Close to the perilously jagged edge was another couple, the pair of them larking about, taking daring pictures of one another, and causing Ruby's stomach to churn. She nodded at them. "They'll be flying over the edge too, if they're not careful."

"You thinking of joining them?"

"Joining them... what do you mean?"

"Well, you've changed direction, you're heading towards them."

Previously she'd steered well clear of the edge but now it was as though instinct was guiding her. Holding onto Cash, who was clearly surprised at this change of heart but not yet objecting, she decided to go with it.

The couple larking about noticed their arrival and at once seized their opportunity. The girl approached Ruby and asked if she could take a photo of them, her accent heavily European. Ruby obliged, wincing again as they stood so close to the edge.

"Why don't you come forward..." she began, her voice cutting off as a flash of memory overwhelmed her – not her memory, someone else's. The sheer weight of grief it was infused with caused her to shut her eyes and turn her head to the side, as if that would somehow shield her from it. "Christ!" she whispered.

Cash noticed immediately. "Ruby, what is it? Is it George?"

"I don't know," Ruby replied, stumbling a bit, trying to understand what was happening. "Not *just* George, it can't be." Rather it was a combined grief that had hit her, the grief of the many, all concentrated in the spot where the girl and her boyfriend were standing – a danger spot – not somewhere to lark about at all.

"Get away from there!" she started shouting, taking a step towards them whilst waving the camera in the air. "You're too close to the edge."

"What?" It was the girl again, her confusion deepening.

"GET AWAY! Don't you understand?"

Not just confused, both the man and the woman showed signs of alarm.

Behind her, Ruby could hear Cash calling.

"Hey, Ruby, stop, it's okay, they're perfectly safe."

They're not!

Nobody was safe where they were standing, the deaths that had occurred – so many of them – had caused the land to become magnetised almost, drawing not just her in this moment but those who had reached their lowest ebb, their despair nourishing the ground more than rain and sunshine ever could – feeding it. And it wasn't fussy; it would claim the innocent too, those that were larking about, just having fun – *stupid* fun so close to the edge of a cliff, but fun none-theless.

Cold fear gripped her. "GET AWAY!"

The girl took a step back, and then another.

"HEY!" It was Cash who shouted now, pushing past Ruby and hurrying to where the girl was standing… no, not standing, she was doing something odd with her arms; they were flailing either side of her.

Ruby ground to a halt, as though paralysed.

What happened next happened so quickly, like a series of dream images too. Jed had re-appeared and was barking furiously at something above his head, something that was dark and swirling. Bats? In broad daylight? It couldn't be, but that's what it reminded her of. *Dark energy,* she realised, stunned to see it, actually *see* it – a swirling, black, glittering mass, really quite beautiful…

A scream pierced the air, followed by a shout. "What is it that you are doing? Leave her, leave her!"

She had to fight to drag her eyes from the darkness, it was so mesmerising, but once she did, her attention was fully captured.

Oh God, she breathed, able to move at last.

The girl was falling, that's why she was moving her arms so erratically, trying to grab hold of her boyfriend, of Cash, anything other than thin air.

"Help! Help!" The girl's voice was thin too, pitiful, and all the while the black mass swooped and swirled, as graceful as a ballerina, as deadly as an assassin. And it was growing too, in width and in height, reaching out, tendrils like claws, greedy... More than that: insatiable – the owner of a thirst that could never be quenched.

"CASH! GRAB HER!"

The girl couldn't fall, she couldn't! If she did, it would be her fault; she was the one who had marched towards her, yelling at the top of her voice, consequently startling her. Why had she done such a thing, why?

"CASH!"

The girl's boyfriend reached out too. For a moment it looked as though the three of them were wrestling with each other – a bizarre dance on the edge of death.

What if... What if...

"Oh, no, no, no, no!" The words were like a chant in her head as she continued to advance, visualising as much white light as possible, an ocean of it, a planet, an entire universe, aiming it at the darkness with laser like precision, trying to beat it back, doing all she could, the *only* thing she could, to combat this potentially disastrous situation. *You won't win this time, you won't!*

Jed was doing his bit too, hurling himself at the descending cloud, over and over again, his fur not the glossy black she was used to but tinged with something, was it gold? Whatever it was it was lighter than usual. *Good boy, Jed, fight it! Fight it!*

Moments had gone by, just moments, but they seemed to last forever, framing a scene in her mind that she knew she'd replay over and over again, that would cause her to shiver every time she thought of it, more than that, much more, if the worst should happen, the *unthinkable.* She'd be hit with a tidal wave of grief, akin to that which had hit her a short while ago; a tsunami that would drown her.

Project white light.

She was doing her utmost, her chant having changed from 'no' to 'please' – praying, as fervently as Mary had prayed, begging for aid from someone, anyone – imagining the rock face crumbling, the waves below, the anguish, the despair, the unfairness of it all. *Please, I'll give anything, anything… I'll do anything…*

That last thought wasn't hers – it was Mary's! She was experiencing another flashback, but now was not the time.

Mary, get out of my head!

The girl's lips were moving, hard and fast, she was praying, begging, pleading… *demanding.*

Please, please, please…

"Mary, stop!"

"It's okay, Ruby, calm down, we're okay!"

Okay? Who was okay? Where was she? *Who* was she? And then it all came flooding back. The girl was okay. Could it be true? So long they'd been teetering on the edge, so long… And not just her, but Cash too, and the girl's boyfriend. She blinked, several times, desperate to believe it, that no harm had been done.

Sure enough all three were standing in front of her, on terra firma, clearly shocked, but alive, gloriously alive. Above, the dark had dissipated, Jed staring outwards, making sure it was gone – standing guard.

Before Ruby could even sigh in relief, the man started shouting at her.

"Idiota! Idiota! What is wrong with you, rushing at us like that?"

"I… I…"

The girl joined in. "We were fine, we were safe, but then you started behaving, I don't know, like some mad woman."

"No, I'm…" again words failed her.

"She was worried, okay?" It was Cash. How many times did he have to defend her? "You were standing so close to the edge."

The girl spread her hands wide. "It may have looked like that from where you were, but we would not do such a thing, put ourselves in danger."

"But if it *looked* like it, you can't blame Ruby for panicking," Cash tried to reason.

The girl vehemently shook her head. "Stupid, so stupid."

"I'm sorry," it was the only thing Ruby could think to say. "I'm so sorry."

"Look, everyone's fine," Cash insisted. "Why don't—"

"Thanks to you," the man interrupted, "but not your stupid girlfriend."

Although Ruby felt she deserved the insult, Cash obviously didn't. She watched as his expression darkened.

"If either of you call my girlfriend that again, I'll push you off the cliff myself, do you understand me?"

"Cash—" Ruby admonished, but he held up his hand to silence her.

"Go on, clear off, you shouldn't be so close to the edge, she's right about that." Ruby was still holding on to their camera and he took it from her and thrust it at them. "Take your selfies somewhere else."

Feeling helpless again, Ruby watched as the man bristled, initially squaring up to Cash but then thinking better of it. Instead, he took the girl's arm and dragged her well away from Ruby, Cash, and the edge of the cliff, only briefly stopping to hurl a few insults in his native language when they were a safe distance away.

When they were mere dots in the distance, she slumped against Cash in relief, Jed coming to sit so close, there was barely any space between the three of them.

"Are you okay?" Cash murmured, still staring after the couple.

"I'm fine, are you?"

"Yeah, yeah, fine."

"I'm sorry..."

"Let's just... forget it."

She moved slightly apart and looked into his face. "I was genuinely worried about them, I thought... But it wasn't the best thing to do, running like that, shouting at them. They're right, it was stupid, really bad."

"This is a bad place," Cash said, looking around. "Tainted."

"You can feel it too, the energy?"

He nodded. "Is this where George Taylor threw himself off?"

"Him and legions of others," Ruby confided.

"Anyone grounded?"

She was quiet for a moment, focusing. "No, I don't think so. Not that I'm able to pick up on, anyway. But there's plenty of residual emotion. It's... ingrained I think."

Like it was at the cottage.

"Okay," Cash said, again his expression was serious, "if

there's no one here that needs your help, let's go back to the pub. I think we could both do with a drink."

"Sure," Ruby said, linking arms with him and trying to blame the look she'd seen in his eyes – no matter how brief – on imagination: that she was tainted too.

Chapter Seventeen

BACK at the Anchor Inn, Cash bought Ruby a double rum and Coke, her hands shaking as she clutched the drink to her. As he'd offered to drive, he opted for coffee, steam rising off his cup as he lifted it to his lips. For a few moments, both of them drank in silence, Ruby glancing at him every now and then, searching his eyes for a reappearance of that look he'd given her on the cliff – and not finding it. Mary wasn't far from her thoughts either and the vision she'd had at the cliff-side of the child praying and those prayers turning into demands. As for George Taylor and co – had they prayed too, at the end? Or had they given up on prayers by then?

Fuelled by the rum as well as a growing need to understand the situation she was in, Ruby stepped outside whilst Cash settled the bill and called Rachel, who'd done her utmost to find out what she could. It was 1903 that the cottage had been divided into two separate dwellings, but it hadn't stayed that way for long. Eleven years later, in 1914, at the beginning of World War One, the property was sold again and, in 1915, returned to its former status as a single household. And that's the way it had stayed until this day, changing hands on a frequent basis, mainly being rented out.

"Did you find out anything more about the London couple from Greg?" Ruby asked, pleased with the information regarding the time-frame Mary had lived – between 1903 and 1914 – but still hoping for more.

"I did," replied Rachel, her tone turning ominous. "They're parents to a couple of teenage boys and, I think I've already mentioned this, they wanted Old Cross as a respite from the big city; somewhere they could escape to at weekends. Also like us, they felt it was haunted, and that idea amused them, Greg said… at first."

"What happened to change their minds?"

"A séance happened."

"A séance?" Ruby repeated. No wonder Rachel sounded the way she did.

"With the four of them sitting at the kitchen table, they started to play. Almost immediately, the glass started to swirl around the board. Initially, they all blamed each other, prompting the mother to insist they take their fingers off the glass, which they did, one by one. And wouldn't you know it, it continued swirling, going crazy. Just before one of them went to snatch it, it started to spell out a word – 'scared.'"

"Scared?" Ruby questioned. *Again.*

"Yes, over and over it did that apparently – scared, scared, scared – and then one final word, which was different to that."

Ruby inhaled, what was it? Mary?

"It was Ward," Rachel said, dashing that hope.

"Ward?"

"Yes, that's right, does it mean anything to you?"

"Yes, yes it does actually. Ward was the last ever landlord of Old Cross Inn, I found out his name from one of the villagers, Thomas Ward to give him his full title."

"Oh my God! I didn't know that. Do you think it's him haunting the cottage?"

If she'd suspected it, this served to reinforce that suspicion. The only fly in the ointment being if the Londoners had heard about Ward, as she had, from one of the locals and it was autosuggestion at work again. If not, the man in the breeches and waistcoat whose shade had appeared in both the kitchen and the double bedroom was indeed Ward. As she'd said to Cash – three spirits, three sets of issues.

Remaining non-committal, Ruby told Rachel that when she got back to Old Cross, she'd try addressing Ward again as well as William, see what response she got.

"William?"

Briefly, she explained about William too.

"Be careful," begged Rachel. "I don't want you putting yourself in danger."

"I'm not in any danger, don't worry." But even as she said it, she wondered at the truth of it. In dealing with emotions, there was *always* danger. Before that thought could develop, she asked Rachel how long Greg had been handling Old Cross Cottage and whether he knew any tenants besides the Londoners.

"No, sorry, before them it had stood empty for a long while, over three years in fact, and it was during that time it came onto their books, the vendor someone who instructed them from afar and whom Greg got the impression had never even stayed there. They lived in the Highlands apparently and it had been an impulse buy." She paused. "Fancy being able to buy a property on impulse, they must have been seriously well-heeled. Anyway, they eventually put it up for sale and that's when the Londoners bought it, asking Greg to sell it on again soon after the Ouija board incident. Again, it stood empty for months and months before we came along."

A thought occurred to Ruby. "Would it be possible to

speak to the Londoners?"

"I asked the very same thing," replied Rachel. "What happened with the Ouija board must have been scary, but *that* scary? Greg's an obliging chap, he really is. He phoned them again and asked whether they'd be willing to chat to us. And the answer was no, categorically no. They wanted nothing more to do with Old Cross Cottage; they just wanted to forget it. Well, he probed a bit deeper, I think as curious as us by now, and he got more information. After the glass had spelt out Ward, it stopped, but only for a moment. Then it was like it was grabbed in temper: it flew upwards and hovered in the air a few seconds before being hurled against the kitchen wall, possibly in the exact same spot where the landlord's been seen. Shards of glass flew everywhere, a largish piece hitting their teenage son and burying itself just below his eye, almost blinding him. *That's* why they left."

"Wow!" exclaimed Ruby. Had Thomas Ward – a formerly much-loved landlord, according to local legend – meant for such a thing to happen?

Rachel sighed. "If we'd known all this beforehand, we wouldn't have bought the place. To be fair, Greg didn't know the full story either. He was pretty shocked too."

"I'll bet."

"You mentioned, didn't you, that you don't recommend using a Ouija board?"

"That's right, we don't. Essentially it's a toy, a game, but it has a universal belief system attached to it, people *believe* it will work and therein lies its power."

"Where does it even come from?"

"The Ouija?"

"Aha."

The answer was shrouded in as much mystery as to where

(or who) Robert Johnson had got his guitar-playing prowess. She'd read up about the Ouija once and tried to recall as much detail as she could. "I don't know where it came from exactly, but it was first sold in a toy shop in Pittsburgh, sometime in the late 1800s – hailed as some sort of magical device that linked the known and the unknown. It was even said its powers had been proven at the Patent Office, which no doubt impressed the heck out of people. The thing is, spiritualism was huge during that time, especially in America, and I think the Ouija was a direct response to that – it *fed* on people's desires – that need to know that something's out there, beyond the life we live."

"Because it's only people like you that know for sure?"

"I only know a certain amount," Ruby corrected. If she'd ever been beyond the light in a previous incarnation, she had no recollection of it, just an instinct, a strong instinct, that it was home, where she belonged – an instinct most people had to be honest, even if it took them forever to acknowledge it.

"I still don't understand how the Ouija got its bad reputation," Rachel did indeed sound perplexed.

"That'd be due to popular culture, films like *The Exorcist* in the 70s, that changed the perception of it from thereon in. Previously, even Christians could use it without fear of reprimand from the church, it was seen as something innocent, a parlour game, nothing more than that. After that film though, it was regarded as a tool for the devil, and that belief just grew and grew, the church jumping on the bandwagon and condemning it too. As I just said, belief is everything, it powers the mind, conjures up stuff, making it hard for us to determine what's real and what isn't sometimes."

"Some game," was Rachel's wry comment, causing Ruby to wince a little as she remembered *Ghost Discovery* and taking that seriously enough. Then again, all this talk of games, that's exactly what she felt she was involved in; one of hide and seek.

Rachel was speaking again. "I'm sorry I can't be more help. I feel a bit useless."

"Not at all. What you've told me could prove very useful."

"I hope so." Again, there was a pause. "You are okay aren't you?"

"Yeah, I'm fine, perfectly fine." Almost causing three deaths on Golden Cap notwithstanding. "Thanks, Rachel, and I'll check in with you tomorrow, if that's okay."

Closing the call, Cash emerged from the pub, checking his own phone for any emails, texts and missed calls, Jed beside him.

"Finished?" he asked her.

"With Rachel, yeah. I've got to call Theo next."

"Let's do that when we get home."

Home? That's exactly what it wasn't; it was a place of transition.

Still, she was eager to return too.

Chapter Eighteen

"HELLO, hello, can you hear me? I'm on loudspeaker."

"Yes, Theo, you're crystal clear."

"Good, good. I've got the team with me. Ness and Corinna say hello to Ruby."

"Hi, Ruby!" Corinna called with her usual enthusiasm.

"Hello," Ness's greeting was more restrained.

"Thought we'd all check in," explained Theo. "Touch base with our leader."

"As well as those who reside in the spiritual world?" Ruby teased.

"Of course. But first, tell me how you are. How is Cash?"

"We're both fine."

"Where is Cash?" Theo asked, obviously expecting a 'hello' from him too.

"He's gone out for a walk, taken Jed with him."

"And he knows he's taken Jed with him, does he?"

"I told him that was the case."

"Aha," Theo acknowledged, booming with laughter.

Ruby smiled but inside she still felt shaken after what had happened at Golden Cap, so must Cash, needing some time alone, or as alone as you could be when accompanied by a ghost dog. As soon as he'd gone, she'd shut the door and walked through the cottage, trying to connect to Thomas

Ward *and* William this time, but getting nowhere fast. The pair of them, like Mary, not ready to reveal themselves.

But I can help you, I can help you all, she'd reiterated, having to admit, when silence was the only thing that responded, that she was having doubts about it. Maybe she needed the team with her, a thought she'd just as quickly dismissed; picturing Cash's face as Theo, Ness, and Corinna pitched up for the remainder of their stay, any pretence of this being a holiday well and truly shattered. She resolved to spend a large portion of the following day doing holiday-type things, steering clear of any cliff-tops, and hunting for fossils on the beach rather than souls long-deceased.

Her mind was wandering again but Theo brought her back to the moment. "Information, that's what you wanted, dear girl, and, well, we've done our best."

Sitting in the lounge, trying not to focus on the hook above her – it still gave her the shivers – hope blossomed once again. "What have you found?"

"I hate to be the bearer of bad news, but not a lot. I checked the National Archives for the early 1900s and, as I thought, census records were thin on the ground. One was taken in 1901 and the other in 1911. Without a surname, a definite occupation, a birth date even, you know as well as I do, it's like looking for a needle in the proverbial. The 1911 one was taken between the second and third of April and if Mary was next door at the time, hidden away, there'd be no mention of her anyway. As for Ellen, there were over nine hundred thousand entries to sift through. I scanned by county of course but there was none in Canonibeare that I could see. What about the timeframe you're looking at, anything more solid regarding that?"

Hope dwindling yet again, Ruby leant back into the sofa.

"Mary and Ellen lived here sometime between 1903 and 1914. 1915 was when Old Cross reverted back to being a single cottage. Before that, as you know, Thomas Ward lived here, until 1900 anyway and he's been seen since, but I suspect only in residual form. However, there's been a development. He might well be here in spirit too." As succinctly as she could, Ruby reiterated what Rachel had told her about the previous occupants and the Ouija board. "And then, of course, there's William."

"William's the one you think tormented Mary during her lifetime?" It was Ness speaking, possessing a similar ability to Theo's – that of being able to detect what was on your mind, even when the miles separated you. Unable to resist testing her further, Ruby nodded rather than answered verbally, and, right on cue Ness asked *how* she knew about William. "Has he made contact?"

"No… well… maybe."

"Curiouser and curiouser," remarked Theo.

Afraid their reliance on *Ghost Discovery* would be treated with disdain, she was surprised when both Theo and Ness condoned the device.

"Yes, it's a game essentially," said Theo, "but so is life. Might as well play it!"

"It's a tool," Ness added, "and like the Ouija it's one that a spirit might utilise in order to communicate. We can't just dismiss it."

"I haven't been," Ruby assured her, although she still felt that relying on it was akin to clutching at straws. "Talking of the Ouija, do you—"

"No!" It was Theo who'd interrupted. "*Ghost Discovery* is very recent, the Ouija… well, as you know, it's far more established."

"But—"

Ness interrupted this time. "Don't be tempted, Ruby, please. Just carry on as you are. You'll get there, you always do. And if you need our help—"

"Hey look, there's a Ouija app on the iPhone!" It was Corinna in the background, sounding genuinely excited at such a prospect.

"Corinna!" Theo swiftly admonished.

"I'm just saying that's all."

"Well, don't," chided Ness too before re-addressing Ruby. "Let your dreams unfold, that's how the child is comfortable approaching you, that's how you'll learn what happened, not through census records, or any other records. Listen to her."

Listen! She was doing her best – but it wasn't a two-way street.

Besides the name William, Ruby also told them about the random words the app kept throwing up. "They're all much of a muchness really. Whether they're significant or not, I don't know. But," she had to admit it, "they're certainly interesting. And occasionally blobs appear on the radar too; they're almost always blue, which indicates a weak presence. Apt you could say as they're all in hiding."

"That could be the reason for it," acknowledged Theo.

"So what happens when they come out of hiding?" Ruby asked, half-joking.

"You deal with them," Ness answered, "and you do so carefully."

"If it gets too much, we'll bomb on down," Theo reminded her.

"I know you will. By the way, what's happened with Brookbridge?"

"I went earlier and did a quick survey," Theo replied.

"Such a lot of turbulence on the estate, those poor, poor souls, so many of them remain grounded. A fair few are in hiding too, but we'll coax them out. Eventually. That's why Ness and Corinna are here actually. I'm briefing them before we all go en masse tomorrow to try and knock it on the head, that case and a couple of other more minor ones."

"Minor ones too?" Ruby queried. "What's the urgency?"

"No reason. I'm just making a stab at efficiency that's all. Aren't you impressed? I also don't want you to come back to a heavy workload. It's a holiday you'll need when you return by the sounds of it, or at the very least, a couple of days off."

The irony of which didn't fail to register.

"As for Ness's earlier comment regarding written records," Theo continued, "I'm not sure I agree." Ruby could just imagine Ness bristle at such words; Theo did tend to make a habit of disagreeing with her. "Census records might not be the way forward but parish records could be."

Ruby's heart sank. The Reverend and she weren't exactly on speaking terms.

"Don't worry about that," Theo continued, "I'm sure Cash is sorting it."

"Sorting it? What do you mean?"

"That's where he went for his walk I reckon, to the vicarage."

"Theo…"

"I know, I know, my intuition is amazing. Tell me too often and my head will swell!"

"I doubt it." Ruby had never met a humbler person.

"I hope your next meeting with Canonibeare's divine overseer proves more fruitful," Theo continued, "and tomorrow try to have some time off."

"I will. I intend to," she replied.

"Just stay away from the cliff tops."

Ruby's mouth fell open. Considering she hadn't told Theo what had happened at Golden Cap that was the most amazing insight of all.

* * *

Later that evening, when Cash finally returned from his sojourn to see the Reverend Martin, Ruby was waiting to ask him precisely why he'd done such a thing.

"Never good to upset the Reverend, Ruby," he'd replied merrily. "Not when his help could be key to solving this case."

"I've told you, parish records are all online nowadays."

"Have you checked the ones for Canonibeare?"

"Actually I have had a quick look, yes."

"And like the census records they're incomplete aren't they?"

That was putting it mildly; there were holes the size of Texas in them.

"Well, the Reverend might have access to what isn't online."

"And he's agreed to look, has he?" she asked, hopeful despite herself.

"He's willing to see you, to talk about it at least."

"Oh, wow, lucky me, I've been granted an audience!"

"Ruby, stop with the sarcasm, he's really very pleasant is the vicar, as is his wife, Jane. She made me really welcome."

Ruby caught a faint whiff of alcohol. "She plied you with sherry more like!"

"Sherry? Don't be so old-fashioned! We had a glass of port actually, well... two glasses, or was it three?" A giggle escaped him. "Actually port is as old-fashioned as sherry isn't it? I'm sure my English grandmother used to neck it. That was it, port and lemon – she loved a tipple in the afternoon, God rest her soul!"

So he *was* drunk – courtesy of the Reverend Martin and his wife, whilst she'd sat at Old Cross pondering whether to download the Ouija app; 'a tool for the devil' as she'd described it to Rachel. That's how desperate she was, desperate enough when morning came around to take the Reverend up on his oh-so-generous offer. Leaving the cottage after breakfast, she had to admit, she wasn't in the best of moods. Expecting Mary's story to unfold further during the night, she hadn't dreamt at all. Time was marching on and at this stage a dreamless night was a wasted one.

Arriving at the vicarage, she took a deep breath and rapped on the door. It was answered not by the Reverend but a woman.

"Jane?" Ruby enquired.

"Oh, hello!" Jane had the same enthusiastic tone as Corinna. About the same height as her husband, she had matching sandy hair, and a tea towel in her hands, which indicated she was in the middle of washing up. "You must be Ruby. My husband did wait, expecting your visit but left about ten minutes ago. Sorry about that."

"Okay, I see, well, not to worry. Thank you…" She turned to go when Jane stopped her.

"He hasn't gone far, he's at the church. I said I'd redirect you."

Before she could reply, suggest again that she might leave it, come back a bit later, Jane started enthusing about Cash. "What a lovely chap you've got there. So polite, so friendly, and greatly interested in the teachings of the Lord."

He was? That was news to her.

"I mean I know he doesn't go to service on Sunday," Jane continued, "he was honest about that, but he does seem to have a great respect for religion."

"As do I!" Ruby stated. Noticing that Jane looked slightly taken aback by her perhaps avid tone, she quickly reined it in. "What I mean is, I'm mindful of all religions too, and believe, that in the end, we all fight the same battle."

"Against the darkness," Jane replied.

"Exactly."

Tucking the tea towel into the band of the trousers she was wearing, Jane clasped her hands together instead. "I do know that, dear. Cash took great pains to explain that. By the way, what a lovely necklace you're wearing!"

Surprised by the sudden compliment, Ruby reached up to touch the aforementioned necklace, an inherited piece from her great-grandmother, Rosamund Davis, that her grandmother had insisted Ruby have and which she wore at all times. Only once had it been ripped off her neck, and that was at Gilmore Street. She'd since had it repaired. "The stone," Ruby replied, "it's tourmaline."

"Ah, the queen of the protection stones," Jane nodded, a knowing look in her eyes. "Yes, I know a little about your religion too, and before you say anything, I use that word very lightly. And Cash, he wears obsidian, another highly protective stone."

Yes he did; a necklace she'd given him when they'd first met – or rather he'd cheekily asked her to give him – and which he never took off either.

"Open-minded, that's the way to be," Jane continued, "and my husband is too, but he's also aware of the modern day attitude towards the church and the controversy surrounding it that's contributed to that attitude. So many are turning away. He just wants to make sure that what people replace it with is genuine, that's all. Don't be too hard on him."

Hard on him? She tried not to baulk at that.

"Anyway, the church is where you'll find him. Good luck."

Having said goodbye to Jane, Ruby couldn't help but smile at the 'good luck' sentiment. Arriving at the heavy church door, she hoped she wouldn't need it as she used both hands to push it open. Once inside, she had to admit, the atmosphere was serene, seductively so, a faint residue of frankincense in the air – an essential oil that she often used during a cleansing, as protective as the stones she'd talked of earlier with Jane. *We're similar in so many ways,* she thought before spying the Reverend close to the altar – a golden cup in one hand and a polishing cloth in the other.

As she walked towards him, he simply carried on polishing. He knew she was there; the church door had made enough noise when it shut behind her.

Glancing at the empty pews either side and doing her utmost to harness that sense of serenity, Ruby made a show of clearing her throat. Still he didn't turn. Well, two could play at that game, she'd veer off, study the stained glass windows instead, of which there were several, their rainbow colours really quite breath-taking with the sunlight behind them. Easily, she lost herself in the depictions of numerous saints.

"Wonderful artwork isn't it?"

Ruby jumped. So he'd joined her at last, his approach, unlike hers, silent.

"Yes, yes, it's beautiful," she answered. "So... you've agreed to see me, to talk about accessing parish records."

"Ah, yes, that man of yours, he can be quite persuasive."

She pondered his words. "Are you saying you had to be persuaded?"

His reply was equally as defensive. "I'm busy, Miss Davis, that's all, preparing for the next event on the church calendar."

"Which is?"

"The birth of St John the Baptist, which we celebrate today in fact. I'm due to hold a service at six o' clock this evening."

Ruby glanced pointedly at the empty pews. "Expecting many?"

"That's precisely why I hold it at that time," the Reverend replied, bristling slightly at her inference, "so people returning from work can join in too."

"So they have no excuse, you mean?" As soon as the words left her mouth, she regretted them. Why did she insist on baiting him? "I'm sorry, I…"

He held his hand up. "I expected little more from you."

Despite that comment grating, Ruby tried again. "What I said—"

"Really, I don't want to hear it, nor do I want to argue. Not with you, not in the House of God."

"I just need your help!" she blurted out. "Please, will you help me?"

Her sudden pleading seemed to unsettle him. "Well… I…erm…"

Ruby turned to the window that she'd been studying and pointed. "Those haloes around the saints' heads, what do they represent?"

Again, the Reverend faltered. "The haloes? Erm… they represent an enlightened person, one who is close to God." With a little more confidence, he added, "The halo is symbolic of the light of grace bestowed on them by God."

"By God," Ruby repeated, "the Higher Power."

"I call him God," the Reverend Martin reiterated.

"So God's a man in your eyes?"

"Yes, no, he's—"

"In each and every one of us, isn't that the case?"

"Yes, of course he is. He lives in all of us."

"Then God *is* the Higher Power, no gender specified. Reverend," Ruby continued, getting into her stride, "what you and I do, as I've said before, it's not so different. Our ultimate aim is to encourage souls towards the light once they've left their physical bodies. In your world they go to heaven, in mine they go home. I'm really not a charlatan and I'm not an atheist either. I believe as much as you do." Dragging her gaze from the windows, she focused on him entirely. "I know you understand what I'm saying, and that beneath that sometimes arrogant exterior there's a good man."

"Arrogant exterior? How dare—"

Ruby refused to let him finish. "I can see the light, I'm not lying. I swear on… on God, I'm not. Surely if I'm lying in His House of all places I'd be struck down by lightning or something! I can *see* it, Reverend," she said again, leaving out the small fact that she could also see the darkness – but that was rare, thankfully, so very rare. "I can see spirits too, the physical representation of those that are grounded. And I understand that as much as I can see the light, they can't, or rather they choose not to. They hide from it instead, and for many reasons, but fear is the big one, it's always the big one. There are spirits grounded at Old Cross Cottage, two for definite, possibly three. And they're hiding, good and proper. But they're also in pain, constantly reliving past events, crucified by them still."

"Crucified?"

"Maybe that's a bad choice of word considering where we are. *Mortified,* is that better? My job is to help them, which is why I believe I've been given this gift. But sometimes I need a little help too. And that's where you come in. I need you to look up names for me, to see if there's any mention between 1903 and 1914 of an Ellen, a William and a Mary, all residents at Old Cross Cottage – particularly Mary, she's the soul that's really suffering, and she's a child, Reverend, just a child."

No sooner had she uttered Mary's name than Ruby did indeed feel as though she'd been struck by lightning. Either that or punched in the stomach.

"Miss Davis—" It was the Reverend, reaching out to her, obvious concern on his face, but she turned from him, back towards where she'd entered the church, the last pew in particular. Mary! She was there, standing beside a woman, her mother, Ellen, no doubt, both with such defiant looks on their faces, staring straight ahead.

Mary!

Would she avert her gaze, look at Ruby? Was this a shade, a waking dream, a vision?

Mary, look at me!

That Mary faded and another took her place – Mary walking down the aisle, with Ellen again, and someone else, someone not as defined as them, a shadow figure – William? Mary looked so small next to the bulk of him and terrified too, glancing at him fearfully every few seconds as if she couldn't quite believe he was there, this man who'd come out of nowhere to overpower them. They were taking their places mid-way down the aisle– a family and as such, respectable, at least outwardly. Ruby caught movement amongst the trio, imperceptible to most, a hand in the small of Ellen's back, *his* hand, delivering a push, slight but unnecessary – wholly unnecessary. Mary noticed too and her whole body shuddered.

Bastard, you bastard! Before Ruby had time to think further, the walls of the church seemed to crumble and fade, disappearing completely. It was as though she were suspended in time and space – listening, just listening.

He's your father now; call him that.

He's not my father! He's not!

You have to, don't you see? It's a sign of respect!

I don't respect him!

Mary!

He hits you, Mam.

I… It doesn't matter. What matters is that he's my husband and your father.

My father is a lord!

Stop it! That's just idle gossip. Your real father, he… We were struggling until William came along; he's changed our lives, changed us. I know some things aren't ideal but we have to endure, Mary. We have always had to endure.

Changed us? That's right. He's changed you, and… and he's changed me…

There was a sob, such a heart-rending sound. Ruby felt tears prick at her own eyes to hear it, the wetness on her cheeks as they started to fall.

"Miss Davis." It was the Reverend again, trying to reach her.

"Wait," she managed, her voice as cracked as her heart. "Please wait."

I don't like sleeping in his cottage, a wall dividing me from you.

We've gone over and over this—

But I hate it there! Something's wrong on his side, he's told me so; it's haunted. I knew anyway. When I shared a bed with you I would lie there, listen to noises from beyond the wall. And now I'm beyond the wall too. Every night, I'm alone in the dark, Mam, but also I'm not alone – there's someone with me. A ghost!

Another sound – a slap, Ruby was sure of it. Ellen had slapped Mary! *Don't,* Ruby cried in her head. *Listen to her, please!* Why did no one ever listen?

No more words now, only emotion. The weight of it so heavy she staggered, just as she'd done on Golden Cap, reaching out blindly for support. Grateful for the Reverend's arm, he led her to one of the pews, where she collapsed down onto it. The sweat was pouring off her, mingling with her tears. As though from far away she could hear the Reverend's voice, talking to her, full of concern, but his words failed to offset the horror, the despair and the anguish she was wrapped up in, thicker than any cottage walls. *I hate you! I hate you! I hate you!* Was that Mary's thought or was it her own? Hate was such a strong word, one she usually tried to avoid, keeping in mind what Martin Luther King had said: *Hate cannot drive out hate, only love can do that.* But in this instance, she hated too, with every fibre of her being. She felt it as though it were a living thing, writhing inside her. It was a snake, and not just one snake, thousands of them, continuously breeding.

She screamed, turned her head to the side, and screwed her eyes shut as she tried to banish the image and the feelings that plagued her.

He ruined our lives!

The child was whispering again, a voice in her ear.

Don't ever forget that!

"I won't," Ruby whispered back.

Promise. You have to promise.

"I do, I promise."

Help me.

Ruby opened her eyes; saw not the Reverend but again that vastness of space – repeated the words that Mary had said when she'd first heard her praying.

"I'll do anything, anything you want."

Chapter Nineteen

WHILE the Reverend Martin rushed off to fetch a glass of water, Ruby continued sitting in the pew, tremors coursing through her. A waking dream, that's what it was; flashbacks into Mary's life occurring randomly now, no longer requiring her to sleep.

As for the whispering, it was as if she was actually here, inside the church.

Or inside your head.

Which was more likely.

Oh, she was tired and little wonder. Experiencing such turmoil, even if it was by proxy, was bound to prove exhausting.

"Here, drink this."

The Reverend had returned and was staring at her, his beige-coloured eyes wide. Ruby didn't look too deeply, but she guessed he was part perplexed, part horrified.

She drank from the glass offered, craving its cleansing properties. More than ever she had to find out what had happened to Mary and draw her out of the shadows, William too, dealing with one at a time perhaps but with the ultimate aim of sending them both to the light. *Not that William belongs there.* Again she screwed her eyes shut. *Don't think like that.* She wouldn't be able to do her job if she thought like that.

"Thank you," she said at last, placing the empty glass down beside her, "and… sorry." She thought she saw a softening of his features when she apologised. Acting on that, she asked, "Do you want to know what just happened?"

The Reverend Martin took his time in replying and when he did his words were accompanied by a courteous nod. "I do but elsewhere perhaps. It… it doesn't seem fitting to talk about such things here."

"Oh, right, okay, I see, because clearly what just happened to me is the devil's work." The words were out of her mouth before she could stop them.

The Reverend's temper flared. "I don't like your attitude, young lady, not at all!"

Ruby pushed upwards to stand before him. "And I don't like yours."

"You're rude, very rude," the Reverend Martin muttered, their eyes engaged in yet another contest, no Cash to referee this time.

"I'm not rude," she denied, "not usually, and neither am I in league with Satan, as I've already tried to point out. What happened just now, the flashbacks I had, they're insights into real lives. *Terrible* lives with terrible acts, terrible deeds, and terrible agonies suffered. There's nothing that can't be discussed in the church, before God. It *should* be discussed before God, because only God – the light – can help."

"No, no, no. I'm sorry no. You'll have to leave. This is a bad idea."

"But I need your help to check who lived at the cottage between 1900 and 1915. I need surnames, professions. More clues basically to build a bigger picture. Don't you want to help Mary? Don't you care about her?"

His hands on her, actually *on* her, he started pushing her towards the entrance.

"Reverend, take your hands off me."

Still he pushed her.

"I'm warning you."

He wants to put his hands on me.

"What?" Who said that? Was Mary back again?

I've seen the way he looks at me.

"Mary?"

He's going to hurt me one day, hurt me so bad.

"Mary, he can't touch you anymore."

He's got his hands on me.

"William, you mean William?"

And the priest has got his hands on you.

"GET OFF ME!"

Spinning on her heels, Ruby faced the Reverend, his expression startled now and frightened too... Oh, yes, she'd spooked him good and proper. He deserved it, deserved everything he got. Full of might, she pushed him back, sent him flying, watched as his fear soared, revelled in it. How dare he put his hands on her! He was no more special than she was. He wasn't special at all. And then it was as if what she'd done hit her too – she'd attacked the Reverend Martin, actually attacked him.

She dashed forward to where his sprawling figure lay. Again, she apologised, over and over. "I'm sorry, so sorry. I didn't mean to... it's just, you were pushing me and in the vision I had, William was pushing Ellen, but he did more than that, so much more, he hit them, he abused them, Mary especially, because as a child, she's an easy target. My colleague Ness mentioned once that it was awful dealing with child cases, and she was right, it is, it really is. I'm sorry, I am. I didn't mean to push you."

The tumble of words having left her mouth, Ruby slumped, sitting on the cold, hard floor beside the Reverend, who'd scrambled into a seated position too.

"You're never going to help me now, are you?" she mumbled.

"And you blame me for that, do you?"

"No," she said, still staring straight ahead.

Silence ensued – he, like her, no doubt trying to come to terms with what had just happened and the strangeness of it all.

"You're not alone," she eventually said.

"Pardon?"

Now she did look at him. "I don't understand either."

With that she got to her feet and left the church.

* * *

Cash wanted to go out that afternoon, to see what else was in Bridport besides the supermarket, or perhaps into Lyme Regis again; to sit and soak up the ambience on the pebbles beside the sea, going for a pint afterwards in one of the bars that lined the promenade. It all sounded so nice, perfect in fact, but Ruby wasn't in the mood, not after the debacle at the church. She couldn't even bring herself to *tell* him what had happened, about the flashbacks, what Mary had said, her subsequent attack on the Reverend. He'd be horrified. *She* was horrified. Embarrassed too. She simply told him the Reverend had agreed to look into matters and that he'd let her know what he'd found in due course. Cash had held her gaze for a few seconds as if suspecting she was spinning him a yarn but he let it go, which she was grateful for. Instead, like

Rachel, he said if she didn't crack this case it wasn't the end of the world.

"Not for me," she'd replied, "but for the grounded that's exactly what it is. How can I leave Mary, Thomas Ward and even William, in purgatory?"

She didn't know what she was going to do with herself to be honest. She longed to sleep – dreamlessly – but that couldn't be guaranteed. Feigning stomach ache, she said she'd prefer a quiet afternoon reading in the living room and Cash had shrugged, said okay, that they could always make up for it the next day.

It was a pleasant afternoon that passed, much to Ruby's surprise. After a bright start, it had clouded over and in the afternoon rain had started to fall, prompting Cash to get the fire going, in front of which Jed duly materialised.

"Temperature's going down. We need to get the room – and us – warmed up."

He was right, it was cold, her hands really quite icy, so she offered to make some tea whilst he threw some logs into the burner. That would help to warm them too.

Outside, it had started to pour, raindrops beating against the windows and causing them to rattle in their frames again. She welcomed it, not feeling so bad about choosing to hide indoors now. *Because that's what you're doing, Ruby, you're hiding.* A wry smile crossed her face. *If you can't beat 'em, join 'em, I suppose.* She, Mary, William and Thomas, they'd all chosen the same place to hide out in.

Whilst the kettle boiled, she wandered over to the kitchen window and peered out. New Cross Cottage, across the way, had no lights on. It was another holiday rental and, like Old Cross, lay empty a large portion of the time. Directly opposite her, the sign for Grange Farm was swaying in the breeze, making a creaking sound, backwards and forwards, the noise growing increasingly louder.

Ruby frowned.

It's a small sign, so why's it making such a racket?

Inclining her head, her gaze was drawn towards the porch, and there, where there'd been nothing before was another sign; this one much larger than the one over the road; a crude picture of a signpost pointing four ways, three words inscribed above it – *Old Cross Inn.* Ruby gasped, it was the pub sign from the late 1800s! Blurred by the rain but clear enough. Her eyes darting to the crossroads just in front, it was the dirt track she'd envisaged once before, and both properties that she'd so recently been looking at were no longer there, as if they'd simply been airbrushed out of existence. Again she gasped. It was nothing less than a headrush, one she was trying her best to understand when the sound of glasses clinking from the parlour caused her to turn in that direction. Not the parlour, not anymore, it must be the bar. Walking forwards, the door was ajar, just as she'd left it and she peeked through. Sure enough, it *was* the bar, ill-lit, with candles flickering on several tables, around which an assortment of customers sat, drinking, talking, or simply nursing their respective tankards. Against the far wall – exactly where she'd imagined it – behind a long strip of oak, as roughly hewn as the tables and beams above, stood a man, tall and rugged, in breeches and a waistcoat.

Thomas Ward! It had to be. The king of all he surveyed.

The atmosphere was jovial, Ward having provided a cosy place to retire to, to escape a nagging wife perhaps, squealing children, or the rigours of a hard day's work. It was a pleasant scene, nothing to cause alarm, one she was enjoying when the scene began to change. Ward was alone, the customers having left. Taking a seat in the bar, he was surrounded by empty tables and chairs, a forlorn figure, his legs apart, his body bent forward slightly and his hands clasped together. He was praying. Just like William and Mary. And he was crying too, Ruby was sure of it.

What is it? What's wrong? Ruby asked but what she was seeing was a recording, nothing more, a scene that had once occurred and which shifted again.

Thomas was behind the bar again, turning his head from left to right, making sure everyone had what they needed. A scene similar to what she'd seen already – what was the point of it? And then the door opened, in the exact place where the door was now, and a man walked in. Not really a man, he was no more than a boy, a beautiful boy, around nineteen or twenty, with dark hair curling around his ears and equally dark eyes. He had on a brown jacket in a rough material and his trousers were brown too. Walking to the bar, he ordered his tankard of ale and that's when Thomas Ward changed – subtly, so subtly – his back becoming a little straighter, his eyes a little wider, his breath almost ragged. The man took his pint and joined some others who were rapidly fading, although not before she saw him lean forward and say something to them, companionable laughter ensuing. She focused on Ward again, noticed him staring after the boy. No, not staring, he was *transfixed*.

"Oh my God, you were in love with him!"

At her words the scene faded and became as it was now, in the twenty-first century – an empty room, a parlour. Ruby cursed. Had speaking out loud caused the image, the *confession* – because that's what it felt like – to fade?

She slumped against the door.

You went to your grave carrying what was for you, in the

times that you lived in, as a man of your status, a secret: that of forbidden love. You were different from other men, and because of that, ashamed, considering the feelings you harboured to be abhorrent, evil even. But, Thomas, I live in more enlightened times. It doesn't matter nowadays. Not here, not in this country. God, you must have felt so alone, so… different. But it's not a crime to be a man and have feelings for another man – if it's love it's never a crime and you loved him, didn't you, that beautiful boy? A love he never knew of and that tortured you, becoming unbearable.

She paused for a moment, feeling his pain as keenly as she had Mary's, remembered when she'd first tuned in, how masculine the energy was in the former bar, no trace of femininity at all. Unusual, but it told her something: Ward was no hypocrite. He hadn't taken a wife and then proceeded to make her life as miserable as his.

Your love for that man is no reason to remain grounded. Go to the light, Thomas, you've done nothing wrong.

Thomas, she pleaded again, hoping he was listening. *You don't have to suffer still. You've suffered enough.*

Thomas?

The air around her was still – even the rain had died down.

Thomas, I know you're here, trying to communicate. There's no need to hide—

"Ruby, Ruby, where are you?"

It was Cash, calling from the living room.

"I'll be along in a minute—"

"You've got to come now. Quickly!"

Damn!

Promising Thomas that she wouldn't leave him either until his soul was at rest, she hurried through 'no man's land', only briefly glancing upwards towards Mary's bedroom before pushing open the door to the living room.

"Cash, if this is about how long I've taken to make the—"

"It isn't. Look at this."

He was holding out the phone, *Ghost Discovery*'s radar spinning round as usual. What wasn't so usual was the list of words it was throwing up – normally one would appear, stay for a while, a minute, two minutes, far longer on occasions, but this time they were appearing one after the other, little more than seconds between them.

Listen, Danger, Bolder, Stronger, Hiding, Scared, Me, Other, Wrong, All, Wrong, You, Different, Danger, Leave, Leave, Leave.

"What the heck's going on?" asked Ruby.

"I don't know, but I've got a feeling it's not William this time."

"Not William?"

Cash shook his head. "It's someone else."

She spun round, stared towards the parlour. *Thomas, why are we in danger?*

Chapter Twenty

MARY bolted from the cottage – there must be someone in the village she could talk to, who'd listen to what she had to say, who'd help her.

He was evil; that's what he was and her mother… oh God, her mother. She didn't even recognise her anymore. No longer full of figure, she was gaunt, skeletal almost, her chestnut hair lank, the shadows under her eyes as dark as any bruise.

He mustn't be allowed to get away with this, he mustn't! Someone would help her. There was Bess, ancient though she was, who lived on the other side of the village. Ellen would sometimes launder and sew her clothes without charging, or at least she used to, and when you did someone a kindness, wasn't a kindness owed?

Above there was a loud crack in the sky – thunder! But no rain as yet, although it would surely follow. Bad weather meant he'd be home early from working in the fields. She had to be quick. Running up the pathway of St Winifred's, she kept her eyes trained ahead, refusing to look at the graves either side of it. She'd had enough of the dead. If Father Gabriel should appear suddenly, she'd avoid him too, and wouldn't feel bad about it. After all, he barely said a word to them at church – he kept his distance when it suited him. It was Bess she'd run to – who was her best chance.

How long had it been since he'd wormed his way into their lives? Two more summers had passed, as rainy as today, the sunshine rare, not producing full crops this time but blighting them along with his mood – making it worse than ever. And now it was autumn, usually a bountiful season, but bereft in so many ways.

She arrived at Bess's in no time. Like the cottage she lived in, it was removed from the others but occupied a single lane, not a crossroads. Of all the people in the village, only they lived at the crossroads. Much smaller than Old Cross, it was nonetheless where Bess had brought up five children. They'd flown the nest now, lived elsewhere in the village, or had moved away entirely.

Bringing her hand up she knocked at the door, banging so hard against the wood she wondered if it might splinter beneath her fist.

"Bess! Bess!" she called, before stopping to put her ear to the door, to listen for shuffling inside. There it was! Slow, but Mary didn't care. She was going to talk to someone at last, break the silence that he'd so often warned her to keep.

As the door opened, she shifted from foot to foot, trying to exercise patience.

"Mary, child!" The old woman blinked her rheumy eyes. "Whatever brings you here?"

On seeing her, on being asked such a question, Mary burst into tears. "I… I don't like him, Bess, I don't like him!"

There was relief in saying it but also disappointment – she wanted to say 'hate' but Ellen had always warned her against the use of such a harsh word.

"Now, now, child, come in, come away in," Bess said, ushering her inside. The cottage might be small but it was warm whereas Old Cross was always cold, the fire running down with neither Ellen nor him ever bothering to stoke it. In her part of the cottage – where she was banished to every night – the cold could claw its way inside you, freeze the very marrow in your bones.

"Sit by the fire and warm up. My, you're like ice to the touch and winter's a way off! I'll fetch you a drink, one of my brews."

The brew was some sort of tea, hot with a slight bitterness to it. Despite that, Mary clutched it between her hands as the circulation slowly returned. Whilst drinking, she had a vision of what life could be like, what it *used* to be like, before he'd come along, and it caused the tears to start again. He was going nowhere, he'd told her that already; told them both, many times, yet still she hoped. An idea occurred.

"Can I live with you, Bess?"

"Instead of your mam?"

Mary's head bobbed avidly up and down. "Please!"

"Oh, wee pet," even more lines appeared on Bess's wrinkled face. "It's not possible. You have a home, a decent home too, with your mam and—"

"He's NOT my father!"

Bess's frown darkened somewhat. "Mary, that's disrespectful."

"I hate him!" There she'd said it.

Bess looked shocked. "Listen to me, I don't know him, that much is true, but he seems to work hard and takes care of you both—"

"He doesn't!"

By degrees Bess's expression hardened. "He's your mam's choice, as a child you've no say in it. And…" Bess swallowed, looked towards the fire, "neither do I."

The tea proving a hindrance rather than a comfort, Mary placed the mug on a flat surface nearby and knelt beside Bess, her hands clasped again, as if she were beseeching a deity rather than a fellow human being. "I can cook and clean and look after you. Now that your children have gone, I can take their place."

"Don't you love your mam?" Bess asked, shock leaning towards bewilderment.

"I do, I do!" She loved her very much, or at least the memory of her mother, the mother that *was*.

"Then away back to her, Mary, you must. You have a family. And, as fond as I am of you, of Ellen too, there's nothing I can do."

"Nothing?" Mary shook her head to hear it. That was a cruel word, so much worse than hate.

"Child—"

There was a sound, the front door opening. Bess looked up. Mary did too, knew it was John, Bess's husband, returning from work or maybe a drink at The Plough. Looking at Bess again, she caught the look in her eyes despite her effort to conceal it. A look that told her she was being a nuisance, and that she should go, that even though they lived in the same village, she was not the old woman's problem.

Mary heeded what she saw, rose to her feet and fled.

* * *

Annie will help!

Leaving Bess's, Mary continued to run. She had to be quick, find help where she could, before he discovered she hadn't been at home, sitting diligently beside her mother, working. Discovered too, that her mother had fallen asleep, that's how Mary had managed to escape. She'd seen her chance and taken it.

Annie was similar in age to her mother and they used to be friendly enough. Like Bess, she wasn't one to criticise, not openly. A mother to three young children, surely she'd listen to her plight. She wasn't old like Bess; she had more energy.

Annie's house was in chaos, two of her three children chasing each other in circles, the third one sitting on the floor alternately screaming and whining, and there was laundry strewn across every surface. Even so it was infinitely preferable to what she was used to. The children weren't riddled with fear, having to watch their every word and Annie was open not furtive, tired but with a spark in her eyes that Ellen no longer had. There was contentment here, happiness, and Mary ached for it.

When she'd first opened the door to Mary, Annie's face was as much a vision of surprise as Bess's had been.

"Mary?"

"Help me! He's hurting my mam, and he'll hurt me too. I know it."

Looking left and then right, Annie had pulled Mary in and closed the door behind her. "Mary! You can't go around knocking on folks' doors and saying such things!"

Couldn't she? Not even if it were true?

Annie turned round, her hands on her hips and shouted at the children behind her. "Will you pipe down, I can't hear meself think!" Facing Mary again, she continued, "You look a fright, you really do. Your face is filthy and your hair…"

A hand reached out to smooth Mary's offending locks but Mary dodged to avoid it. "I don't know what to do. What can we do, Mrs Trenwith?"

"We? About what?"

"About William!" Why did she have to keep repeating herself? Why did they all look the same... as if they didn't believe her?

"William's a good man—"

"He's evil! He locks me away in his side of the cottage, makes my mother do things she doesn't want to. I can hear him, hear *them*. She used to like it, but she doesn't, not anymore. She cries instead of laughs, sometimes she screams. She's got bruises on her. I've seen them, all over her arms. She's not like she used to be, she doesn't even talk to me much anymore, she's... different."

Annie's mouth was agape.

"Your father—"

"He isn't, he isn't I tell you!"

"No, not him, I don't mean him. Who's your real father, do you know?"

"No, but he was a good man. I know it. Not like William."

"But you never knew him?"

Mary shook her head.

"Do you have any other family that could help you?"

"No." It was barely a whisper as she again noticed the children playing behind her, the laughter that burst from one of them, not stifled at all, despite Annie's warning.

In contrast, Annie was silent, clearly contemplating all that had been said. When she spoke, Mary was devastated further. Whatever spark of hope there'd been in her when she'd begun this journey was snuffed out.

"Whatever's going on between a man and his wife is private, Mary. You shouldn't meddle. Try... to distract yourself. Adults' business is adults' business."

"But it won't stop at—"

"Mary!" Annie's voice had grown sterner. She was a small woman, brown hair scraped into a bun and already showing signs of grey but she had a kindness about her, just as Bess did. But kindness was clearly not all it was cracked up to be. It was not the answer. "Heed my words for your own sake. Leave off. Don't make trouble. Keep out of his way if you can. If you have to stay next door, away from it all, then that's a good thing, it keeps you safe."

"His house is haunted!"

"Haunted? Rubbish! There's no such thing as ghosts."

"There is, there is!"

"Mary, there isn't."

"It's the landlord—"

"Thomas Ward? What nonsense! He's long gone."

Mary swallowed, wished she hadn't mentioned anything about ghosts, realised that somehow it had invalidated everything she'd said. Tall stories, that's what Annie would be thinking, that she was telling tall stories. Quickly, she tried to rectify the situation, claw back what credibility she could.

"I'm sorry, I—"

Annie wouldn't let her speak. "What's happening between your parents is their business, no one else's. You should be grateful you have a father now."

Grateful?

"Mary, don't look like that, please, you're a child, you shouldn't look like… Mary, hang on. Where are you going? You wanted advice and I'm giving it to you."

One hand having reached behind her to open the door, Mary continued to retreat.

"It'll get better," Annie said and, unless Mary was mistaken, there was desperation in her voice too. Did she know, deep down, that what Mary was saying was the truth? Had she suspected what was going on? And yet still she wouldn't help.

"It won't get better," Mary spat the words at her.

"It will."

Again Mary shook her head, just as insistent.

It's getting worse.

* * *

"We're alone now, Mary, it's just you and me."

In the corner of the room, as far from him as possible, Mary sat hunched, her gaze averted, refusing to look at him, to give him the satisfaction of seeing the pain in her eyes, the grief that was now an integral part of her.

William stepped closer, the smell that clung to him had a thickness to it, it was cloying, making her eyes water further.

"We'll make it work, won't we? We don't need her. Towards the end, your mother weren't much use to anyone."

How could he say that and to her of all people – Ellen's daughter? How dare he!

"Look at me, Mary."

She wouldn't, she'd refuse to.

"You do as I say, remember? Look at me!"

As quick as a dart, one hand came out to grab her chin, his fingers digging into the skin there and distorting her face grotesquely as he forced her to obey his will. His eyes, she hated his eyes! They were bulbous, boring into the blue of hers, probing beneath flesh and bone to detect what she tried so hard to hide: her fear of him, her complete and utter dread. How he smiled to see it! It delighted him.

She never knew that laughter could sound so terrible, not until he came into their lives. The flesh on her arms began to tingle, and a coldness crept into her heart, seized it as though it were a fist, squeezing until she thought it might burst. Perhaps it was best if it did. She could join her mother then, her poor, poor mother. What was the point of living if this was all there was?

Ellen – how could she leave her alone with this brute? And Mary the one to find her, to cling to her lifeless body as it swayed, screaming all the while, 'Come back, come back!' And then she had run – *Run, Mary, run*. Yet again she'd sought help, practically dragged Annie Trenwith to the door, pointing wildly at the lifeless form that lay within. Although shock had rendered her mute, words formed in her head, ricocheted from side to side. *There! There! See what I said, it was true! And now my mother has done what Thomas Ward did. She's hanged herself.* Not from an oak tree, but from the hook in the middle of their downstairs room, meat of another kind hung out to dry. *This place is cursed.* She wanted to say that too. *We're cursed, and all because of him, because of William. You see what you've done? This is your fault too. You're as much to blame.*

Ellen was taken away, Mary having to be restrained all the while, William looking on with such false tears, his cap in his hands, his head bowed. So many people stood by, but that's all they did, no one came up to her, put their hand on her head, patted her, showed any sign of sorrow, or, more importantly, offered her the help she craved. What they did show was disdain – Ellen had committed suicide, a mortal sin. Like Thomas Ward, her soul could not enter the gates of Heaven. And the priest – Father Gabriel – he was the most disdainful of all, refusing her a Christian burial in consecrated ground. Mary didn't know what happened to her body, no one ever told her, and William, he rejoiced in such ignorance, knowing how much it hurt.

"We'll be happy, Mary, I promise. Once you learn to obey."

No longer shouting, he was whispering now, and in the air around her she heard another whisper. It was the other one, the one who cried in anguish alongside her.

"Until you learn to be a good girl, you'll stay here," William continued. "We don't want you running off again do we, telling tales. I've put a lock on the door this time and only I've got the key – not that I should worry so much, no one will come by. Don't you realise by now they don't care and why should they? Look at you. You're filthy, wild. You'd be an orphan if it weren't for me. You're lucky to have me to look after you, to *discipline* you. Your mother might have escaped but you won't. You belong to me, Mary. It's just you and me," he repeated. "The way I wanted it to be."

The chosen one. She'd thought that once and her instinct had been right.

Straightening up, he let go of her chin although she'd guess her skin was bruised, just as he had bruised her mother's.

Why did you leave me?

She'd asked that question in her head so many times. Ellen was her mother; she was supposed to protect her. But the poor woman couldn't even protect herself.

You should have been stronger!

It was cowardly to have left her, cowardly!

But I have to be strong.

What choice did she have?

William left. But as always the other one remained, the one who was as trapped as she was, the whispers – the prayers – growing more fervent. She'd pray again too. As hard as her fellow prisoner, as zealously, she'd pray for the qualities so remiss in her mother, and for someone to answer... *anyone.*

As her hands came together, as her lips moved, she let the tears flow. But this would be the last time she cried. After this, no more. She would never cry again.

Chapter Twenty-One

"RUBY, it's okay, it was just a dream."

Cash meant well but he was wrong, so wrong. It wasn't *just* a dream, she knew it, and he knew it too. It was Mary, still reaching out, still seeking help, the memory of being refused help by those in the village so strong in her, and how much it had hurt.

"It *was* William who tormented her. I got his name this time."

Cash looked amazed. "Seriously? *Ghost Discovery* was right?"

"It looks like it."

She had to admit, she was amazed too.

"I've also got the connection with Annie Trenwith. Mary had gone to her for help but Annie was a young woman with her own children to look after, she didn't feel she had the right to interfere. Although she sympathised with Mary she turned her away, ultimately scarring them both. It's awful, Cash, it's so awful."

Looking around, she brought one hand up to wipe at her eyes. Yet again she'd woken in the single bedroom – having no memory of leaving the double bedroom and coming here, the second time that had happened. Cash hadn't dreamed, they'd already established that, but he'd woken far from refreshed.

"I don't know, Rubes, it's like I haven't slept at all, but I have, obviously. I just feel… drained."

As did she, with Mary's grief at Ellen's suicide, followed by the terror of being at William's mercy, and locked away, taking its toll. Although Cash had his arms around her whilst she explained, she fixated on the door. William had put a lock on it but a later resident must have taken it off again, only for another to be fitted by George Taylor – both of them trying to contain Mary. George, if he was psychic, terrified of the distress she was in rather than trying to understand it. That was where they differed. Unlike him, and Bess and Annie, and God knows who else, she wouldn't turn her back on someone in need. Although depleted, she'd see it through.

"Oh, Cash," she murmured, a fresh wave of grief washing over her.

"Ruby," Cash's voice was tentative, clearly he knew what he was going to say would not be met with approval. "If this case is proving too much—"

Ruby pushed away from him slightly. "Cash, I'm not leaving until Mary's at peace."

"That might take longer than we've got."

"It might… it won't… I don't care. We're close though, Cash, so close."

"And the others? Thomas and William, what about them?"

"Yes, Thomas too."

"And William?" Cash pressed.

"I…"

"Ruby, you have to think about him too."

"I know I have to, but, Cash, why are some people so

evil?"

"They're not born evil, they come from the light, and that's where they return, regardless of what they've done. That's what you've always told me."

She had – because that's what her grandmother, Sarah, had always told her. She'd had it drummed into her, right from the start. That view later compounded by Theo and Ness. Only Jessica, her mother, had said something different: that evil did exist, that it was very real, and to be careful because if you played with fire, fire could burn you. And Jessica had spoken from experience...

"Ruby, listen to me, if there's atonement, that's taken care of in the light. Your job is to get them that far, nothing more, nothing less, bastards like William included."

And like all jobs it was tough at times, you didn't always want to play by the rules.

But you have to, Ruby. Over and over she told herself that, despite her heart screaming otherwise.

William, she called, from the comfort – the safety – of Cash's arms, *you can't hide forever, you know that don't you? You have to come out some time.*

This room, this damned room, was another in between place; just like the crossroads the cottage was built beside, a place that was... *unholy.*

Ruby shuddered. Who had that thought sprung from? *Mary? Thomas? William?*

Why weren't they answering?

There needs to be an end to this whole sorry mess.

What more was there to find out? Didn't she know enough? That was the thing, with some cases, knowing the bare minimum *was* enough but with others you had to dig, dig, dig, and seize upon the tiniest detail. Only then were you able to coax the spirit forward. You had to get to the *root* of the matter.

What about Ellen? She was a victim too. Was her spirit still here? When she was trying to figure out the identity of the third spirit, she hadn't been able to tell if it was a man or a woman. Sometimes she thought male, at other times she began to doubt that. But now that it was likely to be William, she hoped Ellen's spirit had flown as soon as she'd breathed her last, that she'd found the peace she deserved, the happiness. Her eyes travelled downwards, in the direction of the living room below. Ellen had hanged herself from the hook in the living room, that awful hook that Ruby hated. Is that why she hated it? Why it made her cringe every time she looked at it.

"How old was Mary when Ellen died?"

For a moment Ruby couldn't work out who'd asked the question, she'd been so wrapped up in her own thoughts. She looked at Cash and blinked.

"How old?"

"Yeah, you've got her up to about nine via your dreams, but in that last one, after Ellen had died, was she older than that, a few years maybe?"

"She was still a child!"

"All right, Rubes, I'm just asking. There seems to have been a bit of a leap forward in time that's all, she's a child, but an *older* child."

"Sorry, yeah, it's a good point you're making, I'm... I'm just upset, that's all. To be honest, I don't know how much time had passed, not for sure. Sometimes in the dreams I can't see her, not physically, instead it's like I'm inside her head looking out. There's no mention of Ellen in the 1911 census records so it could be that she died before then, which means Mary was still young, early teens perhaps, no more."

Cash nodded in understanding. "Poor kid."

"Yeah, poor kid and with no one to help her, she was completely at his mercy."

"No wonder you feel the way you do about Will—"

The door to the bedroom flew open as footsteps hurtled across the landing. Looking at each other in alarm, both Ruby and Cash rose at the same time, rushing to see who it was. At the top of the stairs, Jed appeared, forcing himself to tread the floorboards again, but hopping from foot to foot as if they were hot coals.

"What is it, Jed?" Ruby asked. "*Who* is it?"

Jed bolted, straight to the double bedroom.

"Come on," said Ruby, following him.

The door was wide open, and Cash stopped in the doorframe, Ruby to the side of him, his eyes darting around but seeing nothing.

"It's Jed," she told him. "He's at the window, barking."

"And?"

"And nothing else so far. Hang on… there *is* something, I can just make out—"

Ruby stopped speaking in order to concentrate; a shadow, that's what she could make out, looking out of the window.

Who are you? Thomas or William? Answer me.

"What's going on?" Cash's voice was a bewildered whisper.

"Wait," she answered, still focused.

Please, tell me who you are.

The figure, still so faint, started to turn, Ruby held her breath, Jed was quiet too, both of them rigid with anticipation.

Each second that ticked seemed to last an eternity. The

figure was slow, so slow. *Hurry up!* The thought formed but quickly she suppressed it.

Whoever you are, it's okay. I'm here to help. That's all I want to do.

Behind her came another bang, of a door being slammed. She wanted to look but daren't move her eyes from the man in front.

"Cash?"

"I'll go and see," he said, cottoning on to what she was trying to ask. "I think it's coming from the main bedroom."

Jed was growing agitated again, torn between sitting, standing or cowering. Just for a second Ruby took her eyes off the man to look at the dog. When she looked back again she couldn't help but yelp. The man had turned fully – no longer slow but with a swiftness that was so characteristic of the dead.

His face. Oh God, his face.

Rugged features were horribly distorted – mouth agape, a thick slice of tongue lolling at the side of it and black eyes bulging. Although he was far from solid, she got the impression his skin was mottled, decay having found a home. She gulped. There was no noose around his neck, none that she could see. Despite this, he was presenting as if in the throes of strangulation. She struggled to gain control. She'd seen worse, she reminded herself, much worse. Even so, the horror of it mixed in with pity – she had so much pity for him – temporarily paralysed her.

"Thomas," finally she managed to speak, "it's you, isn't it?"

There was no answer forthcoming. All that sounded in her head was a scream, long and protracted, the spirit's arm rising and his finger pointing towards her.

I can help, honestly—

Another scream: an all-too human one – coming from just behind.

What the hell? And then her eyes bulged too as Jed darted past.

"Cash," she yelled, "hold on. I'm coming!"

* * *

"Are you sure you're all right?"

"Seriously, I'm fine."

"How did it get up here, I left it in the parlour?"

"I've no idea, Ruby, only you know that."

"How would I know?" she asked, aghast.

"Because you must have gone downstairs and got it, in the early hours, or whenever it was that you left our bed and came to this bedroom instead."

The object in question was the lump of rose quartz she'd placed in the parlour below when they'd first arrived – meant to encourage love and harmony not violence. When she'd woken, Cash had come in to comfort her, neither of them realising it was in the room with them. When Cash had returned to the single bedroom, however, to investigate the second slamming door, it had flown at him, hurled with so much force that it would surely have rendered him unconscious had he not managed to fend it off with his forearm – his *bruised* forearm. When Ruby had entered the room, she'd almost sent him flying too in her haste to reach him.

The pair of them heading to the kitchen, she'd tended to the blow he'd received with ice wrapped in a tea towel, but it had been a sizeable chunk of quartz, causing a nasty enough injury. Even so, it could have been worse, much worse.

"Cash, why on earth would I bring the quartz upstairs

with me?"

"Because it's needed in the single bedroom more than the parlour?"

"Not if it's going to be used as a weapon." She shook her head. "I honestly don't remember bringing it up. It just… doesn't make sense."

"Who hurled it, do you think?"

Ruby shrugged. "William? Trying to frighten us. He's afraid we're getting too close to Mary. Stuck in the past too, he wants to keep her prisoner still. And…" she faltered slightly, "deep down, I think he senses that I'm angry with him."

"Ruby—"

"Cash, you said yourself it's little wonder I feel the way I do, okay, but I'm doing my best, I'm trying to remain objective. As I said, if I did fetch the quartz, it wasn't a conscious move. I go to sleep in our room, intending to stay there but wake elsewhere. In the first couple of days it *was* a conscious decision, but that doesn't seem to be the case anymore. It's odd, so odd." She thought for a moment. "But the oddest thing of all was Thomas Ward's face—"

"Thomas Ward?"

"Yeah, I saw him, Cash, the figure at the window. When you left the room, he turned, and his face… oh it was horrible. It was so distorted, his expression horrified as he lifted his hand to point. He was warning me, I think, about what was going to happen to you. Which makes me think that you're right when you said that the last voice on *Ghost Discovery* was different to the first. It was Ward again. Perhaps he's been warning us all along, telling us to leave, to get out, to listen. I got that same sense of outrage, an emotion that definitely belongs to him." She paused to consider her words.

"*One* of his emotions anyway. Cash, the thing is he's getting stronger, they all are." Despite what had happened, she began to feel excited. "What we're doing, it's having an effect. Our presence is drawing them out. Yes, we have to be careful, but with a bit of luck, it'll soon be over and Mary will be released."

Cash was smiling too, part hopeful, part trepidatious, when there came another bang, making them both jump despite their optimism.

"Someone's at the front door," Cash said, realising first.

"Oh, thank God, I thought it was all about to kick off again."

"Well, you know what they say; there's no rest for the wicked!"

She smiled. "Hey, be careful who you're calling wicked!"

Leaving him, she went to answer it.

"Hi, Jen, is everything—"

Jennifer's hand shot out and grabbed Ruby's arm. "You have to come quick."

"Why, what's going on?" Ruby asked, slightly startled, she had to admit.

"Stuff's happening at my house, weird stuff."

"Weird—"

"And it's not just mine, Mum's friend from a few doors up came over, said strange things are happening at hers too, and then there's *Heron's Roost*—"

"*Heron's Roost*, what's that?"

"Another house, close to the village. Katharine and Dave live there and this morning, their kid, Freddie, walked into the living room and started screaming."

Ruby's head was spinning. "Screaming, why?"

"Because he saw a ghost, that's why."

Chapter Twenty-Two

"THEO, hi, yeah it's me, Ruby. I… erm… well, you know you offered to drop everything and come down if I needed help? Well, I think that time has come."

If her head was spinning before, it was positively reeling now. What the hell was going on in Canonibeare? As for the Reverend, what was he going to say about all this when he found out? Assuming he didn't know already that is.

Sure enough, when Ruby, Cash, and Jed had gone to investigate the houses that were experiencing trouble, she'd sensed something in all three. Not the same entity – an unhappy wanderer – but separate spirits, grounded for reasons that baffled her.

Despite her bewilderment, she'd assured the worried residents of the houses affected that it was nothing malevolent, although when she'd tried to connect, she'd drawn a blank. Just like those who resided at Old Cross, as quickly as the spirits had come out of hiding, they'd withdrawn.

"It must all be connected," said Theo when Ruby explained.

"But how?"

"That's the million dollar question."

It was – and in terms of an answer, they were flat broke.

"So you'll come down?"

"Of course we will, and Corinna too. It's all subdued at Brookbridge for now, although I think we can safely say that more disturbance will follow soon enough." She sighed. "It's teeming with restless spirits. We send a few on their way and several more roll up to take their place, and the strange thing is, I'm almost certain now that some of them have nothing to do with Brookbridge at all. They're simply troubled spirits, drawn to other troubled spirits; magnetism in action again."

Ruby bit her lip. "Could that be what's happening here?"

"I suspect it's more likely to be connected, which is where analysing parish records would help. You know what the spirits are like, they hold back sometimes."

They certainly did and for a whole host of reasons that could only be understood with hindsight – sometimes not even then. Sighing, Ruby glanced at her watch. She hadn't realised it was so late, it was past six already. "Look, don't worry about coming down tonight. But in the morning, could you leave as soon as possible?"

"Are you sure about tonight?"

"Positive."

"Okay, we'll leave first thing. But if you should change your—"

"I'll call."

There was a slight pause before Theo spoke again. "Talking of parish records, how are relations with the Reverend?"

Ruby winced, quickly burying the memory of lashing out at the priest should Theo pick up on it. "Fine, fine, I... he's on the case I think."

"And he's up to speed with recent events too?"

"I'm not sure, Theo, I haven't told him, but I'm sure someone will soon enough."

And when they did, he'd come banging on her door again.

She could just imagine it – the Reverend Martin marching determinedly through the village in her general direction clutching a flaming cross in her hands, hordes of adoring middle-aged ladies marching behind him, baying for blood... her blood. Again it was an image no sooner conjured than extinguished, Theo didn't need to see that either.

"So you've been busy trying to persuade those long departed to move on today, have you?" Theo continued. "What happened exactly?"

Quickly, Ruby gave her a rundown of the morning's events at Old Cross Cottage, the rose quartz being thrown at Cash having seemingly travelled upstairs of its own volition. And then there'd been Jennifer's house to deal with. The 'weird stuff' she'd complained of when she'd knocked at her door included the TV switching itself on and off, light bulbs flickering overhead, objects being moved at random and the occasional banging of doors, all typical signs of a haunting.

Edyth had looked astounded by it all. "I don't understand," she'd said. "It's been very peaceful here until now."

Ruby had tried not to read anything into that statement – that it had been peaceful until *they'd* arrived in the village – but had failed, despite Edyth looking at her with nothing but concern. Tuning in to the atmosphere, all she could pick up was grief. That and perhaps... guilt. Did someone feel guilty about something?

In Edyth's friend's house, Ruby sensed similar emotions, emanating perhaps from a female – a *young* female. The owner, Helen, similar in age to Edyth, swore blind she'd heard terrible wailing in the night as well as door handles being rattled. Helen's son's bedroom seemed to be at the centre of activity and yet he'd slept peacefully enough throughout the disturbance and all but sneered at his mum's 'hysteria'.

At *Heron's Roost*, a rather grand tile-hung property that stood in its own grounds, again with more tall trees towering above it, something a little different took place.

Opening the door to her, Katharine had greeted them, immediately taking them through to the living room where her son had seen the ghost.

"What did he see exactly?" Ruby asked.

"A woman," Katharine replied, gnawing at her lower lip. "She was standing in the centre of the room, clutching her stomach apparently, her mouth wide open as if she was howling like a banshee. Freddie's ten years old and he's a good kid, not prone to lying and I don't think he was lying about this. He came racing back into the kitchen where I was, shaking as much as I am now." She held out both of her well-manicured hands to prove this. "We've never seen anything in the ten years we've been here, I just don't understand it – why now? Where's she come from?"

Where indeed, thought Ruby.

She asked Katharine to give her a few moments so that she could tune in.

"So you truly are psychic? You can feel her?"

Ruby answered in the affirmative to the first question at least.

As to whether she could sense the woman, she couldn't, not in that moment. But there was definitely a presence, whether intelligent or residual she didn't know, and not just one, but two of them. The crying was faint at first, sounding from far, far away, but gradually it grew louder. It was the sound of two infants! Babies even. Not just in pain, but in agony, suffering vomiting, diarrhoea, blood, and a fever that burned their skin as much as it was burning Ruby's in that moment, making her feel woozy, as though she were going to pass out. Her legs buckling, she reached for Cash, who'd thankfully noticed her dilemma and had hurried forwards. She began to retch too, her throat raw, quite raw, as those around her became increasingly alarmed.

She held up a hand and tried to communicate that she was okay, that whatever was happening would pass, but her words were indefinable; a mere croak.

"We need to call the doctor," Katharine said, Edyth and Jennifer in agreement.

She shook her head in protest as the symptoms continued, silently imploring Cash to act on her behalf and stop them.

Jed materialised and started whining but there was nothing he could do – that anyone could do. It was hopeless, all so hopeless – not her emotion, but the one she was picking up on – grief again, a wall of it.

Katharine had reached the phone when Cash gave in to her wishes.

"Wait! Just… give her time. This sometimes happens, she'll be fine soon."

"She is *not* fine," Katharine denied before only slightly relenting. "Look, I'll tell you what, I'll call Alison instead, she only lives a few houses down, and she's a nurse. If she's at home, she can be here much quicker than Doctor Mead."

A nurse?

Those words hit Ruby with as much force as the physical symptoms.

"Don't call the nurse!" she managed to utter, amazed that she could she was in so much pain. But she didn't want the nurse to come. It was imperative she didn't!

Ruby, calm down!

Why was she getting so het up? Then again, why

shouldn't she? Everything in that moment was overwhelming. Whatever had caused the babies deaths had been awful. But babies, no matter how traumatic their demise, tended to pass into the light with relative ease. So who was grounded here? The mother, or them – or were they all shades, not grounded at all, such suffering entrenched? Again she got a sense of the air around her all stirred up as if someone had taken a big wooden spoon to it.

At last the fire in her belly started to recede, a great gasp of relief escaping her. She could breathe again, the strength returning to her legs. It was over… for now.

Able to assure Katharine herself that she wasn't in need of a doctor or a nurse, Ruby tried to understand what was happening in Canonibeare and drew no conclusion whatsoever. Feeing below par already, she was wary of how much energy these new cases were going to take up – she needed all her strength to deal with what was happening at Old Cross Cottage, hence her decision to call the team in, and to inform the onlookers of that fact, that all cases would be dealt with soon.

"But can't you sort it out now, today I mean? I don't want this kind of thing happening in my house," Katharine protested.

"You're perfectly safe."

"It doesn't feel safe when there's a screaming woman standing in your living room. It puts you off relaxing in here with a cuppa, I can tell you!"

"Spirits can't harm you," Ruby insisted, and it was true, up to a point – *most* spirits anyway. "To be honest I can't detect an actual spirit but there's grief, a mother crying because of an illness that felled her twin babies. That grief is still palpable."

"Palpable? Then how come it's never been palpable before?"

Questions, questions, always questions.

Although the terrible symptoms she'd experienced had been brief, the memory of them was pertinent and she felt like sinking onto Katharine's big comfy sofa that lay a few feet from her. She was so tired of questions.

Intuitive again, Cash intervened. "If Ruby says you're safe, then you're safe. Go about your daily routine and try not to let what's happened get to you. Ruby's just one person. She's good but she can only do so much. When the rest of the team arrive they'll sort out what's going on, lay it to rest. Meanwhile, that's what Ruby needs, a bit of rest. You know where we are if you need us."

Katharine didn't look pleased at all. "Never liked Old Cross Cottage," she muttered, "always full of incomers, people who have no business being here."

"Kath!" It was Edyth intervening now.

"Well, it's true, in't it? I know I've only lived here for ten years but at least I come from a village nearby. Even so, I'm made to feel like an incomer at times."

"You are not!"

"I am, Edyth," Katharine insisted. "But that's a small village for you, it's insular, everyone knows each other, it takes time to be accepted. But that cottage, no one ever stays long enough do they? It's a restless place, and now the village is restless. It's like whatever's wrong with Old Cross is catching, it's diseased."

"You're going a bit far now, Kath." Edyth had started to huff and puff.

Katharine shrugged defiantly. "I'm telling you, that cottage doesn't like being abandoned so often. When you abandon something, that's when trouble starts."

Before Edyth could protest further, Katharine stomped off, presumably into the kitchen. As they stared after her, Ruby couldn't help but agree. Mary had been abandoned – by the entire village, no matter that it was so long ago. And yes trouble had certainly started – those who'd abandoned her perhaps unable to rest too.

Chapter Twenty-Three

RUBY and Cash didn't go back to Old Cross Cottage straight away, they went to the churchyard.

"I just want to see if Thomas Ward's grave is here," she told Cash.

She'd said the same thing to Theo whose response had been 'unlikely.' Ward had died some time before Ellen and if she hadn't been allowed a burial on consecrated ground, what hope did he have? There was no sign of it, so where was he buried? There were so many headstones, stuffed into one small churchyard, it was possible she could have missed it, but even so, Theo's 'unlikely' kept ringing in her head.

Jed was with them, darting in and out of the stone slabs, finally stopping at one and rooting around. Ruby hurried over. Could he have found Ward's grave?

Quickly she read the inscription:

Peter and Sharon Groves
October 1942 – December 1942
Taken too soon

"Cash, look," she said, calling him over. "This belongs to the twins I think."

"You mean the ones who died at *Heron's Roost*?"

"It could be, poor things, just two months old, that's all they were."

Something nagged at her. She'd picked up grief and guilt at Edyth's and Helen's houses – emotions that could be connected to Mary if those they belonged to had known about Mary's plight and yet done nothing about it. Although she hadn't been able to attach a timeframe to the spirits, if it was indeed connected there was no way anyone in the village would have remained ignorant of what was happening at Old Cross. As Katharine herself said, small village life was insular; everyone knew at least something of other people's business. But the twins seemed to be a separate tragedy and therefore an anomaly. The other strange thing was why she'd been so against the nurse being called. She'd got really upset about that and not just because she knew her symptoms would soon pass. Her body had gone cold all over.

Stepping forward she put her hands on the twins' gravestone and closed her eyes – there was so much residual sadness it was like a sharp blow, one that stung as viciously as a wasp. Snatching her hands back she brought them to her forehead, her fingers circling her temples as though it would ease such suffering.

"Come on, Ruby, enough," Cash's voice was gentle. "It's been a long day."

It had, but was there really an end in sight? She was no longer so confident.

As they started walking, Ruby called for Jed to follow. He'd doubled back on himself and was busy sniffing round another grave, cocking his leg up against it to take an imaginary wee. Initially he ignored her, continued to sniff, but she walked on, let herself be guided by Cash, agitation really beginning to get a stronghold. But she shouldn't start to stress, she needn't, the team would be with her the next day, all of them, in Canonibeare, trying to put right what had gone so wrong.

Glancing at Cash, she felt the need to apologise again.

"No worries," he replied, "just leave the holiday locations to me in future, okay? I'm not saying I don't trust you, but…"

"You don't trust me," she finished, offering a weak smile.

"Not when it comes to arranging holidays. I tell you what though, I know this sounds silly, but I'm actually a bit nervous about returning to the cottage."

"It's not silly, I'm nervous too."

"I'm not particularly fond of flying missiles that's all, but I know we have to go back, we can't walk away. We've got to sort out what's happening."

Ruby came to a standstill and stared at him. "Cash, *you* don't have to do anything. This is my job, I'm only sorry there are hazards attached."

"To be fair, there is in any job. Take working at the council for example, you risk being bored to death."

She laughed genuinely this time. "At least my job isn't boring, I suppose."

"No, it isn't and normally I'm fine with that, but I think the problem is I was in holiday mode when I got here. I need to get past that now."

"Oh, Cash, I promise a holiday will mean exactly that in future – a break from work. Somehow we'll manage it, or rather *I'll* manage it." Turning her head in the direction they'd come from, she saw the pub lights twinkling in the distance. "Tell you what, let's not go back, not yet. Let's go to the pub, have a drink and a bite to eat. Later on, we'll return, light a fire, snuggle in front of it, and stay awake all night if we have to. I'm sure we can think of a few things to occupy our time." Deliberately coquettish, she fluttered her eyelashes at him. "If the spirits want to hide, we'll let them. More than that, we'll *encourage* them. They can stay right where they are, because tonight," briefly she glanced around her, "belongs to us, just us."

Cash's smile widened to a grin, the one that she adored. "Rubes, I think we've got ourselves a plan." Grabbing her hand, he pulled her along, as if he couldn't quite get to the pub quick enough. "I take it you're buying?"

"I am," she assured him. "I'm buying all night long."

* * *

It wasn't just Cash who was relieved at the thought of delaying their return to the cottage. Yes, Mary was Ruby's priority, but so was Cash, something she mustn't forget. In fact, she resolved to put him first more often. A man like him – as tolerant – was hard to find, so she didn't want to run the risk of losing him. The dusk deepening, the pub really did look welcoming, like a beacon, drawing them to it.

Despite her resolve, her mind, if not her body, returned to Old Cross Cottage. Not just poor Mary but poor Thomas too. She had to make him understand that in no way did his sexual preference whilst alive condemn him. Not only was he suffering because of that mistaken belief but also because of Mary and William. He must have been witness to all that had happened between them, been utterly stricken by it if his expression was anything to go by – outraged, she realised, the very emotion she'd picked up on in the churchyard. In many ways, he was at William's mercy too.

Oh, William, why did you do it? Why'd you tear Mary and

Ellen's lives apart?

What had happened to make him that way? In her experience there was usually a reason for everything. And what had drawn him to Mary and Ellen in the first place? Their vulnerability? In its way, it was as much a beacon as the lights of The Plough.

"There you go," said Cash, reaching over her head to open the door.

Ducking only slightly, she stepped inside, Jed rushing ahead; no doubt hoping Dollie was there, waiting for him. Ruby's eyes travelled to the bar and she was stunned to see, once again, all the regulars plus the addition of Edyth's husband, Bob, staring at her, their eyes wide and each one, Dollie included, as still as statues.

Cash joined her, raised his hand in greeting but Louisa shook her head, indicating for him to keep quiet.

As still as them, Ruby listened intently whilst also wondering what the heck was going on. Just as they'd done in the double bedroom at the cottage, whilst waiting for Thomas Ward to turn round, the seconds ticked by, each one ridiculously longer than the last. How long were they expected to stand like this?

Ruby couldn't resist. "What's the matt—?"

"There! There it is, it's happened again! Did you hear it?" Louisa suddenly cried.

"Hear what?"

"Listen!" she implored.

Again, they obeyed; there was nothing but silence, an enduring silence and then… there was something else: light chatter, but faint, as though the sound was locked in a distant room. There was a sudden high-pitched moan, which quickly died away; a low sob, barely caught; the chinking of glasses when none were raised.

Cash looked at Ruby who stared back at him. The two dogs were also listening, theirs heads in identical positions, cocked to one side. The sounds reminded her of those she'd heard at Old Cross Cottage, typical pub sounds, but not from this era, from a time long ago. And actually not so typical when she analysed them further – the low sob and the high-pitched moan, both had been gestures of despair.

"Of course! The pub. It's where wakes would have been held, the villagers gathering here after a funeral."

"What?" Cash said. "You think that's what this is?"

"Don't you?" she said, moving swiftly towards the bar. "Louisa, how long has this been going on?"

"The sounds?"

Ruby nodded.

"Ever since I opened the pub tonight. At first, I thought somebody had left a radio playing or something but I searched and found nothing. And then this lot," she inclined her head towards Bob and the other occupants, "they came in, and started hearing it too. It's been on and off you know, just like a radio in fact, someone turning up the volume one minute, then turning it down the next. What is it?"

A scream pierced the air; Ruby screwed her eyes shut, brought her hands up to protect her ears. God, it was intense. Opening her eyes, she realised everyone was looking at her again and slowly she lowered her hands.

"Didn't you hear that too?"

"Hear what?" Louisa asked.

"Ruby?" It was Cash, concerned again.

"I… there was a scream that's all." She took a deep breath. "Louisa, after a funeral is this where the wakes would have been held?"

Louisa looked at Bob and the others, shrugged before answering. "I suppose so, yeah, although that's not the case in modern times. Nowadays, if there's a wake, people tend to hold it in the privacy of their own homes. We're just a normal pub; we have a quiz night, a dance night on occasions too, barbecues in the summer, but mainly people just pop in for a drink before or after dinner, you know?"

Yes, Ruby did know, but in the past it had been a centre for the community, just as Old Cross Inn had been. And, as was happening in the cottages around, that past was waking up and colliding with the present. There was no time for a night off, no peace to be found in the village pub, or anywhere else in Canonibeare for that matter – she had to make the dead speak to her, sleep more if that's what it took, get Mary to shed further light on what had happened, drag her out of the darkness.

"Cash, we have to go back to the cottage. I need to sleep."

"Blimey, Rubes, I know you're whacked but can't we have a pint first?"

Ruby shook her head and turned to Louisa, who'd piped up too. "But what about us? You're a psychic, can't you tell us what's going on in here?"

"I can tell you what I *think* is going on," Ruby replied, feeling her face reddening slightly from being put on the spot. "Something happened in this village to a child called Mary, a long time ago, back in the early 1900s – something bad. And it happened at Old Cross Cottage. Those that lived in the village knew she was in danger but turned a blind eye as people tended to do in those days, and there's a lot of guilt because of that, *still* a lot of guilt, I mean. It's imprinted in the atmosphere." The twin babies came to mind. "There were other deaths too, a whole spate of them. That's what

I'm picking up on, standing here, in this pub, and it's all connected."

"Oh, 'eck!" one of the men at the bar commented. "Helen mentioned there was something strange going on in her house."

Bob joined in. "Edyth phoned me today about summat too. Thought she were mucking about, taken with this one," he nodded towards Ruby, "as much as my daughter seems to be taken with you," another nod, but at Cash this time, "but then I come here and this happens. Maybe she's right, after all."

"Bloody hell!" swore Louisa, initial curiosity turning into fear.

"It's okay, it's okay," Ruby said, fearful too, at the prospect of mass hysteria, "whatever it is, we can do something about it, that's my job. It could be over as quickly as it's blown up, in fact, I'm sure it will be. There's no need to be alarmed."

"But these deaths you're talking about," Louisa said, "you saying they weren't natural? That people were being... *murdered* in the village?"

She hadn't been implying that but was it so far from the truth? Despite her uncertainty, she played it down. "I'm just saying I think it's connected."

"But if murders had taken place here," Louisa continued, undeterred, "several of them like you say, it would have made headline news, even back then. There'd have been a mention of it somewhere. It would be part of the village's history."

She was right. "And there is no mention?"

"Not as far as I know. Bob, do you know anything about it? Ben, Dave? What about you, Paul, have you heard anything? Steve?"

Various muttered replies indicated not.

Then what's this all about?

A loud bang drew a collective gasp. Several lights in the fitting above their head had burst, plunging them into darkness.

"Are you all right? Is everyone all right?" It was Louisa shouting.

"Yeah, yeah, okay, we're okay," replied a chorus of voices.

"Ruby, are you okay?" It was Cash moving towards her, as did Jed.

"What's happening?" Bob was standing up – Ruby could just about make him out as her eyes adjusted. "Can't a man enjoy a quiet pint in his local pub anymore?"

"Bloody hell!" It was one of the other men swearing. "This is all a bit queer, in't it?"

Ruby blinked. She could see other shapes too, more than there should be, much more, and multiplying rapidly. Shadows, shades, whatever they were, beginning to fill the void, of all ages and all sizes, some standing on their own, whilst others were bunched together, their arms around each other as if in support. It wasn't an intelligent haunting as such, none of them showed any sign that they were aware of the living, of her in particular, but what was alive was the emotion, shock this time, disbelief. *'How could this happen, how?'* was the sentiment continually expressed.

How could what happen?

Ruby stood perfectly still as the living, breathing occupants of the pub sprang into action, scrabbling for candles probably or spare light bulbs.

Another figure appeared, a little denser than the rest, hard to tell though whether it was a man or a woman, and slightly set back from the mass, facing away from her.

Is this something to do with you?

As she moved forward someone bumped into her, one of the men, "Sorry, love," he said, "we'll have this sorted in no time, there's no need to worry."

She neither worried nor doubted him. He and the rest of the occupants could address the more technical issues; she alone had to deal with the paranormal.

Turn around and show yourself.

Was it William?

Look at me!

Movement! She was sure of it.

If it is you, then… then…

This was no time to falter. She knew what she had to say: that his sins wouldn't prevent him from going to the light, that that was where he belonged, despite what he'd done. That he wasn't evil, that *no one* was inherently evil.

But he is! He is!

Whose thought was that? Not hers. She was trying to remain objective.

Poor Mary, remember what happened to her, what she endured.

Of course she remembered, she'd never forget.

He's evil!

He's not…

He is! He's evil!

An inner dialogue, but who was conversing with her? Thoughts spun round and round in her head as she continued to investigate, those shades that were closest disappearing, as flimsy as smoke, but not the shade ahead. That remained solid.

A hand gripped hers. Was it Cash, worried about her

drifting away?

She looked to the side. It wasn't Cash, it was a much smaller figure, just the faintest outline, tugging at her.

Look at me, look at me!

Mary? Is it you?

Look at me, only me!

Is this your wake?

But no, it couldn't be, it was a *multitude* of wakes.

Still the girl pleaded for her attention.

Wanting to obey, but needing to identify the second figure too, she focused straight ahead. She was close, so close. With her free hand she reached out.

I've got you cornered, trapped. I'll find out who you are, and what you've done.

ME!!!

No longer by her side but in front of her too, the child flew at Ruby and knocked her backwards. There was a flash of light and then darkness reigned once more.

Chapter Twenty-Four

"CASH, you're going a bit overboard."

"Ruby, I'm not. After you hit your head you were out cold for a good few minutes, or at least it seemed like that. Bloody hell, I thought you were dead!"

"Dead? I'm not quite twenty-seven, remember."

"Yeah, yeah, funny, Ruby, really funny."

In the starkly-lit waiting room of Dorchester County Hospital, a good twenty miles from Canonibeare, Cash was still very obviously in shock, the pupils of his eyes unnaturally wide and his teeth agitating at his lip in much the same manner she employed when upset. Jed too was present, occasional tremors running through his body as he sat and stared at her. They were waiting to see a nurse, after not only Cash insisted upon it, but everyone in the pub too – Louisa particularly, who'd grabbed her keys and driven them here. She'd since returned to the village, despite being nervous about doing so, but made them promise to keep her updated about Ruby's condition. "I'll fetch you when you're ready to come back," she'd said, "but a bump like that, they'll keep you in overnight, I'm sure of it."

The thought of which was intolerable.

Starting to rise, Ruby was going to insist they call a taxi when she was hit by a wave of nausea as intense as any emotion she'd experienced in the village.

A nurse noticed and came rushing towards her. "Easy, Easy," she said. "Let's get you into a cubicle, you need to lie down. Come on, come with me, just take it easy."

As the nurse laid hands on her, Ruby half-expected to flinch, but she did no such thing. Instead, she was grateful for her help as well as Cash's. Between them they got her to an empty bed, her head spinning precariously as she lay down.

"Are you going to be sick?" the nurse asked, a woman not much older than Ruby.

"I... don't know."

"Here, take hold of this if you can," she said, offering a cardboard receptacle. "Or perhaps you can hold it for her?"

"Of course," Cash replied.

Mortified, Ruby's hand shot out. "I can hold it," she said, smiling weakly at Cash. "Some things are beyond the call of duty."

"Never," he insisted. "Just lie still, I'm here with the sick bucket if you need it."

"So romantic," she muttered, closing her eyes and then wishing she hadn't as the room spun wildly. She opened them again, trying instead to remember what had happened. The lights had blown in the pub, causing everyone to rush around finding candles or light bulbs in the darkness... Before that there'd been sounds –woeful sounds – low moans and cries of sorrow. Afterwards, in the darkness, she'd seen shapes, so many of them, not gathering because of one occasion, but many occasions, all occurring at once, the time between them of no consequence, not anymore – they'd become one big angst-ridden melting pot. One shape in particular had stood out, which had more substance to it than the rest but nonetheless she hadn't been able to ascertain whether it was male or female. It could have been William – a man who'd gloat over others' misfortune. One of the wakes could even have been Mary's but if so, why wasn't her body in the churchyard? Surely, that's where she would have been buried, unless... What had he done to her, done *with* her? She couldn't bear to think. And then, of course, there was Mary herself, tugging at her hand, wanting to be her entire focus. Lunging at Ruby, attacking her.

Immediately, Ruby amended that. Mary *hadn't* attacked her. Her actions were borne of desperation, pure desperation. And Ruby agreed, she *should* have listened to her, and because she didn't she was stuck in the hospital, wasting time.

"Cash, we really can't stay here." No sooner had she said it than her stomach heaved. "Oh God!"

Cash was there in an instant, the receptacle placed just below her chin as he held her hair back, bile rushing upwards, splashing her face and him too no doubt.

"Ugh, I'm sorry, so, so sorry."

"Stop apologising, Ruby, this isn't your fault."

The nurse came and took the receptacle away and handed Cash a fresh one, but she was done retching for now, and was lying against the pillow, her heart still racing from the effort. Cash had managed to obtain what looked like wet wipes and was wiping her face with them, tears springing to her eyes as he did so. It was exactly what her gran used to do when she'd been ill in the past.

The nurse returned. "Nausea and vomiting are quite normal following concussion," she said, "please don't worry, or get upset by it. We're going to run a CT scan, and I've got you booked in for that tonight."

"So I really won't be going anywhere?" Ruby managed.

"You really won't be," the nurse replied, smiling to soften the blow. To Cash, she said, "You're welcome to stay with her but I'm afraid there's only a chair to sit on."

"The chair's fine," Cash replied.

As the nurse dashed off to answer some other call, Ruby resigned herself to her fate, but in the morning she'd discharge herself if it came to it, get back to Canonibeare, a village in peril, Mary in particular – whatever had happened there hurtling towards crisis point.

"Don't go to sleep, Ruby."

Having read somewhere that after a blow to the head it was important to stay awake for a certain period of time lest you drift into a coma, she tried to do as Cash asked, but her eyes closed of their own accord, even as her mind continued to swirl.

What had happened when she'd been out 'stone cold'? Had she dreamed or descended into oblivion? She forced her eyes open, squinting at the bright light.

"Cash, I need to sleep."

"Talk to me, just keep talking."

"But I'm tired."

"I know you are, but… look, let me find the nurse, ask if it's okay."

Her hand reached out and clutched his arm. "Don't leave, stay here."

"I'm only going over—"

"No! I don't want to be left alone."

"Okay, okay," he relented.

"Cash, when I was unconscious, what happened?"

"We all panicked a bit to be honest, mainly me I have to admit. Louisa called for an ambulance but they said that if you were coming round, it'd be quicker if we drove, so that's what we did, we got you here as fast as we could."

"Did you fix the lights?"

"Yeah, we found some light bulbs, why?"

"Before I passed out, I saw a flash of light."

"Most likely electric," Cash confirmed.

"And… whilst I was unconscious, did I just lie there? Quietly, I mean."

At that point Cash frowned. "Quiet? No you weren't actually, come to think of it, you were sort of making little yelping noises, and your eyelids kept twitching."

So she had been dreaming, Mary giving her no peace.

The nurse was in the vicinity again and Cash beckoned her over, apparently it was okay for her to rest if she wanted to.

As desperate as she'd been for that option a few moments before she wondered whether to fight against it still as it offered no real respite. But whatever worries she had, they rapidly dissolved. There was no way she could resist sleep, no way at all.

It was coming for her, as was Mary.

* * *

Mary shuffled over to the mirror in the room to check her reflection. Her cheeks looked like they had muddy tracks running down them – the trail of her tears.

No more crying, she reminded herself. And she'd be a good girl from now on, she'd obey, do his will. That way she might breathe fresh air again instead of the rancid smell that permeated this room, the smell of her own fear she realised, choking her it was so potent. Oh, to sit under the oak tree again and make daisy chains, to return to the simple life she'd once had, imagining herself the daughter of a lord. Those dreams lay broken now, obliterated on the rocky shores of memory.

The door… she'd inspect that next. Pushing herself off the bed, she walked towards it, the floorboards creaking, one in particular, stopping her en route.

She knelt down, felt around that floorboard, realised how loose it was. Felt another, that was loose too, this part of the house as unkempt as she was.

Pursuing her original goal, she reached the door, rattled the handle, and tugged at it. It was stuck fast. She fell against it and whispered through the lock.

"I know you're out there."

It wasn't William she addressed, he was gone, but the one who was trapped here with her. The ghost.

"Why don't you help me, show yourself to William and frighten him instead?" A sob burst from her. "Why do you continue to frighten *me*?"

Angrily she brought her hand up to her face, rubbed again at the tears. *You're not supposed to cry, Mary. Not anymore!*

She had to be strong, she had to survive, any way she could.

"You should have helped me." Once again she addressed what lay on the other side. "You *should* have."

* * *

"Good girl, you're being such a good girl."

As Mary filled his bowl with stew, the recipe the one her mother had taught her, she tried but failed not to look at the hook. William caught her.

"You hate it, don't you, Mary? You want it gone?" He

shook his head. "It's not going anywhere. It's a reminder you see. It's how we got to where we are."

Quickly averting her gaze, she focused on what she was doing, breathing calmly and slowly, despite the tightening in her chest. Appease him – that's all she had to do. Ellen had done the same but it hadn't worked – still she'd angered him. 'She was too much like my mother,' he'd said once, his words slurred from the ale he'd been drinking. 'Same build, and that same red hair.' He'd literally spat the word 'red' at Mary. 'My mother never understood me. I'd catch her staring, the expression on her face, whenever she could bear to look at me that is. Yes, Mary, you heard right, my own mother couldn't bear to look at me. 'Tisn't nice, is it? She was happy when I packed up, when I left. Relieved. And so was I, believe me. I didn't give her so much as a backwards glance. Ellen started to look at me like she used to, with that same… distaste. I won't stand for it, d'ya hear? I vowed I'd stand for it no more.'

Just as she'd vowed she'd never cry again.

After this drunken revelation, his hand had reached out to touch her hair, taking a few strands of it between his fingers. "Good job your hair's fair, Mary, not a scrap of red in it. Lucky for you that is. I *like* your hair."

Breathe, remember to breathe.

She'd had to remind herself then and she reminded herself now. As much as she hated to agree with anything he said, he was right; the hook should stay.

"Ouch! This stew, it's scorching."

A hand came out again, this time to deliver a blow across the side of her head, causing her to stumble, to drop the pot she held in her hands. It fell to the floor with a deafening crash, smashed into a thousand pieces, its contents spreading rapidly.

Immediately, she dropped to the floor too and attempted to clean it. In contrast, he jumped up, towering over her, continuing to scream.

"What are you trying to do, burn my mouth?"

"No, no, I…"

"You're supposed to be a good girl!"

"I am, I am."

"Don't answer me back!"

His boot come out, connecting brutally with her stomach, stealing her breath completely before striking again and again. She rolled away from the mess on the floor that had started to congeal, curled into a ball, her hands shielding her head.

It'll be all right; it'll be all right.

She knew the score. He'd exhaust himself soon enough. All she had to do was ride it out.

As the blows invariably died down, as he returned to the table, she glanced again at the hook. And she remembered.

* * *

She'd taken the path that led to the oak tree, once a haven, but no more, it couldn't be. After today she'd never see it again, never sit beneath the swaying branches, looking up at the sky beyond, listening to her mother's voice as she called her home.

"You're a one," she used to say. "Love it outdoors you do, running wild and free."

And free they'd been, until she'd permitted that man entry into their home and imprisoned them both. Strange when she thought about it, not once did she see Ellen shed a tear for her former husband's supposed demise. Was that because she was being stoic in front of her child, or was she indeed lying, as Mary had sometimes suspected? In truth, there'd been no wedding, no father, no legitimacy; she'd been what other children had always called her, what William called her – a bastard; someone who didn't belong, who'd never be accepted, whom society shunned. There was no sadness in that realisation, even though she expected there to be. Just relief. As though she understood at last how others saw her. And that it would never be any different. What had happened to her, what William had done, she'd carry it always. It *defined* her. Happiness was a privilege reserved for other people.

But again, it didn't matter. Not anymore.

The wind was whipping up, not only the branches swaying but also blades of grass rippling beneath her feet. Her last visit to the oak tree, and then it would all be over. A smile played about her lips. Perhaps she'd enjoy what was to come, finding, as he did, such release in it. Sweet release...

Mary... Mary...

Even the wind whispered her name. No, not whispered, it cried out for her.

Mary...

She clutched tighter at what was in her hands.

Chapter Twenty-Five

RUBY sat bolt upright.

"Oh my God, Cash, I think Mary ended her own life! At the oak tree… It looks like she hanged herself too, like her mother before her. And all because of William! He drove her to it. I know I shouldn't, but I can't help it, I hate him, I really hate him!"

Cash was staring back at her, unfortunately so was the nurse, her face a vision.

"Oh, erm…" Ruby stuttered, unsure how to explain the words that had just erupted from her mouth. "I had a dream."

"I see," the nurse replied, looking no less mystified. "Well, now that you're awake I'd like you to stay that way please. It's time for your scan."

An orderly appeared and together they pushed her bed along the corridor to the X-Ray department, Cash going with her as far as he could.

Before she ventured onwards, he leant over to kiss her cheek but also to whisper in her ear. "Don't worry about dreams right now, let's just get you better."

Ruby nodded but there was no way she wouldn't worry. Thomas Ward had committed suicide, Ellen too, and now Mary, and William no less her murderer because of it. She tried to think how old Mary would have been at the time, but like before, she hadn't seen her in that last snapshot because she'd been travelling inside her again, looking outwards – her early teens still? The revelations seemed to be in chronological order so that would make sense. Besides, she wouldn't have had the wherewithal – the *knowledge* – to do such a thing beforehand. Children younger than teenage years had little choice but to suffer and oh, how Mary had suffered. How unbearable it had become. She had to get back to Old Cross Cottage and finish what she came here to do. Find a way. Get this blasted scan over and done with.

Thankfully the scan results proved no lasting damage had been done but they weren't issued until hours later, meaning it was indeed Thursday morning before they were happy enough to let her go. Cash texted Louisa to say they were getting a taxi and going straight back to the cottage so that Ruby could rest.

"Cash, I'm hardly going to be resting, not with Theo and the team on their way."

"They can take over," he said, stifling a yawn. "I'm half tempted not to take you to the cottage at all to be honest, to whisk you away to a hotel, that Premier Inn we were joking about. I don't know, Rubes… this case, it's getting out of hand."

"We can't leave! I mean you can, but not me. I won't. And I'm fine, Cash, really."

She was sitting on the edge of the bed, not feeling fine at all, feeling decidedly wobbly in fact, and doing her utmost to hide it. Cash rose to his feet, stood in front of her, and placed his hands on her shoulders. "Ruby, I've been hurt, you've been hurt. How far is this going to go? As for William, you can't keep doing what you're doing, saying that you hate him, hesitating even when I asked about sending him to the light. I know what he did was wrong, but you're not the judge or jury."

"I can't believe you're standing up for William again!"

"I'm just saying—"

"He abused Ellen and he abused Mary! He may not have killed them but he was the reason why they took their own lives." She paused, shook her head. "I'm not sure which is worse to be honest. And, Cash, he's still there, he's in that cottage, terrorising the child. Don't you think she's suffered enough? I know I do. So pardon me for experiencing the odd surge of hatred, if I'm not as enthusiastic as I should be about sending him to the light, but rest assured, I am aware of what I have to do, even if it doesn't sit particularly well with me, so just… cut me a bit of slack, okay?"

"Would you mind quieting down, please?" It was a nurse, not the one who'd tended to Ruby, a much older lady with a stern expression on her face. "There are sick people on this ward, the last thing they need to hear is other people arguing."

"Arguing?" Ruby responded. "No, we were—"

"Just leave it, Ruby. Let's get out of here, go back to that bloody cottage."

"Cash, I've already said, if you'd rather not—"

"I know what you've already said. Come on."

Although he was clearly pissed off with her, he still held his arm out for her to take. She considered walking ahead without his support, but didn't want to compound the already chilly atmosphere.

In the taxi it was just as strained, only Jed enjoying the trip, hitching a ride in the front seat alongside the driver and looking out of the window with the greatest enthusiasm.

Ruby's head was, as usual, consumed with thoughts of Mary, at what she'd done in order to survive, having to obey a man whose whims were impossible, only to conclude that survival was not so important after all.

As well as cursing William, she found herself cursing religion too. In a village with a church at its centre, even Thomas Ward would have been a regular parishioner, just as William, Ellen and Mary were, listening Sunday after Sunday to so many Christian teachings, some meant to inspire fear and succeeding only too well. Unable to detect Ellen, she must have found the strength to fly – to quite literally rise above it – but Thomas hadn't, Mary hadn't. She had no idea when William died, but he would have known the difference between right and wrong deep down, everybody did, human depictions of hell no doubt vivid in his memory still, of fire, of brimstone, and burning forevermore. He was a coward in life, picking on the vulnerable, and clearly a coward in death, unable to face up to what he'd done.

Her hatred of him wasn't abating. If anything it was becoming fiercer. Cash was right, she'd have to watch it, get herself under control, but as she turned her head to the window, watched the countryside too, she lost the battle over and over again.

* * *

The taxi driver was over-confident. Although Ruby had noticed they were travelling at a fair speed, on the main roads it didn't seem to matter, that's what everyone tended to do, going well over the limit in order to shave a bit of time off their journey. On country roads, however, it was painfully obvious, his foot not bothering to trouble the brakes at all as he flew around blind corner after blind corner.

At last, thoughts of personal safety superseded thoughts of Mary and, despite the lingering atmosphere between them she tried to get Cash's attention. Aiming to be as discreet as possible, she nodded in the taxi driver's general direction.

"It's fine," he mouthed back at her.

It wasn't. They'd already been in a car accident this week, and she didn't fancy another. She squeezed his hand a bit harder this time and he sighed, clearly exasperated, causing her to snatch her hand back. Did he think she was making a fuss? Of course he did. Why did she bother to question it? Tiredness could well be making him irritable, she supposed. She might have slept for a short while but he probably hadn't – plastic hospital chairs hardly conducive to a good night's rest.

Travelling from the south, the cottage was close, but there were still a few more bends to negotiate. With this in mind, she leant forward and tapped his shoulder.

"Excuse me, I think you're—"

"What's that, love?" The taxi driver turned his head to the side. Well into middle age he was also fairly rotund, fitting snugly into his seat, his complexion ruddy and his hair thinning so much he'd do better to shave it off and admit defeat.

"I think you need to slow down a bit," Ruby continued. "I appreciate you're familiar with the roads around here, but—"

"Ruby…" It was Cash, dragging out the pronunciation of her name.

"No, Cash! This isn't a safe speed to go at, not on these roads. Blimey!" her eyes widened as she clocked what had just happened. "That's another bend you've flown around. What if a car had been coming the other way? We'd be history!"

As well as being a speed merchant, the driver was also clearly hard of hearing. "You're going to have to speak up, love."

"Ruby," again Cash sounded peeved, "it's not far now, why make a fuss?"

"I'm not making a fuss, I'm just pointing it out, that's all." Raising her voice slightly, she re-addressed the cabbie, "Could you please slow down?"

To her alarm, he turned again, unable to reply it seemed unless he was making near eye contact.

"Yes, we're almost there, love, almost there," he said good-naturedly, leaving her wondering if he'd actually heard her at all.

"Okay, okay," she relented, "that's fine, thank you."

"Sorry?" he replied, twisting even further.

"I said… Shit! Look out, for God's sake, look out!"

"Shit!" echoed Cash.

The blind bends done with, they were on the home stretch, but still going way too fast. Only slightly further up, Jennifer was walking towards them – also, it seemed, making her way to Old Cross Cottage. Eyes down and shoulders hunched, she looked as though she were on a mission – perhaps there'd been more activity at her house and she was hurrying round to tell them about it. Whatever was on her mind, she was so pre-occupied she completely failed to clock the speeding car, the driver noticing her at least and slamming on his brakes but to no avail. Beneath them, the wheels locked and the car started to slide along the road, as though they were on ice, not tarmac, heading straight towards the centre of the crossroads.

"Jen," Cash was shouting. "Look out!"

Although transfixed by Jennifer, Ruby was aware of other

elements in the picture too – there was another car, travelling from the east – Theo and the team? And further north, just beyond Jennifer, a distant figure broke into a panicked run.

"Jennifer!" Still Cash was calling. Having managed to wind the window down, he was leaning so far out of it she feared for him as well. The driver was cursing; unable to understand why he'd lost control of his vehicle. The other car definitely belonged to Ness, and the figure in the distance was also close enough so that Ruby could identify her. It was Edyth, yelling at her daughter: "Come back, come back!" They were such familiar words, first spoken by Cash when they'd had their near crash, and then by Mary, trying to coax life back into her mother's body. Prompting another memory – no, not a memory: a flashback, someone else's memory – Mary's again, repeating those words – 'Come back, come back.' But to whom this time?

The oak tree, she's at the oak tree.

That didn't make sense. She'd been alone at the oak tree.

The oak tree!

The voice wasn't Mary's. And it wasn't her memory either. This was someone *overriding* Mary. The cottage to their left, she glanced upwards and gasped in surprise. There was the figure of a man in the double bedroom, Thomas Ward, and not just that but hands at the window of the other bedroom too. *William?*

Just as quickly the hands and the figure disappeared. A scream pierced the air, one that everyone heard. Thankfully the car stopped – they seemed to have been skidding forever, although in reality it was seconds. Ruby could hardly bear to look, envisioning all too readily the carnage that lay before her. Cash, however, leapt into action, scrambling onto the tarmac. In contrast, she and the driver sat rigid.

Jennifer was lying in the road.

Oh, no, no, no!

Ness's car had also stopped, and she, Theo and Corinna were rushing forwards.

"Is she all right?" Theo called, her breath laboured. "Is the poor girl okay?"

Ruby dug around in her pocket for her mobile phone, intending to call the ambulance but when she retrieved it, she noticed the battery was completely flat. Thankfully Corinna was speaking into her mobile, doing the deed instead.

Able to move eventually, she joined Cash and Edyth, Cash warning Edyth not to touch Jennifer, not until the paramedics got here and assessed her.

"Is she dead?" Edyth wailed. "Dear Lord, don't let her be dead!"

"Check her pulse." It was Ness. "Make sure she has a pulse."

Taking her hand in his, Cash applied two fingers to her wrist. Waiting for the verdict again seemed to take forever but at last he spoke. "Her pulse is strong."

"Oh, Jennifer!" Edyth continued to wail, not heeding Cash's former words and throwing herself over her daughter's prone body. "Come back, darling, come back."

Her pleading caused Ruby's gaze to return upwards. Did the hands at the window in the twin bedroom belong to William? If so, that was her first sight of him. What was he trying to do, reach out to her – literally – when previously he'd favoured Cash via dreams and the *Ghost Discovery* app?

"Oh, she's moving! Thank God, she's coming round."

Her eyes back on Jennifer, Ruby held her breath, hoping against hope. Sure enough, Jennifer pushed her mother away and with Cash's help sat up.

"What… what happened?" she stuttered.

"You were hit by the car," Edyth replied, pointing to the taxi where the driver still sat gawping.

"The car didn't hit her." It was Ness again, her heart-shaped face even paler than usual. "I saw the whole thing. It missed her but the shock must have caused your daughter to stumble and fall. That's when she fell and hit her head."

"She's concussed then, like I was," Ruby said.

Theo's eyes widened. "You were concussed?"

"Yeah, it's… a long story, I'll tell you later."

The concern on Edyth's face faded and was replaced instead by thunder. "I recognise him in the car. That's Ronnie, that is. What's the matter with him, too afraid to come out, is he?" Her nostrils flared as her lips pursed. "He's a bloody liability, races round these lanes like the young 'uns, nearly bloody killed someone before, he did." She stood up, dusted herself down, and raced over to him. "Ronnie, come on out, you great big lummox! You're responsible for this."

Whilst she ranted, Cash caught Ruby's eye; he was looking sheepish, as if he felt bad about ignoring her earlier worries. Before she could respond, Jennifer sagged against his chest and panted gently. Making the most of having an excuse to do so.

Ronnie had duly stepped out of the car and Edyth continued to berate him as he hung his head in shame. Cash murmured something about an ambulance being on its way and Jennifer protested, "I don't need to go to hospital."

Ruby knelt down. "If I had to go, you should as well. If you've hit your head, passed out, it's serious. They won't take long at the hospital," she lied, "you'll be back in no time. It really is worth being checked out, simply for peace of mind."

"Peace of mind," Jennifer repeated. "That's what I was coming to tell you."

"Oh?"

"The Reverend Martin, he's got wind of what's been happening, not just in the houses but at the pub as well, and he's blaming you. That's why I was hurrying along; I wanted to warn you to expect another visit." She stopped, as breathless as Theo. "Look out, Ruby, the Reverend's creating merry hell!"

Chapter Twenty-Six

WITH yet another person from the village dispatched to accident and emergency, Ruby, Cash, Theo, and the team ventured inside Old Cross Cottage,

"Nasty business," Theo muttered, not moving further than the parlour but glancing upwards at the ceiling.

Ruby stopped too. "You can sense it then?"

"Anyone can, deep down. You're right, the child suffered."

"As did Thomas Ward."

"You'll have to fill us in on his story, every detail."

"That's if the Reverend doesn't come knocking and disturb us."

"If he does, I'll sort him out."

"You *and* me," Ness, who'd ventured into the kitchen, called out.

"Poor man," Theo mused, "he won't know what's hit him."

Ruby hesitated. "I don't want to cause any trouble." Or rather, any *more* trouble.

"No one's here to cause any further upset, darling, we're here to help that's all."

"And believe me I'm grateful," she glanced at Cash, "both of us are."

Theo smiled. "Let's follow Ness. Have a cuppa first, then

we'll do a walk-through."

The tea at least was reviving, Corinna providing a few rounds of toast to go with it and Cash wolfing his down. Meanwhile, Ruby did as Theo asked and filled them in on recent events, Ness, as diligent as ever, jotting down a few notes as she spoke.

"Is *Ghost Discovery* on at the moment?" she enquired.

Cash answered. "No, my battery's flat, I need to charge it. Ruby, where's yours, I'll put them both on charge."

"But the words recorded," Ness continued, "sometimes they're random, sometimes they're more... precise."

"Correct," Cash replied. "Very precise at times."

Theo intervened. "And you think William's manipulating this device, do you?"

Cash nodded. "At first we thought it was Mary but then the phone gave us his name, which was later corroborated via Ruby's dreams with Mary naming him too. So yeah, we've begun to think that it's William's way of getting in touch."

"Through you?"

"Yeah. And just lately, there's been a different kind of tone to the words used, we think Thomas Ward might have cottoned on and is using the app too."

"Wow! Clever Thomas! Any port in a storm, I suppose."

"Different in what way?" Ness ignored Theo's show of enthusiasm.

"Well, they've contained more of a warning."

"Such as?" Ness asked.

"Words like *listen, danger, leave*, that sort of thing."

"Quite a pertinent warning," Ness mused.

"And one that's been issued before," Ruby added. She reiterated what had happened to Rachel in the double bedroom, to her in the churchyard and then finally in the single bedroom, when she'd been thrown against the wall. She also told them about Ward himself and the flashback she'd had, how he'd sat in the parlour, his head low, wringing his hands in such anguish.

"He thought… correction, he *thinks* he's an abomination, not just because of his sexual orientation but also because he committed suicide. Two very grave sins in the eyes of the church."

"And he has to deal with William," Corinna said.

"That's right, another abomination."

"Ruby…" Theo warned. "We're here to help *everyone*, remember."

Immediately Ruby was contrite. "Yes, yes, I know."

"So," Theo continued, "what message do you think William is trying to convey?"

Cash looked at Ruby, "Erm… what do you reckon, Rubes?"

Like Cash she hesitated. "Hard to tell, it really is a series of random words, literally plucked out of the air and nigh on impossible to piece together."

"Maybe not." It was Corinna, her voice held more gravitas than usual.

Theo looked at Corinna. "What do you mean, sweetheart? Enlighten us."

"Well, this *Ghost Discovery* app, it's a bit like automatic writing, isn't it?"

"Automatic writing?" Cash queried.

"It's a method of communicating with the spirits," Ness informed him. "Tuning in and allowing words to rise either from the subconscious or a spiritual source. Either way can prove fascinating." Focusing on Corinna, she asked, "Which one of us would you suggest carries out this practice?"

Corinna blushed – the red in her cheeks the same as her hair. "I've actually got some experience in that particular medium, so… I could give it a go."

Theo raised an eyebrow. "You have experience with automatic writing? Do tell."

Corinna's laugh didn't sound quite as genuine. "Oh, Theo, not now, let's concentrate on William shall we? I'll tell you about it another time."

"I look forward to it," Theo replied, eyeing her still.

Ruby remembered one of the dreams she'd had in the hospital. "Actually, Corinna, you might not be the best person to channel William, I don't think he likes redheads. His mother was one and I don't think there was any love lost between them."

"What colour hair did Mary have?" Ness asked.

"She had fair hair."

"Well then, he's not keen on blondes either is he, if he drove her to suicide?"

Ruby stuck to her guns. "Even so, it does seem like William favours Cash, another man instead of a woman. Perhaps…" she paused, wondering if she was pushing her luck, "you could give it a go, Cash?"

Cash shrugged. "Yeah, anything to help."

"Theo, Ness, Corinna, would that be okay?" she checked.

"We could let Cash have the first stab at it," answered Theo, "see what happens?"

"Sounds good to me," Cash replied.

Theo leant back in her chair, her substantial bulk causing it to creak slightly, and with one hand patted at her hair, the same colour as the rose quartz she favoured. "Now, talking of apps, I've had a little look at one myself."

Cash looked at Ruby, who looked at Ness and Corinna,

wondering what she was going to come out with.

"Oh, I know, I know, just because I'm seventy, you think me a cotton headed ninny muggins when it comes to technology—"

"A what?" Ness asked, completely flummoxed.

"It's from the film, *Elf*," Corinna informed her. "It's what the giant Elf calls himself."

Theo chuckled. "Love that film, watched it again the other day."

"But it's not Christmas!" Cash stated, pointing out the obvious.

"Some things should be savoured all year round, dear boy. Anyway, returning to my point, I've been looking at ley lines."

"There's a ley line app?" Cash was impressed.

"Well… it's more of a resource," Theo answered. "I found it on the internet, not on my phone. Rather grandly, it's called *The Amazing Mystical Ley Line Locator*!"

"*The Amazing Mystical…*?" Ruby queried. "Theo, are you serious?"

Theo held up her hands. "Hear me out," she insisted. "Now, first up, I take it all of you know what ley lines are?"

Ness rolled her eyes. "Of course."

"Cash, do you?" Theo checked.

"Yeah, they're ancient trackways, usually straight and passing through sacred sites such as Stonehenge and Avebury. They sort of connect various power points."

"Correct! And my first hunch regarding Canonibeare was that it was built on the St Michael's Ley Line, being as it's turning out to be such a paranormal hotspot."

"St Michael's Ley Line?" Cash asked. "You might need to explain that a bit more."

"I'd be only too delighted. Basically, it's a long distance alignment that runs from St Michael's Mount in Cornwall all the way to Hopton-on-Sea on the Norfolk Coast. It's the country's spiritual backbone if you like and so called because various shrines along it are dedicated to the archangel St Michael."

"The church in Canonibeare is dedicated to St Winifred's," Ness pointed out.

"My dear, you can't be too pedantic about these things, there's always an anomaly somewhere." Glancing specifically at Ruby, she added, "Wouldn't you say?"

An anomaly? It reminded her of the haunting at *Heron's Roost*. How it was different to the other hauntings. Staring back at Theo, Ruby nodded in agreement.

"Besides, Ness, I said various shrines, not all of them. This mother of all ley lines links several significant sites such as Glastonbury Tor, Avebury, which has just been mentioned, and the abbey at Bury St. Edmunds as well as various other stone circles and barrows dating back to the Neolithic period. Is this mere coincidence? Not in my opinion. Long ago, when people built such structures they were more in tune with the earth's energy. They knew how to harness it, or shall we say, *encourage* it. These were all places of worship and collective prayer, as we know, is a powerful thing."

Cash looked truly awed. "So is Canonibeare on the St Michael's Ley Line or not?"

Theo paused for a moment, letting their hopes build up and then shook her head. "No, it isn't and I was disappointed by that too. But, believe me, there is a point to what I'm saying. During my online research I came across the resource I just mentioned and all it required me to do was Google the postcode for Old Cross Cottage, type it into the explorer and voila! The cottage *is* on a ley line and one that runs directly off of St Michael's. It starts at Hadrian's Wall, runs through Liverpool, Chester and Bristol, straight through Glastonbury and Stonehenge before ending a few hundred metres from here." Turning her head towards the window, she wagged her finger. "And that there crossroads sits smack-bang in the middle of it."

There was quiet as all sat in contemplation of this revelation.

"Wow!" Corinna exclaimed at last.

Ness was a harder nut to crack. "Did you test it, Theo?"

"Test it, what do you mean?"

"Type in other postcodes, see if miraculously a ley line runs through them as well."

"As a matter of fact, I did," she replied, smugly. "And no, a ley line does not run through every single address I could conjure up. Surprisingly, being as I live there, not even through my humble abode! And yes, I have to admit there is a disclaimer on the site, which says that ley lines don't actually exist, but that's just there to cover backsides. Of course they exist, and for a purpose too, and crossroads, as Ruby and I have already discussed, are another key feature. They're a place of worship and superstition, representing so much to man, both in a literal sense and a metaphorical one. That's why the membrane could be thin at sites such as this, simply because man *expects* it to be. Cash, we know what happened to Ruby at the pub, but tell Ness and Corinna how you got that rather nasty bruise on your arm."

Cash explained about the quartz. "Ruby has no idea how it got from the parlour to the single bedroom, but she's been sleepwalking a fair bit since we got here."

At his words, Ness was alarmed. "What does he mean by

that, Ruby?"

"It's just a couple of times actually," corrected Ruby, "I've started off in our bedroom and woken up in Mary's, with no recollection of how I got there."

"Mary's?" she queried.

Her eyes flickering upwards, Ruby nodded. "I suppose you guys want to carry out an initial survey?"

Ness and Theo rose simultaneously. "You suppose right," Ness answered.

Chapter Twenty-Seven

IN the parlour, Theo went straight to the far end of the room and placed her hands out in front of her, palms down.

"This is where the bar counter was, where Ward's body was laid out."

Remembering the flashback she'd had, Ruby nodded. "That's right."

"And bar sounds reverberate sometimes?" Ness checked.

Again Ruby nodded. "But it's mainly residual. This cottage retains a lot."

"Yes," Ness agreed, "like the little boy behind you that's dashed towards the door. A modern day chap judging by the way he's dressed, in jeans and a jumper and not even dead yet, I'll bet. He's just a memory, nothing more than that."

Ruby looked behind her, couldn't see anything out of the ordinary, the memory having vanished.

"And what about Jed, does he like it here?"

At his name, Jed materialised and started wagging his tail. "He doesn't like it upstairs," Ruby answered. "It's the floorboards that put him off, I think. Other than that, he seems happy enough, he comes and goes as he usually does."

"Ah, the coffin lids," Theo said, cottoning on to what Ruby was saying, "must get a gander at those too. Poor Jed, they offend his sensibilities, do they?"

Walking past the staircase, all three of the newcomers stood and stared upwards. "I don't blame, him," Corinna muttered. "I'm not too enamoured of them myself."

"Before we go up, let's go through to the lounge," Ruby suggested, "it's past this area, 'no man's land' I call it, a bit of a wasted space really. A cloakroom slash utility space I suppose, although directly above it is Mary's room."

"*Was* Mary's room," Ness corrected.

"That's what I meant," Ruby replied but Ness continued to look grave.

Standing in the living room, all eyes were drawn directly to the hook. "Yet another charming feature," Theo commented.

"That's where Ellen hanged herself from," Ruby informed them.

"Oh?" Ness walked over to it. "That's not the impression I get."

Ruby joined her. "What is your impression, Ness?"

"When Old Cross was a pub it was used to hang meat, nothing more than that."

"No, Ellen hanged herself from it. Mary showed me."

"Well, let's not argue," commented Theo. "One of you is bound to be right…"

"Yes, me!" Ruby insisted.

"Let's just… carry on with the tour, shall we?"

Slightly bewildered that they both seemed to doubt her, or rather Mary, Ruby showed them the tiny winding staircase, which Theo wouldn't even contemplate negotiating. "I'll get stuck," she declared, turning in the direction of the main staircase instead. "I'll take my chances with the coffin lids any day."

Once together on the landing, the five of them vied for

space.

"Over there is our room," Ruby pointed, "and that's a twin room. Behind us is the single bedroom." Quickly, she reminded them of the cottage layout during Mary's lifetime. "In the single bedroom there's now a doorway in the wall that leads to the main bedroom, and that's where she slept with Ellen, before William came along."

Although Ruby made to enter the single bedroom, Ness went in the direction of the twin bedroom, the one where Ruby had so recently seen hands at the window.

As the rest followed Ness, Ruby had no choice but to do the same.

In front of the twin beds, Ness closed her eyes, everyone affording her the silence she needed to tune in and make a connection. After a minute or two, she opened her eyes and spoke. "William certainly is in hiding, and he's very afraid."

"Of retribution?" asked Ruby.

"Retribution of sorts," Ness replied enigmatically. "But he's desperate to reach out, that's a plus point. As you've told him many times, Ruby, he can't hide forever."

Again, Ruby couldn't help but bristle. She got the impression that Ness seemed to think she meant it in a *threatening* way. Ness's gaze remained on her and Ruby was sure she'd caught that thought. If that was the case, however, she didn't comment.

The first to look away, Ruby suggested they go into Mary's room at last.

Shoulder to shoulder in the tiny room, Ruby was sandwiched in between Theo and Corinna. Eventually, Theo broke the silence. "I agree, the atmosphere's heavy in here. The emotions more intense than I've felt in a long while."

"Because she was a child," Ruby replied. "Children are

ruled by their emotions."

"True," Theo concurred, whilst Ness broke rank and crossed over to the mirror, the floorboards creaking under her feet, as loose now as they ever were. "See anything interesting?" Theo asked her. "Discounting your reflection of course."

"It's too dark to see properly."

Ruby frowned. What was Ness talking about? There wasn't a great deal of light upstairs, granted, but there was certainly enough to check your appearance in a mirror. Confused, Ruby led them through the door and into the main bedroom – where sweet seduction had so quickly turned into terrifying abuse.

"This was the room I was initially drawn to," she explained. "As soon as William came on the scene that changed to the single bedroom."

"Of course," Theo responded. "It would." Then, before Ruby could reply, she clapped her hands together. "I think we've seen enough for now. Later we'll need to spend time connecting more fully, but before we do that I believe we've several houses to visit, a pub, an oak tree and the vicar. Best start delegating tasks, I think."

* * *

Ruby had wanted to visit the Reverend Martin with Theo. If he had it in for her still, she'd prefer to fight her own battles. But Theo wouldn't back down.

"Take Cash and go and find the oak tree. I'll bet it's at the end of the ley line, a few hundred metres from the cottage, in a direct line south—"

"Its east, Theo, I'm sure of it, that's the direction in which she ran towards the cottage."

"And you've explored eastwards?"

"Well… yeah."

"Did you find anything?"

"Nothing significant, no."

"Then appease an old lady and try the south this time."

"I…" About to protest, Ruby faltered. Perhaps Theo was right.

"Without wishing to sound supercilious, darling, I certainly am right. And don't worry if there's a zillion oak trees that way too, trust to instinct, you'll find it."

Ruby nodded in defeat. "So, you're going to see the Reverend are you? What about the houses and the pub?"

"Corinna and Ness have agreed to deal with those initially, and then I'll join them, once I've steered him off the warpath. We can reconvene later this afternoon. Now," The briskness of Theo's voice indicated that as far as plans went, theirs was set in stone, "let me check those addresses with you again then we'll all be on our merry way."

When the team had left, Ruby stood staring at Cash. "I feel a bit… out on a limb. I know I wanted their help but it's like they've come down and taken over. They get to deal with the interesting parts and I get left with finding an oak tree!"

"Ruby, you've had a major blow to the head, remember? Let them do the hard work. The weather's good, a walk will be nice. Where's Jed?"

"He's here."

"Good, then let's enjoy a bit of time together, whilst we can, just the three of us."

Like we were supposed to, that was the intimation.

"Okay, okay," she sighed, "let's go. We'll search for an

hour or so but if we're on a highway to nowhere, like we were when we went east, then I'm going back into the village to help out, whether the Reverend likes it or not."

Cash nodded once in acquiescence and then grabbed his jacket.

"Have you got your phone with you?" Ruby asked as they trudged along the road they'd travelled previously in the taxi.

"Of course. You?"

"Aha." After a slight pause she asked him if *Ghost Discovery* was running.

Taking his phone out of his pocket, he fiddled with it. "It is now."

"Good," she said, aware that things perhaps were still slightly off between them but unsure what to do about it. She was too tired to tackle it alongside other issues, to be honest. She just wanted to focus, get as much done as possible.

A lovely day, the sun was shining, warming her skin – you could almost smell that summer was on its way; that lovely, balmy scent that held so much promise.

"It's pretty here, isn't it?" she said, almost to herself rather than Cash.

"It's lovely, what we've seen of it."

"We should come down again, explore a bit more."

He nodded. "If we can find the time."

If *she* could find the time. Again she caught the hidden meaning. Perhaps it was best if she just walked and didn't speak at all.

A few hundred metres was soon up – they'd need to veer off the road, to the right if they were to follow the cottage in a straight line, find an opening into one of the fields that lined the road – fields that were also full of oaks.

Coming to a standstill, she felt the same frustration as before.

"What were you saying about a highway to nowhere?" Cash muttered.

"Oh, all right, Cash, give it a rest!" she snapped. Strangely, Cash looked surprised by her reaction.

"I was just saying."

"That's just it, you're *always* just saying."

"Ruby—"

"Hang on," she interrupted, holding up a hand.

"What is it?"

"It's Jed, he's heading into that field over there." She pointed slightly southwest. "There's a clump of oaks right in the middle of it."

"So, what are we waiting for?"

Ruby continued staring. He was right. What were they waiting for? She needed to get moving, force her feet to work, place one in front of the other. *Force?*

It certainly felt like an effort, each leg as heavy as a block of stone. She also felt dizzy again and slightly nauseous, having to blink rapidly to try and clear her head.

"Come on, Ruby," Cash said, heading to where she'd pointed.

"All right, okay." *Thanks for helping,* she thought as he rushed forward. He hadn't noticed her predicament at all when usually he noticed everything.

"Ruby!"

"I'm coming!" she shouted.

Oh God, what was wrong with her? Stupid question. She *knew* what was wrong with her. She was still concussed. She might have got the all-clear, but the doctor had said symptoms could persevere for quite a while longer. She tried to remember what those symptoms could be: nausea, yep, that had returned. Dizziness, confusion – was she confused? Possibly. Cash had looked surprised that she'd snapped at him, was she misinterpreting the tone in his voice?

Taking a few steps, she stumbled slightly. Jed stopped barking to look at her instead as she did her utmost to reach him.

Was that someone hovering above his head?

Ruby blinked again, shook her head but gently, as the movement served only to increase her nausea. Yes, there was a figure. Thomas Ward?

Jed jumped up as she thought it and started pawing at the ground, not just one of him, but two. *Damn, I've got double vision now.*

Strange that symptoms of concussion should be assaulting her so suddenly, she'd been fine when she left the hospital, just a bit sore-headed. Certainly, she hadn't been suffering anywhere near as bad as this.

Again, she took a few steps, her hands held out either side for balance. There was definitely the body of a man swinging from the boughs of the tree – a man in similar clothing to the figure that had stood at the window of the double bedroom. It had to be Ward. In which case, where was Mary? She'd hanged herself too.

Listen! Leave!

The words were flung at Ruby, confusing her further.

Thomas? What's wrong? Why do you want us to leave?

Listen! Leave!

The words were hissed this time, echoing through the chambers of her mind.

Despite feeling so wretched, Ruby held firm.

No, Thomas, we're not leaving. I can see you, your body

hanging from the boughs. Jed is digging at the ground below. A thought struck her. *Is that where you're buried, Thomas? Underneath the tree where you died?* His body had lain for a week at Old Cross Cottage, whilst it was decided what to do with it. Had that been the final decision, to bury him there? In which case, was Mary buried there too? And how many others before them, whose bodies had also been cut down? Occupying the site where the ley line ended, the oak tree may well be a magnet, just as Golden Cap, as Beachy Head, as Old Cross Cottage were magnets. A death site. If she started digging, what secrets would be discovered?

LEAVE!

The word slammed into her as though it were a physical entity.

She closed her eyes again and was surprised when she opened them to find the ground so close. What was happening? Was she falling?

Once again she couldn't prevent herself from succumbing to darkness.

Chapter Twenty-Eight

"I'M warning you, Cash, don't you dare call the ambulance. I don't need to go to hospital again."

"Then we go back, and you rest. I'm not taking no for an answer, you blacked out."

"Just for a moment, that's all."

"It's enough."

"It's fine, *I'm* fine. That tree, the one Jed was sniffing around, the one that's set slightly apart, I saw Ward's body hanging from it."

"What about Mary?"

"No, I didn't see her. Here, help me up."

Where she'd fallen was still a fair way from the tree, she hadn't managed to get far at all. Despite the pain shooting through her head, she continued to stare, hoping to see something relating to Mary (if hope was the right word to use).

"There needs to be a dig under there, you know," she said.

"To find their bones?"

Ruby nodded.

"That's best left to the police."

Theo had said much the same thing regarding digging at the crossroads. But here, it was off the beaten track, not so obvious. "It's only really *her* bones I want."

"How would you know whose they were?"

"By handling them, hopefully."

"No, Ruby, it's just not ethical. Besides," he said, staring at the tree too, "they're beautiful trees, in a lovely setting. It's not a bad place for a body to be buried."

In a way, he was right. At least there was no swirling black mass hanging around, like there'd been at Golden Cap. "I wonder who decided to bury Ward there?"

Cash shrugged. "If Mary's here, someone would have to have buried her too. Who would have done that? And something else is bothering me…"

"What?"

"How does a kid go about hanging herself? How would she know what knot to tie in the rope, for instance? Also, what did she stand on before kicking it away?"

All of those questions had bothered Ruby too, but in her dreams Mary had stood in despair at the foot of the tree, not only that, but full of dark intent.

"William," Ruby answered. "It could have been William."

"Who hanged her?"

"No, who buried her."

"How would he have known where she'd gone?"

"Because it's where the desperate go, it's a magnet. If she'd disappeared, it wouldn't take a lot to work out where."

"But like I said, she'd have needed to be quite savvy to hang herself."

Again, Ruby tried to find answers. "Time had definitely passed in the dream, I'm not sure how much, but maybe she was thirteen, fourteen, around that age anyway. Teenagers have been known to hang themselves in the history of mankind, Cash."

"I know but it's usually in their own homes and a chair or

a desk is involved – I hardly think she'd have dragged something to stand on all the way out here."

"That would depend on how desperate she was."

"Ruby, come on—"

"Cash, I don't know," she admitted at last. "It's not *impossible* though, whereas her situation was." Having slumped, she tried to straighten. "I've got to go there, tune in."

"I'm getting you back to the cottage."

"Cash!"

"I either take you there or I take you to the hospital. No more digging around, in both senses of the word, not right this minute."

Her stomach heaving, she retched, but thankfully it was dry.

"See? I'm taking you back."

"You're trying to stop me."

Cash drew back. "I'm not, Ruby. I'm just being sensible."

She retched again. "Sorry, what are you talking about?"

"You said I was trying to stop you."

"Stop me doing what?"

"I don't know. Going to the oak tree I presume."

"Did I? I don't remember." Clearly, her confusion was getting worse. "Okay, okay, just… take me home."

It was the first time she'd called it that.

"Good, you're seeing sense at last."

"To be honest, Cash, I don't know what I'm seeing anymore."

* * *

Despite it being a warm day, it was chilly in the cottage, Ruby shivering as soon as she entered, Cash too. Jed had hesitated at the door, clearly enjoying the sun.

We'll get the fire going, she promised, wanting to keep him close and he duly stepped over the threshold.

She didn't need to instruct Cash regarding the fire; he led her through to the living room, made her sit down and then headed straight to the inglenook.

Settling herself, she looked again at the hook, tried to detect the shade of Ellen hanging from it, but was unable to. In the dream she'd been told *that's* what had happened but it wasn't a scene she'd actually witnessed. Just as she hadn't actually seen Mary hang herself. The oak tree too, the impression she'd been given regarding its location had been the wrong impression.

But Mary wouldn't lie to me, what would be the point?

"Fuck!" It was Cash swearing, jumping backwards at the same time.

"What is it, Cash, are you hurt?"

"Yeah… no… I'm all right. One of the flames sparked, that's all."

"Be careful," she warned.

"Yeah, I am. Don't worry."

The fire, crackling away, did little to take the chill off the atmosphere.

"Your phone," Ruby said, when Cash sat beside her. "Any activity on it?"

Inspecting it, he shook it a couple of times. "The radar seems to be stuck."

"Really?" she said, taking it from him so she could look too. "How strange. It could be a glitch. Try downloading it again or something?"

"Yeah, or an app that's similar. Give it back and I'll try."

After a few minutes, he cursed again.

"What's wrong now?"

"The battery's low. I've managed to download the app, but I'm only on about five per cent, I'm going to have to recharge it. What about your phone?"

"Hang on, let me get it. Here you go." Noticing his face as he looked at it, she asked what the matter was.

"You haven't got much battery left either but we'll give it a go. What's your password for the app store?"

She told him and he typed it in. Frowning, he asked her to repeat it before shaking his head.

"It's no good, it's not accepting it. Ah, and now your phone's dead as well." He sighed. "I'll go and put them on charge, we'll do it later perhaps."

"Okay."

"Cup of tea whilst I'm in the kitchen?"

"That'd be lovely, thanks."

She watched him as he stood up, a phone in each hand. Before he left, she called his name.

"Yeah?" he said, turning towards her, the light from the fire reflected in his eyes.

"I... I love you."

His surprised expression was almost comical, and then he broke into a grin. "I love you too. Any reason why you're making a point of it right now?"

"It's just... I know it's not easy being with someone like me."

"Believe it or not, Ruby, easy doesn't interest me."

She swallowed, tried to make light of it. "So you're not denying it then?"

He shook his head. "If you want me to patronise you, Ruby, you're out of luck. You're right, you're not easy to be with at times, but what you are is fascinating, funny, and ultimately kind. Everything you do, whether it's right or wrong, you do because of good intentions. But if you're angling for me to say what does annoy me about you, it's this. Forget good wolf, bad wolf, you're a lone wolf at times. There was never any need to lie to me about this cottage, I might have been pissed off at first but we'd have reached some sort of compromise about it, we always do. You have a team, people who love you, just remember that and don't shut us out."

His words seemed to hang in the air, long after he'd left the room.

* * *

It took a while for Ruby to understand what she was hearing. At first she thought it was Mary, whispering in her ear again, or praying, as she'd done so many times. In fact, she was sure it was but then, as she graduated to full consciousness, she realised there were two voices, both of which she knew well.

She was in the living room and clearly she'd been sleeping, as far as she knew without dreaming. It wasn't quite dark, but the day was definitely on the wane. In the fireplace, the flames had bedded in, not leaping about, trying to catch each other, lazier than that. Jed wasn't lying beside it, as he loved to do, perhaps he'd gone to sit with Cash as he talked to… Ness. That's it, that's who was in the kitchen with him, although she was keeping her voice low, as was Cash. Yawning, Ruby crept from the sofa to the door and opened it slightly so she could listen more intently.

"It's… village… happening… tied… okay?"

"Okay… unwell… sleeping… tree… what's… on?"

In a way the conversation reminded her of the *Ghost Discovery* app – words being thrown out at random and the user having to work to make sense of them. Corinna had suggested automatic writing in order to harness a similar energy, with Ruby volunteering Cash to take the lead in that particular activity, because he was William.

What?

Quickly she corrected herself: because he was *channelling* William – apparently. It could certainly prove interesting; they should try it tonight. This case was supposed to be wrapped up within twenty-four hours, so it was time to pull out all the stops.

"Theo… Reverend…"

Again, Ruby's ears pricked up. What had happened between Theo and the Reverend? Was she still with him?

"Theory… explore… Reverend… helping."

A theory? Who had a theory – Theo? And if so, the Reverend was helping her with it – actually assisting? That was a turn-up for the books.

"Interesting… Ruby… what… seems."

Ruby sighed in frustration. What was Ness saying about her?

"…worry… leave… "

Leave? Was someone going to leave?

"Keep…eye… stay."

What a relief! They were going to stay, of course they were. Why doubt it?

"Danger."

She frowned. Had Ness just said 'danger'? Her curiosity was at critical, but they'd lowered their voices further, making it even more difficult to hear. It was so quiet in fact that she heard whispering, just as she thought she'd done upon waking. And the temperature was dropping again; the room was cold, *she* was cold, causing her to shiver. The whispering was yet another series of words. Rapid. *Fervent.*

She swung round.

Mary?

There was a shadow, a shape, just beneath the hook, staring upwards – a child's shape, but fleeting, so fleeting, like the words she'd been listening to, barely caught.

She darted over to where the figure had been, felt the ground sway beneath her, as though she were on a ship's hull. Forcing herself to stand still, she listened again. Overhead there were footsteps – a *child's* tread – running across the main bedroom, a door opening and then slamming, the footsteps coming to a halt in the single bedroom – the in between room – somewhere as lost as this entire place, as the crossroads – caught between two worlds. And that's where Mary was, waiting…

The front door slammed. Clearly Ness had said all she wanted to say for the time being and gone back into the village to deal with the unrest. Upstairs, there was unrest too. Floorboards creaking now, not just from directly above, but the entire upstairs, the sound a ghastly chorus played especially for her.

Mary, tell me what you want.

The answer flew back at her.

You!

There were more footsteps. Cash was on his way back. With Mary's reply ringing in her ears she bolted to the sofa and jumped back on it, her eyes closing just before the door to the living room opened, adding its own creak to the cacophony in her head. Immediately Jed started to sniff around her, jumping up and nose-butting her a few times. There was no fooling him. But Cash was a different matter. She listened as he walked towards the fire and stoked it, sensed the flames jump to his command – *cold* flames – sensed too when he settled himself, not on the sofa, wary of disturbing her, but on the armchair, as close to the fire as possible.

Jed continued to nudge, to whine, clearly bewildered by her lack of response.

Just… go and sit by Cash, there's a good dog. I'm fine. I need to do something, that's all.

Go upstairs and see Mary, that's what. The child had shown herself – only the second time she'd done that – found the courage to step forward and not just within a dreamscape. But, at the risk of upsetting Cash again, she had to see her alone, because that's what Mary wanted. To do otherwise might cause her to hide again. Yes, there was danger, as Ness had said, but there was also the hope of an end in sight – at last. Although she hadn't heard fully the exchange between Ness and Cash, she'd been able to get the gist: *Don't leave Ruby, stay with her, until we get back.* But when would they get back? There was no telling. As for Theo's theory, what could she possibly know that Ruby didn't? After all, she was the one who'd been in the firing line all week, not just channelling Mary, *becoming* her at times.

Just as she'd hoped, Cash was snoring, a light but regular sound and proof that he was asleep – his body finally seeking reprieve from the events of last night and today. She opened her eyes and saw Jed staring at her, *pleading* with her.

Again she reassured him.

I'll be fine. Stay downstairs, you hear? Stay.

Tiptoeing from the room, she went towards the kitchen, the gloom of early evening having settled, casting shadows everywhere she looked, and in amongst them Thomas Ward, no doubt fearful, as William was fearful – but of what?

Thomas, I'll deal with you, she promised. And William. She'd deal with him too.

In the kitchen, she found her phone, checking it was fully charged. Shoving it in her pocket, she left the kitchen and parlour behind. Jed was at the bottom of the stairs, a pitiful expression on his face, doe-eyed almost, but she passed through him. He wouldn't follow; he'd been given his command.

As she climbed the coffin lid stairs, the creaks continued, the cottage coming to life around her. On the landing, a door opened, not William's room – that remained firmly shut. Only the door to the double bedroom was open, just a fraction, Thomas Ward having shifted upstairs alongside her, but only daring to peek.

You're all so afraid!

The thought occurred with glee. No, not with glee, there was triumph in it.

Ruby!

The sound of her name being called startled her.

"Cash, is that you?"

No, she was confused again, her mind a quagmire. It had to be Mary.

Me… Find Me.

As she turned to the left and pushed open the door that had once been locked, she heard Ward for the umpteenth time begging her to leave.

Chapter Twenty-Nine

THE room was empty as Ruby stepped inside. No matter. She'd expected it to be. Such a small room, a corridor really; a room that should lead somewhere but instead held you captive. The epicentre, or at least it had become so, ever since Mary.

Poor Mary.

The thought seemed to have a life of its own.

"I'm here now," Ruby whispered. "And I won't leave. I promise."

But she had to coax her out first.

Lock the doors!

Yes, of course! That might help her to feel more secure; it was, after all, what she was used to. But how could she do such a thing? There were no locks, not anymore.

Barricade yourself in.

That would work. She'd haul the chest of drawers against one door and the bed against the other.

Putting the idea into action, she winced as the feet of both the bed and the chest of drawers scraped against the floorboards. Surely such a racket would wake Cash up? Then again, she often thought he'd sleep through an earthquake.

With both exits blocked, she sat down, caught her breath, and let the darkness in the room take hold. It was strange how the spirits preferred darkness, even though they were so in need of the light. It offered plenty of hiding places she supposed, so she'd let the darkness be; perhaps it suited her purpose too. Sitting in the middle of the room, she focused on her phone. Should she do this, was it a mistake?

Do it!

Whose was that thought? Hers, or Mary's? As in dreams, the boundaries were blurred. Releasing her breath, she accessed the app store and typed in *Ouija*. Several options came up. Corinna had planted the seed of this idea, and now it was growing in substance. Theo and Ness would never approve and in truth, neither did she, but if it was a way to get Mary to communicate more fully, she had to try.

In the end, she opted for *Spirit Board,* only mildly amused by the warnings that came with it: '*Welcome to the world of the paranormal, proceed with severe caution. The secrets Spirit Board reveals can sometimes be treacherous. Men and women have gone mad because of it, lost forever in the demon realm.'*

God, they liked to ham it up the people who created these apps! Then again, she supposed, such words would have the desired effect on some and put them off for life. Others, however, were not so easily deterred.

Waiting for it to load, she read the instructions – they'd be different to that of a physical board. Apparently she was to hold the Spirit Board flat and place her thumbs on two of the four Spirit Disks located at the corners of the board, in order to connect with it. She must not attempt to hold the Spirit Board still or make the planchette go where she consciously wanted it to go. All pretty standard stuff so far. Instead, she had to focus on the issue in mind and allow herself to enter a meditative stage, letting the planchette move freely, guided by forces she might not understand.

A wry laugh escaped her. She understood all right.

There was one more instruction – a recommendation not to undertake this 'perilous journey' alone, but to have a 'trusted friend' in tow. It was sound advice but again, she couldn't go against Mary's wishes – not if she wanted results.

Placing the mobile on the floor, she tuned in, the light from it eerie and causing more shadows to accumulate. She should really spend some time focusing on light of a spiritual kind, surrounding herself in it, but she was conscious of the time, that Cash could wake any minute and notice she was gone again; that Theo, Ness and Corinna might not be as long as she thought, and if they found her doing this…

She had to remind herself that Mary was a child, an abused, tortured, and betrayed child. She had nothing to fear from her.

And likewise Mary, you have nothing to fear from me. I'm here to help you, I've promised you and I won't go back on that. If you come forward now, I'll take your hand, I'll walk with you to the light. You're not alone, not anymore.

The silence was maddening – Mary had said that once.

Then speak to me via the Ouija. You can do that, I know you can. We're safe in here. It's just you and me, like you wanted. Please communicate, don't be scared.

Incredibly the planchette started to move – randomly at first, gliding over the letters of the alphabet, the numbers from 0 to 9. *'Yes'* and 'no' were either side of the board and 'goodbye' at the bottom – all very traditionally laid out against a sepia background. 'Good luck', that's what Ouija was supposed to mean – an innocent enough sentiment, depending on which way you looked at it.

Relaxing into the game, she let the planchette go where it wanted. Tried not to influence what was happening in any way.

S C A R E D

That was the last word on her mind – her subconscious influencing it after all?

Moving the planchette back to base, she tried again.

Mary, I understand you're scared but there's no need.

Again the planchette moved.

H E R E

If you're here then come forward, take my hand. This can end now.

S A F E

You are safe, I'm with you, and I won't leave until you're in the light.

D A R K

You were never meant for the darkness, Mary.

Without warning the mobile span round and shunted forward a few feet as if it had been pushed, landing in the centre of one of the floorboards.

"Mary, why did you do that?"

When there was no reply, she shifted onto her knees and crawled across the floor towards it, placing it back down in front of her again, her thumbs in position.

Mary, if I'm here with you, what are you so afraid of? It's time to leave this place.

Nothing happened and then, to her relief, more words were spelt out.

Y O U

Yes, Mary, I'll guide you.

M E

We're together now.

H I M

Don't be afraid of William.

H U R T

I won't let him hurt you. Walk with me to the light.

N O

Mary…

N O

The light is home.

S U F F E R

You don't need to suffer anymore.

H I M

Or be afraid of him. Trust me.

S C A R E D

I know, darling, I know you are.

H U R T

You've been so hurt. The thought formed in her head again, *Poor Mary, poor, poor Mary.*

C O M I N G

What do you mean? Who's coming?

O T H E R

Ruby frowned. *What other?*

S C A R E D

Mary, listen…

L I S T E N

Ruby stiffened. That word. Was it again a reflection of what was in her subconscious, or had the 'other' somehow managed to connect too.

Who is this? Is this Mary, or someone else?

Q U I C K

Again Ruby was stumped. Was she the one who had to be quick, or the spirit that was responding?

L I S T E N

"I am listening!"

L E A V E

It wasn't Mary. Around her the atmosphere had changed, strangely it had become less oppressive. It was one of the others, chasing poor Mary away.

S C A R E D

And yet Mary had used that word too. What was going on?

"Who is this? Who's here?"

H U R T

"Thomas? William?"

Y O U

"Which one is it?"

M E

"I don't understand."

H I M

The planchette moving rapidly, she stopped asking questions, had no time as more words were spelt out.

D E V I L

O N

H E R

B A C K

What was that supposed to mean?

Again the planchette whirled round the board.

P O O R

M A R Y

P O O R

P O O R

M A R Y

Yes, poor Mary, of course poor Mary.

N O

Y E S

N O

Y E S

N O

Ruby stared in disbelief. "Thomas or William, try and understand, I need to contact Mary first. I'll help her, and then I'll help you. She's a child, just a—"

N O
N O T
C H I L D
Y E S
C H I L D
N O
Y E S
N O

It seemed to be some kind of tug of war and she the one caught in the middle. "Whoever else is here, step aside, Mary comes first. *Poor Mary, poor, poor Mary*—"

Ruby inhaled.

Those last few words, they'd been pushed into her brain, forced through her mouth. The concussion aside, she was more confused than ever.

"What's happening?" she whispered, as much to herself as to anyone.

Whatever doubts she'd had, they began to magnify. She shouldn't have done this, come in here and dabbled with the Ouija of all things. Okay, she was desperate, but she'd been desperate before and not resorted to such measures.

T O O
L A T E

No longer cold, heat swamped her, beads of sweat breaking out on her forehead. It *was* too late, concerning the Ouija, but she'd employed it because a child was in peril. Even so, did that give her license to be so reckless? *Playing with fire...* Just like her mother had done before her, the consequences of which had been severe.

N O T
C H I L D

No sooner had the words been spelt out then the mobile flew upwards. Ruby rocked back on her heels, again with no clue as to who the entity was that had snatched it, watching as it rocked from side to side, the fight continuing.

"Show yourselves, please. Let me see what's going on here!" Ruby pleaded, having to swerve to avoid the increasingly violent movement. In her chest her heart was hammering so loudly it seemed to deafen her and then suddenly, quite suddenly, the phone was still, albeit hovering just a few inches from her face.

Was the fight over, she wondered, the other having fled? That hope was dashed when the phone was flung with considerable force at the mirror.

Fully expecting the next sound to be that of shattering glass, the phone missed and hit the wall instead, falling to the floor to lie discarded.

Ruby got to her feet. The mirror – she remembered taking pains to avoid it before but she couldn't do so again. Whoever had thrown the phone, wanted her to look, to see what was in it, the gloom not a hindrance for her as it had been for Ness.

Her breathing erratic, she began her approach. The phone was laying screen side up and again the glare that it cast was eerie, somewhere in between the light and the dark, as Mary was, as William and Thomas were, as she was too. On it, the planchette was counting backwards from 9 all the way to 0, slowly but surely.

Dragging her eyes from the phone to the mirror, she leaned forwards and peered. At first she recognised the reflection: the brown hair was her own, her skin pale, her eyes wide, haunted almost, and full of expectation. Then slowly it began to change – like a scrying mirror might change as you continued to stare at it, features growing hazy, blurring, forming again. No longer her face, but that of someone else's.

Ellen?

Was the dark, elusive presence her all along? The downtrodden, beleaguered mother? Her spirit grounded when she'd thought it had flown.

But Ellen had had red hair, cascades of it. The person staring back at her was blonde, and not a child. She was all grown up.

Ruby's heart lurched, understanding what the countdown signified.

Here was a woman with the devil on her back, a woman who'd prayed and prayed when she was young, who'd begged someone to listen, anyone, and they had. Because there was *always* someone listening – even when you didn't think so.

There was no point in hiding, in pretending, not now that she'd been seen. As soon as the planchette landed on zero, Mary stepped forward – a portal having been wantonly opened. Closer she came, closer still, stopping in front of Ruby – the same height and stature as her, but older, much older – before moving forwards again.

It didn't start here.

No, it had started in the room next door.

But this is where it will end.

Before consciousness faded, there was a noise – in the distance somewhere – a dog barking, becoming more and more agitated, and then Ruby heard no more.

Chapter Thirty

"RUBY, Ruby, where are you?"

It was the man. He was coming. Standing in the centre in the room, she looked around and blinked a few times. At her side she flexed her fingers, as if circulation was poor and she needed to revive them. Her legs were as unsteady as a foal's, but rapidly she gained in confidence, taking a step forward, and then another.

Beside the bed that was blocking the door to the landing, she waited as patiently as she'd ever done.

The man came to a halt outside the door, perfectly still as if he was listening too – just like the other one used to... the one that was here before her... that was still here – silent at times but not at others, whispering continually about damnation. Oh, how terrified she'd been at first, how she'd wanted to run from the room, from the cottage, into the arms of the night, find some sort of sanctuary, away from demons both living and dead. And then slowly, over the years, all fear had left her, replaced by anger instead and a thirst for something else, for vengeance of course, on her mother, on William, on everyone. Damned? They all were. And she'd happily damn them further.

"Ruby, are you in here again?"

She stared as the door handle twisted, first one way and then the other, imagined the puzzled look on his face as the door refused to open. A physical barrier against a physical body but it was what was inside him she wanted: the one that hid.

"Ruby, what's going on? Open the door!"

He was banging now, his shoulder against the door as he pushed against it, still calling Ruby's name, no longer cool, but panic beginning to set in; an *awareness*.

"Hang on," she found her voice at last. "Wait a minute. The bed is in the way."

She'd let him in, of course she would. That was her aim: to draw William out, to make him suffer, just as he'd made her suffer, and for so long.

Poor, Mary, poor, poor Mary.

Words she hated but which, ultimately, had proved so useful.

"What's the bed doing in front of the door?"

"I'll explain, in just a minute."

"Hurry up."

"I am hurrying, the bed's heavy, that's all."

William, William, William. With their arrival he'd reached out, not to the girl, the one who could see, but to the man, growing bolder after all. He'd tried to 'connect' as they'd put it, to explain his plight, wanting someone to understand him, seeking to be absolved. No! All their talk of the light, she'd borne it, but no more.

Putting her hands on the steel frame of the bed, its coldness shocked her. Such a strange sensation after all these years: the feel of something solid. But there was no time to revel in it. She had to hurry. The girl was strong and fighting back. *Poor, Mary, poor, poor Mary.* Immediately the girl's struggle ceased.

There! He could enter. The way was clear.

Within seconds the door flew open, banging against the side of the bed and flying back to hit him although he lifted his arm to soften the blow.

"Thank God! Ruby, are you okay?"

"I'm… I'm fine."

He shook his head as though perplexed. "One minute you're downstairs asleep," he paused for a moment, shrugged slightly, "admittedly so was I – the next minute I've woken up and you've gone again. Do you remember getting here this time?"

"I remember everything."

"Oh, good, that's good." There was relief on his face. "Shall we… erm, go downstairs and wait for the team to come back?" A shiver ran through him, as well it might. "God, this cottage is cold. Come on, Ruby, let's go downstairs."

"I don't want to go downstairs."

That surprised him. He looked around, saw that the chest of drawers had been moved too, his eyes widening before suspicion set in. "Ruby…"

"Yes?"

"What's going on in here? That door's been blocked off, this door too until you moved the bed. Had you locked yourself in or something?"

She nodded.

"Why?"

"It's what I'm used to."

"What *you're* used to? You mean it's what Mary was used to?"

Again she nodded.

He reached out. "Rubes, I'm thinking it might be worth getting you checked out again. At the hospital, they said to

301

come back if symptoms continued or got worse."

"There's nothing wrong with me."

"Ruby—"

"We are who we are. Even in death."

Again, the confusion was all his, fear creeping in too, as it always did, even in those you thought that fear could never touch.

"I think I'd better call Theo, you know, get her to—"

She waited until the phone was in his hand and then reacted like lightning. Dashing forward, her fist smashed it from his hands, both of them watching as it crashed to the floor. Next, she banged the door shut, obliterating the light from the landing, the darkness she'd grown used to wrapping itself around them.

"You're going nowhere, William."

"William? What are you...? I'm not William, I'm Cash."

"I know you're in there."

"Who? William? Ruby, just come downstairs."

She stepped back as he reached out. "Don't touch me. Don't you dare touch me!"

At once the man's features hardened. "I don't know what's got into you, Ruby, but this is ridiculous. We're going downstairs." He quickly reconsidered. "Actually, we're going outside, you need some fresh air, we both do. It was cold but now it's... stifling in here." Leaning forward, he seemed to scrutinise her. "You don't seem yourself, Ruby. I'm not taking no for an answer. We've got to get out of here."

As quick as she'd been when she'd slapped the phone from his hands, she darted to the bed. Lying hidden beneath the covers was what she wanted. What she'd snatched from the kitchen whilst the girl had fetched the phone.

Only briefly did she have to force her fingers to close

round the handle – *poor Mary, she suffered so much, remember?* The hand relaxing, she brought it upwards. She didn't want him to die straightaway, not this time. That had been a mistake; one she'd rectify. And Ellen? That had been a mistake too, setting her on this path.

Just his eyes had time to react to her actions, such disbelief in them. They were dark whereas William's had been midnight blue, but he was in there somewhere, he'd come to the fore. He wouldn't want her to destroy his only chance of salvation.

A satisfying scream as the knife slashed the skin on his left arm, not sinking into bone and sinew, not yet. His body remained something to toy with first. Staggering backwards, he lost his footing and fell against the door, clutching his arm as he fell.

"Ruby, what the... why did you do that?"

"Ruby's gone."

"Gone?" He had to stop, catch his breath again. "Then who are you?"

"Mary."

"Mary?"

"And you're William."

The man shook his head. "No, no I'm not, I'm Cash. Oh, shit, my arm. That hurt, Ruby!"

With his good arm he tried to push himself upwards but she issued one simple command: "Don't," the knife held aloft again, a clear threat that she'd use it again. After some hesitation, he obeyed.

"Ruby, stop this. The others—"

"Are busy, you said so."

"But they'll be back soon."

"By which time it'll be too late."

He looked up again, those eyes wide, so wide. "What do you mean too late?" A snort, derisive almost. "Surely you don't mean to kill me."

"Not yet, not straight away, not like last time." She stopped, her own breathing becoming erratic as she remembered. "You escaped so easily didn't you? One blow to the head was all it took. I kept yelling at you, 'come back, come back', screaming at the top of my voice but it was no good, no good at all. You're the real bastard here, William! I had such plans for you, out there in the woods. You're such a bastard! It was you responsible for Mam's death and for all the deaths that came thereafter. They were all because of you." Tears threatened to explode but she blinked her eyes, refusing to let them fall. "I know you're in there, William. You think you've found a way out, an escape route. But I told you, just before you closed your eyes for good, that you were damned as much as me. Remember? I told you only hell was waiting. That's why you fled to the cottage, wasn't it, so you could hide from the devil? You found your way back so easily. When I realised, I was so surprised…" She shook her head, still surprised. "But I'm worse than the devil. That's what I became when you stole my dreams, stole everything. I prayed and I prayed, just like the other one that's here prayed, and at last someone listened – but not God. Oh no, not him, the *opposite* of God, but he became my god nonetheless. Such promises were made. I could kill you again, just as long as I fed him whilst I was still alive, so that's what I did, year upon year. I fed him well."

There was a light sheen on the man's face as he stared at her, took in all she was saying. "I'm not William, I'm Cash, just Cash. Don't take your anger out on me."

"GET AWAY!" she screamed, making him jolt. "GET

AWAY FROM THE DOOR!"

"The door? Why? What are you—?"

"MOVE!"

As quickly as he could, he shuffled along, keeping his back close to the wall.

Grabbing the bedframe she moved it across to block the door again, just as another banged elsewhere.

"It's not your friends," she said, desperate to snuff out any hope in him. "It's the other one, getting agitated, but there's nothing he can do, he's afraid of me too now. There's no one to stop me. I'm dragging you down to hell."

As quick as she'd been, the man lunged forwards. Making contact with her, the knife dropped to the floor and so did she, with each of them making a grab for it. He reached it first but she struck out with her foot, hitting him square in the face and causing him to lose his grip. She flailed around. Where was it? Where was the damned knife? When her hand closed around it again, elation surged. Bringing it round in an arc, she drove it into flesh this time, relishing the cry that emerged.

"Suffer, William, like I suffered! And in hell I'll make you suffer more."

He rolled away from her, clutching at his shoulder now, and groaning. "Ruby… Ruby… Stop this! Come back… you have to come back."

"My name is Mary!" she hissed. "Get against the wall."

He obeyed, pain distorting his face as he shuffled backwards.

"Let me go, Ruby. I'll get help, I promise. We both need help."

Flying towards him again, her face was mere inches from his. "I don't need anything, except to hurt you, when will you understand that?"

"In hurting me, you hurt yourself."

Such harsh laughter escaped her. "What's this? What's this? Are you trying another tactic, William? To get me to see the error of my ways?"

"No... I—"

"What about the error of *your* ways?"

"Mary..."

At the use of her name, she gasped, fell back a little. "William, it *is* you, isn't it?"

"Yes, it's me."

"I knew it! I knew you were in there. You can't hide forever, none of us can. We have to pay for what we've done."

"I'm sorry."

"You're sorry?" she screeched. "Sorry isn't good enough!"

The man lifted his head to look in her eyes. "But, Mary, it's all I've got."

Chapter Thirty-One

"RUBY, Cash, where are you? Jed came to find us. Where are you? Cash, answer me if you can!"

The shouting from downstairs caused her to falter as her head whipped towards the door – it *was* his friends. The shadow dog, the one that accompanied the girl, had warned them. No matter, the doors were barred, the prisoner held within.

Turning her head back, she repeated, "They can't stop me, William. They couldn't then and they can't now. People are stupid, so stupid. They only see what they want to see, not what's plain, what's obvious. They're easy to fool and they're easy to hurt." Her breathing had grown ragged again. "The pain in their eyes... Oh, it was wonderful to see. It was like a salve, a comfort. Strange, that pain can be such a comfort; it was a revelation, something to warm a cold, cold heart. My God made me realise what a pleasure it could be and I'm grateful, *eternally* grateful. That's the deal, you see: I'm his forever, willingly. You are too, although not as willing as I."

"Mary," his voice was tired, laboured even. "You did *not* make a pact with the devil, and you're not damned, nor is William and nor is the other one, Thomas Ward. You just *think* you are. No matter what you've done, you belong in the light."

"SHUT UP! SHUT UP! SHUT UP!" she screamed, unable to help it, his words as much a blow as any he could deliver physically. "JUST SHUT UP!"

There were footsteps on the stairs, several pairs of them, her screams having alerted them to their exact location. There was scratching and sniffing too, it was the dog braving the floorboards, detecting what was beneath them perhaps? So what. Let them find out what's there, the names that she had scratched, the dates. They were coffin lids and so she'd made use of them, their deaths recorded at Old Cross Cottage as well as on headstones in the churchyard.

Outside they were continuing to call, banging as he had done, heaving their weight against the door, but it held firm. And then one of them gasped. "Oh my God! Oh my God!" It was the younger one, the one with hair so like Ellen's. "There are names on the underside of these boards, and look at this, it's a scrap of clothing, seems to be made of linen I think, and a tassel, the kind you'd find on a baby's shawl. There are other things too, a rattle, a silver chain, some spectacles. Relics. Is… is that what you'd call them?" She hesitated again, "Or souvenirs?"

There was silence for a moment and then another woman started talking, the eldest of the three. "So my theory's correct, although there's no joy in that, in any of this. Mary, is William in there with you?"

So she knew who they were, their true identities? And yet the one in front of her slumped against the wall, violent shivers coursing through him, repeatedly denied it.

"Mary." It was the older woman again, the one they called Theo, her voice calm, melodic almost. "Is William speaking to you? What's he saying?"

Turning her attention from him, she looked towards the

door. "Lies is what he's saying, all lies. Ha!" She spat the word out. "He's even said he's sorry. Can you believe such a thing? But he's not, and I'm not either, I'm not sorry at all."

"Does he deny who he is?"

Deny? "Yes, he does, sometimes, I—"

"Does he pretend he's Cash?"

Looking back at him, she said, "Cash?"

Again, there was hope in his voice. "Ruby?"

No, I'm not Ruby, I'm not! "William, you're William!"

In the darkness, she could sense he was doing his utmost to rally. "I'm Cash, and you're Ruby, and you love me, remember? You said so, before... before all of this."

Love?

"And, Ruby, I love you. Whatever happens, whatever you do, I love you."

She closed her eyes. That's what William said. When he was hurting her, taking what he shouldn't. How dare he say such a thing? How dare he!

"YOU DON'T KNOW WHAT LOVE IS!" The spittle flew from her mouth.

"Mary, let him speak. Let William speak," Theo implored.

"NO!"

"Mary, you've waited for William all these years, now see what it is he has to say before you... deal with him. That's all I'm asking."

There was another voice, male – words tumbling from his mouth, reminding her of the other one, how they'd tumbled from his mouth too.

"Who's there with you?"

"My colleagues, Ness and Corinna, and also the Reverend Martin."

"The Reverend?"

"That's right, of St Winifred's Church, in the village."

"Is he praying?"

"Yes, for all of you."

She scrambled to her feet and ran towards the bed. "I DON'T NEED HIS PRAYERS!"

"Yes, you do, Mary, for what you've done. But you're not a demon, even so. None of you are demons. The only hell that exists is the one you've created."

"No hell? So he gets away with it, does he? With everything he did?"

"No, Mary, he won't. He'll feel your pain as keenly as you do, and he'll feel the most terrible remorse. I think he's remorseful even now. William, am I right? That's why he's grounded you see, why so many remain grounded. Death has this way of putting so much into perspective, of making you realise the effect your actions had on others, of making you suffer them too. If you let him speak, you'll see that he's sorry. That's what he's been trying to tell you, through Cash, just how sorry he is."

"If you knew what he'd done, what I've done…"

"We do know what you've done," another voice, more sombre in tone, belonging to the woman with black hair. "And yet still we want to help. You *deserve* help."

"But the children, all the children…"

"Are at rest now, their parents too, we've seen to that. Now it's your turn."

She took a step back. "You know nothing. There's no rest for the likes of us."

It was the elder lady again. "Ellen didn't end her own life, despite her despair. When you were alone with her, you tried again to get her to listen to you, didn't you, to escape from William, to find a way. But she was so beaten, so cowed, she refused. Where would you go, she wondered. What would you do? She'd made a fresh start once and it had ended in disaster. Who's to say it wouldn't happen again? And so you grew angry, rightfully angry in my opinion – she was your mother, in charge of your wellbeing – and in your anger you pushed her, as you pushed Ruby, rushed at her and she fell back, hit her head against the stove door, the blow proving fatal. And he came back, William I mean, and saw what you'd done, saw his chance too – to stop you from ever seeking any more help. He hung her body from the hook and sent you into the village to say your mother had committed suicide. She'd left you both alone, and yet still you hoped that someone would ask *why* she'd done such a thing. But no one did. And so his plan worked, you were at his mercy."

A tear! Damn it, there was a tear on her face. With both hands she palmed her eyes, silently threatened to gouge them out if they betrayed her again.

"Ellen's death was recorded in the parish records, 1907 it was, so was her marriage, to William Cannon in 1904. There was no mention of you, Mary, not at that point. William's death was also recorded, in 1914. Murder; a passing vagrant probably held responsible rather than you. Why would anyone suspect you? They'd pity you, wouldn't they, the villagers? They always had. *Poor Mary, poor, poor Mary.* They might even take a bit more notice of the orphan from thereon in, especially if you were doing something valiant, such as training to be a nurse, showing incredible dedication, rising, like a phoenix, in their eyes anyway, from the ashes of such a broken childhood. In 1914, what would you have been, seventeen, eighteen? It was the year that war broke out and there were very few if any resources to investigate William's death, but on the other hand, plenty of resource for a girl like you to learn about medicine and to use that knowledge in the darkest of ways."

"They buried him in the churchyard," she spat, "on *consecrated* ground."

"Yes, his gravestone's there, Mary, but it's a simple marker, and the inscription on it is fading, making it hard to read. I'd give it a couple more years before it fades entirely. Another good thing, it isn't next to your gravestone, it's nowhere near."

Again, she had to screw her eyes shut to stop the tears. That *was* one good thing, the thought of lying close to him again intolerable.

"Mary," the old woman continued, "between 1939 and 1945 – during World War Two this time – there were a high number of deaths in and around this parish, something our friend the Reverend here was well aware of and had always wondered about. A few adults but mainly children, as they're easier to kill I suppose – more vulnerable, just as you were vulnerable when you were a child. You identified with them more."

She swallowed, her chest heaving. How strange to hear it all again.

"Once more the war detracted from the truth, gave you leeway. What poison did you use, Mary? Was it arsenic? Similar to another serial killer in history, one that didn't get away with it, who was named Mary too; Mary Ann Cotton. She was hanged for her troubles. But then she was just an ordinary woman, not someone held in high esteem, working for the community, as you were. In so many ways nurses and doctors are like gods, no one thinks to question them, everyone trusts them... Well, they did back then, not so much now, to be honest. Someone might think, fleetingly, that their child, their mother, their brother or their sister, should have survived, that they hadn't been *that* ill, but if you don't overdo it, if you space the deaths out, again people turn a blind eye, believe what they want, what they need to, in order to survive the grief. Any guilt that might surge is suppressed... for a while at least. You were clever, Mary, such a bright little girl. That's how you presented yourself to Ruby isn't it? Not as the adult you grew to be. So much easier to manipulate her that way."

Tears! Damn them for falling! And the girl within her – Ruby – was stirring again.

"How did you die, Mary, a couple of years after the second world war? Not of natural causes, you were only fifty. Did you poison yourself?"

"Stop him praying!" she screamed in answer. "The Reverend, stop him!"

"Okay, okay." There were more whispered words and then silence.

"I couldn't wait anymore," her voice was a whisper too at first. "I knew William was here, I knew it. I'd come visiting, you see; whenever the cottage lay empty, jemmy a door open, or a window. It wasn't hard. Most of them were rotten anyway. I'd wander from room to room; it was neglected, but it wasn't empty, far from it. I'd sense William, as well as the other one. He was still here, still full of anguish. I'd threaten them both; tell them I was coming for them too. I promised, I did, as I sat and carved the names of my victims – relishing that I wasn't the victim any longer. I'd been one for long enough. In 1946, I called Old Cross Cottage home again – a dream come true in many ways. Ironic isn't it, that it should be so? But once I was back I could torment my tormenters more fully, be as relentless as they'd been, as merciless."

There was only one room she'd shunned since her return, the room with the hook in, because of Ellen. *Poor, poor Ellen...* No! She mustn't think that! She mustn't weaken. Her mother was the one who'd invited him in. She'd deserved to die!

"Mary, what happened at the oak tree?"

The oak tree? Where vengeance was exacted and proved so... disappointing.

"I lured him there..."

"William?"

"Of course William! He followed me like the dog that he was as I promised such delights. Whilst he unbuttoned his trousers, I bent down, retrieved a heavy stone I'd hidden, one I could stun him with and then... well then, the torture could begin. Out there, even further from the village, no one would hear him scream. I wanted to savour the fear in his eyes when it dawned on him that his life was in my hands, just as mine had been in his, to bask as I took that life from him, destroyed it as he'd destroyed mine, as I took my revenge. God, I wanted revenge, on everyone who'd ever hurt me and if not them directly, I'd hurt those they held dear. They'd feel what I'd felt for so many years – the *despair*." She stopped, choking on her own tears. "Such a big man he was but he fell so easily. I fell too, onto my knees, I cursed him and damned him, I told him that it wasn't over, that the only gates open to him were the gates of hell, that I'd find him there, I'd hunt him down. He thought he'd be safe at the cottage. What a fool! As soon as I realised he was here... that my god had listened, *really* listened... Oh, it was a miracle! Like I said, I couldn't wait any longer, I had to force the issue, turn my hand against myself – end my life too. Because

I'd promised, you see. And like my god, I don't break promises."

"But, Mary, you're breaking a promise right now."

"What?" she spluttered. "What do you mean?"

"You're crying, which is something you vowed never to do again. And it's okay to cry. Do you know why? Because some promises should never be made."

"I… I'M GOING TO KILL HIM!"

"Mary, calm down!"

"I WANT HIM DEAD!"

"He's dead already."

"I… I…"

"Mary, listen, please listen, you've got to let go of all this hurt inside you."

Again her head whipped from side to side, it wasn't just the old woman who'd said those last words but other voices too, a chorus of them, coming from inside her and in the air around – imploring, begging, demanding that she let go.

Thrashing her head from side to side, she tried to rid herself of their unwelcome instruction but instead they increased in volume, deafening her. Enraged, she rushed to the bed and thrust her knife into the mattress, over and over again, ripping it apart, feathers flying into the air like dozens and dozens of frenzied angels.

"Ruby, Ruby!" Another voice added to the mix, the man behind her.

"I'M NOT RUBY!"

"You are, you're Ruby, *my* Ruby."

His? She'd never belong to anyone but her god, only he deserved such loyalty.

"Mary, the Reverend wants to pray for you, and for all those trapped at Old Cross Cottage. And I'm going to pray with him."

Pray? Why did she keep insisting? Didn't they realise their god was useless? Worse than the devil, he glorified in suffering, *her* suffering. He'd allowed it.

"Mary, for me, God is the Higher Power, the Light. I know what you're thinking, that he abandoned you, when you needed him so much, but the Light never abandons anyone, it's always there, waiting for you to come back to it."

Shut up! Shut up!

"Reverend, are you ready? Hail Mary, full of grace…"

The mattress annihilated, she span on her heel, went over to the curtains, tore them down and with her bare hands ripped them into shreds.

"Our Lord is with thee…"

She remembered praying to her namesake as well as God. Such a futile gesture.

"Blessed art thou among women…"

She was cursed, and so she'd cursed others, fed her god as she'd promised. *And I don't break promises, I don't!*

"… and blessed is the fruit of thy womb, Jesus."

Wasn't *every* child supposed to be blessed, to be cared for? Even bastard children!

"Holy Mary, Mother of God…"

Unholy Mary, that's what she was… what she wanted to be. She would never go to the light. She would never forgive.

"… pray for us sinners…"

The light would expunge her because of her sins, the deaths she had wrought.

At the chest of drawers, she pulled every drawer out and kicked at them, not heeding the pain, slipping only once on the floor, on the blood that had been shed.

"… now and at the hour of our death."

The hour of her death, so swiftly it had come. In this room, this tiny cell-like room, she'd drunk poison too, increasing it day by day until she was drowning in it, her life playing out before her, even as her stomach convulsed, in a series of images, some she couldn't bear to relive, not again, and none that brought the satisfaction she'd craved. So she'd find satisfaction in death, was *still* seeking it.

"Amen."

She fell to her knees, prised her fingers in between the gaps of the loose floorboard, pulled, and pulled, working it loose – ignoring the splinters that embedded themselves in her hands, until finally it was free. *Amen.* It was the same word she'd scratched on there, not as an adult, but as a child; a lonely, hurt, and bewildered child. 'Agreed', that's what it meant. She'd asked her mother once, who in turn had asked Father Gabriel after service one day. And she'd done just that, agreed a pact with her god, who was Satan – the fallen, an outcast, as she was an outcast. No heavenly father for her, no earthly father, and no wretched stepfather!

Rocking back and forth, she hugged the floorboard as though it were the most precious thing in the world. "I promised," she said. "I promised."

"Cash, Cash, are you all right?"

"I'm all right, Theo, I'm all right. Keep doing what you're doing, keep praying."

The man, who'd been sitting in the corner, watching her silently, started crawling towards her. "Don't," she said or tried to say but her voice caught.

"Ruby—"

"I'm not Ruby."

"You *are* Ruby. That's why you didn't stab me again, why you took your anger out on the bed instead, why you tore down the curtains, wrecked the furniture, anything but hurt me anymore, but you're also Mary. And yes, perhaps I'm William too; he's been channelling me, speaking through me, *reaching* out. Whilst... whilst you were at the door, whilst Theo was telling you what she'd found, I've been writing, or rather my hand – I can still use one thankfully – took on a will of its own. I was *compelled* to write, not on paper, I haven't got any, so I improvised. I found my iPhone, used the notepad app. I... erm..." he stopped, the effort of speaking proving too much perhaps but quickly he rallied, swallowing deeply before continuing. "I recognise some of the words, they're the ones from *Ghost Discovery*. But there's more now, complete sentences. It's from William, I know it is. Let me read it to you, please, while I still can."

About to say no, her head nodded, as if that too had a will of its own.

"Okay, good, that's really good, here we go... *It's dark where I am. It's cold and cramped. I get confused, mixed up. Does my heart still beat? Sometimes I think so. Other times I realise. This is wrong, all wrong. I'm wrong. I'm tormented, by her: the child and the mother too. I'm so tormented! I pushed her out, she said, ruined her. Did I? Was I responsible for what she became? Surely not! I can't be blamed!*"

Seeing the look in her eyes, the man held his hand up. "Wait, don't do anything," he implored again. "Hear me out, hear *him* out." He began reading again, his manner more rushed. "*They were irresistible, the two of them, alone, as I was, as different. They didn't belong. I was drawn to this place, to them. I knew, from the minute I saw that child running towards the cottage, heard her mother calling her, that they'd be mine. And what an appetite they gave me! One I indulged as though I were a king. Staking my place in the world, when I'd wandered for so long, finding a home at the crossroads. But that child, she threatened it all! There was such venom in her eyes. Selfish, selfish child! I had to find a way to break her. And so I banished her, to my side of the cottage, filling her head with tales of creatures that walked the creaking boards at night, telling her to listen for them whilst her mother slept. I'd listen too, for her screams of terror. But she was stubborn, so stubborn, she wouldn't cry out. Not like my wife, an altogether more malleable creature. Desperate you might say. And they did, those around us, quick to judge but never to help, a blessing in my eyes. I wanted to own them both, possess them, but that child, she aligned with the devil the minute she killed her mother. Yet still she made me want her, growing taller and finer whilst Ellen withered in the ground. But that defiance, that evil, it was always in her eyes, I could never knock it from her. Try as I might. It wasn't my fault what she became! I'm a man, just a man. And she was so tempting. It was her fault! Hers!"*

The board she was holding crashing to the floor, she grabbed the knife again. She'd show him whose fault it was!

"Just listen, please, Ruby, if you're in there, let me speak. There isn't much more to go, we're coming to the end. Mary, like Theo said, you've waited a long time for William to come out of hiding, hear what he has to say. If you still want to stab me afterwards, well… so be it. Just… let me get to the end." Hugging his bloodied arm to his chest, his eyes looked as though they were starting to glaze. *"Dark, so dark. I don't like it, I want to come out, but I'm so afraid. As much as I used to want her, I don't now. She's not content with what she's taken from me. It's not enough. Always different, she's become something else. Craven. And it's my fault, she says, and keeps saying. It's because of me. Am I as bad, as lost? Images float towards me, memories. They must be. Each one so vivid I can hardly bear to look. But there's no choice. They're everywhere, even when I shut my eyes. There's me, the child, her mother, the longing, the fear, the pain, the bewilderment, the anger. It's like looking at a terrible stranger, an actor on a stage. But it's me. Something craven too."*

The man stopped, crept closer, held her gaze but he needn't have worried, it was as though those last words had weaved some kind of magic, she was spellbound. "Mary, this is the bit I want you to hear, it's something new I think, the most important bit. It's the realisation... *The truth dawns, slowly at first, then in a rush that almost blinds me. I was that man. I made those choices. Not just capable, I was gluttonous. But I'm no longer blind. In darkness I can finally see. I'm on fire with the grief I've caused. I'm burning, and it hurts, much more than the twist of any knife. Even so, I won't hide anymore, from you or the truth. It was my fault, everything. It began with me. I'm sorry, I am. But in sorrow there's hope. The darkness is receding, there's the light that they talk of, it burns too, but it causes no pain. If I can see it, Mary, so can you. Just look. That's all you have to do. We're not damned after all."*

As he finished speaking, there was silence. Even the prayers had stopped. It was as though they were caught in time, as if there was no time at all.

"Has he gone?" she asked.

"Yes."

"To the light?"

"I think so."

"You're not him anymore?"

"I'm Cash," he stopped, gasped for breath. "Just Cash."

"If I kill you, it'd be for no reason?"

"None at all."

The tears were relentless.

"He's defeated me, again."

"No, Mary, you defeated the darkness in him. Look towards yourself now."

"Cash! Cash! Can you open the door? Move whatever's obstructing it?"

Despite the distraction, the man never took his eyes from her.

"Is that okay, Mary, can I open the door?"

Reaching out a hand, the bloodied one, he touched her, tenderness in the gesture that was alien. No, not alien; it stirred a memory.

"Mary?"

She nodded, watched, as with great difficulty he got first to his knees and then to his feet, staggering slightly whilst he crossed the room.

What was the memory that was nagging at her? What was it? Of course! How could she forget? There was sunlight, the branches of a tree swaying overhead, a carpet of daisies around her and the anticipation of the evening to come, of lying in her mother's lap as she stroked her hair, flames in the log fire dancing. Content, she was so content. Her eyes closed as she began to drift, thinking of her father. Who was he? A lord perhaps? How she loved that idea! Her mother smiling, well aware of her dreams, and continuing to stroke her hair – her touch always so gentle.

As the man did his utmost to move the bed aside, she rose too. The door bursting open, she raised the knife high and, with all her might, plunged it inwards.

Chapter Thirty-Two

"YOU'RE all right, darling, you're all right, we've got you now. She's gone and William's gone too, you're all right."

"Wh…where am I?"

"In an ambulance, on our way to the hospital."

Her hands came up and clutched at her stomach. "Am I? Did she—"

"No," Theo said, cradling her still, "Cash, dear boy that he is, despite the state he was in, looked back, guessed Mary's intention and threw himself at you, knocked the knife from your hand, knocked you backwards too. You blacked out."

"Blacked out? Again? Cash? What do you mean, the state he was in?" No sooner had she said it then visions filled her mind, strange visions, like picture postcards that were frayed at the edges, coming into view and then fading again. Cash, she'd stabbed him, she'd slashed at his arm. "Oh my God!" she whispered.

"Not you." Ness was on the other side of her. "It was Mary, she'd possessed you."

"Possessed me?"

"After a fashion, yes."

"After…? Is Cash all right?"

"He will be," Theo answered. "He's in the ambulance in front, Corinna and the Reverend are with him… and Jed."

Jed was with him? That was good, that's where he should be, by his side.

"Jed warned you, didn't he?" she asked Theo.

"Yes, he came to warn us that something was happening, which is why we rushed back. I'll explain all about Mary to you later, right now you need to rest."

"You said she's gone." She looked down the length of her own body. "Has she?"

"You're not possessed any longer," Ness explained. "And yes she has gone."

"To the light?"

"Ruby, you really do need to rest."

* * *

Ruby was released from hospital after twenty-four hours. Cash was kept in. The police were called and, when they were able to, questioned him regarding what had happened. His reply? A masked intruder had broken in and attacked him, having fled when his friends burst into the cottage, alerted to the fact that something was wrong by their dog.

"What dog?" the Police Officer asked.

"The dog that belongs to my girlfriend, she...erm... she must have got one of the villagers to look after him or something, being as we're both in here."

At the mention of his girlfriend, they'd pointed out she'd been covered in blood too. "That's 'cos she was beside herself," he'd answered. "Threw herself at me rather than the attacker. Bless her."

The Police Officer had paused whilst taking notes. "But, Canonibeare, it's a quiet village, isn't it?"

"It is now, Officer."

"Now that he's gone?"

"He? Yeah, of course, now that he's gone."

All this Theo had relayed to Ruby before taking her to see him.

"I don't think they believe a word he's told them," she'd said. "They're suspecting some kind of domestic between you, but if he's not going to press charges, there's nothing more they can do about it. They'll want statements from us too. My advice? We back Cash to the hilt, and, yes, that means you too, Ruby. I know I'm always saying honesty is the best policy but actually sometimes it's not."

When at last Ruby was reunited with Cash, Jed sitting faithfully by his side but wagging his tail upon seeing her, she burst into tears, wanting desperately to do what he'd told the policeman she'd done and throw herself at him.

"I wouldn't," Theo second-guessed her. "He's a bit delicate at the moment."

She contented herself with holding his hand instead. "I'm sorry," she whispered. "I'd never hurt you, you know that. I love you."

"Ruby, you weren't responsible for what happened. Don't cry."

Sniffing loudly, she'd had to release his hand so she could retrieve a tissue and blow her nose. "It doesn't hurt though does it, to apologise?"

"It doesn't," and then with a glimpse of his trademark humour, he'd added, "You know how to wound a man, Ruby. I said it on the way down and I'll say it again."

Incredibly, neither of them could stop laughing.

The nurse said he could leave hospital in a few days time; thankfully the wounds inflicted were largely superficial. Even so, the amount of stitches he'd needed seemed horrendous.

Leaving him in the nurses' and Jed's capable hands, no matter how reluctantly, she went with Theo back to the cottage, where not only Ness and Corinna were waiting but Rachel and Mark too. Having not heard from her in two or three days they'd become worried and driven down.

Corinna put the kettle on to make tea. The rest of them took their places at the kitchen table where between them Theo and Ness filled in the gaps.

"We'll start with the Reverend," Theo decided. "Ooh, he's a stubborn one he is. It took his lovely wife, Jane, to cajole him into helping us, despite me adopting my most winning smile." She demonstrated it to them at that very moment. "See? How could he resist? Anyway, whilst Ness and Corinna were sorting out what was happening elsewhere in Canonibeare, doing a sterling job I might add, he and I got down to business amongst the dusty tomes." She laughed coquettishly as she said it, a sound that again caused Ruby to smile, even though she still felt so hollow inside. *Poor Mary.* Where had she gone if not to the light?

Ness took over, po-faced at such innuendo. "When we arrived, we got the impression that what Ruby had seen, courtesy of Mary, was not quite what had actually happened. In other words, Mary manipulated Ruby, right from the beginning. Via dream connection, she presented as a child, probably because people tend to empathise more with children than adults, thereby only ever showing half the story."

"As in what happened to Ellen for instance?" Ruby said. "I only saw the aftermath."

Ness nodded. "That's right. And later, it was Mary that stopped you from approaching the oak tree too, playing on both the warnings you'd heard already and the symptoms of your concussion. The last thing she wanted was for you to see what had really happened there. Oh, the power she had over you, Ruby, when you thought that she had killed herself. It was immense! She also used the Ouija to manipulate you further, although Ward tried so hard to wrestle with her over that."

Before Ruby could comment, Rachel piped up. "Excuse me, did I hear correctly, you used the Ouija board? Why, when you warned us against it!"

Ruby could feel her cheeks burning. "I'd still warn against it, but…" How could she explain? She'd called the vicar arrogant, but she'd displayed arrogance too in using such a tool alone. All she could do was promise she'd never do it again.

"Promises, promises," Theo said but it was good-natured enough.

"The hook in the living room," Ness continued, "that's what first alerted me to what was going on, and Theo too. We knew as soon as we set eyes on it that it was an innocent enough object, only ever used for purpose, which was of course hanging meat from in order to feed patrons of the Inn. An original feature, nothing more."

Rachel screwed up her face, shuddered slightly. "Nonetheless, I've made up my mind, along with those floorboards, it's going." She turned to her husband. "In fact, put it at the top of your 'to-do' list, Mark, finding someone to remove that hook."

"But if it's an innocent enough—"

"No, Mark! Even the mere thought of a body hanging from it is bad enough."

"And thoughts, as we know, are powerful things," Theo agreed. "Take William for instance. He thought he was damned, not least because Mary told him so as he drew his dying breath but because having passed he realised what he'd done, the gravitas of it, and therefore couldn't believe there was hope for him. Thomas Ward, a homosexual, also believed himself to be an abomination in the eyes of the Lord, his preference for his own gender and the pain of unrequited love driving him to take his own life, which, of course, is another grave sin, or at least it was widely considered to be during the time that he lived." Solely addressing Ruby now, she continued, "Ness and I have talked with Tom at great length in your absence, even Corinna got in there and put her tuppence worth in. It always helps to have a modern view, I think. He's a good man, we told him, as angry as he was about what Mary had endured as a child – as *outraged*, he knew that she'd become something dangerous and so he took it upon himself to warn the ever-rotating residents of Old Cross Cottage about her. He wasn't scared for himself, despite what Mary thought, he was only ever scared for the living. He mentioned the Ouija board again, the time that it was used by the Londoners." Another laugh escaped her. "He gave them a good fright he did, repeatedly spelling out 'scared' and his surname, but it was Mary who really saw them off, grabbing the glass, and throwing it so viciously, the intent to cause damage of some sort. Tom would never go that far. Although when he thrust you against the wall, Ruby, in the single bedroom, he was beginning to lose patience."

"So that was Ward?"

"It was, and the car accident you had on the way here, it might well have been just that... an accident. Then again..."

"It might have been Thomas, or Tom as you called him, reaching out."

Corinna sat forward. "But how would Tom have known you were on your way?"

"The power of thought once again," Theo answered. "Ruby had Old Cross Cottage on her mind and it acted as a magnet to those on the same wavelength."

Corinna sat back, looking as stunned as Rachel and Mark.

"But what about Golden Cap?" Ruby asked. "What happened there?"

Theo looked at Ness, who frowned before speaking. "You said you saw a black mass hovering over the cliff edge that drew you to it, perhaps with dark intent?"

Ruby nodded, closed her eyes briefly. If it hadn't been for Cash and Jed...

"I think you can work out what happened," Ness continued, "or rather what *didn't* happen – thankfully – and not just because of Cash and Jed, but because of you, Ruby, and the light within you. It's strong, it honestly is."

Yet despite that she was vulnerable, she succumbed so easily at times.

"Strength and wisdom come with age and experience," Theo commented, "as does resistance. You have to remember that, Ruby. To quote the most famous prophet of them all, *'He that is without sin among you, let him cast the first stone at her.'* We've all made mistakes, the only crime is if we never learn from them." Taking a moment to let her words sink in, she returned to the subject of Thomas Ward. "Like William, he's gone now too. Having had his body laid out for a week on the bar of the Old Cross Inn, it was eventually decided what to do with him: he was to be laid to rest under the oak tree where he'd hanged himself. I asked Tom who'd decided on that and he couldn't seem to remember. So I continued nagging until he did." Theo stopped, her eyes becoming misty all of a sudden. "The man he'd fallen in love with, it was his suggestion. He said it was a beautiful spot, as good as any churchyard, something I tend to agree with. Afterwards, as Thomas lay beneath the ground, his spirit hovered, and the man – his name was Edward – made a vow."

"A vow?" queried Mark, caught up in the story too.

"To visit the burial site… often."

"Often?" Ruby repeated. "Do you mean…?"

"Yes," said Theo, "that's exactly what I mean. Thomas Ward was so ashamed of his feelings that he'd buried not only that memory but also the possibility of the man he loved being in love with him too. When we pointed that out, when we told him how beautiful we thought it was, I think he finally believed us. He was still hesitant about leaving, in case Mary comes back. He's the landlord of Old Cross, you see, the overseer, and like our Jed, he takes his responsibilities very seriously." She shook her head. "Once a proprietor, always a proprietor I guess, but I convinced him he'd stood guard long enough. If she returned, the living would have to deal with it."

Mark's gaze became less enthralled. "If she returns? What do you mean? I don't want her coming here again, she sounds like a lunatic!"

"She wasn't a lunatic," Theo's voice was stern. "She was a child who'd been scarred by cruelty. When a child suffers in that way, there are two choices: she can turn from such cruelty, renounce it entirely by thoughts, words and deeds, or she can embrace the bitterness and the hatred that such injustice invokes in her, following the perpetrator down that very same path, in some cases overtaking them and becoming worse, much worse. Mary, sadly, opted for the latter. She killed her mother, although…" Theo inclined her head towards Ness, "we tend to think that was an accident. But as an adult, the deaths she caused were premeditated for certain."

"Which makes her a monster!" Mark insisted.

"No," Theo shook her head. "You see, I don't think she walked so far that she lost herself entirely and I'll tell you why. Ruby, when you were at the pub, you saw a figure, one of many I know, but it was more solid than the others, just ahead of you."

"That's right," Ruby replied.

"Can you tell us again what happened leading up to when you were pushed?"

Ruby shifted. "Erm... yeah... I asked the figure its name, realising it wasn't just a shade but much more than that."

"An intelligent haunting?" Rachel said.

"That's correct," Ruby answered, smiling at her. "I couldn't tell if it was male or female – that's significant actually. Before it finally became clear we were dealing with the grown-up Mary, I sometimes got the impression of a woman at Old Cross, but it was always so vague. Regarding the figure in the pub, I kept asking who it was and getting nowhere. The next thing I knew, there was a child by my side, desperate for my attention. Because I remained focused on the other one, she grew angry and pushed me. Before she did, she screamed 'Me!' After that, it all went black." She inclined her head in Jed-like fashion, "What are you reading into that, Theo?"

"That she was asking for help, deep down, in her own way."

"How?" Ruby asked.

"Yes, how?" echoed Ness.

"Because she showed you the real her before deciding against it. You see, in many ways, Mary *is* still a child. And, as a child does, she panicked and lashed out. But the adult

Mary knows she's in need of help, even if she can't fully admit it."

"So where is she?" Ruby asked, leaning forward, desperate to know, caring so much about the answer that it hurt, something Theo could sense well enough.

"Ruby, she may not surface again in my lifetime or indeed yours. The first step to redemption is forgiveness but that's something she's finding very hard, not just regarding William but herself too. And so she's in hiding again, even deeper than before, believing that the supposed pact she made with her god – the devil in other words – is forged in iron. As for where she is she's not in the cottage anymore. Feel for yourself how much lighter the atmosphere is." Turning her head, Theo stared out of the kitchen window. "No, she's somewhere much darker than this."

"She's in hell?" Corinna breathed.

"Yes, her version of it."

"That's terrible."

"It is," Theo acknowledged, "but we're not entirely powerless, there's something positive we can do. It might not seem like much but it is. It's a great deal, in fact. Rachel, Mark, we're going to need you to take over where we've left off and your fellow villagers too, who will hopefully help out whenever you're absent. Jennifer Campbell's a good girl. She'd be more than willing to help, especially after what's just happened."

Mark was clearly perplexed. "What do you mean? What are we supposed to do?"

Theo regarded him solemnly. "You do this. Every night, in one of the windows overlooking the crossroads, leave a light on. When you're not in residence, either use a timer or get one of the neighbours to pop in and flick the switch.

Ideally, the light should burn from dusk until daybreak. And, if you sell up, pass that instruction on to the next person, and the next, make them understand the importance of it."

"Why?" Rachel's voice was but a whisper as everyone stared just as solemnly back at Theo, Ruby in particular, holding her breath as she waited for the answer.

"Because, dear friends, one day, Mary might turn around and come back to the crossroads, see that there's a light burning and finally leave the darkness behind."

Exhaling, Ruby closed her eyes.

To that end she could only hope... and pray.

Epilogue

THE Reverend Martin turned out to be a bit of a gem. Taking the case as personally as Ruby, he went on a bit of a mission, pulling some strings with local parishes to find out the identity of Mary's father.

Ruby already knew from her first dream encounter with Mary that she and her mother had hailed from a village further west, one with a name the child had found as difficult to pronounce as Canonibeare. With those two clues to go on, as well as the name of Ellen, the Reverend had researched a number of villages and at last found evidence of an Ellen Dyke having been born in Coombnarbor in 1877 and having married Robert Weaver in 1896 when she was 19. Mary Weaver was also recorded as having been born a year later in 1897, the year that Robert had died.

When he'd rung to tell Ruby, she was so surprised she had to grab the nearest chair and sit down in it. "What was the cause of his death?" she asked.

"A fire, in the village school of all places, and some controversy over it too."

"Oh?"

"Robert Weaver occupied the position of caretaker at the school and the blaze started one morning, when the school was fully attended, originating from the room he occupied it was thought. A timber school, the fire spread quickly, cutting off two classrooms in particular. There were several resulting deaths, including his."

"I see," Ruby replied, her heart sinking.

"It was only some years later that the truth was revealed."

"The truth?" Her heart stopped its descent and fluttered instead.

"The fire had indeed started in his office but not by him, by a group of boys who'd gathered there whilst he was busy elsewhere, warming themselves by the stove, the doors to which they left open after returning to class. It sparked, caught alight, and… the rest is history as they say. As is human nature, people sought someone to blame and Robert was an ideal candidate, one who could no longer protest his innocence."

"That's awful," commented Ruby, "little wonder Ellen had to take flight."

"Indeed, but the burden of guilt is a heavy load to carry, for some anyway. One of the boys that had been in Robert's office eventually came forward. It was a few years later, he was a young man by then, and he confessed all. He also stated that Robert, far from being the culprit, was something of a hero that day, that he personally witnessed the man helping so many to safety, rushing back into the fire again and again to save those he could, unable in the end, to save himself."

Ruby closed her eyes, her heart not just fluttering, but also dancing. "So he was a hero?"

"He was."

"Which is better than being a lord."

"I'm sorry?"

"Nothing, nothing, just something Mary said, but that's great news, Reverend Martin, the best. I hope the village made some sort of reparation towards Robert."

"Oh, they did, they do. They make a point of never forgetting, holding an annual memorial service for him and for all those who died, there's standing room only apparently, even today. I'm thinking of doing the same, Miss Davis, you know, for all those that died in this village," he paused for a second, before adding, "unnaturally."

"Will that include Thomas Ward, William Cannon and… Mary?"

"It will include all lost souls," the Reverend replied.

Ruby nodded, Mary needed all the prayers she could get. As for Ellen, her heart went out to her. She'd concealed Robert's identity from Mary in order to protect her, but one thing she always did was insist he was a good man, because he was, and she never for a minute doubted it, unlike so many.

After their phone conversation, Ruby returned to Canonibeare on several occasions, all for very brief periods of time and with one clear purpose in mind – to stand at the crossroads and share with Mary the name of her father, what he'd done and how brave he'd been. She'd implored her to follow her father's example, to be brave too and come out of hiding, face up to what she'd done, accept the consequences, and thereafter find peace.

Unfortunately, there was never any hint that Mary was listening.

During her last visit, Cash and Jed came with her and she'd visited Mary's grave instead – the one under the yew tree that she'd been drawn to when Grace Comely had come by and captured her attention. Standing at the headstone, she'd laid her hands on it but sensed nothing. Her body might lay here but her spirit never had.

Although they'd come on business, Cash had nonetheless booked a room at The Royal Lion Hotel in Lyme Regis for the three of them, despite their 'No Dogs' policy.

"Ruby," he'd said, "Saturday belongs to Mary, but Sunday's mine."

On Sunday, they'd had a lie in then gone to the beach for more of the region's famous fish and chips, of which Jed couldn't get enough, of the smell at least.

It was October and not the most clement of days, so they'd eaten in a pub instead of on the beach, but after that they'd braved the weather and headed towards the Cobb, there was an aquarium on it, which was home to a sea mouse apparently.

"Come on, Ruby, we've got to see that."

"Cash, I'm just going to walk a bit further. I... I've got things on my mind."

"Mary?"

"Yeah, her as well."

He reached out a hand. "There's always next time."

"I know, I know."

"Don't get upset."

"I'm not."

"Really?"

"Really."

"You're not going to hurl yourself into the sea or anything?"

"Cash!"

He grinned before turning serious. "Ruby, stop beating yourself up. If you hadn't done what you did with the Ouija, the case might not have been resolved at all."

"So, what are you saying, two out of three ain't bad?"

"Hey, that reminds me of a song—"

"Cash, no! The last thing I need is for you to start singing again."

"It's okay, don't panic, I can't remember the tune anyway."

"That's never stopped you before."

"Oi!" Letting go of her hand, he tickled her sides instead, causing her to squeal. "Right, that's quite enough of that," he said, mercifully stopping after a few moments, "I'm going to check out this creature from the black lagoon. Is Jed coming?"

"Of course, he is. He's probably wondering if it's edible."

"Now there's a thought."

Watching their backs as they walked away, Ruby pulled her coat tight around her before turning round again. Her hair wild, she walked to the end of the Cobb and stared outwards at the horizon, admiring the might of the waves as they raced towards the shore. They'd found out the identity of Mary's father, but the identity of her own father was still the biggest mystery in her life. He was a policeman – that was all she knew – and as such, an upholder of the law, sworn to truth and justice, the same as she was albeit in a more spiritual sense. Did she even look like him? Have the same colour hair; the same shaped eyes, a similar curve to the mouth? Married to another woman whilst having an affair with her mother, he'd known Jessica was pregnant, and consequently abandoned them both. But surely he must think about his bastard child – perhaps not quite as often as she thought about him, but sometimes, in the quiet reaches of the night, or even whilst busy – a random burst of curiosity coming to the fore. Had she any brothers or sisters – *half*-brothers or *half*-sisters she reminded herself. What were they like? She'd inherited her psychic gift from her mother's side, so what had she got from her father?

Normality?

Maybe. At the very least, finding out about him might help her to understand that side to her she always found so baffling – her *lost* side. Her occasional recklessness was again something she had in common with her mother. But did she get her hot-headed ways from him, her enthusiasm too and her dedication to the cause – *blind* dedication at times? Part of her job was to find out about others, to chip away until the bigger picture emerged – the truth able to set you free, most of the time anyway. What about her truth, her history? Was it possible it could do the same?

Ruby, you're not looking to excuse yourself again, are you?

She honestly wasn't. She just wanted to evolve, as Theo had said. Avoid making the same mistakes twice, becoming a liability even. The danger she'd put Cash in…

"You've got to come and see this sea mouse, Ruby, it's incredible, like some sort of alien! I'm not taking no for an answer this time."

Ruby blinked, wondered what the hell he was talking about, and then remembered – the sea mouse, that bloody sea mouse.

"Okay, okay, I will, on the way back."

Before she could turn round to face him, he came up behind her, entwined her hands in his, and lifted them to shoulder height.

"This is very *French Lieutenant's Woman*," he said, whispering into her ear.

"How do you know? You still haven't seen the film."

"I'm presuming it is."

"It's not. Meryl Streep stood alone. What we're doing, it's a bit *Titanic* if you ask me."

"*Titanic?*"

"Oh, come on, there's no way you haven't seen that. This is how Rose and Jack stood on the bough of the ship as they sailed to New York."

"Never got there though, did they?"

"Rose did." In the end.

"Well, whatever we're doing, whoever we are, it's very romantic."

"It is," she agreed, Jed materialising to sit by her side, all three of them at the end of the Cobb, but at a crossroads too – at least she was – still.

Whoever we are…

As the gulls circled round them, as the waves continued crashing to shore, as the world rotated on its axis, she came to a decision. But no more acting the lone wolf, not this time; she'd enlist her team, Cash too if he was willing, every step of the way. Together they covered all bases – they completed her… almost.

The sea wasn't the only thing responsible for the moisture on her cheeks.

I need to know.

The next case on Psychic Surveys' books would be her own.

The End

Also by the author

If you've enjoyed Old Cross Cottage and want to read more paranormal fiction from Shani Struthers, check out the rest of the books in the Psychic Surveys series (if you haven't already!): Book One: The Haunting of Highdown Hall, Book Two: Rise to Me and Book Three: 44 Gilmore Street – there will be six books in total, including Book Four: Old Cross Cottage. There's also a prequel to the series: Eve: A Christmas Ghost Story and a companion novella, Blakemort. If you prefer romance with a hint of the supernatural, there's the ghostly Jessa*mine* and the first in a brand new series: This Haunted World Book One: The Venetian, which mixes fact with fiction and is set between Venice, 'the world's most haunted city' and Poveglia, in the Venetian Lagoon, 'the world's most haunted island'. They're all available from Amazon in e-book format and paperback.

Eve: A Christmas Ghost Story
(Psychic Surveys Prequel)

What do you do when a whole town is haunted?

In 1899, in the North Yorkshire market town of Thorpe Morton, a tragedy occurred; 59 people died at the market hall whilst celebrating Christmas Eve, many of them children. One hundred years on and the spirits of the deceased are restless still, 'haunting' the community, refusing to let them forget.

In 1999, psychic investigators Theo Lawson and Ness Patterson are called in to help, sensing immediately on arrival how weighed down the town is. Quickly they discover there's no safe haven. The past taints everything.

Hurtling towards the anniversary as well as a new millennium, their aim is to move the spirits on, to cleanse the atmosphere so everyone – the living and the dead – can start again. But the spirits prove resistant and soon Theo and Ness are caught up in battle, fighting against something that knows their deepest fears and can twist them in the most dangerous of ways.

They'll need all their courage to succeed and the help of a little girl too – a spirit who didn't die at the hall, who shouldn't even be there...

Psychic Surveys Book One:
The Haunting of Highdown Hall

"Good morning, Psychic Surveys. How can I help?"

The latest in a long line of psychically-gifted females, Ruby Davis can see through the veil that separates this world and the next, helping grounded souls to move towards the light - or 'home' as Ruby calls it. Not just a job for Ruby, it's a crusade and one she wants to bring to the High Street. Psychic Surveys is born.

Based in Lewes, East Sussex, Ruby and her team of freelance psychics have been kept busy of late. Specialising in domestic cases, their solid reputation is spreading - it's not just the dead that can rest in peace but the living too. All is threatened when Ruby receives a call from the irate new owner of Highdown Hall. Film star Cynthia Hart is still in residence, despite having died in 1958.

Winter deepens and so does the mystery surrounding Cynthia. She insists the devil is blocking her path to the light long after Psychic Surveys have 'disproved' it. Investigating her apparently unblemished background, Ruby is pulled further and further into Cynthia's world and the darkness that now inhabits it.

For the first time in her career, Ruby's deepest beliefs are challenged. Does evil truly exist? And if so, is it the most relentless force of all?

Psychic Surveys Book Two:
Rise to Me

"This isn't a ghost we're dealing with. If only it were that simple…"

Eighteen years ago, when psychic Ruby Davis was a child, her mother – also a psychic – suffered a nervous breakdown. Ruby was never told why. "It won't help you to know," the only answer ever given. Fast forward to the present and Ruby is earning a living from her gift, running a high street consultancy – Psychic Surveys – specialising in domestic spiritual clearance.

Boasting a strong track record, business is booming. Dealing with spirits has become routine but there is more to the paranormal than even Ruby can imagine. Someone – something – stalks her, terrifying but also strangely familiar. Hiding in the shadows, it is fast becoming bolder and the only way to fight it is for the past to be revealed – no matter what the danger.

When you can see the light, you can see the darkness too.

And sometimes the darkness can see you.

Psychic Surveys Book Three:
44 Gilmore Street

"We all have to face our demons at some point."

Psychic Surveys – specialists in domestic spiritual clearance – have never been busier. Although exhausted, Ruby is pleased. Her track record as well as her down-to-earth, no-nonsense approach inspires faith in the haunted, who willingly call on her high street consultancy when the supernatural takes hold.

But that's all about to change.

Two cases prove trying: 44 Gilmore Street, home to a particularly violent spirit, and the reincarnation case of Elisha Grey. When Gilmore Street attracts press attention, matters quickly deteriorate. Dubbed the 'New Enfield', the 'Ghost of Gilmore Street' inflames public imagination, but as Ruby and the team fail repeatedly to evict the entity, faith in them wavers.

Dealing with negative press, the strangeness surrounding Elisha, and a spirit that's becoming increasingly territorial, Ruby's at breaking point. So much is pushing her towards the abyss, not least her own past. It seems some demons just won't let go…

Blakemort
(A Psychic Surveys Christmas Novella)

"That house, that damned house. Will it ever stop haunting me?"

After her parents' divorce, five-year old Corinna Greer moves into Blakemort with her mother and brother. Set on the edge of the village of Whitesmith, the only thing attractive about it is the rent. A 'sensitive', Corinna is aware from the start that something is wrong with the house. Very wrong.

Christmas is coming but at Blakemort that's not something to get excited about. A house that sits and broods, that calculates and considers, it's then that it lashes out - the attacks endured over five years becoming worse. There are also the spirits, some willing residents, others not. Amongst them a boy, a beautiful, spiteful boy...

Who are they? What do they want? And is Corinna right when she suspects it's not just the dead the house traps but the living too?

This Haunted World Book One:
The Venetian

Welcome to the asylum…

2015

Their troubled past behind them, married couple, Rob
and Louise, visit Venice for the first time together, looking
forward to a relaxing weekend. Not just a romantic destination, it's also the 'most haunted city in the world' and
soon, Louise finds herself the focus of an entity she can't
quite get to grips with – a 'veiled lady' who stalks her.

1938

After marrying young Venetian doctor, Enrico Sanuto,
Charlotte moves from England to Venice, full of hope for
the future. Home though is not in the city; it's on Poveglia, in the Venetian lagoon, where she is set to work in
an asylum, tending to those that society shuns. As the true
horror of her surroundings reveals itself, hope turns to
dust.

From the labyrinthine alleys of Venice to the twisting,
turning corridors of Poveglia, their fates intertwine.
Vengeance only waits for so long…

Jessa*mine*

"The dead of night, Jess, I wish they'd leave me alone."

Jessamin Wade's husband is dead - a death she feels wholly responsible for. As a way of coping with her grief, she keeps him 'alive' in her imagination - talking to him everyday, laughing with him, remembering the good times they had together. She thinks she will 'hear' him better if she goes somewhere quieter, away from the hustle and bustle of her hometown, Brighton. Her destination is Glenelk in the Highlands of Scotland, a region her grandfather hailed from and the subject of a much-loved painting from her childhood.

Arriving in the village late at night, it is a bleak and forbidding place. However, the house she is renting - Skye Croft - is warm and welcoming. Quickly she meets the locals. Her landlord, Fionnlagh Maccaillin, is an ex-army man with obvious and not so obvious injuries. Maggie, who runs the village shop, is also an enigma, startling her with her strange 'insights'. But it is Stan she instantly connects with. Maccaillin's grandfather and a frail, old man, he is grief-stricken from the recent loss of his beloved Beth.

All four are caught in the past. All four are unable to let go. Their lives entwining in mysterious ways, can they help each other to move on or will they always belong to the ghosts that haunt them?

A note from the author

Keep in touch via my website – www.shanistruthers.com - where you can subscribe to my occasional newsletter and keep up-to-date with book releases, competitions and special offers. I'm also active on Facebook and Twitter, it'd be great to hear from you!

CPSIA information can be obtained
at www.ICGtesting.com
Printed in the USA
LVOW13s1739180517
535011LV00011B/1195/P